# AMBROSIO DE LETINEZ,

OR

# THE FIRST TEXIAN NOVEL,

EMBRACING

## A DESCRIPTION OF THE COUNTRIES BORDERING ON THE RIO BRAVO,

WITH

## INCIDENTS OF THE WAR OF INDEPENDENCE.

A FACSIMILE REPRODUCTION

of the 1842 edition

With an introduction by

WILLIAM D. WITTLIFF

To which has been added

**SAM HOUSTON AND TEXAS**

By DORMAN H. WINFREY

# AMBROSIO DE LETINEZ
## AND THE EARLY TEXAS NOVEL

Texas, its enduring land, its highly diverse peoples, its
mighty themes of iron and lead, hoof and horn have from
the aimless wanderings of Cabeza de Vaca provided a
tremendously rich lode of raw material for the novelist.
But the originators of the authentic indigenous literature
of Texas were talkers rather than writers, and one good
listener for them was audience enough. For every frontier
has been a land of storytellers who, mostly through raw,
ribald, humorous yarns, provided necessary antidotes to the
cold realities of frontier life. And though they naturally
enlarged on fact and embellished stories of contemporary
characters and events with their own personalities and
abilities—J. Frank Dobie said that a story belongs to whoso-
ever can tell it best—they seldom left the thread of truth
completely behind. The best of these old-time tales vividly
reflects the indomitable frontier spirit. What citizens of
the Republic of Texas did write—that is, for public consumption—was restricted to political pamphlets (with lots
of fire) and personal accounts of various expeditions against
Mexico. With the exception of John C. Duval and Noah
Smithwick, both of whom wrote after Texas had become
a state, and a handful of others, the citizens of early Texas
produced no substantial body of native literature.

The writing of novels they left to outsiders and foreigners—and for that matter the reading of them, though by no
means were the old-time Texians illiterate (Bugbee esti-
mates that by 1833 fully two thirds of the Texas population could read and write). What few personal libraries
existed in early Texas revealed catholic though utilitarian
tastes, with books ranging from geography, philosophy, and
history to midwifery and medicine. But the novel, with the
possible exception of Sir Walter Scott's, held little interest
for Texas readers; William Hogan, in his *The Texas Republic: A Social and Economic History*, a book that ranks with

Smithwick's *The Evolution of a State,* tells of one Texas reader who claimed that his mind had been ruined by the reading of novels and that

> a parent should never permit his child to pursue a work of fiction, as long as he has any regard for his mind, his morals, or his happiness. Novels, in my opinion, are the most fruitful sources of unhappiness and discontent in the world. Even drunkenness, with all its sickness and loathsome horrors, does not engender more pure and unmitigated misery. They portray unreal and over-wrought images of perfection, and inspire wishes in our bosoms which can never be realized . . . . They clothe vice and immorality in the hues of the rain-bow . . . . Finally, they create a distempered fancy, and morbid sensibility, which renders us totally unfit for collision with the cold and uncharitable.

What the first American writers of Texas "historical" fiction took for fact they lifted out of articles in the popular press or picked up from acquaintances who had traveled near or through Texas. These they blended with their own pre-conceived ideas based on traditional sources, equally as erroneous as the popular press; then further corrupted the whole by pandering to the literary tastes of a whoopla-hungry reading public, or using what they considered facts of the Texas experience as weak vehicles on which to hang their own tirades for or against this or that. And it is precisely here—and from like works not labeled fiction—that what has come to be called the Texas myth got credence, for people, by and large, throughout the centuries have trusted the printed word, most especially in book form. Regarding Texas material, early Texans chewed what they heard or read, whereas readers outside the state swallowed whole—and many Texians (like Bigfoot Wallace who gave the folks back home in Virginia the only thing they were willing to believe—fantasy) were doing a bit of the feeding.

The first Texas novel, written in French by an anony-mous Frenchman and published in Paris in 1819, was based on the abortive attempt of exiled Bonapartists to establish a colony, Champ d'Asile (Camp Refuge), on Texas soil.

Though chronologically *L' Héroïne du Texas* is the first novel based on an actual Texas experience, it can hardly be considered a Texas novel in any real sense, most of the action being what Lon Tinkle called a "pressed-flower sentimental romance occurring in Paris." As few copies ever reached America and as the work saw no publication in translated form until 1937—and then produced in handsome format by the Book Club of Texas, Stanley Marcus' noble venture—it had no influence on Texas fiction to follow.

The second Texas novel, and the first originally written in English, was *Francis Berrian, or The Mexican Patriot,* by Timothy Flint, a protestant minister from Massachusetts who got as close to Texas as New Orleans. Issued in 1826, *Francis Berrian*—like the novel presented here and *The Cabin Book* (1844) by Charles Sealsfield (English pseudonym for Karl Anton Postl, a one-time priest), which includes perhaps the longest after-dinner speech (sixteen chapters) in world fiction—gets wrapped up in religious controversy, being a combination of "exposing" Catholic abuses and generally attacking Spanish-Catholic society.

*Ambrosio de Letinez* was first issued as *Mexico versus Texas, a Descriptive Novel, most of the Characters of which consist of Living Persons,* in 1838—the same year that saw publication of Hugh Kerr's *Poetical Description of Texas, and Narrative of Many Interesting Events in that Country,* acknowledged by most Texians with the couplet: "O, Kerr, Kerr, Kerr/What did you write those poems fur?"

Authorship on the title page was given simply as being "By a Texian," and in place of a standard copyright notice the following statement was offered:

> The author being a Texian cannot take a copyright, yet he forewarns all roguish booksellers against printing his work; for he has an infallible means to render any spurious edition useless, and this he will not fail to do, if necessary.

It was true enough that, in 1838, a "Texian" could not obtain a copyright as the United States at that time did not grant copyrights to non-American citizens. But had the author in fact been "a Texian," with all the concern he evidenced by the preceding quote, he certainly would have applied for a copyright in the Republic of Texas (which issued but one copyright in its history, that to George William Bonnell's *Topographical Description of Texas* in 1840). But he did not; the fact is that the author of *Mexico versus Texas,* for various reasons, wished to remain anonymous.

The book apparently enjoyed enough distribution to warrant a second edition, for in 1842 it was reissued in two volumes under a more romantic title: *Ambrosio de Letinez,* this time giving the author as A. T. Myrthe, and holder of the copyright as Anthony Ganilh. The second edition, the present volume being an exact facsimile, follows closely the first, with the addition of verses to the chapter headings, slight changes in diction, and the inclusion of the peculiar chapter on Flambeau, "a quateroon boy" from Louisiana, which in no way fits into what little plot there is to the novel.

Scholars have long debated the identity of the author. No evidence whatsoever has been found substantiating the existence of "A. T. Myrthe." Sister M. Agatha Sheehan, in her dissertation, "A Study of the First Four Novels of Texas" (May, 1939), presents strong evidence that authorship of both editions belongs to Anthony Ganilh, Frenchman by birth and later Catholic missionary in the United States:

> This novel is evidence in itself that its author was one of the most learned and capable of early Texas writers. It is also proof that the unknown author, styling himself "A Texian," was a person who was thoroughly grounded in Catholic doctrine and ceremonial, if not too firm in his faith. Nobody except a priest, or one who had studied for the priesthood, could have written *Mexico versus Texas.* No secular would have been capable of the theological and philosophical disputation. And no protestant clergyman would have had the necessary training in Catholic apologetics.

Sister Agatha finds the first traces of Ganilh in America around 1817, in which year he was ordained a priest in Kentucky. Ben J. Webb, in his *The Centenary of Catholic-*

*ity in Kentucky* notes that Ganilh "was a man of excellent mental gifts and of great learning," but that he "was regarded by his associates of the clergy as somewhat erratic and shiftless."

By 1826 Ganilh was in the Diocese of New Orleans as priest in charge of the Church of the Immaculate Conception at Mobile, Alabama. Two years later he was in New Orleans where he preached the sermon on the occasion of a celebration in honor of General Jackson. Between 1828 and 1838, when he returned to St. Joseph's College in Kentucky, there is no known record of his whereabouts. It is possible that he was then in Texas, working on *Mexico versus Texas;* it is possible that he had returned to France. The fact that he returned to the Catholic Church gives good indication of why he wished the author of *Mexico versus Texas* to remain anonymous, for his presence there would certainly not have been tolerated had his superiors realized that he was the author of such an anti-Catholic work. His readers too most certainly would have considered him highly hypocritical had they known a practising priest had written *Mexico versus Texas.*

But if earlier he was simply wavering in the faith, by 1841 he had made a complete break, for in that year he left St. Joseph's College and the priesthood, supposedly to return to France. The following year, however, he was still in the United States where he took copyright in his own name for *Ambrosio de Letinez.* Though not giving himself as author, he had, in a fashion, committed himself.

It is most probable then that Anthony Ganilh, a capable yet disillusioned priest, and A. T. Myrthe were one and the same.

At the time the book was written, all the world was interested in the stirring events of the Texas Revolution and in its hero Sam Houston—to whom the author offered a highly patronizing introduction. And though he ostensibly used events of the Texas Revolution for his story element, the book itself is wholly concerned with theological disputation (as were *Francis Berrian* and *The Cabin Book*), the loose plot being entirely coincidental.

Set from about 1814 to 1836 the story begins in the state

of Durango, where Maria Letinez Faring, a Mexican lady of high rank who with her American-protestant husband is fleeing ecclesiastical jurisdiction, dies in childbirth. Before she dies she makes her husband promise that their child will be raised in the Roman Catholic faith. The father then leaves for the United States. The child, a boy, takes his mother's name, as was the Spanish custom, is raised first by the kindly priest who attended his mother at her death, then by his mother's parents, until at the age of eighteen we find our hero, Ambrosio de Letinez, "a tall, handsome, young man, with a pair of epaulettes, and at the head of cavalry, under Urrea" during the Texas Revolution. In a run-in with the Comanche Indians he, by chance, rescues an American girl, Sophia Linton, and takes her to Matamoros to board ship for the safety of New Orleans. But the ship sinks and Letinez finds safety for her with an Irish woman in San Patricio, then rides off to Goliad where he saves her father who has been captured with "Fanning's" forces. By this time he is, of course, hopelessly in love with Sophia—she an American and a protestant, he a Spaniard and Catholic. After a great many emotional and religious conflicts and other difficulties, including his capture after the Battle of San Jacinto, the two, who by this time have discovered by an odd coincidence that they are cousins, are reunited and marry with a great gathering of family in attendance.

As a collector's item the book, in either edition, is extremely rare. *Mexico versus Texas*, privately printed for the author by N. Siegfried in Philadelphia, no doubt in a small edition, can be located in no more than a half a dozen libraries in the country and is listed as number nineteen in Graff's *Fifty Texas Rarities*. For the purpose of this facsimile reprint the second edition was chosen as it includes the additional material mentioned earlier. With the exception of the republication, though in translated form, of *L' Héroíne du Texas* no other early Texas novel has thus far been reissued.

Deeply graven on the face of the William L. Clements Library in Ann Arbor is this sentence: "In darkness dwells the people which knows its annals not." It is unfortunate that for our earliest novels we must listen to voices with no ties to our soil, but even these aptly illustrate the fact that though early American novelists did not understand the Texas character and experience, they at least recognized that here was a unique experience on which a mighty literature could be built—and step by step through our native chroniclers and novelists, Noah Smithwick, John C. Duval, George Sessions Perry, J. Frank Dobie, Tom Lea, William Humphreys, Fred Gipson, and others here and to come, that mighty material is being hewn into a mighty literature.

William D. Wittliff

Austin, Texas
October 16, 1967

*The Statue of General Sam Houston, to whom the original edition of AMBROSIO DE LETINEZ was dedicated is the work of Raoul Josset, French sculptor. It was cast in Italy in 1956-1957, and was presented to The State of Texas by Grand Lodge of Texas A.F. & A.M. on October 28, 1961.*

*The Statue may be seen in the lobby of The Texas State Library, at Austin, Texas.*

*The inscription on the pedestal reads as follows:*

GENERAL SAM HOUSTON
1793 - 1863
PRESIDENT OF THE REPUBLIC OF TEXAS
CHAIRMAN OF THE CONVENTION OF
FREEMASONS THAT ESTABLISHED THE
GRAND LODGE OF THE REPUBLIC OF
TEXAS, A. F. & A. M., IN THE SENATE
CHAMBER OF THE CAPITOL, HOUSTON
DECEMBER 20, 1837

GENERAL SAM HOUSTON
1793-1863
PRESIDENT OF THE REPUBLIC OF TEXAS
GOVERNOR OF THE STATE OF TEXAS
A BROTHER WHO GAVE HONOR TO THE
CRAFT, GRAND LODGE OF TEXAS HONORS
HIM AS ONE OF THE FOUNDERS OF TEXAS
A SIGNER OF THE TEXAS DECLARATION
DECEMBER 20, 1836

# SAM HOUSTON AND TEXAS

Texans have always been quick to honor the heroes of their past history, but when they recall Sam Houston, it is almost as if they see encompassed in the form of one man the character of Texas herself. Other men have left their mark on the course of Texas history; some have made contributions nearly as great as his, but none has so captured the imagination or the devotion or been so inextricably linked with Texas as he. The only man ever to be elected governor of two states, he was a towering figure on the national as well as the state scene. But though he "left an indelible trace in the pages of the nation's history," he is above all a Texan, so much so that his name has become almost synonymous with that of the state he loved so well.

In the Texas State Library in Austin, Texas, is a gigantic mural depicting the major figures and events which mark the growth of Texas as a nation and a state. In the foreground and directly in the center of the panoramic scene is the face of Sam Houston. No position could better express his place in Texas as for nearly thirty years he stood unyielding while all around him raged the chaos and confusion of passing events. When the Alamo fell, when the field at San Jacinto beckoned, when annexation was debated, and when the guns at Fort Sumter broke the peace, Rusk, Austin, Fannin, and a score of other noble men rose to answer the challenge; but ultimately it was Houston that Texans came to look upon as the pillar of strength by which they could measure the conflicts of the times as well as gather the strength to meet them.

Perhaps Sam Houston is more closely identified with the state than other Texas heroes because his personal destiny was so intimately linked to her own. The state and the man rose together, one from the depths of obscurity as a Mexican province, the other from the disgrace of a lost reputation, to the heights of glory and acclaim. From the time Sam Houston settled in Nacogdoches in 1833 until his death thirty years later, he was an outstanding figure in Texas. A leader in the movement culminating in the Texas Revolution, he won his first and greatest glory at the Battle of San Jacinto, where as Commander-in-Chief he led Texans to victory and independence. For the next twenty-five years he was almost never out of public office. Elected first and third president of the new Republic, he served in the Fourth and Fifth Texas Congresses, and when Texas entered the Union, he served as one of her first senators. In 1859, when the secession question was raging throughout the state and the nation, he won election to the office of governor. A year later he relinquished the office rather than represent a government he could not countenance. In 1863 he died, still looking to the day when he would again serve his state.

Though few men have served Texas so well or so long, it was not his deeds alone that have given Houston his singular place in the state's heart. Rather, what Houston possessed that could not be matched was his indomitable character. In a letter to Andrew Jackson he once wrote, "I have often reflected upon the trials through which you have passed, and admired the firmness with which you met and triumphed over opposition." Andrew Jackson and the Roman consul Marius Gaius were the men whom Houston adopted as his personal heroes, and his life was an emulation of theirs in principle as well as deed. Like them, he was a champion of the common man and of government that gave him honest representation. "Assemblies and deliberative bodies have often destroyed liberty; but no individual, while deliberative bodies have remained honest and incorruptible, has ever overthrown the liberties of any people. . . ." Houston was intensely concerned with personal character and honor; when faced with a choice between losing a reputation and acting dishonorably, he said "If my character cannot stand the shock let me lose it."

The romantic and dramatic qualities of his character particularly suited Sam Houston to become the symbol of

Texas' greatness. From the age of sixteen when he abandoned civilization to live with the Cherokee Indians to his sixty-eighth year when he rode out to camp with the Confederate troops, he never chose the life of complacent luxury and idleness which could easily have been his. Always a man of action, daring in word and deed, striking and even flamboyant in appearance, yet with a high regard for personal honor and integrity, he represented the virtues that the West valued most. Henry Steele Commager said of him that "What is most striking is that Houston seems made to order not only as a nation builder, but as a repository of all of those qualities which we associate with his time and his country." "A magnificent barbarian, somewhat tempered by civilization," he was described in Washington, and so he was. But Texas, too, was a young and energetic state, not too constrained by the edicts of the polite world, and no man could have better represented the combined qualities of Texas in his day and Texas as she would come to be. For Sam Houston demonstrated in the "democracy of his habits, and the aristocracy of his ideals" the potential as well as the actuality of Texas and showed to what she could aspire.

It is because of these qualities that Houston has become more than a hero to those who now command the legacy that he bequeathed. His place in Texas history could never be captured in a title; though he has been called "the Hero of San Jacinto," the phrase is descriptive and not definitive. Houston was more than a military hero or an outstanding public leader; even when they most energetically opposed him his contemporaries recognized that Sam Houston was a man apart from the ephemeral issues of the moment, even while he dominated them. No better indication of his central place in the history of Texas exists than the fact that his fellow countrymen in the days of the Republic divided themselves not into political parties, but into pro-Houston and anti-Houston factions, apparently believing that they need seek no further for an object of their allegiance or resistance.

Houston has become a living representation of what Texans hold as their ideals, and since ultimately these have no meaning beyond the human, it is fitting that "Sam Houston" and "Texan" should be mentioned in the same breath. His name must always stand at the center of any representation of Texas history, for it was around his solid figure that the embryo state took shape and strength. Many monuments have been erected to honor him, in Texas and other states, but they pay tribute to his deeds rather than to the essential spirit of the man. His greatest monument rests in the history, legends, traditions, and ideals that have taken root in the state to which he dedicated his entire being for three decades and to which he bequeathed the stature of his character as an inspiration and a goal.

*Dorman H. Winfrey*

DORMAN H. WINFREY
DIRECTOR AND LIBRARIAN
TEXAS STATE LIBRARY

# Acknowledgment

For his extensive knowledge of early Texas books, and his counsel in helping us decide upon this book, for the careful study and many hours of research which went into his preparation of the scholarly preface found herein, we are grateful to Mr. William D. Wittliff. He is a 27-year-old ranch-bred Texan whose budding Encino Press is making for him an enviable place in Texas letters, and whose ambition is to publish books that are not only handsome but worth reading, keeping and cherishing. His growing stature and outstanding accomplishments make us doubly appreciative of his efforts in making the presentation of this book more interesting to our readers.

No one could be better qualified to write about Sam Houston than Mr. Dorman H. Winfrey, Librarian, Texas State Library. His great insight into the qualities and character of Sam Houston make the dedication of this book take on a new meaning, and make us take greater pride in the name "Texan." Mr. Winfrey seems to have walked midst the great volumes written about this man until they have given him an awareness almost equal to a personal relationship with this great leader and shaper of Texas destiny. We cannot express too warmly our gratitude for his contribution to our effort.

When it was learned that the original two-volume edition of Ambrosio de Letinez listed by a New Orleans dealer had been sold, we were fortunate to obtain reproduction privileges from Mr. James Day, Director of Texas State Archives, for the set which they own. We express our sincere appreciation to him for his kindness and cooperation in allowing us to make negatives from this rare edition. It is indeed a pleasure to work with such dedicated people who have appreciation of our desire to perpetuate this book.

To all these, we say a grateful thank you.

*Jack C. Vaughn*

CHAIRMAN OF THE BOARD
THE STECK COMPANY

# AMBROSIO DE LETINEZ,

OR

# THE FIRST TEXIAN NOVEL,

EMBRACING

## A DESCRIPTION OF THE COUNTRIES BORDERING ON THE RIO BRAVO,

WITH

## INCIDENTS OF THE WAR OF INDEPENDENCE.

BY A. T. MYRTHE.

"The fourteenth century pitted against the nineteenth."
DON DIEGO DEL CHILE.

VOL. I.

NEW-YORK:

PUBLISHED BY CHARLES FRANCIS & Co., 252 BROADWAY.

GEORGE W. WOOD & CO., PRINTERS, 45 GOLD ST.

1842.

TO HIS EXCELLENCY,

# SAMUEL HOUSTON,

## PRESIDENT OF THE REPUBLIC OF TEXAS.

---

THE country which your valor and prudence were mainly instrumental in raising to the rank of a nation has, a second time, called you to the executive chair, and thus presiding over the destinies of a new people, you cannot remain a stranger to the first efforts made to unfold the national character. It is this consideration which has emboldened me to inscribe to you the present work.

Nothing is so well adapted as literature to develop the genius of a new country, and the struggle of Texas against Mexico affords a noble subject for a work of imagination, in which the utmost power of description may be taxed, without fear of sinning against probability. The Texians may be considered as leading a crusade in behalf of modern civilization, against the antiquated prejudices and narrow policy of the middle ages, which still govern the Mexican Republic. The eyes of the world are upon them. The north of Mexico expects its deliverance at their hands, and if Texas be faithful to the call of Providence, power, glory, and immense wealth await her among the nations of the earth.

To accelerate the epoch when *her star* will reign para-mount from the Sabine to the Vermillion sea, and when millions of human beings, now degraded through ignorance, will learn to bless the name of the New Republic, as that of a benefactress, and rejoice in her success, as that of an adop-tive mother, should be the aim of every Texian. It is the object I have had chiefly in view in writing this work. I cannot flatter myself with the idea of having done justice to the subject, but I will find some indemnity for my labor, if you look favorably on the attempt.

Your Excellency's most humble

and obedient servant,

THE AUTHOR.

# PREFACE.

In considering human events as they pass under his eye, the statesman is seldom able to take in at one view all their bearings, and justly to estimate the alterations they are likely to introduce into the civil polity of the race in whose fate he happens to be interested. But, if it be a perplexing task to trace such changes, through the vista of futurity, among the people in the midst of whom they originate, how much more difficult must it prove to point out their connection with the destinies of different nations and distinct races? There are, however, occurrences of so singular a nature, as fully to authorise a reflecting man to foretell results, which, at first sight, appear to bear no proportion with the causes that are to produce them. Events like these are intended by Providence as germs of mighty revolutions in which the happiness of millions is concerned, and that can be relied on with a political faith as strong as the confidence placed by the most acute reasoners in demonstrations *a priori*.

No revolution has hitherto taken place better adapted to illustrate the proposition here laid down, than the establishment of Texian independence. A few years ago, Texas formed but an insignificant appendage to Mexico, and though its soil was known to possess exuberant fertility, with facilities for inland navigation which nature had refused to the rest of the Mexican provinces, the government entirely neglected it. With the apathy of ignorance they made concessions of its territory to men aliens to them in language and religion, whose habits of social life were diametrically opposed to theirs, and whose spirit of adventure and ardent love of freedom rendered them mortal foes to arbitrary rule ; while their acquaintance with modern improvements in arts and sciences pointed out a separation as inevitable, at no very remote period. Had the Mexican government known what mighty change they were preparing by their

generosity to the Anglo-Americans, instead of inviting them
to colonize Texas, they would, no doubt, have prevented their
entrance into that country ; and yet we question whether
any thing could have taken place more conducive to the re-
generation and improvement of Mexico than the success of
the Texians.

By the Machiavelian policy of Spain, Mexico had been
kept in a complete state of pupilage and ignorance, almost
entirely isolated from the rest of mankind, and deeply imbued with prejudices calculated to render a communication
with foreigners repugnant to her national feelings. From that
political lethargy she could never have awakened by her un-
aided energies. Much less could she have reached the high
road of modern civilization, had she been left to grope her
own way. But by her contest with Texas, she is now
brought into a *moral* strife with modern lights, the necessary
result of which will be the overthrow of the semi-barbarous
system of polity that has hitherto prevented the development
of the capacity of her people. The gates which illiberality
and bigotry had closed against the introduction of foreign
improvements and science are unbarred, and in spite of the
opposition of the privileged classes against the spreading of
knowledge, or their puerile attempts at reaction, darkness
must ultimately be dispelled. Like a man who, from the
obscurity of a subterranean dungeon, suddenly finds himself
exposed to the glare of a meridian sun, and is, by that in-
stantaneous transition, deprived of the faculty of vision, till
the pupil of his eye adapt itself to his new situation ; Mexico, emerging from the darkness into which Spanish policy
had plunged her, sustains as yet with difficulty the brilliancy
of modern civilization—she is wincing and making awry
faces !—still the pupil of the national eye is *dilating*, and a
mighty change is hastening on.

It is this contest between the imperfect civilization of the
fifteenth century, which sways the land of Anahuac, and that
of modern times, which has already effected an entrance
into the country ; that we have in the present work undertaken to depict. As the collision between the two opposite
systems became more strongly developed during the war
against Texas, we thought that by connecting the information we could communicate on this subject, with the adven-

tures of an officer who, during that sanguinary struggle, highly distinguished himself, we would render our work more instructive and entertaining.

It will not be denied that the subject offers both interest and originality. We are aware it required greater talents than we possess, to do it justice; yet we hope we can claim some merit for having pointed it out, as well as for the labors which the composition of this work has rendered indispensable. Our observations are the result of protracted travels through Mexico. Nearly all the localities mentioned in these pages have been personally visited by us, and as most of them lie in the northern provinces, never till now described by travellers, we may presume that our remarks possess, at least, the merit of novelty.

Some fastidious critic may object to our work that the story is loosely put together, and presents in its plot none of those complicated imbroglios, accounted so essential, in modern novel writing, for stirring the imagination of the reader. To the first count we plead guilty, but answer with Sir Walter Scott, " Who, the devil, minds the frame of a picture, provided the painting itself be well executed ? " To the second accusation, we answer that we should rather think it a subject of praise, should we be found capable of interesting our readers by faithful delineations of nature, or exact descriptions of the workings of human passions. We have long been of opinion that the precept of Horace, " Sit simplex dumtaxat et unum," should apply to a novel, as well as to a play, for the legitimate object of the latter is the same as that of the drama.

A friend who has obliged us with numberless corrections suggests the idea that the ceremonials and clergy of the Romish church are too frequently introduced on the scene. The charge, if it be a defect, is well founded ; yet we must plead in self-defence, that we cause those reverend personages to act in so diversified a manner, as will, we hope, afford amusement to the reader. Moreover, the church has so much sway in Mexico, and the practices of bigotry are so closely interwoven with every kind of business, civil, criminal, military and commercial ; that, in justice to the proportion things bear to each other, we could not allot a lesser space to the *padres*, nor fulfil, otherwise, the project we had in view of giving a detailed account of Mexican manners, and the thousand curious incidents resulting from the moral contest in that country, between modern civilization and antiquated prejudices. Under whatever other defects this work may labor, we hope we have impartially fulfilled these two objects, which, we are not aware, had even been aimed at, by any book published on Mexico, since its emancipation from the Spanish yoke. In pointing out the influence which the independence of Texas is likely to exercise on the population of the northern provinces, and what are the destinies in reserve for the new republic, we may have been more sanguine than the present state of affairs could warrant, yet we have no doubt our predictions will prove true.

The political details with which we have connected our descriptions, in order to impart to them that species of literary interest which results from a dramatic form, are of too recent a date, and have made too much noise in the world, to have left us at liberty to introduce the alterations which our fancy might have suggested. It is what will happen to any novelist attempting to interweave his fiction with any point of history not yet mellowed by time. But is this a defect ? can our work be less estimable because the political events it relates are narrated with historical exactitude ? We should suppose not. But how far we have met with success in conquering the difficulties of our undertaking, is not for us to say. More than once we have applied to ourselves the famous line of Horace, " incedis per ignes suppositos cineri doloso." Now, let the public pronounce whether we have succeeded in picking our steps along this dangerous path without damage to our socks.

# AMBROSIO DE LETINEZ.

## CHAPTER I.

> Interminable meads
> And vast savannahs, where the wandering eye,
> Unfixt, is in a verdant ocean lost;
> Another flora there of bolder hues
> And richer sweets, beyond our gardens' pride,
> Plays o'er the fields, and showers, with sudden hand,
> Exuberant spring.
>
> *Thompson's Seasons.*

In that singular region of Mexico, where the high table land begins to sink by gradual descent towards the valley of the Rio Bravo, there extends through a space of more than four hundred miles in length, and three hundred in breadth, a desert, known under the name of " Bolson de Mapimi," so utterly destitute of water and vegetation, as to be intransitable. Its interior is, of course, entirely unknown, and though it is supposed to contain metallic riches to an immense amount, no one, except every now and then, some wild Indian, ever ventures upon crossing its skirts. Nature, however, which often delights in contrasts, has blessed with fertility and enriched with perpetual verdure a small district on the southeast verge of the dreary wilderness. This enchanting oasis is fertilized by the waters of the river Nasas, which, rising in the mountains of Zacatecas, flows in a northeast direction, until it loses itself in the lakes of Parras and Mapimi. The various channels into which it branches off, and by means of which its beneficial influence pervades every part of this beautiful plain, form a thousand meanders. Groves of tall and elegant saplings, interspersed with trees of gigantic size, adorn their banks, and offer to the traveller's contemplation a spectacle which may be said to be *unique*, in a journey from the mouth of the Rio Bravo to the foot of the western chain of the Sierra Madre ; (¹) while the intervening prairies are thickly enamelled with blossoms of the brightest hues, richest fragrance, and utmost elegance of configuration.

In the spots which the scanty population of the country has already begun to cultivate, many productions of the temperate zone are richly blended with those of tropical climates, and the equable temperature, together with the perpetual absence of frost, insure to the laborer the varied reward of his toils. Here, luxuriant fields of wheat are enclosed by quick hedges of orange trees, and vineyards are guarded against the inroads of wild animals by thick-set rows of cacti, upon which the cochineal insect multiplies in myriads of millions, or the varied species of the Indian fig grow in abundance. In the orchards, the avigato pear, fig and pomegranate, alternate with the dwarf apple, peach, plum, apricot and other trees of the north. On the banks of the streams, the arundo gigantea is extirpated to make room for the sugar-cane, while the driest spots are made to produce crops of fine silky cotton, equal to the best sea islands. In a word, the agriculture of this fertile plain, although yet in its infancy, may be considered as the richest and most varied it is possible to imagine.

But nature, as if desirous to impart to her gifts a greater value by contrasting them with scenes of the most awful aridity, has raised, on every side of this rich district of country, except the south-eastern edge, a circumvallation of mountains, the jagged summits of which tower in chalky nakedness, above the neighboring level. Not the least tree or bush adorns their sides. Hardly can one find, here and there, a sturdy agave, or half-withered opuntia, sadly vegetating in the rocky crevices. Generally belonging to the trap formation, these rocks assume regular shapes, and mostly rise in perpendicular ledges, so that their summits are frequently inaccessible. There are, however, at intervals, deep cuts, called *puertos*, in the language of the country, through which nature has opened a communication from one valley to another, and it is at the entrance of one of those narrow passes, by which the inhabitants of the delta of the river

Nasas communicate with their neigbours, that is situated the little town of Phelipa, where the scene of our story opens.

This place could, at the period to which we refer, boast of some illustration rather uncommon in the north of Mexico. Its first magistrate, who had been *Alcalde Mayor* of part of what now forms the state of Cohahuila, was a man of education, who, having in his youth studied divinity with an eye to a rich benefice, in the gift of one of his uncles, had, when the war of independence broke out, abandoned it for the study of law, but who still plumed himself upon his double knowledge, and used sometimes to boast that he was "*in utroque jure laureatus.*" Among the members of the *Ayuntamiento*—anglice, the board of aldermen—there were four or five persons well acquainted with Latin, and possessing some knowledge of Spanish literature. Two foreign physicians, the one an American, the other a Frenchman, exercised the healing art in partnership, and their learning imparted a zest to the social tone of the place, while the parish priest, who was accounted a prodigy of erudition, by his influence and polite behaviour, harmonized the whole, and by the exercise of an enlightened charity, always succeeded in repairing what little breaches of good manners, jealousy, or illiberality might produce among those worthies.

This dignitary was a great and good man, in every sense of the word, and as he plays a distinguished part in our history, it will not be improper to make our readers minutely acquainted with his character.

Don Fernando de Larribal (such was his name) was the youngest son of a Biscayan gentleman, who having but a slender fortune to leave to his children, had despatched our Fernando, yet almost an infant, to Mexico, to be there brought up, under the patronage of his elder brother, who had been an inhabitant of that country for several years previous, and had already realized a considerable fortune. It was in the post of secretary to the Bishop of Durango, to whom he had attached himself, after entering into holy orders, that his powers of insinuation and conciliating manners had gained him an influence and credit superior to his wealth. That credit he employed for the advantage of his brother, immediately after his arrival ; by procuring his admission, as one of the king's bursars, ([2]) into the college of San Juan de

Leteran, the best seminary of learning at that time extant in Mexico. Here, young Fernando made great progress, and by his good conduct, so highly recommended himself to the rector of the institution, that, upon his brother's benevolence growing too scanty for the purchase of books and works of literature, which the young man thought necessary for the improvement of his mind, he was assisted out of the director's private purse. Thus protected, he went through what was, then and there, supposed to constitute a complete course of education ; that is to say, he thoroughly learned Latin and Arithmetic—went through Algebra, as far as the equations of the third degree—dabbled a little in geometry and Spanish literature, became a proficient in metaphysics and theology, and was solemnly admitted to the degree of bachelor of arts, in the university of San Ildefonso, by receiving with great pomp and formality, the power of "*interpreting Aristotle throughout the whole world.*"

Being thus invested with academic honors, he was by his brother's interest presented to the living of Phelipa, which, in point of income and respectability, might be accounted the fourth or fifth in the large diocese of Durango. There he had by his zeal, learning and charity, recommended himself to the universal love and respect of the inhabitants. Out of an income of six thousand dollars a year, he spent for himself barely what was sufficient for the actual necessaries of life, and employed the remainder in supporting a public school, and relieving private distress. Not content with these benefactions, he kept a little pharmacy, in order to administer gratuitously remedies to the poor, and even, when requested, practised medicine, with which he was well acquainted. It is true, that as he had not the Pope's permission to that effect, he was scrupulous in prescribing for the sick ; yet he never could withstand the calls or tears of the poor, and this was, as his vicar observed, a greater stumbling-block to him, than all the other canons of discipline, put together. Furthermore, at his leisure hours, he taught Spanish and Latin grammar to the children of several of his rich parishioners, who were desirous of having them prepared for college, free of expense —a thing not more infrequent in Mexico, than in other countries.

This man, thus endowed with the spirit of philanthropy,

was entirely free from the moral defects which are but too frequently found to disgrace the Mexican clergy. He possessed a great zeal for the good of souls, without intolerance ; great learning, without pride—and, to say all in a few words, he was a *holy priest*, and yet an honest man. It was no wonder, then, that he was respected and loved by his parishioners. They were the more attached to him, by comparing him with his fellow clergymen, of other parishes, and they had, in order to express their attachment, generally adopted an Indian epithet, which they applied to him, by way of eminence. They called him *Tata padre*, an endearing expression, by which Mexican Indians designate a degree of moral excellence almost superhuman, and which, in the halcyon days of religious fanaticism, they thought it was a great honor to confer upon the illustrious Don Vasco de Quiroga, first Bishop of Mechoacan, after he had, by arduous labors, civilized the Tarascos, and introduced among them agriculture and the mechanical arts. (³)

To our benevolent and virtuous clergyman, Providence had afforded numerous occasions of exercising his charity, by placing him at the head of a large parish, chiefly consisting of Indians, who, although partly civilized and acquainted with the arts necessary to social life, were still ignorant, improvident and apathetic in the extreme. The numberless calls made upon him, at all hours, by night and by day, seldom tired his patience, and though he sometimes grumbled, he always hastened to the assistance of his parishioners, whenever they insisted upon being attended by him, rather than by his vicar—which was generally the case, and rendered the latter's office almost a sinecure.

On the day in which the hero of our story was ushered into the world, our worthy clergyman had been called to the sick, four times already ; and, feeling much fatigued by his repeated rides, he was resting himself and enjoying the cool of the evening breeze, under a spreading orange-tree, in his *huerta*, when his servant, a silly old Indian, called Tio Pedro, precipitately, rushed towards him, with a countenance in which astonishment, mingled with terror, was depicted, and exclaimed in a hurried voice, " Now, Tata padre, may the most Holy Virgin of Guadelupe defend us, (⁴) but there is another sick call !—And in the most strange manner ever seen in Phelipa.

A four wheeled coach, Señor, has just stopped at the main
gate of the court yard; and, to my notion, it was never
made in this republic.—The wheels are so slender!—And
with bright iron bands, all of a single piece!—And the body
of the coach, Señor,—oh, it is a sight!—Varnished all over;
—olive green, picked out with yellow! The grand carriage
of the Bishop of Durango, himself, when he came down to
give confirmation, last summer,—was nothing to it! And
he who rides in it is a strange gentleman, Señor,—very
strange! He is dressed like the Alcalde's son, when he returned from Mexico, and wears a narrow brimmed hat, like
the one your worship brought from Durango, at your last
trip.—And his face, Señor,—oh, it is so white and smooth!
The man must be a Jew!—I am much mistaken if he is not
an American. He cannot be a Christian, I know. He looks
so much like one of those pictures which Tirilla brought from
France and wished to palm upon the people for images of
saints. Now, Tata padre, I hope you won't go. The man
is certainly a Jew, and there is no knowing what he might
do with your worship."

This address was delivered with so much volubility by Tio
Pedro, that his master had not the chance of uttering a single
word; but, rising up from his seat, he directed his steps
towards the parsonage, when he was met at the gate of the
huerta, by the gentleman whom Tio Pedro had described.

The stranger was a man of twenty-three or twenty-four
years of age, of a striking beauty; but evidently a prey to
the most violent grief. He accosted the priest with politeness, and informed him, with tears in his eyes, that a lady,
who was travelling towards Bexar, had been seized with the
pains of premature labor, and compelled to remain at a village
of the name of Larza, three leagues distant, and that *he* had
come in haste, to seek both for medical and spiritual assistance.—She was in imminent danger, and he wished to know
whether there was any physician in the place.

To this, the priest answered that they had two medical
men, in Phelipa, but that, unfortunately, both were absent
and at a considerable distance. At this piece of information,
the stranger seemed to be thrown into a paroxysm of grief.
He wrung his hands,—looked up towards heaven and then
upon the priest, with such an air of supplication, that the lat-

ter was unable to withstand its eloquence. He had resolved within himself to send his vicar, to administer spiritual con-solation to the sick lady, for he felt so much tired from his preceding rides, that he did not think himself adequate to the task ; but he could not resist that dumb appeal, and imme-diately changed his resolution. He knew, indeed, that spirit-ual ordinances conferred by his vicar would be as efficacious as his own ; but in the physicians' absence he was the only person able to administer medicine. He, therefore, consoled the stranger in the best way he could, and added he would go himself to the lady's assistance, and that, as he understood something of physic, he hoped to be of service. There was, also, he said, an old *partera*, in the place, who had often, in difficult cases, acted under the direction of medical men. They would take her along with them, and in the meanwhile despatch messengers to the physicians, to hasten their return.

By this time they had reached the dwelling house of the clergyman, who immediately sent his servant to bring, with all possible speed, Tia Rachela, the above mentioned priestess of Lucina, who was to accompany them. But the servant, disliking the errand, manifested some repugnance and even undertook to reason the case with his master.

" Tia Rachela," said he, " will hardly be prevailed upon to come, when she finds out in whose company she is to ride."

" How !" said the priest ; " you forget yourself, Tio Pe-dro. My kindness has spoiled you. Am I not good com-pany enough for Tia Rachela ?"

" Ah, Señor," resumed the servant, " sure, your worship is good company enough, but it is not of *you* I speak—and if a poor servant might presume to give an advice," added he in a whisper, " I think you would do well to send your vicar, rather than go yourself. Consider, Señor, as I told you, that the man—"

" And consider, Tio Pedro," resumed his master, waxing wroth, " that, as your parish priest, I do command you to go immediately and fetch Tia Rachela hither, and answer not a word—not a syllable."

Overawed by his master's decisive tone, Tio Pedro obeyed, but not without grumbling. Having got to Tia Rachela's house, he informed her of his errand, in such a manner, as inclined her rather to conceal herself, in order to eschew the contamination attending a ride in the same coach with a man suspected of being a Jew, than to perform what, in other circumstances, she would have considered as an act of charity. She was arguing and debating the matter with Pedro, when the clergyman, tired waiting, came to decide her by his authority. His commands, delivered by himself, in person, she could not resist, and donning her best shawl, she reluctantly went with him and entered the coach. The Tata padre and the strange gentleman mounted afterwards, and drove with great speed towards the *rancho,* or village of Larza.

They were no sooner gone than Tio Pedro flew to the house of Doña Salas, an old beata, who, having buried three husbands, had, at the age of sixty-three, made a vow of celibacy, and through a desire of participating in the merits of the order of St. Francis, taken the habit of the *terciarias.* Merely by wearing the gown of the institute, and reciting a few additional prayers, every week, she became possessed of an individual share in the large stock of spiritual graces and indulgences which are the exclusive property of the Franciscans, and was in full community of merit with the Capuchin nuns themselves.

This beata, though sufficiently faithful to her religious vows, by which she had got a cheap bargain of salvation ; had, nevertheless, a mortal hatred against what is generally accounted the monastic observance most painful to a female— I mean silence and recollection. Her house was the newsroom of Phelipa, and the place of rendezvous for all the gossips of the vicinity. This, being well known to Tio Pedro, was the secret, though unavowed motive, which prompted him to resort thither, in order to give a quicker and wider spread to his suspicions and surmises. He found at Doña Salas' a little club of female gossips, who had seen the coach drive up to the priest's house, and had immediately met, in order to deliberate upon the purport of that strange incident.

Tio Pedro's countenance indicated that his tongue was pregnant with some extraordinary piece of news, of which it longed to be delivered, for he kept his mouth shut up with great rigidity, and wagged his head to and fro with no less solemnity. There is a kind of freemasonry among newsmongers, to what degree soever they may belong, which enables them, at one single glance, to guess when a brother or sister of the craft has something worth knowing in his budget, and their natural eagerness to get at it is not a little heightened by a consciousness of their penetration.

Upon Tio Pedro's entrance, therefore, they did not fail to assail him with a confused medley of queries, to which, however, he, out of a sense of his own importance, declined answering, until he had been regularly invited to sit down by the lady of the mansion, and was categorically interrogated by her.

" Now, Tio Pedro," said Doña Salas, who knew well how to manage him, " you have been running up and down the town in a great hurry, for I saw you passing by, several times, and you will not, I think, be the worse off for a little glass of *vino mescal*." (⁵)

" Indeed, Señora," answered Pedro, " I hardly ever taste it, for the Tata padre can smell it, should I swallow but a thimblefull, but as he will not return till to-morrow, I think I can venture it without any danger."

" He will not return till to-morrow !" resumed Doña Salas. " Is he then gone so far ?"

" He is not gone farther than the village of Larza," replied Pedro, " but for all that he will not return till to-morrow night ; that is, if he return at all."

" If he return at all !" exclaimed all the women, alarmed. " Mercy on us, Pedro ! What is the matter ?"

" The matter, Señora," returned Pedro, " is that my master is gone off with an outlandish kind of a man, who is no Christian, I am sure, for he speaks rather broken Spanish, and when he came to the door of the house, he knocked and knocked, without ever calling out *Ave Maria*. His wife is unexpectedly brought to bed, yonder, at Larza, and if he be a Jew, she, of course, is a Jewess. So, master is gone to give her extreme unction, and Tia Rachela to assist her, in her own way. But I am afraid it will turn out worse than we think. They may kill my poor master—and for Rachela, they may throw a spell upon her, and even should she escape unhurt, by whom can she expect to be employed, after assisting a Jewess ?"

Upon hearing Tio Pedro's surmises, the female senate
2*

became horrified, and thinking, as well as he, that their beloved Tata padre was in danger, they began to deliberate
upon the means of rescuing him. Doña Salas proposed to
send the sacristan, beadle and singing-boys, armed with
swords and daggers ; but Tio Pedro remarking that the boys
were too young to fight, and the sacristan too old, it was,
after mature deliberation, agreed to go to the Alcalde's, and
lay the matter before him, not doubting but he would send a
party of civic guards to insure the priest's safety.

The first Alcalde of Phelipa, although he had, in his youth,
studied divinity, was by the knowing ones, supposed a little
inclined to *modern philosophy*, and of all the women in town,
the one he hated most, was Doña Salas, on account of her blue
gown and white cord of St. Francis. He was, therefore,
most disagreeably surprised, when he saw that female entering his office, accompanied by four or five of the most med-
dlesome gossips in the whole parish ; but when they laid before him the subject of their visit, he became still more displeased, for he had no mind to make himself ridiculous by
acceding to their wishes, and yet he knew that a refusal would
give them occasion of prattling against him, and representing
him as inimical to religion.

Unwilling, therefore, to incur the odium of a flat denial,
he represented to them that there was not the least probability of their beloved Tata padre's life being in danger, since
the person who had called appeared to be a gentleman of
respectability—that the village of Larza was populous and
the road to it quite safe, and that he could not concur in a
measure, which, without any adequate motive, could not fail
to create an unusual excitement, and perhaps alarm the person
to whose assistance the priest had been so ready to fly.

All these plausible reasons did not, however, satisfy our
pious women, and least of all Doña Salas, who entered into
an elaborate argument with the Alcalde, in order to prove
the reasonableness of her proposal. She belaboured him
with her tongue, but that magistrate's mind being made up,
and seing that all her eloquence availed nothing, she, at last,
lost patience, and left the office, in a pet. The female
squadron who accompanied her participated in her displeasure,
and they were no sooner in the street, than they held a council
among themselves, and it was agreed to go to the captain of

the civic guard, to beseech him to do what they, under the present circumstances, judged necessary. They found this functionary more tractable than the Alcalde ; yet, not thinking any great display of military force necessary upon this occasion, and, also, for fear of committing himself with the Alcalde, who was very jealous of his power ; he contented himself with summoning, as secretly as he could, eight privates, whom he rather begged than commanded, to go, without noise, towards Larza, and watch over the priest's safety. This was accounted a signal service rendered to religion, by Doña Salas and the other *comadres*, who attended upon her, as humble satellites revolving round a primary luminary. In order, the more leisurely, to descant upon the Alcalde's impiety and their own attachment to religion, they adjourned to the house of one of their number, who had some excellent chocolate, of which they wished to partake, as it was now about five o'clock in the afternoon, and there we will leave them, to enjoy their fragrant beverage, seasoned with scandal.

## CHAPTER II.

There, grim fanaticism, with gory hand,
His poniard shakes, and by his serpent looks,
Freezes the human mind,—to lasting infancy
Binding a race, for highest thoughts designed.
*Don Diego del Chile.*

WHILE the members of the civic guard are trotting on, on their errand, we will overtake the priest and the strange gentleman, who are riding ahead of them, in order to listen to their conversation. After a long silence, during which the stranger's grief seemed, at every moment, to increase in intensity ; the priest, desirous of alleviating it by consolation, observed, " My calling, Sir, which makes it binding upon me to keep secrecy in every thing relating to the spiritual welfare of my fellow men, and my desire of being useful to you, persuade me that I cannot be thought indiscreet in manifesting a wish to be informed more in detail of your present circumstances. It may enable me to be more serviceable, than I could otherwise expect to be—yet I would not be thought to court a confidence which you may have powerful reasons to withhold—much less would I violate the sacredness of misfortune, by an importunate curiosity. I make the suggestion, merely because you seem to be struggling with yourself, and your mind appears weighed down by an oppressive burden."

"It is true, father, you have guessed aright," answered the stranger. " I have a communication to make, for I shall want your counsel and aid. This communication is painful ; yet I fully rely upon your generosity and discretion. From your reputation, your charity is known to me, and I am also aware of the sacredness of the seal of confession, under which alone I will communicate to you the cause of my grief and fears. It is, indeed, urgent that you should be informed of all, before you reach the bedside of her whom you are going to visit—but how shall I unbosom myself within this woman's hearing ?—Is there any language unknown to her which we could use ?"

" Are you acquainted with Latin ?" interrupted the priest.

" Too imperfectly for the purposes of conversation," returned the stranger, " but perhaps you understand English or French."

" English," replied the clergyman, " if you will articulate slowly, I think I shall be able to understand your meaning, for I read, and have some practical knowledge of the language."

" Well, then, father," resumed the stranger, " we will converse in English, for it is my vernacular tongue. I am an American by birth—the youngest son of a planter of the state of Maryland—of the name of Faring. Having, in my youth, embraced the mercantile profession, I was sent to the city of Mexico, by a commercial house of New York, with which I was connected. I had not been living long in that city, when certain affairs obliged me to undertake a journey to the state of Mechoacan. The persons with whom I had business to transact lived in the city of Pascuaro, and I found the scenery of the environs so picturesque, that I prolonged my stay in that town, somewhat more than I would have done, had it not been for that attraction. (⁶)

" I took so much delight in studying the beauties of nature, which are there revealed with a perfection of which I had no previous idea, that I made the banks of the lake the theatre of frequent rambles, and the islands which stud its surface, the objects of frequent visits. I was, I believe, the first American ever seen in that part of the country, and although this circumstance naturally made me an object of curiosity for the inhabitants, yet, on account of my supposed difference of religion, it was mingled with a certain degree of hatred, which, not unfrequently, broke out into open insults. The people, in their ignorance, looked upon me as a person by whose contact they would be defiled, and with whom it would be a sin to be in habits of intimacy, or to exhibit the common civilities of life. My neglect in paying to the ceremonies of religion the external marks of reverence which are exacted from all—though proceeding from mere ignorance—was constructed into open disrespect, and being accidentally present, one day, as the host passed by, without taking off my hat, I was stabbed by an ignorant shoemaker, near whose booth I was standing.

" I was left in the street, weltering in my blood, till, happily for me, the coach of Count Letinez passed by, and his daughter, who was riding in it, with her governess, seeing me thus abandoned, out of compassion, caused me to be carried to her father's house, which was not far distant. The old Count was absent, and the servants, in the idea that the wound I had received was a just punishment for what they considered a sacrilegious act, would not have waited upon me without disgust ; but I was indebted, for a more humane treatment, to a clergyman, a brother of the Count, who, during the latter's absence, superintended his house-hold and governed his family. My eternal gratitude is due to that worthy priest. He had a mind enlarged by reading, perfectly free from bigotry and prejudice, and he sincerely lamented the fatal effects of the intolerant ideas planted in Mexico by the Spanish government. He had been conver-sant with Humboldt, was fond of the company of foreigners, and acted towards me with genuine philanthropy ; since, notwithstanding my being a Protestant, he took the best care of me, and did not disdain to administer medicine to me with his own hands. His conversation was interesting, and he was passionately fond of literature. A similarity of taste, on my side, formed between us a bond, which, in a short time, ripened into intimacy, and as soon as I was able to rise from my bed, he introduced me to the distinguished visiters of the house, and installed me, as it were, a member of the family.

" I had not been long in the house of Count Letinez, be-fore his only daughter, Maria del Carmen, made an indelible impression on my heart. Her beauty was of a superior or-der, and though she had not enjoyed the advantage of an education corresponding to her rank, the goodness of her heart and delicacy of her feelings, in great measure, sup-plied the deficiency. She soon reciprocated my sentiments, and our growing attachment did not seem, for a while, to attract her uncle's notice ; which made me believe he did not intend to oppose an union between his niece and me. There was, however, an obstacle to the accomplishment of our desires, which I was sometimes afraid would prove in-vincible—the difference of religion. No marriage between a Protestant and a female of the country had ever taken place, and though the objection could be removed by the

Pope's dispensation, still the Pope was so far distant, and the communications with the Holy See were so difficult and precarious, that it might be considered as insuperable.

" Notwithstanding all the difficulties we foresaw, our mutual love kept increasing, and at last, her uncle, becoming alarmed for the consequences, in a polite, but firm manner, signified to me that I could not continue an inmate of the family, adding, that, as an union with his niece was impossible, all further intimacy between us must cease.

" Overpowered with the most poignant grief, at an intimation which I considered as cutting off all my hopes, yet unable to renounce her whom I loved more than my own life, I had, before my departure from the house, a private interview with her. Her uncle had already announced to her his resolution, but I found her less grieved than I had reason to expect. Fully acquainted with the extent of his love for her, she hoped to induce him to change his determination, and she imparted to me a scheme she had already sketched out for that purpose. In order to give her plan (of the success of which she was very sanguine) time to take effect, she requested me to absent myself for some weeks, and not to show myself in the neighborhood, until I should hear from her. I expostulated, but in vain, for she insisted on my immediate disappearance, prescribing, at the same time, that I should remove to the Island of Tzintzonzan, situated in the middle of the lake of Pascuaro, where the ruins of the ancient capital of the kingdom of Mechoacan are still to be seen, inhabited by a few Indian families. ([7])

" Implicitly following her directions, I took a boat, that same evening, and caused myself to be ferried over to the place of my temporary exile. I had no idea of the artifice to which she had recourse, in order to work upon her uncle's fears, and induce him to accede to our mutual wishes. But, on the twenty-second day after my departure from Pascuaro, I received from her a letter, in which she informed me that matters being made up, her family were going to remove to Valladolid, the capital of the province, where they had a house, and that I might make my appearance, in that city, with renewed hopes. She had availed herself of my absence, to feign a violent grief, which seemed rapidly to terminate in a decline. In the meantime, her old nurse (who still lived with her in quality of dueña, but entirely devoted to her wishes) had played her part admirably well, incessantly speaking of her mistress' approaching death, and hinting that her state was owing to the repulse I had met with.

"Many persons now began to blame the old uncle for his cruelty, and he became himself alarmed for the life of his niece. He tried to console her and sought to dissipate her melancholy, by the recreations most adapted to her age, but she remained inconsolable, until, at last, the old gentleman, relenting, promised that he would no longer oppose our marriage.

"The old Count might start objections to the alliance of his daughter with a Protestant, but, as he was, in all things, directed by his brother, it was not supposed a very difficult task to overcome them. A more formidable obstacle resulted from the religious impediment. We needed a dispensation from the ecclesiastical authority, and without it, our marriage could not be celebrated. It was for the purpose of soliciting that permission, the family had taken the resolution of removing to Valladolid, where Maria directed me to meet her, in order (*) that my efforts might be joined to theirs.

"At the first interview I had with her, she informed me of the artifice she had employed, in order to overcome her uncle's scruples, and I must confess that I was not a little surprised; for I believed her too plain and unaffected to be capable of what could not be considered in any other light than duplicity. But as she had been actuated by an ardent affection, of which I was the object, I could not possibly resent her conduct.

"We now abandoned ourselves to the most delightful anticipations of future happiness, and the old Count, who soon returned to join his family, though he made, at first, some show of resistance, was, at last, persuaded by his brother's entreaties and his daughter's tears, to ratify our mutual promises. I should never come to an end, were I to relate in detail all the solicitations we were obliged to have recourse to, and all the formalities we had to undergo, to obtain from the ecclesiastical authority permission for the celebration of our nuptials. The Bishop of Mechoacan was absent, but he had delegated his jurisdiction to the Dean of the cathedral, who happened to be a particular friend of the family of Letinez and under great obligations to them. This dignitary was sufficiently disposed to grant us the favor we sued for, but it was thought by many above the power even of episcopal authority, such dispensations being, by the canons, commonly reserved to the Pope himself. The Count, however, found various divines of great authority who decided in our favor. In order to oblige us, a particular point of the canon law was strained. It was said that when recourse to the sovereign pontiff is either physically, or morally impossible ; the Bishops are, in their dioceses, authorised to grant all the dispensations commonly reserved to the Apostolic See. In our case such a recourse was *morally* impossible, because in the present disturbed state of affairs, both in Mexico and Spain, it was extremely difficult to communicate with his Holiness. These reasons prevailed over the Dean's mind and he granted us the dispensation. There were several other formalities, which we should have been obliged to comply with, had not the indulgence already shown us rendered it ridiculous to exact things of minor importance, and we were, therefore, married, without any publication of bans, or any other disagreeable delay.

" The ceremony took place in the Count's domestic chapel, and the Dean himself, in his quality of Vicar General of the Diocese, did us the honor of officiating. Never was there a couple more happy than we. Every day, our love seemed to increase and the old Count with his brother blessed, a hundred times a day, the happy marriage which betokened peace and happiness to their old age ; but our felicity was disturbed by a cause we had the least reason to suspect. The Bishop of Mechoacan, who had been long absent, returned at last from Europe and being informed of our marriage, was highly displeased at the authority which the Dean had arrogated to himself, during his absence. He immediately interdicted him the exercise of his ecclesiastical functions, and not content with this, his Lordship declared our marriage null and void, and the spiritual court issued a mandate for our separation.

" The family of Letinez obliged me to abscond, but, as the Bishop was informed that I still continued to visit my wife, in secret; by a strange stretch of authority, he caused her to be shut up in the convent of St. Clair. It was only at

the end of six months, when her advanced pregnancy rendered it absolutely impossible that she should any longer continue
among the nuns, that she obtained leave to return to her father's.   Once at liberty, she was the first to propose to me
to take her to the United States.   Our intention was, immediately after reaching the frontiers of Louisiana, to send a
trusty messenger to her father, to inform him of the place of
our retreat, and she doubted not but he and her uncle would
come to join us.   This hope rendered the moment of her
departure less bitter than it would otherwise have proved,
but now, that the period of her confinement has overtaken
her, in the midst of our journey, the fear of being pursued
by the emissaries of the Bishop has created a paroxysm of
terror, and I anticipate the most fatal consequences.

" Now, father," continued the stranger, " I have briefly
imparted to you the history of my marriage.   It is under the
holy pledge of secrecy I have reposed this confidence in you.
I am afraid my wife's misgivings are but too well founded.
If we are arrested, at this juncture, the fright will prove fatal.
Could she be but removed to some convenient place, at a
distance from the high road, my fears would be less excruciating.   If you can aid us, by your counsels, or influence
over the villagers' mind ; oh ! I beseech you, in the name of
that religion, of which you are so worthy a minister ; take
compassion upon an innocent woman, most unjustly per-
secuted."

The good clergyman was moved even to tears, by the
stranger's appeal, and promised to do every thing in his
power.   He entered upon the discharge of his promise, by
endeavouring to reconcile Tia Rachela with her task.   The
reader may remember that this worthy matron had set out on
the present errand, with great reluctance, and the priest was
afraid, that, if she were not soothed and her suspicions lulled
asleep; she might acquit herself of her functions in so careless,
a manner as to endanger the lady's welfare.   He, therefore,
translated for her edification a part of the stranger's communication, and left her completely satisfied that the person
she was called to assist was no Jewess ; but a Christian and
a Count's daughter, to boot.   He, moreover, became security that she should be well paid for her trouble, particularly if
the safety of the lady and her child was the result of her at-

tention and skilful deportment ; and Tia Rachela, who had,
till then, manifested her displeasure, by a very sulky demeanor, condescended to illumine her countenance with a certain
sunshine of satisfaction, which proclaimed that her former
suspicions were entirely dissipated.

In the meantime they were drawing near to the village of
Larza—for they had driven with the utmost speed—and
upon their arrival, Mr. Faring, alighting from the coach,
begged the clergyman with Tia Rachela, to await his return, and entered the cabin in which his wife was lodged, in
order to prepare her for the interview.   There was no need
of much art, or eloquence, to dispose her mind, for, indeed,
far from being impressed with any sentiment of awe at the
idea of the priest's visit, she manifested, on the contrary, an
earnest desire of seeing him, because, being persuaded that
her death was drawing near, she earnestly wished to receive
the last sacraments of the church.

When the good clergyman entered the cabin, he was
shocked to see the absolute want of comfort in that miserable habitation, in which a lady of her high birth had been
reduced to take shelter.   It might be said with truth, that
the poverty of the Mexican peasant was visible, there, in all
its nakedness.   There was neither table, nor bedstead, and
had it not been for a matress which the travellers had
brought with them, the sick lady would have been necessi-
tated to lie on the bare earth.   Two or three low stools sup-
plied the place of chairs, and some fragments of dried
gourds, that of crockery ware; while the only two articles
that bore any resemblance to furniture, were a block of grit-
stone, shaped into a kind of mill, with its corresponding
roller, to grind maize into a soft pulp, and a circular plate
of iron, to bake that pulp into thin cakes—a species of Indian bread which is the main article of food of the population of that country.   But in order to give a more exact
idea of the wretchedness of the Mexican peasantry, I am
bound to add that this *comal*, or griddle, being of cast metal,
was considered, in such a place, as an article of luxury.

The priest had no sooner entered the apartment, than all
those who were present approached him with marks of the
deepest reverence, and devoutly kissed his hand.   He kindly
blessed them all, and directed them to withdraw, in order

that he might hear the sick person's confession, during
which, he administered not only spiritual comfort, but also
all the other consolations her present state seemed to require.   He told her that, provided her situation should allow her to be removed to the town of Phelipa, he would procure for her a convenient house, with proper furniture and
attendants, and, at all events, protect her against the attempts of any one sent in pursuit of her.   Moreover, he
assured her that her marriage was valid, and that she had no
longer any thing to fear from the Bishop of Mechoacan, and
he concluded by holding up to her hopes the pleasing prospect of a happy termination of her journey, when she would
find in her husband's love, an indemnity for her present
sufferings.

The good man's representations soothed her mind to comparative calm, and when he had exhausted all the motives of
consolation which his Christian charity could suggest, he recalled the company, and they all sat down in expectation of
the moment fixed by nature for the lady's delivery.   Tia
Rachela, now highly interested in her behalf, by her beauty,
youth, and piety, selected from among the oldest and most
prudent matrons of the neighboring cabins, those by whom
she desired to be assisted in her functions, and every thing
promised a happy issue, when, unfortunately, a considerable
noise was heard in the street before the cabin, and the news
that a party of armed men had arrived from Phelipa, reached
the lady's ears, and caused the catastrophe, which we will
attempt to describe in the following chapter.

## CHAPTER III.

Pasce l'agna l'herbetta, il lupo l'agna,
Ma il crudel amor di lagrime si pasce.
*Metastasio.*

THE commander of the little party of the civic guard, who had, at the instance of Doña Salas, been sent towards Larza, in order to watch over the priest's safety, rode hard with his men, and arrived at the village, shortly after the carriage. Their arrival created a kind of alarm in the *rancho*, and its indiscreet announcement within the lady's hearing induced her to believe, that her worst fears were realized, and that her pursuers had, at last, overtaken her. Seized with consternation, and uttering a loud shriek, she fell into hysterics, which brought on a premature crisis. Thereupon, Tia Rachela gave the signal for all the men to withdraw, who, in consequence, retired to a neighboring cabin, where, after two hours, anxious expectation, it was announced to Mr. Faring that he was the father of a fine boy, but that the mother was in the most imminent danger.

Aroused by this fatal news, from a kind of stupor into which he had fallen, he hastily entered the cabin where his wife lay; and drawing near the bed, gave vent to his feelings by a flood of tears. Taking one of her hands, which lay motionless on the pillow, he kissed it, while she cast upon him a look, in which love and grief were mingled, in an inexpressible manner. That kiss seemed to reanimate her sinking frame, and summoning all her remaining strength, she addressed him in the fervid and impassioned tone of the daughters of the south, " *Esposo de mi corazon y de mi alma,*" said she; " I must leave thee !—Oh, my well-beloved, and the only beloved upon earth, what wilt thou do, deprived of me ?—Alas ! that our happiness has been so transient !—that I have known thee, but to be separated from thee, in so cruel a manner !—thou weepest !—Bend thy face to mine and kiss me, before I die,—and bathe my face with thy tears, —their moisture will be a balm to me in my grave."

Her husband having assented to her wishes, she continued ; " Our love has been reciprocal, and now I do not aban-
3*

don thee, altogether. I leave thee a precious deposit ;—but oh, for my child !—in what religion is he to be brought up ? —Alas ! thou wast not united with me by the bands of the same faith. Thine differs from mine, as much as earth differs from heaven—I cannot die in this uncertainty, about the fate of my child—swear to me, dearest, that thou shalt cause . him to be brought up in his mother's religion—swear it by my heart, which has been so true and faithful, and thy oath shall be recorded in heaven !—I must see him made a Christian, before I die, and the padre must baptize him under my eyes. I cannot die in peace, without it."

Her husband interrupted her, in order to give his solemn promise that the child should be brought up as she desired ; but was unable to allay the torrent of feeling, or soothe the state of excitement which could only accelerate her dissolution. The priest felt great scruples at the idea of baptizing the child in a private house, it being in no danger, and the rubrics of the Church prescribing that, except in cases of impending death, this Sacrament should be administered only in consecrated places of worship ; yet, thinking that the ceremony might have a soothing effect upon the mother's mind, he overcame his own repugnance. Every thing was, therefore, made ready for the administration of this ordinance, and though the utensils made use of to hold the blessed salt, the baptismal water, and other requisites were of the poorest description ; the solemnity and devotion with which the minister performed the service of the ritual, hallowed the ceremony with a dignity, which it would not perhaps have possessed, had the child been christened at the baptismal font of the Cathedral of Valladolid, with all the pomp suited to the heir of the house of Letinez.

The mother beheld the whole in silence, and with self-possession ; but when, after the ceremony, they presented the child to her, she again broke forth into a torrent of impassioned expressions, which all the efforts of those who surrounded her could not repress. The mental excitement to which she abandoned herself increased her weakness, and feeling her strength giving way, she took out of her bosom a diminutive miniature, representing the Virgin of Guadelupe, and hung it round the child's neck, by means of a light gold chain, to which it was appended. Having made her husband promise that he would cause the child to wear it constantly, in remembrance of his mother, she next requested Rachela to cut two locks of her hair, which she directed her husband to send to her father.

During this interval, Mr. Faring endeavored, by gentle admonitions, to prevent the manifestation of her awful forebodings ; but when he saw her removing her wedding-ring, and presenting it to him, with the solemn words, " *Adios !* and never bring my child under the empire of a step-mother !" he was no longer able to control his feelings. Throwing himself on his knees before the lowly couch, he called out, in accents of despair, " Maria, what art thou doing ?— Thou art hastening thine own death !—Wilt thou leave me to despair ?—Oh ! I beseech thee, calm these transports.—For my sake--for the sake of thy babe ! Have mercy upon us all."

To these endearments of her husband she answered not, but lay speechless, and without motion. The efforts she had made seemed to have exhausted her frame, and it was evident that death was on the point of completing his work. Tia Rachela, who (to her honor be it said) had, during this scene, shed a flood of tears, no sooner saw her fainting away, than, judging that swoon would be her last, she called upon the padre to administer extreme unction. The husband was by force removed from her bedside, and the preparations for the administration of the last Sacrament were quickly made.

Whatever may, by various classes of Christians, be thought of the spiritual efficacy of this rite, it possesses a moving simplicity, and a kind of patriarchal grandeur, which are eminently calculated to impress the beholder with lively sentiments of faith, and to excite in the patient deep feelings of repentance. In the present instance, the interest might, to a vulgar eye, have been diminished by the absence of that pomp and glitter which are generally its accompaniments in so wealthy a country as Mexico ; but, to a man of feeling, it would have been heightened by the dignity and solemn fervor with which the worthy clergyman graced the ceremony. Truly did he appear an angel of mercy, when, robed in his white flowing surplice and purple stole, he drew near to the little altar, erected by the dying lady's bedside, and stretching forth his right hand over her head, according to the rubrics, he called upon God, in the words of the ritual, " Look down, we beseech thee, O Lord, upon thy handmaid, whose strength is failing fast, and take compassion upon a soul which thou hast created. Holy God, Father Almighty, who, by infusing the grace of thy blessing into the suffering bodies of thy faithful, vouchsafest to restore thy creatures to the enjoyment of health, hearken unto the invocation of thy holy name ; strengthen her by the help of thy right hand, fortify her by thy virtue, and defend her by thy might."

The cabin in which the ceremony was taking place, though poor and destitute of every kind of ornament, save some clumsy images of saints, was full of sincere worshippers, whose sympathies condoled with the husband's grief. There was not a dry eye among them, and their tears were mingled with their prayers, as they bent, in breathless anxiety, towards the Tata padre. They were only poor Indians, hardly half-civilized, yet, notwithstanding their poverty, every one had found the means of procuring a slender wax taper, which he now held lighted, in his hand, in order to honor the last breath of a sister in the faith. These tapers had been blessed on the festival of *Nuesta Señora de la candelaria*, and there was a virtue in them, to smooth the passage of a departing soul into the nether world, and though the blessing had cost two shillings, they did not grudge it to the strange lady !— This might be superstition, but it was charity.

The priest went on.—The holy oil was applied to her eyes, and they were shut to the light. The sign of the cross was signed over her lips, and they were closed—closed for ever :—she had breathed her last, murmuring the name of her husband !

She was no sooner dead, than the supplications for the living soul ceased. The priest knelt down, and, lifting up his eyes, and stretching forth his hands towards heaven, seemed, in a moment of rapture, to offer up that pure spirit, thus untimely cut off from all earthly affections, before the throne of immortal providence ; but as his looks returned to the earth, and fell upon the inanimate corpse, reminded of his ministerial duty, he put on the black stole, and slowly began to recite the *office for the dead*.

Mr. Faring was too deeply affected to take any of the

measures necessary in the present circumstances ; in consequence of which, the worthy clergyman, after having scrupulously recited all the prayers prescribed by the ceremonial of
his church, kindly took upon himself the office of undertaker.
A coffin was out of the question, this being a luxury in which,
in Mexico, none can indulge, except in large cities—a necessary consequence of the great scarcity of plank, every one
of which, for want of saws, has to be fashioned, with the axe
and adze, in the true Robinson Crusoe's style, out of a solid
piece of timber.   A fair piece of linen was, however, procured, in which the body of the Count of Letinez's daughter was
shrouded with decency, by Tia Rachela, and deposited upon
high trestles, where it lay the remainder of the day, in a kind
of mock state, with its face uncovered, a blessed candle burning at each corner, and a vase of holy water with a sprinkler,
at the feet.   The corpse was visited by the villagers, every
one of whom, in his turn, piously sprinkled it, out of the vase,
and then signed it with the sign of the cross, reciting, at the
same time, a fervent prayer—generally a *De profundis, or a
Salve Regina*.

The next day, a sufficient number of men was engaged to
carry the body to Phelipa, where it was to be interred, and
the order of the funeral procession was arranged, when there
arose a dispute between Tia Rachela and some of the women of the rancho, about the kind of dress in which the corpse
should be arrayed.

In order to make our readers understand the drift and importance of this dispute, we must premise some few observations on certain monastic observances and institutions, still
extant in Mexico.   The mendicant friars were established
in that country, immediately after the conquest, and, as by
their constitutions, they were debarred from the right of possessing real property, and reduced to live on alms, they obtained from the Holy See certain privileges and special
graces, which, in point of spiritual merit, raised them high
above the rest of the clergy.   These were granted them, as
a kind of indemnity, for their renunciation of temporal blessings ; but they were not found sufficient to quicken the charity of the faithful, which, in process of time, grew so luke-
warm, that those religious bodies were threatened with starvation.   To remedy this inconvenience, therefore, they

obtained from the Pope the faculty of granting the indulgences peculiar to their order to such of the laity as they might think proper.

The Franciscans, the eldest of the mendicant friars, eager to enhance the right conferred, and to derive therefrom the greatest advantage, instituted what was technically called the *third order* of St. Francis ; that is to say, a confraternity of lay persons, entirely distinct from the nuns and friars. The members of this brotherhood live in the world, or even enjoy a married life, if they choose ; and yet, upon their wearing a little badge of the institute, and reciting a few additional prayers, they participate in all the merits of the members of the first order. Though the acquisition of so much grace, at so cheap a rate, be a capital speculation, in spirituals ; still, such is the supineness and negligence of the people, that many forego the immense advantage, during their lifetime. The means of forcing it upon them, after their death, has, however, been piously found out. This is done by burying the body in the gown and hood of the order ! During the middle ages, it was usual to put these badges on dying sinners, before they expired, and it was what the writers of that period styled "mori in domino ;" but now-a-days, it is equally efficacious, if performed before they are committed to the grave.

The order of St. Francis, that acquired a vast influence in Mexico, extended this pious practice all over the country, and even, at this day, few persons are buried, in the interior of the republic, without this formality. The Franciscans do not, however, enjoy a monopoly ; for all the other orders, seing the prodigious advantages derived from it, imitated the practice. The Carmelites procured for the scapular, so great a reputation, that even the wealthiest religious fraternities saw themselves obliged to don it over their own conventual garments. The Dominicans, also, extended far and wide the credit of their white tunic, and though they never could cope with the Franciscans, still they proved formidable rivals. This multiplicity of blessed garments for the dead, and the difficulty of making a selection agreeable to all the relations of the deceased, not unfrequently occasions unpleasant debates, in Mexican families, and has, more than once, changed the grief incidental to the death of a friend, into bitterness against the living. In the present instance, it brought about a ridiculous squabble between Tia Rachela and two of the comadres of the Rancho.

The *partera*, who was a very zealous devotee of the order of St. Francis, had, immediately after the lady's death, sent a courier to Phelipa, in order to bring a *mortaja* of her own choice. But when the aforesaid funeral garment was unfolded, the two old women, who had assisted her in laying out the body, vehemently exclaimed against the choice she had made.

Doña Juana Merino was the first to raise the outcry. " And what !" said she, " is it in this habit of the nuns of St. Clair, you intend to bury a lady of her rank ? A Count's daughter !—Pshaw !—when I lived in Guadalaxara, all the ladies who died were buried in the fair white gown of the Dominican nuns. It was a pleasing sight to behold them in that dress ! Ah, many a one I have helped to lay out !—The hood was always made of the finest English flannel, lined with white silk and trimmed with Flanders' lace. When a lady was fixed in this trim, with her hands meekly crossed on her breast, and a gold rosary between her fingers, it was a sight for the Lord Bishop himself, though it was but seldom that his most illustrious lordship would take the trouble of pronouncing the blessing upon the mortaja ; except when it belonged to people of distinction."

" Hold your peace, woman," replied Tia Rachela. " Do you think that all the lace and silk, which you ever saw in Guadalaxara, are worth a share in the suffrages of the order of our father St. Francis, in which this unfortunate lady will participate, by our putting on her this mortaja ; besides a plenary indulgence, applicable to her soul, on the festival of our blessed lady of the *Portiuncula ?* Talk like a Christian, and cease your palaver about white silk and Flanders' lace."

" Talk like a Christian !" replied Juana Merino, incensed ; " that is to say, then, that I talk like a heretic, or a Comanche Indian ! And what do you mean, yourself, by making light of St. Dominic's habit ? The Dominicans are something better than your Franciscans, I trow. Had you seen as much of the world as I have, you would know, that while the king of Spain held his own, undisturbed, in this kingdom, *they* had the inquisition under their jurisdiction,

and could shut up in their dungeons the viceroy himself.
And as for indulgences, I wish to know in what the Dominican habit is inferior to the Franciscan ? Go to, Tia, you
know nothing—why, there is a hundred years indulgence
for the mere kissing of the hem of a Dominican friar's gown !
—show me the same among your Franciscans. Ay, you
may bring together the *Guadelupanos* of Zacatecas, and the
*Cruciferos* of Queretaro, and I defy you to show the same."

"Doña Juana is in the right," interrupted the other matron, whose name was Rita de Marfil, "and I am of opinion
that we must give to the lady a white mortaja of St. Dominic. My daughter-in-law has one, which was blessed in
Quatorce, five years ago, by a holy preacher. We can get
it, I dare say she will charge very little above prime cost,
and the widowed gentleman is rich enough to pay for it."([9])

"Ah," replied Rachela, "you come out plainly now, and
I have found you out. You have a mortaja to sell—have
you ? And it is the reason why you prefer St. Dominic's ;
but, as sure as my name is Rachela, the lady shall be buried
in the one I have sent for from Phelipa, and if you do not
want to help me, you may go about your business—I will
inform the Tata padre of your charitable intentions."

The threat which the wise woman had thrown out immediately dissipated the opposition of the two matrons, who,
without further resistance, submitted to her direction. The
dead body was, therefore, soon deposited on the bier, and
the funeral procession set out for Phelipa. The march was
opened by the coach, in which rode the priest, Tia Rachela,
Mr. Faring, and a woman of the Rancho, whom they had engaged to take care of the infant, until a regular nurse could
be procured. Next, came the corpse, borne on the shoulders
of four men, followed by eight more, who were to act as re-
lays, on the road ; for it is accounted indecorous, in Mexico,
to convey the bodies of Christians to their grave, in vehicles
drawn by animals—a piece of funeral etiquette which ob-
tains also in some parts of the south of France. Lastly came
all the servants with the sumpter mules that had accompanied Mr. Faring in his journey, the priest having directed
the former to pack up their master's equipage and to follow.
The march was closed by the armed men that had come from
Phelipa, at the instigation of Doña Salas, and who, having

found their expedition a work of superogation, had, nevertheless, remained at Larza, in order to accompany the Tata
padre back to his house, and give to themselves, in the
eyes of their fellow-townsmen, the merit of having been of
some service to him.

The march lasted five hours, and the procession entered
Phelipa, just before twilight. The greatest part of the population came out to behold their entrance, but the priest addressing them a few words in reprehension of their indiscreet curiosity, they immediately dispersed, and the corpse
was carried to the church, where it was deposited to remain
until the following day, when the funeral obsequies were to
take place.

After complying with these pious duties, the clergyman
turned his attention to the present forlorn state of the stranger, whom circumstances had thus thrown upon his protection. He immediately sought out a nurse for the infant, and
fortunately succeeding, he placed her and her young charge
in the house of a respectable lady, who, reverencing the
*padre*, gladly undertook to watch over both. Mr. Faring
and his servants were lodged in the priest's house, and the
best part of the night was devoted by the latter to the consolation of his guest.

The motives usually suggested to the sorrowing mind, in
order to assuage its grief, appear, at first, to make but little
impression upon it, and many are, on this account, for leaving nature to take her course, as they term it, and abandon
the distressed in heart, to the bitterness of their own thoughts.
This is, however, nothing but a specious cloak to conceal
their own selfishness, which makes them indifferent to the
sufferings of a fellow-creature. Surely, though the consolations bestowed upon the unfortunate should not prove efficacious to heal sorrow, the manifestation of the tender sympathies of a feeling heart cannot fail to lighten the weight,
which, incubus-like, oppresses the sufferer. By appearing to participate in his grief, we help him to bear its
burthen.

Up to this rule did the charitable priest act. There was
no consolatory motive, whether drawn from religion, or from
the contemplation of terrene things, which he did not repeatedly press upon Mr. Faring's consideration ; and, though

his efforts had no visible effect, still he knew they would not
be altogether unavailing.

These charitable cares were interrupted by sleep, to which,
however, a very small portion of the night was allotted, as
on the next morning, the body of the unfortunate Maria del
Carmen was to be committed to the grave. When the time
appointed for the burial had arrived, the widowed husband
could by no means be persuaded to remain in the house, but
insisted upon attending the funeral, which was performed
with all the magnificence that could be afforded in so remote
a place as the town of Phelipa. The parish priest himself
officiated, attended by a deacon and sub-deacon. The *cata-
falque*, in the middle of the nave, was covered with black
cloth, and adorned with a profusion of mourning escutcheons
and wax lights. The very altar was hung with sable ornaments, and the singing-boys were clad in deep mourning,
while the incessant tolling of the numerous bells published
to a great distance, that a grand funeral, *con lujo y pompa*,
was being celebrated.

The service to which this outward exhibition served as an
accompaniment is eminently beautiful, and probably the
sublimest portion of the ritual of the Church of Rome. It
begins by the ninety-fourth psalm, sung in a plaintive tone,
by a single voice, which, for the sake of effect, is always a
contralto, where it can be got, while, at the end of every
verse, the whole choir responds, in a low solemn bass voice,
as though it proceeded from the bosom of the grave. The
lessons, taken from the book of Job, are read in a recitative
tone, intermingled with solemn pauses, when a death-like
silence prevails, and the whole is crowned by the grand
dirge, " Libera me, Domine, de morte eterna," &c., with a
harmony and power so piercingly stirring, as to be almost
too affecting for the human heart. It is a perfect *Onomato
peia* of the scenes in purgatory, wherein are imitated, with
the utmost perfection, the low and humble entreaties for
mercy—the suppressed groans of the suffering souls below ;—nay, their very shrieks of wo, and their writhings
under the chastising hand of God. It had, in this instance,
a powerful effect upon the stranger, who, being a Protestant,
had never before witnessed such a spectacle. The singing-
boys, in full chorus, had just intoned the famous anthem,

" *Miseremini mei, saltem vos, amici mei, quia manus Domini tetigit me !*" when, Mr. Faring, overpowered by his feelings, sank to the earth, in a deep swoon, and the good clergyman, his friend, had to disrobe himself, in order to attend him home, while the service was continued and concluded by his vicar.

Mr. Faring was immediately put to bed, but the priest found it difficult to recover him from his fainting-fit, and when, at last, he was restored to the use of his senses, the first expressions he uttered showed that he was delirious. Greatly alarmed, and fearing the most fatal consequences, the clergyman would not trust to his own knowledge of the medical art, but immediately sent for the two physicians, neither of whom had yet returned. Forced, therefore, to rely upon his own individual skill, the priest ordered bleed-ing, which had a favorable result, and caused a revulsion from the head. The two physicians, however, arrived be-fore the end of the day, and relieved the worthy ecclesiastic from the anxiety to which he had been a prey, by assuring him that they did not consider the state of the patient as dangerous. They chiefly prescribed mild remedies, and rather directed their efforts to what the Frenchman styled " *un traitement moral*," than a pharmaceutical one. For that purpose, they prescribed that the child should be fre-quently brought to his bed-side, and that the father should be indulged in bestowing upon him his parental caresses.

This had the desired effect. Though Mr. Faring shed tears the first time the child was presented to him, yet he felt there was something left to fill up the vacuum which his wife's death had created in his heart. His affection began again to expand, and in a few days he was able to rise from his bed. Little by little his health improved, and at the end of six weeks, thinking himself sufficiently recovered to re-sume his journey, he broached the subject to his kind host, who, by this time, had conceived a strong attachment for him, and could not think of a separation without regret.

The worthy clergyman had been, at first, greatly inter-ested in behalf of the stranger by the frank confidence with which he had entrusted to him his wife's condition and the ecclesiastical persecution she had been undergoing. Then, the various proofs of tender love, he had manifested towards

her showed that his heart was actuated by the noblest feelings. Lastly, the priest had found out his guest to be a
man well versed in literature, to which he was himself passionately addicted. He made it the subject of the many
conversations, that, during Mr. Faring's convalescence, he
held with him, in order to avert his thoughts from the consideration of his late loss ; and thus he became fonder of his
society, in proportion as he discovered the extent of his
knowledge.

There are no bands so pleasant as those which this kind
of intimacy forms between men of learning. The mutual
enjoyments they communicate to each other, in their intercourse, may be compared to the effect of friction, in physics,
that produces both heat and light, and it is with no less precision, than sublimity, that a great English poet, in a short
sentence, of the deepest meaning, styled them, " the feast of
reason and the flow of soul." The unexpected points of
view, under which one is brought to consider a subject, by
the novel reflections which are elicited, and the peculiar
tinge that each idea contracts in a kindred mind, when its
possessor, in the full confidence of friendship, permits one to
dive into its recesses—the zest of the quick repartee, in conversation, when unobscured by the stiff and formal veil of
wordly etiquette—the brilliancy of the sally, resulting, like
a spark, from collision ; all these are the refined enjoyments
with which a beneficent providence rewards the cultivation
of the mind. All this, ennobled by self-respect and mutual
esteem, generally enriches and adorns the friendship of men
of genius and renders it durable.

The parish priest of Phelipa began to realize, in Mr. Faring's conversation, the charm which we have attempted to describe, and was desirous of insuring to himself its continuation.
The only pleasure he had known, during a long series of
years, was that of reading ; but what is reading, if one is
condemned to perpetual silence about the works one peru-
ses ? It is true, as we have already said, that the Alcalde
as well as some other worthies of Phelipa, had received a
collegiate education ; but then their knowledge went no further
than the dog Latin into which the metaphysics of Aristotle
have been translated by father Goudin, and a few scraps
from Spanish writers of the sixteenth century—such as the

Araucana and the eternal Don Quixote ! The conversation of those literati could not fill up the void in the priest's mind, and it was with no less wit than truth he used to say of himself that he had been " Damnatus ad bestias."

He, therefore, pertinaciously insisted upon Mr. Faring's settling in Phelipa, laying before him, in detail, all the advantages he might derive from commerce on a large scale, in a place, where, for hundreds of miles around, he would have no competition to fear ; but his guest's resolution was not to be shaken. He could not forego the hopes and inducements that his rank, standing and instruction held out to him, in his native country ; in order to settle in a strange land, the manners of which were vastly inferior to what is found in more civilized regions. He could not think of embracing the religion of the country, without which, he knew, there was but little personal security ; and lastly, he was aware that his friend, though liberal and well bred, aimed, nevertheless, at his conversion, and the attempts he foresaw he would not fail to make for its accomplishment would engender bickerings between them, and diminish that friendship, which he really thought it an honor to himself to have inspired in so good a man. He, of course, persisted in his determination.

When the priest saw it was impossible to detain the father, he earnestly begged that he might be, at least, permitted to retain the infant and bring him up. He could not think of Mr. Faring's journey and the dangers incident to it, without fearing that it would prove fatal to the little creature. He dreaded, besides, that he should not be educated in the Catholic faith, and the mere thought was intolerable to the good man. As he had baptized him, he believed himself answerable to God for his salvation.

It was, in fact, utterly impossible for Mr. Faring to carry the infant with him, to the United States, and he was glad to grant as a boon, what he would, otherwise, have been obliged to ask as a favor. He knew the worthy man well enough to be sure that his child would be as tenderly taken care of as if his mother were alive. He, therefore, agreed to leave the babe in the hands of the nurse to whom he had been entrusted, under the superintendence of the lady in whose house both had been placed ; but as soon as he should be able to

4*

walk, he was to remove to the priest's house, where the old
"*Ama de llaves*,"* a very snug and motherly Indian woman,
who had served the priest, in quality of house-keeper, more
than twenty years, would take care of him.

Mr. Faring generously paid the nurse, beforehand, made
very valuable presents to the lady in whose house the child
lived, and would, also, have bestowed proofs of his liberality
on the clergyman's house-keeper, but she would accept nothing, save a small painting of " *Nuestra Señora de los dolores*," which was precious in her eyes because the Bishops of
Durango and Monterey had conceded a forty days' indulgence,
for every pious look that any one of the faithful should cast
upon it.   This was a real treasure, for she might be casting
sheep's eyes at it, a hundred times an hour!—It was one of
the spoils of the deceased lady, and though the priest had especially forbidden his house-keeper to accept any gratuity,
he was not sorry, when he discovered the picture had been
secured from the profanation it might have incurred, by
being carried away into a heathenish country, such as the
United States were supposed to be.

* Literally, " the mistress of the keys."

# CHAPTER IV.

Trust not, my friend, the softness of the land.—
Have your good sword well girt, and e'er at hand,
Your pistols,—your spontoon, with double load,
For through a dangerous region lies your road.

*Anonymous.*

ALL things being now arranged to the mutual satisfaction of both parties, and Mr. Faring's preparations being completed, he took his departure from Phelipa, with the promise of returning, if practicable, at the end of three years; and, tearing himself from his kind host, set forward on his route. He rode alone, in his coach, armed to the teeth, and accompanied by six servants, who drove ten sumpter mules, loaded with his trunks, bed, provisions and a tent. Taverns, or inns, there are none in the country and even the villagers are so scantily supplied with comforts, that, unless a traveller be disposed to live in an Indian fashion, he must go provided with the necessary equipage, down to the cooking utensils. It is true that the owners of cabins, in the ranchos, generally grant permission to travellers to sleep in their dwellings; but these, from the scantiness of the population, are not always to be reached, and even, when reached, it is commonly found preferable, from the uncleanliness and narrow dimensions of those buildings, to sleep out of doors. All travellers, therefore, *bivouac* as they go, unless when they chance to have letters of introduction to wealthy families, whose means enable them to exercise hospitality.

Mr. Faring's journey was a specimen of the manner in which the better sort of people perform their travels, in Mexico. The march was opened by three servants, on horseback, each armed with a long sword, a short musket depending from his saddle-bow, while a large dagger, called, in Spanish, *belduque*, was stuck in the leather wrappers which served him for boots. Each carried, besides, a pair of holster pistols and the *lasso*, indispensable for catching their mules, after feeding, and which might, in an emergency, be

used as an offensive weapon, and one, too, of the most formidable description. Next followed the coach, drawn by
four mules, with outrider ; and the remainder of the men,
equiped and armed as the foremost ones, brought up the rear.

In this way, they rode, forty or fifty miles, every day,
under a trusty guide, whom they had engaged at Phelipa ; as
Mr. Faring's servants were strangers to that part of the
country, and, of course, unacquainted with the roads. The
guide acted, also, in the capacity of cook, and it was his business to provide, on the way, fresh meat, or other provisions,
at the ranchos through which they passed, or from the shep-
herds whom they happened to encounter.

For that purpose, he would frequently leave the party, and
strike to the right, or left, through thickets of *nopal*, or *car-
denche*, so thorny and closely interwoven together, that a
foreigner would have judged them absolutely intransitable for
any human being. Thoroughly encased in a leather dress, he,
nevertheless, aquitted himself with little or no damage to his
skin. The same feat was frequently performed by others
among the servants, when in pursuit of any capricious mule
that chose to leave the main road. In fact, the habits of the
Mexican peasants seem peculiarly adapted to the management of the horse species. There is no mule, how fractious
soever, which they cannot tame in half a day ; and their
sobriety and tough powers of endurance are a match for those
of the animal. The mule will trot the whole day, under a
burning sun, bearing a burden of three hundred weight, and,
at night, fare sumptuoulsy, upon the dry grass which may be
picked up, among bushes and briars, in regions, where, frequently, there does not fall a drop of rain for six months.—
But the Indian will stand the same fatigue and lie down con-
tentedly, beside his pack-saddle, after a scanty supper of
brown beans and *tortillas*,* with a burning sauce of red
pepper, as condiment. With this regimen, he can resist the
fatigues of the longest journeys and without any other provision, he sets out on his march.

The country through which our present party were travel-

* For the preparation of tortillas, the maize is first steeped into water
slightly acidulated with lime, and when ground on the *metate*, or mill,
the pellicle is carefully separated from the dough, which is, next, flat-
tened to the thickness of paste board, baked and eaten hot.

ling soon lost the smiling aspect of the fertile oasis which we have described in the beginning of this work, and they enter-ed upon a lonely waste of fifty leagues in extent, destitute of vegetation and, consequently, of inhabitants. At a great distance, to the right, they could descry a chain of mountains, running parallel to their road, but from which flowed neither brook, nor rill, to relieve the dreariness of the scene. They found it necessary to carry water for their use, in small kegs, with which they had provided themselves for that purpose, before leaving Phelipa, and when, at night, they came to their encamping place, the mules had to be driven to various muddy puddles, sometimes at the distance of three leagues from the road.

The night scene was picturesque and presented a spectacle analogous to patriachal manners. As soon as the mules were unloaded, the first care of the servants was to erect, with the pack saddles and loads, a kind of rampart, in the form of a parallelogram, and then set up Mr. Faring's port-able dwelling in the centre of that species of fortification. Of stout canvass, and firmly secured by means of ropes and wooden pegs driven into the ground, it was comfortable enough, in a country where there are no dews and seldom any cold. In this tent were spread mats, on which the cloth was laid by the servants, though, afterwards, a trunk was used as a table. At the further end, was placed the bed, so that Mr. Faring might, with an eye to greater security, cause some of his servants to sleep under the same shelter, in case he should apprehend any danger. There he could also read, write with a certain degree of comfort and enjoy cleanliness, by no means the distinguishing characteristic of the cabins, at the ranchos, or haciendas ; where fleas, and, not unfre-quently, something worse, are found a complete preventative of repose.

At a few steps from the tent, the cook made a fire, un-packed his cooking utensils, and set about preparing the sup-per, while the rest of the men, after driving the mules to water ; hobbled them for the night, and turned them among the bushes, to graze upon the few blades of grass which had escaped the heats of the summer, or the voracious tooth of the goat, immense flocks of which constitute the wealth of the proprietors of the soil in those parts.

The morning scene was still more lively and distinguished by a peculiar air of bustle. While Mr. Faring was drinking his chocolate and strenghthening his stomach with some of the cold relics of the supper of the preceding evening; his men set about collecting their mules, and when these were driven together, the *lassoing* began. Taking in his hand the rope, at the end of which dangled the running noose, and forming it into large coils, each man, with unerring aim, threw it over the head of the mule he had selected—though at a considerable distance,—nor were the restiveness and capricious movements of the animal obstacles to the precision of the *arriero's coup d'oeuil*. The mule being thus caught, the rope was, with similar promptitude, adjusted in the form of a halter, and the animal led away to be saddled. The whole operation hardly ever took more than five minutes, and two men were adequate to the task of putting on a load, and securing it by tight girthing. The whole baggage thus loaded, two or three of the *peones* proceeded, with the sumpter mules, while the remainder prepared the carriage, which being promptly ready, set off with great rapidity, and soon overtaking the vanguard ; caused them, in their turn, to fall to the rear.

In this manner did Mr. Faring journey on, until he reached Parras, a considerable town, in the province of Cohahuila. This place, which has, since the epoch to which we refer, acquired a certain importance, in consequence of considerable establishments in the manufacturing line, undertaken by a wealthy English banker, is situated in the centre of a frightful wilderness, and owes its existence to the ancient Mexican Jesuits. In the very heart of that desert, at the foot of one of the spurs of granite mountains that stretch into the arid plain, abundant springs of the purest water gush out and fertilize a few leagues of a soil which would, otherwise, have remained condemned to perpetual aridity. It is a situation like that of Tadmor, in the Oriental wilderness—serving as a resting place for the caravans that pass from the table-land, to the sea-shore, and affording abundance of provisions at a cheap rate.

The reverend fathers, who were the pioneers of civilization in those remote regions, found a few Indians, wandering about through the waste, and soon brought them under their spiritual empire. The influence and credit of their order in Europe, enabled them to obtain from the king of Spain, permission to cultivate the grape-vine, and they formed, here, two splendid haciendas. A town grew round their conventual establishment, consisting almost exclusively of their dependents and laborers ; for the good fathers were not disposed to admit strangers amongst their neophytes. They gave for reason of this policy, the necessity of guarding the morals of their converts, against the contagious example of Europeans. Some of their enemies have, since, pretended that this jealous and exclusive spirit had, for its object, to keep the Indians in more complete subjection ; but, whatever may have been the cause, the effect, in the north of Mexico, resulted in the introduction of an improved system of husbandry, and a knowledge of the principal mechanical arts, among rude and ignorant savages, who, had it not been for the efforts made by the Jesuits and mendicant friars, would yet, like the Lipanes, Comanches, and Apaches, live in a state of nature.

Some of these missionaries were, no doubt, actuated by selfish considerations and worldly views. Many a friar, weary of the hard life, rigorous poverty, and strict obedience of the convent, would solicit a *mission*, as a measure of relief, and, upon finding himself comfortably lodged in a snug parsonage-house—surrounded by hundreds of Indians, who looked upon their padre as a kind of demi-god, and revered his very failings—he could not be so blind as not to prefer such a situation to the naked cell of a Franciscan, or Capuchin friary. Such motives did, probably, frequently stimulate many of those propagators of the faith ; but it must also be confessed, that there were among them, many truly apostolic men, actuated by the purest religious zeal, and the most sublime philanthropy.

Even these, however, could not have taken a sufficient hold on the minds of the Indians, naturally fickle and little susceptible of permanent impressions, had not the Spanish government, whose policy, in the management of its colonies, was singularly provident, made it a rule to send on the steps of each missionary, a party of soldiers, who never failed to erect a fort where he built a church. These' soldiers protected the priest, and, by degrees, accustomed the

savages to the dominion of the whites. Sometimes, however, the Indians proved refractory and deaf to the missionary's instructions, and in those cases, the government had
recourse to a singular artifice, the idea of which, seems to
have been borrowed from a certain mode of quail hunting,
peculiar to the southern regions of Europe. In those countries, fowlers make use of tame quails, in order to inveigle
wild ones into their nets, and in imitation of this, the Spanish government made use of colonies of Tlascaltecans to
draw in the wild Indians.

The powerful republic of Tlascala, that resisted all the
power of Montezuma, and which Fernando Cortes thought
himself happy in forming an alliance with, has, by such arts
as these, dwindled away and is now diminished to a territory
of thirty miles square. Travellers are apt to wonder at the
disappearance of this once powerful people, and to manifest
a philanthropic indignation at their supposed annihilation.
But the Tlascaltecans were not annihilated. They are, probably, at this day, more numerous than ever. True, their
nation has been broken up, but they exist, like the Jews, in
a scattered state.

Near all the towns of any consequence, in the internal
provinces of the north of Mexico, you find a large village of
this race of Indians, generally bearing the name of Guadelupe, and adorned with a church of special sanctity, in which
is kept a statue of *Jesus Nazareno*, more miraculous than
any the white people possess in their own houses of worship. In the greatest emergencies, and particularly in cases
of drought, the whites of the neighboring cities are obliged
by custom to resort, in solemn procession, to those villages
and borrow the venerated statue, which they carry with solemn pomp and devotion to their own temples, in order to
obtain from heaven the favor sued for. The superior worth
of this holy thing, engenders in those Indians, a kind of nationality, which the remembrance of the past glory of the
republic of Tlascala would not effect. It binds them together, and serves to persuade them that, in some respects, at
least, the whites are confessedly their inferiors.

In many places, they have retained the use of their primitive language, which was the same as the Mexican, and
they distinguish themselves above the rest of the inhabitants

of that country, by a neater system of husbandry. Their
fields are better tilled, they have finer orchards, their inclo-
sures, in particular, are delightfully green, and similar to the
live hedges of European farms. Among them, you see a
better distribution of water for the purposes of irrigation;
more industry, more activity and life, and a certain look of
independence, very different from the cringing glance of the
other aborigines of the country. Such villages were colonies settled by the crafty Spaniards,—first, to have the advantage of the labors of the Tlascaltecans; secondly, to
make, by their means, upon the minds of the wild Indians,
an impression favorable to the domination of the white race.
These Tlascaltecans were the *decoy-birds* made use of to
inveigle new subjects under the dominion of the king of
Spain, and this system of colonization served, besides, to
break up the Tlascaltecan nation, whose territory was too
close to the city of Mexico, not to give the government
some umbrage, as long as that people retained a distinct social existence.

The scheme was well planned, like most of those which
proceeded from the Jesuits' store, and it succeeded accordingly; but the inventors have not reaped the fruit of their
labors! They acquired millions of leagues on the earth's
surface, for the crown of Castile, and that foolish government dissolved their order and exiled its members, for the
sake of the trifling plunder to be obtained from their farms
and colleges. It was, in very deed, killing the goose that lay
the golden eggs! But the old Spanish monarchy is gone to the
tomb of all the Capulets. Peace be to its manes! A better
fate, perhaps, awaits the founders of civilization in those
parts. Phœnix-like, the Jesuits are rising from their ashes,
and repairing in crowds to the favorite haunts of the first
patriarchs of their order. They are already numerous in
the Mississippi valley, and cast many a tender glance at the
golden regions of New Mexico. They will, probably, resume
the lead there, but never more to draw the chesnuts out of
the embers, for his Catholic Majesty.([10])

It was at one of those decayed *Jesuitical* villages that
Mr. Faring put up, about three leagues from the city of Parras. A large vineyard, three miles square, irrigated by a
limpid stream, and surrounded by lofty walls, flanked the

village on one side. On a rising ground stood the chapel, which, for its size and internal decorations, could vie with many of the parish churches of the country ; and the habitation of the owner, who might, with more propriety, have been styled Lord of the manor, occupied a plat of level ground, by the side of the babbling brook.

Bringing a letter of introduction for the master of the house, Mr. Faring went to ask hospitality, which was granted with all the courtesy and ceremony proper to a Spaniard of the old school. The mode of receiving travellers, in that country, is, however, so singular, that our readers will not, we are sure, be sorry to peruse, here, a detailed account of what is, on such occasions, practised in the most wealthy families. The principal building, at the *Hacienda de Abajo,* (such was the name of the village,) was a vast quadrangle, including a paved court-yard, with a well in the centre, and decorated with various shrubbery. To this inner court, there was but one entrance, opening upon what might be termed the public square of the village. To this portal the coach drove up, and Mr. Faring's baggage, when unloaded, was piled up in the passage, and left exposed to the curious gaze of the passer-by, while, in the same *Zaguan* was established the temporary abode of the traveller's men, peones, cook and postillion. There they remained, day and night, when not attending to the mules, and for the convenience of their class, the architect who built the house, had provided two stone benches, along the walls, on which they might sit, or lie down, as best suited their conveniency.

As for their master, he was conducted, with great ceremony to a large hall, round two sides of which, ran a low divan, in the Asiatic form, but not with Asiatic luxury. There was there, neither silken pillow, nor golden fringe ; but the *estrada,* which consisted merely of a narrow and uncomfortable wooden bench, was covered with cushions of coarse brown velvet. In order to prevent the clothes of those who sat upon this divan being soiled by the white wash of the walls, along which it was ranged, a piece of showy calico, two yards wide, figured as tapestry, which made the nakedness of the walls, above and below the narrow strip, more glaringly conspicuous. Six heavy wooden chairs, and a table of coarse pine plank, unpainted and unvarnished, were all the furniture this apartment could boast. The floor was brick, and the windows were almost blocked up, with thick wooden bars, which served, rather to exclude the light, than to increase the safety of the inmates.

Into this pleasaunce was Mr. Faring introduced, with an infinity of bows and scrapes, that out-vied a Frenchman's ceremonial, and there he found the mistress of the house, with her two daughters, gravely sitting on the estrada, as stiff as if they had been carved out of a block of marble, each with an immense tortoise-shell comb stuck on her head, and a saltillo *rebozo* (shawl) hanging from the comb and tightly wound round her neck and shoulders, which gave to their figures as ungainly an appearance, as if they had been prepared for strangulation. This is a bad substitute for the Spanish mantilla, and the Mexican ladies, who have not lost the elegant carriage, nor *airs-de-tête* of their grandmothers, would do well to look to it.

These three females, though belonging to the most distinguished class, were entirely devoid of instruction. Their acquirements were limited to reading and writing, which last was considered a great attainment for persons of their sex, and is, indeed, exceedingly rare ; but their ideas extended not to polite literature, nor knew they the elements of history, or geography. Their conversation was, therefore, dry and uninteresting, and Mr. Faring felt all the weight of dulness creep upon him, when chocolate was served. It is customary to offer a cup of that beverage to guests, in Mexico, whenever they happen to visit in the morning, or evening, and it would be accounted grossly impolite to neglect this mark of hospitality. To the chocolate succeeds a tumbler of clear water, after which, *cigarritos* are handed round.

These cigarritos are more than half paper, and the smoke they produce is a kind of luxury to which our traveller was not very partial, still, in compliment to his host, he offered violence to himself and continued to smoke, till he was invited to pass into the *gran sala*, which was the most splendid apartment in the whole mansion. The furniture of this hall was, in point of magnificence, superior to anything else in that part of the country, and as the family we are now describing was one of the most wealthy in the state of Cohahuila, it may, upon the whole, be taken as a sample of what was then, and is even yet, in the northern parts of the Mexican republic, accounted luxury and comfort. The pavement consisted of indurated mortar, painted red, and as highly polished as the surface of a mirror, which is done by a process hardly understood, or, at least, seldom practised in the old continent. It looks nearly as beautiful as stucco work, and is as durable as the *chunan* of the East Indies. It were a desirable thing to introduce such pavements for ground floors, into the architecture of the United States. They would prove a great addition to the internal decoration of the houses of our southern planters. They are easily kept clean and possess the coolness and brilliancy of marble. In this instance, however, such a piece of magnificence was not in keeping with the bareness of the walls, which were, indeed, white-washed, but devoid of every ornament, except some prints, in gilt frames. The windows, too, were without curtains, and the eternal estrada, itself, without the accompanying strip of calico. Along the walls, on each side, were ranged some rush-bottomed chairs imported from New Orleans, but the most sumptuous piece of foreign furniture was a mahogany table, in a corner, upon which were placed three small statues of Saints, exquisitely carved, decorated with gems, and in full dress of gold and silver tissue. These were " *los Santos de la casa,*" the household saints,—something like the penates among the old Romans.

Our traveller attracted by the delicacy of the sculpture, drew nigh to those saints, and began to examine them with attention ; whereupon the lady of the house, mistaking his curiosity for a religious feeling, explained to him, at great length, all the miracles they had performed in behalf of the family ; and, in order to manifest how grateful she had been for the benefits she had received, displayed, before him, a complete wardrobe, which she kept in one of the table drawers, for the use of the little figures. There were white satin gowns, with silver fringe, to be used during Christmas and Easter weeks ; red, for whitsuntide ! purple, for lent and advent ; nay, black ones for holy week !—She had necklaces and ear-rings for them, and treated them just like little girls treat their dolls. From her careless prattle, he even gathered that she attributed to them human passions, and thought them accessible to vanity and resentment ; for it was not without some self-complacency that she detailed how many times she had punished them, when deaf to her petitions, by taking away their finery, or stimulated them, by promises of costly ornaments.

Many of our readers will, no doubt, think the present account exaggerated, but we can assure them that, far from being overloaded, the sketch has been greatly weakened— through fear of wounding *Protestant* notions of probability. It is, in fact, what we have done, all along, in describing Mexican manners, and the peculiar features which modern civilization has assumed, in that singular country ; for, had we adhered to a close and rigorous description of both, the result would have been accounted incredible.

Strange as the assertion may appear, Mexico contains in itself all the germs of a great nation ; but they are still in embryo. The transition from a despotical to a republican form of government has been so sudden, that it has caused civilization, among the upper classes, to take a leap backwards— in order, probably, that it might gather more impetus, to clear the intervening chasm.

But though we are resolved to soften down certain crudities,—not to say enormities—which might, if exhibited, impart to our work an air of improbability ; we will, nevertheless, closely adhere to fidelity of expression. As to the modes of civil life—as they are, of themselves, indifferent, or, at best, but remotely connected with morality ; we make it a point to depict them with the most scrupulous exactitude, and in this, we think the present work may lay claim to some originality. For that purpose, we must continue the journal of Mr. Faring's travel, on his return to the United States ; and should our kind reader imagine this an *hors d'oeuvre ;* he must forgive the slight irregularity it introduces into our story, in favor of the information it conveys.

The company remained in the gran sala, of which we have attempted a description, till half passed ten, when it was announced that supper was on the table. Crossing, therefore, the court yard, they repaired to the eating room—another hall, nearly similar in dimensions to the one we have described, and where they found a plentiful supper. The viands were delicate, consisting of lamb, kid and fowls ; but the
5*

cookery was a strange mixture of the old Morisco and Indian styles. There were chickens, stuffed with almonds and raisins !—Pigeons, fricasseed with sugar and white wine !—Pork, stewed in a red pepper sauce, sufficiently strong to excoriate the palate of an Englishman, and each dish, besides, so profusely condimented with garlic, as would have turned the stomach of a Genoese. But, above all other spices and condiments, figured, in awful pre-eminence, the *chille piquen*, a kind of bird's-eye pepper, the taste of which is intolerably fiery. Poor Mr. Faring suffered severely by this good cheer ; but besides the abominable cookery of the dishes, the means of enjoying the festive board with comfort were scanty. Chairs there were none, and two long narrow benches, without the addition of cushions, supplied their places. Three knives were accounted sufficient for nine persons, so that our traveller was frequently obliged to have recourse to the implements of nature, as a substitute. This was not, however, so repugnant as being constrained to drink out of a tumbler, in common ; but as there were but four glasses on the table, he was also obliged to submit to that inconvenience.

If comfort was wanting, there was a great display of magnificence, to make up for it, for every thing which could be silver about the table was of that metal, and no less than six servants waited upon the guests. As soon as supper was over, one of them recited a long grace, in praise of the Blessed Sacrament of the altar, and the immaculate conception of the Virgin Mary, after which Mr. Faring retired to his couch, which consisted of the mattress and clothes he had brought with him,—spread on the floor of the gran sala. There we will leave him to his repose, while his servants, stretched on their blankets, are enjoying the benefit of the cool and bracing night air in the open court-yard, during their slumbers—a manner of lodging servants generally practised in Mexico, and which the mildness of the climate renders tolerable for them.

Our American had purposed to continue his journey on the following day, but his host was urgent to induce him to prolong his stay, and his servants represented to him that his travelling mules were much fatigued, with their hurried march and stood in need of recruiting themselves in the rich pastures of the Hacienda, so that he made up his mind to tarry there, two or three days longer.

# CHAPTER V.

The friar has walked out, and where'er he has gone,
The land and its fatness are marked for his own.
He may roam where he lists, he may stop when he tires,
For every man's house is the barefooted friar's.

*Walter Scott.*

BEFORE Mr. Faring's departure, some new travellers arrived at the manor house. They were two Augustinian friars, from Durango, bent upon a pilgrimage to the shrine of *nuestra Señora del chorro*, in the mountains of Tamaulipas —a place of devotion just then starting into celebrity, but whose destinies, which promised to be so brilliant, have been since blasted, by the Yorkino government of that State. Of these two friars, one was lame, and the other labored under a chronic rheumatism, and both expected to be restored to healthful vigor, by the intercession of the virgin del chorro.

They no sooner heard of Mr. Faring's journeying that way, than they conceived the idea of palming themselves upon him as travelling companions, being persuaded that they would much more conveniently perform their journey in a vehicle, than on their hard trotting mules. Communicating their wishes to our host, a man most religiously inclined to oblige any one who wore a shaven crown, he broached the subject to Mr. Faring and easily convinced him that it would be desirable for him to have such fellow-travellers. In case of an attack from robbers, they would be a protection to the whole party, and besides, might prove useful in the way of obtaining provisions, along the road,—the country people, not always disposed to sell victuals to ordinary travellers, never refusing them to clerical ones, and even dutifully presenting them, every now and then, with delicacies, without any compensation. The Friars' company was, therefore, willingly accepted, the more so, as Mr. Faring knew that his being a heretic was a circumstance involving no little danger, and he could not rely upon the secrecy and discretion of his servants,—these being qualities in which Mexican Indians are generally deficient.

On the day of his departure, therefore, he mounted his
coach with a greater sense of security, and when sitting between the two friars, felt more comfortable than before.   On
their part, the *religiosos*, though not a little disgusted at the
idea of riding in the same carriage with a Protestant, either
mastered, or disguised that feeling, and scrupled not to entertain Mr. Faring with their conversation.  He was not
backward in addressing them with queries, and the subject
he selected was peculiarly calculated to awaken their collo-
quial powers.

"Be so good, reverend fathers," said he, " as to give me
some information touching the place of devotion to which
you are bound.   I am a foreigner, uninformed of the peculiarities of the country, and as I have never, hitherto, heard
that place mentioned, I would be glad to learn something
about it."

"Why, Señor," said the elder of the two clergymen, " it is
a sequestered glen, on the eastern ridge of the mountains of
Tamaulipas, one of the branches of the Sierra Madre, some
few leagues from the city of Linares, where it has pleased
the Holy Virgin to manifest herself in a miraculous manner—which promises to that place, in future ages, as great
a fame as it has been the lot of any other sanctuary in Mexico to acquire.   I should not even be surprised if it were to
become as celebrated as the collegiate of Guadelupe.   That
glen being very deep, and flanked on either side, by steep
marble rocks, is diversified, here and there, by deep caverns, in which are found great quantities of fine alabaster
and curious petrifactions.   It happened, one day, that two
masons and a sculptor, who had undertaken to erect an altar
piece, in the church of the Hualawises, (a tribe of converted
Indians,) resorted thither, in quest of materials for that purpose.   Finding a satisfactory selection difficult to make, and
having already visited several caves and fissures in the
rocks—still undetermined in their choice, they came, at last,
to a wide opening, in the side of the mountain, from which
flowed a rivulet of limpid water.

"It being the dinner hour, they concluded to enter the
cave, in order to enjoy their meal in the cool shade, and behold ! upon entering it, they found the place incrusted with
the very materials they were in quest of—and of the finest

quality—resplendent, and as white as the driven snow ! The
grotto was perfectly beautiful, and disposed like a large *sala*,
as if dug and fashioned by the hand of man.    At the farther
extremity, a splendid cascade, falling from a height of thirty
feet, formed the rivulet already mentioned.

" They drew near it, but judge of their surprise, when
they saw, between the *chorro* of water, and the alabaster
wall, the image of Our Lady gracefully hovering over them,
in the air.   They were struck dumb with terror—as they
well might, poor sinners ! for, who were they, that heaven
should especially favor them with such a vision, in preference to so many priests and religious men in the country ?
But so it was, and, at last, recollecting themselves and falling down on their knees, they devoutly crossed themselves,
and recited the litanies—not daring to look up for a time.

" They expected to hear some verbal revelation ; but no
voice issuing from the sacred image, they, at last, ventured
to look up again, and beheld it in the same place, and with
a smiling countenance, which encouraged them to approach.
They even ventured to pass between the water and the alabaster wall, which they found brilliant and polished to a pre-
ternatural degree, but lo ! the blessed image had become
settled and had fixed itself on the stone, where it remains
visible to this day—as if engraved—though, no doubt, it was
never carved—save, perhaps, by angels, in a miraculous
manner."

" Oh Maria Santissima !" piously ejaculated the other
friar, " how much is not Mexico indebted to thee, that thou
vouchsafest to bless us in such a manner !"

" And that place, no doubt," interrupted Mr. Faring,
" has, since these events have transpired, attracted considerable attention, from the whole neighbourhood ?"

" Indeed you may say so," returned the friar.   " Not
only from the neighbourhood, but from a vast distance, multi-
tudes resort to it, and wonderful is the number of cures
wrought there.   You may judge how far the fame of the
blessed cave has already extended, since brother Villamil,
there, and my unworthy self have come all the way from
Durango—a city more than a hundred and fifty leagues
distant.   We had, indeed, heard of the place, long ago, and
felt a desire to perform the pilgrimage ; but our prior, good

man, had a notion that it was an artifice of Sathanas, and a temptation, in order to divert us from the spirit of prayer and contemplation so essential to a religious life. God, however, has been pleased to take the prior to a better world, and we were very careful, in the election of his successor, to covenant, before giving him our votes, that he should grant us the permission to undertake the pilgrimage. For more than ten years, I have suffered under a severe rheumatism, so that I can very seldom attend divine service in the choir, or even preach, as I was wont to do, before my ailment; but I hope that at the Chorro, the most pure and holy Queen of Heaven will cast upon me an eye of compassion. And, in fact, it is, as one may say, for her own interest, that I am now travelling, as much as for my advantage. The convent of San Augustin, of Durango, is of some note, and should two brothers of that house get cured at this new sanctuary, it will greatly increase the number of pilgrims, no less than the value of votive offerings. Durango is the country for silver and gold, and the pearls of California are adjacent! Our state could, in one month alone, furnish more *preciosi-dades* to the Sanctuary del Chorro, than Tamaulipas, Nuevo Leon and Cohahuila together, in ten years. I will duly explain this to the pious anchorite, who is the keeper of the blessed cave, in order that his fervent prayers be addressed to the mother of God in our behalf. Oh, the special blessings bestowed upon this country by these signal apparitions! There was, first, that of Guadelupe, near the city of Mexico, shortly after the conquest. It was especially vouchsafed to the Indian race, which it was necessary to win over, and the miracle occurred on the identical spot where had stood the temple of their famous idol *Tonantzin*.* An Indian, even the pious Juan Diego, was its honored voucher; but now a second witness of our immaculate faith has risen in these Northern parts. It is, undoubtedly, to bear testimony against the heresy and unbelief which threaten to invade us from the side of the Anglo-Americans. Yea, it is, in my opinion, a sign unto *them!* And what other land can, now-a-days, boast the same favors and heavenly visitations! Truly we may say, as the Guadelupe medals have it, "Non fecit taliter omni nationi!"

* Tonantzin was the Mexican Ceres, the Goddess of maize.

"Your discourse edifies me, reverend father," said Mr. Faring, "yet, methinks, before this new place of devotion can obtain as much fame, and inspire as much veneration, as the collegiate of Guadelupe, there are certain formalities to be undergone, at Rome, and the whole history of the apparition must be approved by the Holy See, before it can be admitted by the faithful."

"Are you, indeed, aware of that?" interrupted Father Villamil. "It shows that you have studied our religion, and paid some attention to the constitution of our church! But your observation is correct. The testimony respecting the apparition must be scrupulously examined, at Rome, before the sacred congregation of rites, and a solemn office composed! It costs as much as the canonization of a Saint. If modern times were like past ages, it would be easy to collect the money wanted, at Rome, for the fees of office incidental to the process and other duties; but with the suppression of the Holy Inquisition,([11]) charity has grown so cold, and the looseness of private opinions so prevalent, that we are afraid no sufficient effort will be made. Well may the daughter of Zion weep, at seeing the inroads of heretics, schismatics, unbelievers, Jews and impious men of every sort, who roam through our land, and have brought the curse of Heaven upon us. How different matters went on when we had the Holy Office among us!"

Mr. Faring, who felt that the friars were taking with his feelings, as an American, greater liberties than their situation warranted, thought proper to change the conversation. The two holy men possessed but little instruction, except in matters of divinity, and of course their company proved uninteresting; but, towards the middle of the day, the weight of dulness was alleviated by the view of a splendid phenomenon, unknown both in Europe and the United States.

They were drawing near a little village, of the name of Tinaja, built at the foot of a huge mountain, which lies perfectly insulated, in the centre of an immense plain, when the most lovely prospect imaginable broke upon their sight. There lay a beautiful lake, the limpid waters of which, sparkling in the sun, extended afar their broad expanse, till lost in the mists of the horizon, and were diversified with delightful groups of Islands, covered with shrubs of the greenest hue.

Their road conducted them, in a direct line, towards its banks, but in proportion to their approach, the lake appeared to re-cede, as though it had been a scenic illusion, to tantalize the weary traveller. It was high noon, and the vast plain through which they were riding, consisted of what, in Mexico, is termed *barrial,* that is to say, indurated clay, which, con-stantly exposed to the rays of the sun, attains almost the consistency of stone. As it was entirely destitute of vegeta-tion, the charm resulting from the contrast, when the eye, after wandering over the barren superficies, rested on the translucent waters, was inexpressible. Mr. Faring was de-lighted, and declared his intention of stopping on the banks of the lake, to take his afternoon meal, and enjoy the luxury of a cool bath. He was not a little surprised when the friars laughed at his eagerness, and told him that if he were not to dine till he should reach it, he ran a great risk of fasting a long time. He thought they were jesting, and even felt some rancor for the liberty they were taking, until his ser-vants affirmed the same thing, to wit, that what he saw was merely the effect of an optical illusion.

This recalled to his memory the mirage of the eastern regions, described by several travellers, and he could easily conceive how a state of the atmosphere similar to that of Arabia, or Egypt, should also produce this phenomenon, in the barren plains of Mexico. Our friars had never heard of the mirage, their reading having been very limited, but they had frequently beheld the curious spectacle which now excit-ed Mr. Faring's surprise, and one of them even undertook a philosophical explanation of it, by referring to the laws of optics, a smattering of which he had acquired, from a Latin work of Jacquier, on physics.

From the borders of that beautiful but imaginary lake, they continued to pursue an easterly direction, and encamped for the night near a little hamlet, called *Alamo mocho.* No sooner had they pitched their tent, than a numerous company of country people was seen approaching the place where they had put up for the night; and, apprehensive that they were robbers, Mr. Faring and his men seized their arms and re-solved to defend themselves, while the friars, confiding in the influence of their priestly character, walked towards the intruders. The latter, recognizing the sacred habit, approached the padres with marks of deep reverence, and, upon drawing nigh, devoutly kissed their hands and walked bareheaded by their side.

The business which had brought them together was of a singular nature. A man, who lived at a considerable distance from Alamo mocho had arrived there the preceding night, pretending to have received a revelation that a corpse was buried near the hamlet, at a certain spot, which he described with so much minuteness and precision, that the villagers immediately knew the place. The disinterment of the corpse was not his sole object, for he affirmed that a sum of six thousand dollars was secreted in the grave, and for the purpose of its extraction the company were now convened and marching towards the spot. Though it seemed strange that he had collected for such a purpose so many witnesses, yet this was a necessary precaution, to enable him to prove the honest acquisition of the money, should he ever be questioned about it.

Mr. Faring listened to the story with an air of incredulity, and could not, at the conclusion, restrain his risibility ; but he was assured, by one of the friars, that such events were by no means rare, in Mexico, and were not by the shrewd ones accounted miraculous. Being still inclined to consider it as a hoax, or a gross instance of superstitious credulity, the friars proposed to him to accompany the stranger to the place indicated, and witness the search. Assenting thereto, they soon reached the spot—a dreary looking ravine, thickly overshadowed by acacias and ebony-trees. At the foot of a large palm-tree, between two stones, planted upright, as if to mark a grave, the stranger, assisted by the villagers, began to dig. They had no sooner penetrated one foot and a half in depth, than they discovered a corpse, not yet entirely putrefied. The sight was disgusting and the stench so intolerable, that Mr. Faring was obliged to remove to some distance, while the assembled villagers broke forth into loud shouts of joy,—calling, at the same time, upon our friars, for prayers, in behalf of the dead.

" Alas, for the poor murdered soul !" exclaimed one of the peasants, who stood gaping, on the brink of the grave ; " to have lain here, heaven knows how long, without ever receiving the rites of sepulture—or having so much as a *De pro-*

*fundis* sung over it—or some drops of Holy Water sprinkled
for its repose! Ah, me!—Now, when l think of it, l have no
doubt it is the ghost which my wife saw, by moon light, walking at the cross roads *del cerro*, on all Hallows night. Its
head was wrapped round with a bloody handkerchief, and it
groaned frightfully!—By St. Corolampio, I must do something for the poor soul.—Fathers, here are two rials.—Kneel
down, if you please, and say some *responsorios*—just as much
as the money comes to."

"This is well thought, indeed," interrupted another
rustic, fumbling in his pocket, and adding a sixpence, to the
two rials, which father Villamil had already pocketed, "I
will have a share in the merit of this good work. Not that
my wife has seen any ghost; but my ewes and goats *have*,
and if they could speak, they would tell a strange tale. I
never had so many of them to miscarry, in a single season!
The poor soul, here, was restless, and rode them in the night,
till they cast their kids.—*Vaya!* I thought somebody had
bewitched them!"

"And do you think," said his wife, who was present,
"that a sixpence is going to lay a ghost like this? A stranger in the country, I warrant you—and murdered with cold
lead, too—which is not a Christian-like death—certainly not
the way to do the thing in Mexico! The ghost will never
mind your sixpence, man. It is a mass you must give—
nothing less than a mass."

Thus incited by his more generous spouse, the man made
an effort, and handed the friars a dollar for a mass, and his
example had such an effect upon the spectators, that every
one began fumbling in his pocket, to contribute to the general offering for laying the ghost. They were particular,
however, in their selection of prayers for that purpose. One
called for a *Miserere*, another for a *Libera me*, while a third
one who had but two cents to offer, modestly contented himself with an *Hail Mary*, &c.

In the meantime, the digging went on, and the clergymen,
on their knees, kept muttering their prayers. When the
offering of money ceased, however, it was found that the sum
made up was too trifling to compensate for the joint labors of
both friars, so that father Garces, who was the superior, got
up, and left brother Villamil to discharge the worth of

the *Jolas*, (copper coins) while the search was briskly prosecuted.

The corpse was soon extracted, removed to another spot, and the grave it had lately tenanted, ransacked and examined. In it they found money, sure enough! A few inches below the corpse, there had been secreted a leathern valise, which contained, not six thousand, but six hundred dollars in silver, with an ingot of gold that might be worth about five hundred more. A pair of pistols accompanied the valise, and though rusty and damaged, Mr. Faring easily ascertained them to be real Mantons. The boots and some rags of what had been the apparel of the deceased yet re mained, which convinced him that they must have belonged to a foreigner, probably a countryman of his, or an Englishman. Seized with great emotion, he conquered his repugnance, and approached the corpse, which, though decayed, still preserved marks of having come to its end in a foul manner. The skull had been penetrated by two balls. It was, therefore, evident that some one had been inhumanly murdered, but when, and by whom?

Suddenly the idea flashed upon Mr. Faring's mind, that the man who pretended to have had the revelation, and had come from a distance with so exact a description of the place of interment, must have been privy to the horrid deed, or, perhaps, the perpetrator, and he immediately formed the resolution of arresting him, and delivering him over to the authorities of Saltillo, a city, situated not far from Alamo mocho. He, nevertheless, thought it prudent to consult the eldest of the two friars, who seemed possessed of more sense than his companion.

For that purpose, he took father Garces apart, and said to him, " Father, I cannot reconcile myself to the idea that this man knew the existence of this corpse, buried in so lonely a place, by revelation! It is, evidently, a traveller who has been murdered, and here secreted, with his money, to be disinterred at leisure, at a time when the excitement produced among his friends, by his disappearance, should be allayed; in order to screen the murderer from the retribution of the law."[*]

" Your suspicions are probably just," replied the friar,

---

[*] Such adventures as these are not unfrequent in Mexico.

"yet heaven has frequently made such revelations, either by dreams, or by unequivocal signs, to poor and worthy men., in order to relieve their necessities, and, also, that the treasure, which would otherwise have uselessly remained concealed, in the bowels of the earth, might benefit the poor murdered soul, by being partly spent in prayers and masses *de requiem.*"

"Father," interrupted Mr. Faring, "though I do not pretend to deny the existence of miracles, still I cannot admit, for one single moment, that there was any thing supernatural in this affair. The fellow was too well acquainted with the place, not to have visited it previously. Rely upon it, either he was the assassin, or knows who perpetrated the deed. I think public justice requires that he should be arrested, and delivered over to the Alcalde of Saltillo, in order that the crime may be judicially investigated. I have a sufficent number of men to apprehend him."

"I advise you," replied the friar, "not to meddle with this man, nor to do what would be accounted exceedingly foolish, and subject you to considerable delay and expense. Why, it would be acting the part of Don Quixote, who went about, avenging wrongs and redressing injuries! What should we come to, in this country, if it were thought necessary to apprehend all those who act similarly with this man?—I have known, in my time,—that is, since I was a novice,—no less than twenty-five, or thirty corpses, thus disinterred, between Zacatecas and Durango, and never heard that any body interfered; though, to be sure people would, sometimes smile and significantly shake the head, when a fellow returned enriched from one of those expeditions. Moreover, I think you wrong the poor man, by your suspicions: he is innocent, I dare say. He appears very mild, and is certainly very charitable, for he has bestowed forty dollars, out of six hundred, for masses, to be said on behalf of the deceased. A robber would hardly have thought of the like, I am sure."

Mr. Faring, seeing that it would be impossible to persuade the friar of the propriety of his design, and aware, also, that it would be exceedingly difficult to execute it without his concurrence; gave up the idea. In the meantime, the stranger made liberal donations to the rustics who had assisted him in his search, replaced the corpse into its earthly tenement, and departed carrying off his prey.

Our traveller spent the time which elapsed till supper, in the most uncomfortable manner, being haunted by thousand doleful ideas ; but the friars seemed indifferent to the melancholy spectacle they had witnessed. The inhabitants of the hamlet felt greatly honored by their presence, and the women obsequiously gave them several little *regalos*. One humbly brought a couple of chickens, and, with many low reverences, begged that they might be roasted for the supper of their *paternities*. Another presented a kid ; a third one, a jar of fresh cream, and by this means their commons were not a little improved. Upon the whole, and despite of Mr. Faring's feelings, they spent not only a cheerful, but even a festive night. Before retiring to repose, they held a consultation on the direction they should pursue the following day.

By far the greatest part of the territory which constitutes the Mexican republic consists of an immense plain, raised six or seven thousand feet above the level of the sea, and buttressed by two distinct chains of mountains, each of which is known by the name of the Sierra Madre ; this denomination extending even to the range that pervades Texas. These two mountainous ridges spring out, from an immense chain which is a continuation of the Andes of Peru, and after entering the states of Puebla and Mexico, and shooting up towards heaven the enormous volcanic peaks of Popocatepetl and Istacihuatl, divides itself into two arms, which embrace the high plain already alluded to, styled, in the language of the country, " la mesa de Anahuac." The singular topography of this mesa imparts to it a certain resemblance with the *steppes* of great Tartary, and the mountainous chains by which it is bounded, being almost every where precipitous, render an access to the upland country extremely difficult, except at a few spots, where deep-cut puertos open an entrance for carriages.

The western chain runs due north. Throwing out lateral spurs, here and there, it forms the immense volcano of Colima, and the still more surprising, though less gigantic *hornitos**

* The hornitos of Jorullo are small conical mounds of earth, ten or fifteen feet high, emitting an incessant smoke and a fetid odor. They are several thousands in number and cover an immense plain. That country has been volcanised since the Spanish conquest.—A considerable river of hot water has taken the place of two fine streams, which, before, watered the plain, now known by the name of *mal pays*.

of Jorullo.   But the main ridge pursues its course, at an
average distance of three hundred miles from the Pacific
ocean and the gulf of California, until it ultimately reaches
the northwest territory of the United States, where its prolongation is known by the name of the Rocky mountains.

The Eastern branch runs at about a distance of two hundred miles from the sea coast, following its sinuosities, in a
northeast direction, until it enters the state of Cohahuila,
where it is lost, in the immense plains watered by the Rio
Bravo.   This chain, without being so high, or precipitous, as
the western one, is sufficiently so, however, to prevent any
carriage from crossing the proud circumvallation with which
the interior of the republic is fenced round, unless its northern extremity, be *turned*, which can be effected only at Saltillo.   This circumstance will always secure a paramount
importance to that city.   From the *camino real*, anciently
constructed, by the Spanish government, from Vera Cruz, to
Mexico ;  this chain of mountains, extending to Saltillo, forms,
for the space of eight hundred miles, a grand wall, or national
fortification, rendering the access to the interior, exceedingly
difficult and precarious, till one reaches the latitude of the
last mentioned city.

Our travellers had now reached the point which has, on
that account, become the great Eastern thoroughfare, between
the high and lowlands, and they had to determine what road
they should pursue.   One, that passed through the city of
Saltillo, was both shorter and more transitable, but so dread-
fully infested by robbers, that it was next to a prodigy to
escape being attacked by them.   The other, which crossed
the main ridge of the Sierra, nine leagues to the northward,
was accounted more rugged, but better watered, and had not
yet become the resort of banditti, being seldom frequented by
travellers.   Mr. Faring preferred the latter, being chiefly
influenced by the opinion of his guide.

The next morning, therefore, they set out early, intending
to cross the gap, before night, and reach the head of the valley
of Nicamole, which is six thousand feet, at least, lower than
the table land west of the Sierra.   Nothing can equal the
magnificence of the spectacle which, upon a nearer approach, this chain of mountains exhibits.   The atmosphere
of Mexico is so clear and transparent, that the peculiar tints

which these ridges display, are distinguishable at a vast distance, and their colors appear as vivid, as if just laid on by the pencil of a skilful artist, with their various shades melting into each other by gradual transitions. New Spain is the country where the primary formation most frequently appears upon the superficies of the ground, and the primitive rocks having been there less disturbed by subterranean commotions, than in any other part of the globe; sulphur, the grand *mineraliser* of metals, imparts, on that account, a more brilliant tinge to the bodies with which it is combined. Though one cannot help regretting the absence of vegetation, yet the sight of the shining streaks, by which metalliferous veins are indicated—following the undulations of the various ridges in which they are imbedded—amply repays the curious observer, and promises a richer harvest to the geologist.

Shortly after leaving the village of Venadito, where they took their breakfast, our travellers entered the gap of the mountain. Their road followed a rapid declivity, and the lofty ridge, transversally divided by a tortuous glen, towered, on either side, to the height of several thousand feet, above their heads; exhibiting the most fantastic shapes. Every thing was on a gigantic scale—the castellated peaks, —the perpendicular precipices—the gaping caverns!—yet every feature bore an air of rigidness which inspired horror and deadened that sentiment of mental elevation, which is the natural result of the contemplation of sublime scenery. No trees, waving in the breeze—no birds, warbling among the foliage—no shepherd's reed, attuning the surrounding echoes! The scenery was sublime, but it was the sublimity of death! Even the few plants which found a scanty supply in the crevices of the rocks were of an anomalous, and if one may say so, of a ridiculous shape, and every one thorny! And such thorns as are not to be found any where else, on the face of the earth. Thorns, that can neither be cut with a knife, nor torn from the parent stem, without breaking it to pieces—thorns that seem not to participate of the nature of wood; but rather, appear like so many vegetable cock-spurs, uniting the incorruptible durability of horn, with the sharpness of steel. There flourish, in pernicious variety, the multifarious species of the cactus plant, save those which produce the cocheneal and the edible figs called *tunas*. The dwarfish opuntia with violet colored leaves spreads its useless bunches throughout every bottom. The viznaga, or cactus melo cactus, peeps out of every cranny, assuming every hue, from dark green, to pale grey, and carpeting the surface of the trap rock with a triple row of prickles, as sharp as needles, while the *organo* shoots up in singular prisms, from every loamy nook, but produces no pitaya.*

At long intervals, some trees appear, but even *they* are fenced round with thorns, that render them nearly unapproachable ; while their growth is so stunted by the lengthened droughts to which the country is subject, and their trunks are so knotty and contorted, as to render them any thing but pleasant objects to the sight. In a word, the vegetable kingdom seems to exhibit itself, there, under the most repulsive forms ; in order, as it were, to be in keeping with the mineral one. Through this defile, Mr. Faring had already proceeded a considerable way, when one of his men learned from a cowherd, that a large company of robbers lay in wait, two leagues distant.

---

* A delicious fruit, of a globular form, about the size of a walnut, and of a deep red color. The juice is sweet and abundant, dying all the secretions of the body of a bright purple. The organo flourishes most in California, where, in many localities, it furnishes their only means of support to the few miserable Indians who roam through that barren peninsula.

# CHAPTER VI.

My kingdom—my city of Tenochtitlan !—What have you done with it, Señores ?—Civilized, you say ?—Let me see. Why, yes. There is your Mexico,—It is pretty. It would make a handsome suburb to my ancient capital. But let us look further.—Where is justice ?—Freedom for the exercise of industry—security for travellers—a sufficiency of food for the lower classes ?—Ah, ah ! a curious civilization ! By Vitzliputzli, I could have done better than that, in the same space of time.

*The Ghost of Montezuma, a tragy Comedy.*

Upon receiving the unwelcome intelligence mentioned in the preceding chapter, the whole caravan came to a halt, and a consultation was held upon the measures most proper to be pursued in such an emergency. It was, at first, proposed boldly to proceed and defend themselves, sure that the banditti would prove pusillanimous, and that, as soon as two or three of their number should fall, the rest would retreat ; but the friars decidedly opposed such a plan. They believed that the robbers, upon a near approach, would respect their habit; but they were not so sure that the bullets of their guns, fired from a distance, would show the same discrimination. They voted, therefore, for proceeding in a pacific manner ; but Mr. Faring did not relish exposing his effects to pillage, out of zeal for peace ; neither did he anticipate much danger from resistance, as he had a considerable number of men, all of whom were well armed. The question was, whether the latter would face the robbers and support their master. Mr. Faring resolved, at all events, to make a trial.

Assembling together his *peones*, he communicated to them his resolution, and in an inspiriting tone, commanded them to form in the order best calculated to render their resistance effectual ; but his measures were thwarted by father Garces, who insinuated that a passive conduct was likely to prove their best safeguard. He succeeded in his design, for, notwithstanding the show of bravery which Mr. Faring's servants had evinced, they were in great trepidation, and manifested a wonderful docility in following the padres' counsels. This was a serious vexation to poor Mr. Faring, who bitterly repented having allowed the pusillanimous friars to travel in his company. There appeared, however, no means of extricating himself from the present difficulty, except by retracing his steps, and proceeding to Saltillo, where he made a vow to leave the two children of St. Augustin. Accordingly, he gave orders to return.

Upon learning his resolution and seeing the friars' obstinacy, the guide informed the company that he knew a secret path, over the brow of the hill, by which loaded mules might reach Nicamole, without incurring the danger of an attack, although they would be exposed to perils of another description, from the extreme narrowness of the road, and the tremendous precipices along the edge of which it was conducted. This path is called " *El paso de los Angeles,*" not from its pleasantness, as the inexperienced reader might imagine, but because it had originally been supposed impassable by any one except beings of an ethereal nature. Now, the guide proposed to drive the mules that way, accompanied by the peones ; while the coach and friars should continue on the common route, and if they should encounter the banditti, he argued, that, provided no resistance were made, the carriage would run very little danger of being detained, and they would reach their destination in safety. Mr. Faring did not perfectly approve of this arrangement ; yet it appeared, under the circumstances, the most prudent plan they could adopt. He, therefore, determined to accompany the mules, and trust the vehicle to the guidance and management of the two friars. Every valuable article which he had in the carriage was transferred to the back of a spare beast, and recommending himself to the prayers of the two holy men, he left them to provide for their own safety in the best way they could, promising to rejoin them, early, the ensuing morning, at the head of the valley of Nicamole.

The guide led him back about a mile and a half, up the glen, and then, leaving the beaten track, began to ascend the side of the rocky ridge, which appeared so precipitous, that, at a distance, one would have judged the path hardly practicable for a goat. But the mule is a wonderful animal, no less sagacious than inured to fatigue, and especially serviceable in mountainous and rocky countries. Still, notwithstanding all the confidence which Mr. Faring placed in the

instinct of the one he rode, he had not proceeded three hundred yards, when he became alarmed, and, overcome by
dizziness, he declared that he should prefer continuing his
journey on foot, to undergoing so imminent a danger.
Alighting, therefore, he walked the remainder of the way,
with a gun in his hand, to the great surprise of his servants.
After severe fatigues, they crossed the ridge, and, marching
until the afternoon of the following day, they reached the
valley of Nicamole ; where they were surprised to receive
no intelligence of the friars.

The poor religiosos had met with signal misfortunes, and
the confidence they had placed in the highwaymen's reverence for the habit of St. Augustin had been most awfully disappointed. After their separation from Mr. Faring, order-
ing the postillion to drive as quickly as possible, they hoped
to be enabled to pass the suspicious ground with such rapidity, as to elude the watchfulness of the robbers, who were
posted at a narrow pass, above a mineral spring, bearing the
ominous name of " *los Amargos.*" But the sight of a travelling carriage, at that time, a rare occurrence in those parts,
was, of itself, sufficient to awaken the attention of the highwaymen, and induce them to anticipate a rich booty. As
soon, therefore, as the postillion was within hearing distance,
they bid him stop, at his peril, threatening, with a volley of
oaths and curses, to blow out his brains, if he should refuse.
The poor postillion, perceiving a numerous gang obstructing
the passage, was forced to obey, and the robbers, coming up,
soon surrounded the coach, and took possession of the two
mules rode by the servants.

The captain of the banditti was the first to open the door
of the vehicle, where he expected, no doubt, to find some
family of distinction, well provided with cash ; but great was
his surprise to behold, instead, the two friars, whom terror
had almost deprived of the power of speech.

" What have we, here ?" exclaimed he, in the discontented
tone of a disappointed man. " Padres, who are you, and
where are you going ?"

" Alas, señor," answered Father Garces, trembling with
fright, "we are two unworthy brothers of the order of the
Heremites of St. Augustin, of the convent of Durango, bound
for the sanctuary of the Virgin ' del chorro,' in the mountains

of Tamaulipas. We are both priests, and, of course, under the special protection of the ecclesiastical law, which prohibits, under pain of excommunication, *latæ sententiæ*, to offer violence to a person in holy orders."

"Are you indeed, friars?" replied the outlaw, with a look of incredulity, either real, or affected. "Many persons put on a religious habit, now-a-days, in travelling, in order to fare better on the road, or to deceive gentlemen of our profession."

"Indeed, we are," replied father Garces, still more alarmed, "and if you do not believe our habit, you may well credit our letters of ordination, as well as the letters of *obedience*,* from our worthy prior, by which we are recommended to the charity of the faithful." So saying, he put his hand into a pocket, concealed in the large sleeve of his gown, and opening under his armpit, and drew out two large pieces of writing, looking like notarial acts, with the appendage of a huge seal, and presented them to the robber.

The highwayman, who knew not how to read, was, nevertheless, ashamed to confess his ignorance, and looking over the papers, pretended to examine their purport; after which, folding them up and returning them to the friar, he said: "Well, well, this will do. You are privileged men and we will do you no bodily harm. God forbid that we should draw down upon us the curse of an excommunication. We will treat you with all possible civility; but come, it is necessary to speed the matter, for we expect new travellers, every moment, and two jobs at once might prove embarrassing."

"Well," resumed the friar, "you can despatch us in a trice. Be so kind as to return the two mules to our servants, and the matter is all sped. We will not long cumber your grounds with our presence, and yet," added he, with a paternal smile, "we will not fail to pray for you."

"How is this, *Padre mio?*" interrupted the robber; "you expect that I will return your servants' mules—*Voto a Dios*, you are an unreasonable man. This is too childish, for one of your cloth!—You may think yourself lucky to escape with your life, and thank our delicacy of conscience which makes

* Letters declaratory that the bearer was a regular member of their order.

us unwilling to shed the blood of anointed clergymen. But make haste, for it answers no good purpose to be uselessly parleying, on the highway, and my company are growing impatient."

"Upon my honor," replied the clergyman, (who, now thinking that he had nothing to fear for his life, was growing bolder,) "I never was more desirous of making haste, than at this present moment. Since you wish to retain the mules, keep them, in God's name, and let us go."

"Let us go!—oh, padre, padre !" exclaimed the robber, "is it possible you do not understand me !—Do you think we can let this coach proceed, without previous search ?—People of your profession seldom stir out without a handsome provision of doubloons. Therefore, I say, alight from the coach, reverend fathers ; we should be sorry to have to recur to force."

The two clergymen obeyed, reluctantly enough, yet without any fear of a discovery, on the part of the robbers, as they had no money secreted in the vehicle. They viewed, therefore, with perfect indifference, the search, prosecuted most minutely and in the strictest manner ; but which produced no favorable result. Not a little displeased at his want of success, the captain muttered, eyeing the friars askance, " If you were *common* folks, a little twine twisted round your thumbs, with a slow match, would soon make you *sing out,* and we would be saved all this trouble,—but we must reverence you, forsooth, and handle you as nicely as if you were delicate china ware ! Still, you must have *it* some where, and since it is not deposited in the coach, it must be secreted about your persons. Come, I will commence with you, who are the youngest," addressing himself to father Villamil ; " sit down upon this block of rock, and allow me to take off your sandals. My hand is quite light, and you will see what a nice valet-de-chambre I make."

Upon receiving this polite injunction, father Villamil raised the outcry. "How, now !" said he, " Bethink you that this is bodily violence, and comes precisely within the canonical provisions of the council of Trent. By such a conduct, you incur excommunication in the same manner as if you were to maltreat, or even to murder me."

" Padre," replied the robber, sternly, " I beseech you,

make no resistance. Our patience is somewhat of the short-est, and if our excommunication is certain, as you say, we may be tempted to enhance its worth, by treating you more roughly. If you behave yourself mildly—and as becomes a worthy son of St. Augustin—we are not unwilling to do the handsome thing by you. Come, we will not fleece you to the quick. Only throw off your sandals,—and also,—if you have no objection—I will help to disrobe you of this cumber-some black gown, which is, probably, too heavy for your paternity. We will see whether we cannot lighten it, a little! There are many curious little seams about these habits of yours, and many a golden peseta can lie perdue in the pad-ding of the cowl.—*Vamos, Padrecito!*"

So saying, he pulled off father Villamil's sandals, and not-withstanding some resistance, on his part, two other robbers divested him also of his gown. The captain found nothing concealed between the two pieces of sole leather of which the conventual *calceamenta* of the friar consisted; but his lieutenant was more fortunate. Sewed in the lining of the hood, or *cucula*, were no less than nine doubloons. This discovery was hailed with loud shouts by the robbers, who now turned their greedy eyes towards father Garces. Upon seeing in what manner they were proceeding with his com-panion, this worthy was seized with a violent cholic, and earnestly requested the robbers not to search him; proffer-ing, at the same time, six doubloons, which, he said, were all he possessed. The highwaymen diverted themselves, for a while, at the sight of the grimaces he made, in order to persuade them that he was really suffering horrid pains; but his shallow stratagem availed him not. He was search-ed, as well as his fellow traveller, and every seam of his gown which contained any coin, ripped open.

By the time the robbers had examined to their satisfaction, the apparel of the two holy men, they found themselves pos-sessed of nineteen doubloons, in gold, and a fair string of pearls, destined for *Nuestra Señora del chorro;* but which they sacrilegiously appropriated to themselves. The poor friars wrapped themselves up in their black gowns again, which, having been ripped open in so many places, present-ed a ludicrous appearance. The pieces dangled about their limbs, in so strange a fashion, that one would have supposed the good fathers were acting a shrove-tide mummery at the expense of the religious orders. Their sandals having been cut open, also, they remained barefooted, and their destitute situation moved the compassion of the robbers themselves, whose captain proposed to restore four doubloons, out of the nineteen they had deprived them of, to which the whole company assented. They abstained also from appropriating to themselves the mules that drew the carriage, and replacing the friars in it, dismissed them without any further molestation. The servants who accompanied them lost their riding beasts, however, and were obliged to mount the vehicle with the padres.

They continued their journey along the gap in the uncomfortable plight which we have described, but, as misfortunes seldom come single, they had hardly proceeded two leagues, when the coach was overturned. By this accident one of the fore wheels was broken, and the night setting in very dark, the whole company were obliged to stop at that unlucky spot, without any thing to appease the cravings of hunger, except some jerked beef.

When day dawned, they contrived to bind up the broken wheel together, with leathern thongs, and slowly dragging the carriage along, the whole company walked on foot, save the postillion. In this guise they arrived at the spot where Mr. Faring was awaiting them. The deplorable plight in which they got there, precluded all idea of continuing their journey before the coach should be repaired. This was, however, an operation likely to prove difficult, for the nearest place which boasted a wheelwright was Pesqueria, a town more than thirty miles distant. Thither they had to despatch an express, by whom the two friars conveyed to the parish priest a written account of their melancholy adventure, supplicating the loan of clerical garments, in order that they might enter the town in a condition suitable to persons of their order. That clergyman immediately sent them two cassocks, with a pressing invitation to come and lodge at his house. Along with the messenger, who brought this token of brotherly feeling, there came a wheelwright, with tools and materials to repair the broken wheel, and in five hours after his arrival, the caravan was ready to pursue its march.

These various cares, nevertheless, had detained them nearly two days at the place where Mr. Faring had halted, a delay that had given him time to indulge his passion for sublime scenery, of which very few spots upon earth can afford more splendid specimens than the valley of Nicamole. That scenery continues to be, in great measure, of that stern and rugged character, which we have described as belonging to the western chain of the Sierra Madre ; but the accidents of nature are so varied, the forms of the mountainous peaks so novel, and cast into so well ordained proportions, the hues of the rocky strata so splendid, and yet so softly blended toge- ther, and the whole spectacle unfolds itself so progressively to the traveller's eye, as he descends the gap, at the foot of which the valley commences, that the line of harmonious relations is not marred by the least flaw. The vast pano- rama gradually swells into the most exalted magnificence, without overwhelming the imagination.

A handsome river issues from a deep glen, on the right hand, and meanders through the vale. A double row of evergreens adorns its banks, and affords a contrast to the brilliant tinges that seem to flame on the towering ridges. The crystalline stream now purls over a pebbly bottom, now divides itself into several channels, and irrigates smiling or- chards of aguacates, orange, lime, pomegranate and other trees peculiar to tropical regions, the fragrance of whose blossoms vies with the splendor of their colors. Large flocks of sheep are seen grazing in the pastures, while the distant crags of porphiry rock resound with the bleatings of the scrambling goats. Indian cottages, of a round form, peep from among the green boughs of the perfumed *gui- sache,* or elegant *retama,** and the whole forms a scene so tranquil and so fair, that, as the traveller descends the gap, and lifts his eyes up towards the superb cliffs which tower aloft, on either side, and then suffers them to rest on the en- chanted valley at his feet, he is forced to exclaim, here beauty sleeps in the lap of the sublime !

In mountainous scenery, nature seems almost every where to have *dashed* the sublime in a wild mood, but here, she

* The broom, in the lowlands of Tamaulipas, grows to the size of a large tree. Its blossom is smaller than that of the European kind.

has brought it out with method and reflection. Here, you see, in the midst of the utmost grandeur of configuration, a chasteness of form, a symmetry of proportions which perfectly harmonize the whole, and impart to it that character of unity, no less desirable in natural beauties, than in the works of art; and yet we question whether the Alps themselves can boast higher spires, or more craggy peaks than some of those which indent the two chains that bound the valley of Nicamole.

As you proceed, the vale widens, until it attains the average breadth of eight leagues; but this vast plain is relieved from the reproach of monotony, which almost always attaches to far extended levels, by ranges of low and gently undulating hills, (*lomitas*) with beautifully rounded tops, covered with verdure,—generally running at the distance of two or three miles from the main chain,—and seemingly mounting guard at the feet of their gigantic neighbors. The highest of the peaks which surround the valley is the *Cerro de la Popa*, that rises, like an immense gothic castle, with crumbling towers and ruined battlements. Though the hand of Science has not yet measured the elevation of its summit, it cannot be less than nine or ten thousand feet above the level of the sea; but what heightens still its imposing appearance is an immense spire of one single block of glittering rock, which shoots up from a corner of the vast mass, so similar, in its configuration to an ancient steeple, that, at a distance, the eye is easily deceived by the similarity, and it requires the repeated asseverations of the inhabitants of the country to inure the traveller to the belief that what he beholds is not a work of art. This stupendous spire is appropriately styled, in the language of the country, " *la Aguja*," (the needle.) Towering, perpendicularly, five hundred feet above the adjacent crests, its pinnacle forms the most commanding object in this splendid amphitheatre, and Mr. Faring could not resist the temptation of taking a sketch of it with his pencil, as well as embodying the poetical beauties of it, in an ode, which we would cheerfully give to the public, were the versification a little more harmonious.

Leaving, at last, the contemplation of those wonderful scenes, our travellers crossed the valley diagonally, and soon arrived at the town of Pesqueria grande. It was precisely on Holy Wednesday. As the three following days form, in Catholic countries, a season of great solemnity, devoted to religious exercises, the friars were very importunate with Mr. Faring, to remain during Easter, so that, partly to oblige them, and partly to rest his mules, which had greatly suffered in the passage of the Sierra, he consented to prolong his stay till the following Tuesday. For that purpose, he rented a house, with a spacious courtyard, for the use of his animals, and in less than two hours' time, his bed and furniture were arranged in order, and he had procured for himself a kind of temporary home, sufficiently comfortable.

The two friars assisted the parish priest in the ecclesiastical ceremonies and processions with which the latter part of Holy Week is over-crowded, while Mr. Faring, who had nothing to do, sauntered about—from the church to the market-place, and from the market-place, to a spruce sanctuary, just erected, in honor of the virgin of Guadelupe, the great patroness of the Mexican republic.

He was much entertained in witnessing the various religious exercises by which these people solemnize our Saviour's passion, and we will, here, detail some particulars, which, on account of their singularity, were the peculiar objects of his attention. Maunday Thursday is, in Mexico, as in all other Catholic countries, distinguished by a solemn high mass, in the morning ; but there, the *Alcalde* and the *Ayuntamiento*, that is to say, the Mayor and board of Aldermen, officially assist at it, in great ceremony, and receive the Sacrament. After this, the chief magistrate of the town, kneeling at the foot of the altar, receives from the hands of the parish priest, the key of the tabernacle, which he wears, the whole day, suspended from his neck, by a ribbon adorned with splendid embroidery. This is accounted a great honor and a high privilege, which costs the church very little and wonderfully flatters the vanity of these people. Before the conclusion of the morning service, the public officers already mentioned present their gold headed canes, which are their badges of office, to the sexton of the church, to be deposited in the sanctuary, close to the altar. This is done by way of solemn homage, which, in their corporate capacity, they pay to the dogma of transubstantiation, and is a rite prescribed by the Spanish statute law.

In the afternoon, all the magistrates assist also at the *pe-diluvium*, and bear a part therein. This is in imitation of our Saviour's washing his apostles' feet, at his last supper. Twelve beggars are seated in two rows, in the nave of the church, and the parish priest with his whole clergy, robed in white, washes their right foot, while one of the city magistrates pours the water, mixed with wine, and another wipes it, with a towel; after which the foot is devoutly kissed by the whole board of aldermen. This, if performed with gravity, might become impressive, and though the kissing of the feet should be now dispensed with, as no longer in accordance with the modern sense of propriety, it is, at all events, a practical lesson of Christian humility and civil equality.

Late in the evening of the same day, a grand procession is formed round the town, in which a crucifix of gigantic dimensions is carried, in a reclining posture, by eight men. But this exhibition is rendered repulsive, and even shocking, by *penitentes*, who walk at the head of the procession, naked, from the waist upwards and bare legged, tottering under the weight of a huge piece of timber, to which their arms are fastened in the form of a cross, and having their faces covered with a black veil. As they are commonly Indians who perform this part, the deep dark hue of their skin increases the disgust which such an instance of barbarism is calculated to inspire; yet it is the part of the ceremony most admired, and it is accounted more or less splendid, in proportion to the greater or lesser number of penitents who appear therein. This mummery is closed by a sermon, and the church remains open all night, during which, a crowd of devotees of both sexes fill the chapel where the Eucharist is exposed for the adoration of the faithful.

The ceremonies of the following day are far more complicated, for new and multiplied processions and exhibitions succeed each other, with such rapidity as to leave the clergy hardly time to breathe. In the morning, they carry out a large statue of Christ, bearing his cross. It is dressed in purple velvet, embroidered with gold, and set on a kind of triumphal car, borne on the shoulders of the most qualified men of the place. This figure is styled *Jesus Nazareno*—unappropriately enough, as it purports to be a representation of our Saviour walking to Calvary, after his condemnation.

Another figure, as large as life, representing the Virgin Mary, in deep mourning, (yet with a profusion of sparking jewels, about her neck and ears,) immediately follows the statue of her Son, and is pathetically called *la Madre dolorosa*. After leaving the church, the two statues separate, and each is made to perambulate an allotted circuit, followed by a numerous retinue, with abundance of singing and incensing, after which, meeting in some *plaza*, a kind of tragic pantomime is acted, and the two images are made to salute each other and condole on their mutual grief. They return to the church, in company, and preparations are immediately made for a new procession. It is only a repetition of that of Maunday Thursday, of which we have already given a description.

On concluding this ceremony, a third spectacle is exhibited for the purpose of representing the dead body of our Saviour inclosed in a bier. This recumbent statue bears the name of *Jesus muerto*, and the exhibition is prolonged till long after twilight, in order to honor Christ's sepulture. A number of men in masquerade attend the procession, some personating the Scribes and Pharisees ; others in the garb of Roman soldiers, and each acting in character ; the whole resulting in so heterogeneous a performance, that it looks like a parody and a burlesque of the worst kind upon the Christian religion. In some Catholic countries, processions are conducted with a grace and majestic gravity which render them impressive, and really favorable to religious feeling ; but every part of the ritual of the church of Rome which the Spanish genius has modified, it has so far twisted and perverted from the original design, as to render it shocking to common sense. This service of Holy Week, which, in the Roman missal, is full of grace, simplicity and pathos, they have so far degraded, that it would hardly be fit for Vitzliputzly !

These exhibitions are intermingled with sermons and exhortations, generally as pitiful as the ceremonies themselves, and with the most ridiculous titles it is possible to imagine. In such religious exercises as these is that holy day spent, to the exclusion of every other occupation !

On Holy Saturday, the mass is prolonged till a late hour, but so soon as the blessed fire is lighted, an immense quantity of rockets is fired, in token of spiritual joy—a manner of evincing their religious feelings, so congenial to the character of Mexican Indians, that there is no pious ceremony of which it does not constitute a part.

At the conclusion of those solemnities, Mr. Faring prepared to pursue his journey ; but, being earnestly requested to remain another day, in order to witness the commencement of the fair, which is held in Easter-week, he consented to gratify the friars' curiosity. In Spanish times, there was, in the North of Mexico, but one great fair, that was held in the city of Saltillo, in the month of September. Being an affair of great importance, not only to the inhabitants of that city, in particular, but also to those of a wide spread district, who resorted thither, in great numbers, to barter their precious metals for the commodities of Europe, it was thought proper to solemnize the opening of it, by religious ceremonies of an imposing description. A glittering banner, blessed with pomp, by the highest ecclesiastical dignitary of the place, was carried about by a herald gorgeously apparelled ; an immense quantity of rockets was fired, and maskers and mummers perambulated the streets in wild glee. Since the beginning of the revolution, every town of any pretensions, in the three or four surrounding provinces, becoming anxious to enjoy the same privilege, the various sovereign legislatures, intoxicated by the first draught of supreme power, granted their petitions with thoughtless facility. The town of Pesqueria had consequently its own fair, and the solemnities with which it was opened, were in imitation of those of Saltillo.

We will not weary our readers with a description of the blessing of the banner, nor of the firing of rockets, in which there was nothing remarkable, except the waste of holy water and gunpowder ; but an Indian dance, that formed a leading feature of the revels, may prove of greater interest, inasmuch as it is a remnant of the old system of policy practised in Montezuma's court, before the Spanish conquest, and serves to illustrate the primordial manners of the aborigines. We allude to the dance of the *Matachines,*—originally a sacred performance, emblematical of the Mexican system of Astronomy, and of the manner in which this ingenious people had regulated their calendar ; but which Montezuma, who, though a barbarian, was a natural adept in king's-craft, found means to turn to his own honor, by becoming the chief performer therein, and making himself and his empress the objects of the adorations that were, before, paid to the sun and moon.([12])

Some time previous to the arrival of Cortes in Mexico, this monarch married the daughter of the old king of Tezucco, and in order to solemnize his nuptials with greater pomp, ordered that this dance should be holden at his court, when he would himself, dressed in his imperial robes, personate the sun, and his wife the moon, while the rest of the performers, consisting of the principal caciques and tributary kings, would represent the signs of the zodiac, and the principal constellations of the heavens. It was afterwards repeated, at stated intervals, and considered as an imperial function.

The attitudes and figures have nothing remarkable, being evidently of Tartaric origin, and limited to hopping alternately upon each foot; but the postures exhibit, or, rather, are emblematical of the most cringing servility imaginable, a refined species of self-abasement, hardly credible in a semi-barbarous people.

The dance is opened by the boy who personates Montezuma, accompanied by his bride, who is distinguished by the name of Malinche. The former, gaudily dressed, in silks and ribands, with a splendid crown on his head, hops with a galliard step down the apartment, while his spouse walks by his side, with a grave and dignified demeanor, waving a rattle, the noise of which is an apology for music. The dancers follow their monarch, and imitate his motions. Proceeding in two parallel rows, they reach the goal, and return to the starting point, one line wheeling to the right, and the other to the left, so that there are four rows of dancers, moving in contrary directions. A man, in a hideous mask, personating the evil genius, with a whip in his hand, rules the dance, and not unfrequently applies the lash to the caciques and grandees, the monarch alone and his Malinche being exempt from his jurisdiction.

At stated intervals, the emperor and his bride sit down in two arm-chairs, and the whole party, in two rows, kneel and make low prostrations before their majesties. Their obeisance is the most servile imaginable, for they bend down, till their foreheads touch the dust—all the while waving their rattles. In advancing towards the throne, this ceremony is repeated nine times, and the same number in receding ; but, as they retire, they punctiliously avoid turning their backs upon royalty, and walk backwards, which increases the ludicrous effect of the scene. I never witnessed so deep a sense of humiliation from man to man ; still this dance has a wonderful attraction for the aborigines of New Spain, and inspires them with an air of exultation, for which it is difficult to account, except, perhaps, on the supposition that its symbols awaken in their mind the remembrance of a nationality, now irrevocably lost, and shed a faint halo round the traditions of the past glories of their race. The name of Montezuma is to them typical of every thing which was honorable to the Aztecs ; and, singular as it may appear, the northern Indians, whose progenitors had never heard that name mentioned—nay, the Tlascaltecans, who were its bitterest enemies,—have caught the infection.

This exhibition would have had but little interest for our traveller, had not one of the Alcaldes of Pesqueria, a man tolerably well acquainted with Mexican antiquities, and who presided over the revels, undertaken to act as his *cicerone*, and explained to him the signification and meaning of the figures and postures of the dance. " Those eighteen low prostrations," said he, " are typical of the eighteen months into which the ancient Mexican year was divided ; and the irregular steps by which they were followed represented the five intercallary days, called *nemonteni*, that the Aztecs ingeniously added to their eighteen months, to make their civil year agree with the solar revolution. Now, pay attention ! They are forming the zodiac, round the sun. Look at the constellations, as they whirl round. This fellow, who pretends to butt, with his head, is *Aries*. That other, yonder, who waves his arms about, with his ten fingers expanded, and garnished with nails, which a hawk might envy, represents *Cancer*, and imitates well enough the movements of the crab. Next come the Couguar and Pecari. These are not classical names, neither are they to be found in the nomenclature of Ptolomeo. The former is the Mexican tiger, and the latter, —I am almost ashamed to mention the name,—is our wild hog ! But such as they are, they figured in the calendar of the aborigines, instead of the *Leo* and *Virgo* of astronomers."

But we must put an end to the prattle of the old Alcalde, for our reader would not probably have the same indulgence for his garrulity, as was manifested by Mr. Faring. The latter, happily endowed with a philosophical turn of mind, was not sorry to have had the chance of witnessing a genuine remnant of ancient Aztec customs, and he felt grateful to the friars for having, though unconsciously, procured him this additional stock to his information.

The two holy men, having nothing else to do in Pesqueria, and finding themselves pretty well rewarded by the parish priest, for the little assistance they had rendered, were anxious to set out for Monterey, the metropolis of the province of Nuevo Leon, that the grandiloquence of the Spaniards had dignified with the name of kingdom.

This city which is a bishop's see, boasts a population of about twenty thousand souls, and is built in a very picturesque situation, at the foot of a high mountain, whose jagged summit gives it some resemblance to a mitre, and whence flow numerous rivulets, which spread fertility through the plain, below. The style of building is the Morisco, as throughout the rest of Mexico; that is to say, the houses are almost universally one story high, only; with flat terrace roofs and few windows to the street. They are frequently built in the form of a quadrangle, round a small courtyard, decorated with evergreens and a fountain, or a little purling stream—a refinement, borrowed by modern Mexicans from their Andalusian conquerors. The houses of the poor, however, are nothing but miserable hovels, built of reeds and plastered with clay.

Having already mentioned some remnant of Morisco taste still lingering among this people, I must, in order to corroborate this statement, inform my readers that the same is to be traced in their style of dress. The men seem to regret the turban, and avail themselves of every trifling pretence, either a little wind, or a slight headache, in order to wrap round their head, a white linen, or some showy piece of silk. It is not even rare to see clergymen, in their ecclesiastical functions, or military men on parade, decorated with this strange kind of commode. The low people manifest also a fondness for the broad Turkish trousers; and, in imitation, their *calzoneras* are slit at the sides, from the hip down to the

ankle, and the broad white drawers allowed to float in the
air, which is as strange a fashion as any invented, since the
*souliers a la poulaine*, of the middle ages, and impedes as
much their walk.

In the north of Mexico, the whites are, proportionably
speaking, much more numerous than in the south of the Republic ; yet not so much as stated by Humboldt, in his political essay on New Spain.   This great writer has, on this subject, as well as on some others, been led into error by those
upon whose testimony he relied, for he never visited that part
of the country, and the descendants of the European race do
not certainly amount to a fifth part of the population of Durango, Chihuahua, Cohahuila, Nuevo Leon and Tamaulipas,
nor to the seventh of that of Sonora and California.   They
are rather a handsome people,—even fair-complexioned,—
stout, and well made, and superior, in physical qualifications,
to the Spaniards, from whom they are descended ; but they
have, to a certain degree, contracted the habits of the Indians,
which has greatly tended to weaken that moral fortitude, con-
stancy, and fixedness of purpose, for which the Castilian
character is so eminently distinguished.   One would, also, be
tempted to believe that the whites have imitated the timidity
of the aborigines.   The very alterations which they have introduced into the pronunciation of the Castilian language
seem to evince the progress of effeminacy.   The Spanish
LL, as if too hard for their palate, has been softened into Y,
and the elegant Z has dwindled into a common S.   The mass
of the people, and even frequently men of education use, in
conversation, the diminutive form, for every substantive that
enters into the discourse, a circumstance which communicates to their conversation a most preposterous and intolerable monotony.   This was a singular rule of the Aztec grammar, and passed for a token of servile submission, from an
inferior to a superior ; but now it is universally practised and
towards every class.   But I am unconsciously wandering
astray from my subject !   Alas, a novelist is often like a cook,
who, in order to make a respectable looking dish, out of small
materials, has to eke it out with some sauce, into which are
admitted different ingredients that could never have figured
by themselves !   Pity me, therefore, dear reader, and benig-
nantly pursue the narrative of Mr. Faring's journey.

## CHAPTER VII.

Here our two races meet,—here is the field
Where ignorance and anarchy shall yield
T' enlighten'd rule and profitable laws.—
Onwards we must,—nor ever shall we pause,
Till the Vermillion wave reflect our star.—
Fair California hails us from a far,
And *this* sweet vale shall be our Runnymede,
From whence our prosperous arms, with Freedom's speed,
Will soon enforce the charter you betrayed.—
Against your tyranny we stand arrayed,
T' assert the code of Nature, and our name
Shall to the conquer'd be—a blessing.
                              *The Texian, a Poem.*

At Monterey, the two Augustinian friars separated from Mr.
Faring, for they were now to travel in a southern direction,
while his route lay due east.   He remained in that city, four
days, to visit the few curiosities it contains, but found nothing
worthy of admiration.   The cathedral is a flat and unmeaning edifice, surmounted by a multiplicity of diminutive cupo-
las, painted with gaudy colors, and resembling more a
Turkish mosque, than a Christian temple.   The new church,
begun by Bishop Valdés, stands out of the town, in the
same state in which it was left by its founder.   Without
roof and without lateral walls, it presents to the eye the spectacle of a ruin, and the two rows of Gothic arches, destined
to support the roof of the nave, are not grand enough to be
impressive.   The Bishop's country-seat, on a high rock,
near the western suburb, looks dreary, and seems more fit for
the habitation of ghosts and bansheas, than for the abode of
a prelate enjoying an income of forty thousand dollars a year.
No wonder, then, that our traveller was disappointed in his
expectations.   He left the Metropolis of New Leon in bad
humor, which, however, vanished, when he reached Cadereita,
another considerable town, belonging to the same state.   In
this neighborhood, the country is under exellent cultivation.

Immense quantities of sugar are raised and a prodigious variety of fruit-trees embellishes the skirts of the place, the houses of which are in better style and of finer materials than those of Monterey.

From Cadereita, Mr. Faring continued his journey without stopping at, or taking notice of any other town, through which he passed, until he reached Refugio, at the mouth of the Rio Bravo. It was then hardly more than a large rancho ; but, from its situation, began already to attract considerable attention. That place having since become a populous city, its name has been changed into that of Matamoros, in honor of one of the most distinguished heroes of the revolution, and its locality will, in spite of the sand bar at the entrance of the harbor, render it, in times to come, the principal sea port of the Mexican republic, and secure for it an extensive trade.

The Rio Bravo has a course of sixteen hundred miles, being, like the Mississippi, subject to periodical inundations, and flowing in a variable estuary, which has formed, in many places, shallow lakes, similar to those that are so conspicuous in the delta of the Mississippi. Rising in the country of Taos, a region fertile in wheat, and abundantly timbered, it receives the Rio Conchos, an important stream, by which the mineral riches of Chihuahua might be transported to its mouth. The river San Juan, to which most of the creeks that flow from the glens of the eastern range of the Sierra Madre are tributary, disembogues also into the Bravo, and its waters might be rendered available, for the exportation of the produce of two states already abundant in sugar, and the soil of which is well adapted to the cultivation of cotton.

A rapid but comprehensive glance enabled Mr. Faring, who was endowed with a peculiar turn for commercial speculations, to notice all these natural facilities, and many a splendid plan of future enterprise was then conceived ; but he reckoned, as one may say, without his host, for the Rio Bravo has continued, till now, a *virgin* river, and though a population of nearly one million of souls might be benefitted by its stream, in the exportation of their surplus produce, yet neither the sail, nor the oar, has disturbed its tranquil surface. A steamboat has, indeed, made its appearance in the port of Matamoros, but has been considered an intolerable nuisance,

having a tendency to ruin the interesting land carriage, by
means of mules or ox-carts, now in general use ; nor is there
the least probability of the like encroachment, on the part of
any designing foreigner, being tolerated a second time ; but
this by the bye.

At the epoch of Mr. Faring's arrival at Refugio, one or
two schooners from New Orleans, used to perform stolen
trips, between those two places ; for the mouth of the Bravo
was one of the *debouchés* that the pirates of the gulf had discovered for their goods, and several of Lafitte's men had become
the patriarchs of the place.   In one of those schooners Mr.
Faring designed to take his passage to the United States, as
he had abandoned the project of continuing his journey by
land.   But, in order not to trespass upon our reader's patience, we will abstain from enumerating all the difficulties
he found, in accomplishing his purpose, and, taking a temporary leave of him, we will return to the hero of our story,
whom we have left in the charge of the parish priest of
Phelipa.

The servants who had escorted our American on his journey, being dismissed, followed, on their return home, the
same route they had pursued, while in his company, and did
not fail, in passing through Phelipa, to call upon the priest.
To him Mr. Faring had addressed a letter, accompanied by
valuable presents, informing him of the deep regret he had
felt in parting with his child, and that he should have been
tempted to recall his word, had he not reflected, that, were
the little boy carried out of the country, such a circumstance
might endanger his rights to the inheritance of the house of
Letinez, whose property was immense.   He, therefore, besought the priest to open a correspondence with the old Count,
or his brother, and to give them frequent intelligence of the
child's state and welfare.   This request was very unwelcome
to the excellent Don Fernando.   He did not set the least
value upon riches, and could not understand how he would be
conferring a benefit on his ward, in trying to secure for him
his grandfather's wealth.   On the other hand, he was apprehensive lest the family of Letinez should take the child away,
if they once knew where he was.   He felt, in consequence,
a considerable perplexity as to what course he should pursue.
His innate sense of justice, nevertheless, at length prevailed

over all selfish views and private affections, and he gave to the servants who were returning to Mechoacan, the following letter, addressed to the Count of Letinez, together with the official certificate of his daughter's death and her child's baptism, which latter document was, according to the laws of the country, necessary to secure the little boy's legal rights.

" Escelentisimo Señor,

" As it becomes a pious Christian to be prepared for all losses with which it may please Almighty God to visit him, I doubt not but your Excellency will receive with resignation the afflicting intelligence I have to communicate. Your heart had, no doubt, been deeply afflicted by the untoward events which obliged your son-in-law and daughter to seek for safety in a removal to the United States. That separation, though only temporary, must have been keenly felt by your Excellency; yet it has pleased Almighty God to send you now a far heavier trial; and circumstances over which I have had no control, render it my duty to inform you of your loss. Your excellent—your accomplished daughter, has been called to a better life, where she now is, undoubtedly, interceding for your welfare. Her death was truly edifying, and after receiving the Sacraments of the Church with the greatest piety and resignation, she left for you a *token*, which the bearer of the present letter will hand to your Excellency. Your worthy son-in-law was so afflicted by her death, that a dangerous sickness was the consequence, and after his convalescence, which was tedious and painful, he has thought proper to continue his journey for his native country, whence it is his intention to return in three or four years. He has entrusted to my care his little son, for whom I have procured an excellent nurse, and who, I rejoice to say, is in good health and highly interesting. It was not without great difficulty I could obtain your son-in-law's permission, that the infant should remain with me; but having, previous to your daughter's demise, pledged my word to her that the child should be brought up in the Catholic faith, I was resolved to carry this point. I send you, by the bearer, an authentic certificate of your daughter's death, and grandchild's baptism, of which I beg your Excellency to acknowledge the receipt.

8*

" I remain, with great respect, your Excellency's humble servant and *devoted chaplain*, and *kiss your Excellency's hands, &c., &c.*"

In six weeks' time, the parish priest of Phelipa received an answer from the Count of Letinez, in which that nobleman thanked him, with deep expressions of gratitude, for the services he had rendered his daughter, and declared his intention of taking charge of her child. He could not think of the heir of his family being reared among strangers, as if he were a foundling, and the honor of his house, no less than his personal duty, required that the infant should be brought up under his own eyes. He did not precisely state when he intended to send for the boy ; but the priest gathered, from some of his expressions, that it would be as soon as the grief resulting from the unexpected news of his daughter's death should be a littte assuaged.

How powerful soever the Count might be, the priest had no mind to deliver up his charge to him. He had received the little boy from his father, whose natural right to dispose of him was unquestionable, and no law could oblige him to resign the deposit to any one, without his consent, or order. He, therefore, in a letter, written in a polite but manly tone, imparted his resolution to the Count ; beseeching his Excellency not to put him to the necessity of refusing his messenger. Old Señor de Letinez and his brother were, nevertheless, resolved that their intentions should not be frustrated, and scrupled not, in case milder means should prove ineffectual, to resort to coercive measures, to obtain their object ; yet, before recurring to force, the family were desirous to employ the conciliatory interposition and persuasion of Abbate Letinez, who consented to take a journey to Phelipa, for that purpose. It was an arduous undertaking on the part of the good ecclesiastic, and it required all the love he bore his family, now centred in the only scion left by his niece, to induce him to venture upon so hard a task.

When this projected journey to the state of Durango became known to the family of Letinez, all the servants were put in commotion, and the report of such an extraordinary circumstance, being spread through the city of Pascuaro, became the subject of all conversations. In the meantime, preparations were made for the expedition, and on such a scale, that one might have supposed it was question of providing for a small army. The grand family coach—a vehicle large enough to answer the purposes of a room,—was furbished anew, its elaborate decorations of sculptured wood were regilt, the seats were restuffed, and its ponderous wheels, strengthened, by having their spokes wrapped round with tough thongs of leather, besides being carefully watered every day.([13]) The most trusty and skilful servants, on the several Haciendas of the count, were ordered to select the best travelling mules, from the immense herds belonging to the family, and several cooks busied themselves in preparing provisions of the best quality—*fiambres*, of every description,—Estramadura saussages,—venison, *tassajo*—chocolate perfumed with vanilla—*pinole*,* and what not? At last, the day of departure having arrived, the whole party went to church, to hear a mass *pro itinerantibus*, celebrated by the Abbate himself; after which he bid adieu to his brother, but not without many embraces and tears, and set out on his journey.

The upper classes of the Mexican population are remarkable for a certain helplessness, or rather, feminine languor, that renders them averse to the least fatigue. Wages being prodigiously low, and the common people fond of servitude—which saves them the trouble of providing for themselves—wealthy houses generally retain a number of domestics which, in Europe, would be accounted out of all proportion. In this respect, Mexico may be compared to the East Indies, where people keep a particular servant for every species of domestic work, and where each menial confines his care to his specific occupation. Children, being from their most tender age, surrounded with so many attendants, are, of course, much indulged and flattered. They contract a habit of calling upon their servants, for the most trifling wants, and consider the performance of any little service for themselves as unbecoming persons of genteel standing, and as an intolerable hardship.

No idea can be formed, from the servility of the negro

---

* Pinole is made with fine corn meal, pounded almonds, sugar and various spices.

slaves, in the south of the United States, of that of the low
classes, in Mexico ; for, the negro, while he crouches before
his master, does it with an air of fear, and visible signs of
terror, which show his humiliation to be extorted ; and this
naturally disgusts a man of sensibility.  The Mexican, on
the contrary, fawns upon his master, with a look of *love*,
which seems to be spontaneous, and there is in him an appearance of devotedness, superior to any thing ever beheld
in other free servants, which has undoubtedly some foundation in the idiosincracy of the Aztec race.

With these premonitory remarks on the peculiarities of
the serving classes, in Mexico, before their eyes, our readers
may imagine the deep reverence, the obsequious care and
minute attention of which Abbate Letinez was the object,
during his journey.  No less than five servants and ten Mo-
zos de mulas waited upon him,—all proud of their charge,
and never failing, when passing through a rancho, to inform
the villagers, in a whisper, of their patron's condition, and to
add some slight hint on the object of his expedition.  Whenever the good ecclesiastic alighted from his coach, no less
than five or six of the servants would run to help him down.
It seemed as if they thought the wind committed a sacrilege
by blowing upon his person, and the earth was too much
honored by being pressed by his feet.

Notwithstanding the tender officiousness of the servants,
and the good cheer daily provided for him, father Letinez
felt horridly fatigued, and after the first five days' ride, was
obliged to stop, some time, at the house of the parish priest
of Temejuatlan, who had been one of his scholars, while he
taught metaphysics in the university of Guadalaxara.  At
that clergyman's, he was informed that a part of the *Bajio*,*
through which his road lay, was in a most deplorable state
of civil commotion—this rich district being, then, overrun by
different parties of insurgents, on the one hand, and of
Spanish troops, on the other —and that the prosecuting of
his journey would, perhaps, endanger his life.  This piece of
intelligence greatly alarmed our pacific ecclesiastic, and he
was, several times, tempted to retrace his steps ; still he felt

---

* The Bajio is a district of great fertility, lying on the skirts of the
state of Morelia, and running into several of the adjacent *departamentos*.

ashamed to return, without accomplishing the object he had in view, and after long reflections pro and con, he resolved upon proceeding.

Having imparted his final resolution to his friend, the latter told him, that, since his mind was absolutely made up, he would try how far his safety could be insured by means of a passport, which would prove of some service, in case he should fall into the hands of certain parties of the insurgents, with whom he confessed that he was secretly connected. Father Letinez, however, was alarmed at the idea of a passport, and told his friend that prudence would not permit him to accept his offer, for it might prove as dangerous, should he encounter the royal troops, as serviceable with the insurgents. To this his friend replied, that his objection would be removed, upon a view of the instrument provided for his security, and so saying, he opened a closet, out of which he brought a bundle of walking-sticks, every one of which had a small effigy of the Madona of Guadelupe carved on the top.

"These," said he, presenting his friend with two of them, "will insure your safe passage through my parish, that extends twenty leagues to the north-east of this place, and even procure you any little succor which my parishioners can afford. Beyond the limits of my spiritual jurisdiction, they will, I am afraid, prove of little value, for it is a private signal and particular token agreed upon with my men, yet some of them may be wandering a little further north. At all events, keep one of these sticks in your left hand, and give the other to the leader of your caravan, and instruct him to carry it in such a way that it be easily perceived by any one he may chance to meet on the road. Ah! Bless the good virgin of Guadelupe! without her we could not have moved those silly masses; but she has given the Spaniards the trip! Has she not? They little thought when they got Juan Diego's vision put in the breviary, that, one day, this blessed Lady would play them such a trick!"*

Father Letinez, who did not think a belief in the virgin of

* The first insurrection in Mexico was carried on in the name of the Virgin of Guadelupe, by Hidalgo and his associates. Hence her image is set up in the hall of Congress, and she is considered as the great protectress of Mexican independence, and chiefly hostile to Spanish pretensions.

Guadelupe an article of faith, (though it would be a dangerous thing publicly to deny it in Mexico) laughed heartily at
his friend's remarks, and inquired how he came to possess
so much credit with the insurgents, that they should reverence to such a degree a cane coming from him.

"Credit among them," replied the other, "Who should,
if not I ? I can tell you under the rose, that I direct their
movements, and while I am snugly sitting here, in my parsonage, they stir no where without my orders. And yet, I
frequently receive the royal officers, when passing this way.
Oh ! I am sure my secret will be kept, though it is known to
a considerable number of people. Had the rattle-brained
fellow of Dolores, thus cunningly kept the match burning,
without letting the smoke escape, he might have been still
quiet in his cure, or, perhaps, have obtained a yellow cap to
cover his tonsure with.([14])   But my empire does not extend
far, as I have told you, and this is the misery of those who
do not come out boldly. I am horridly cramped by the wild
*armadillo* of the hills. By my santiguada, you must beware
of him ! Should you fall into his hands, there is an end of
your journey, I assure you."

"And who is he ?" inquired father Letinez.

"Padre Torres," replied the other, in a whisper, and looking
round, with a suspicious air, as if afraid to be overheard.

"Yet, you do not imply that he would murder a fellow
clergyman, or offer him personal violence ?" resumed he of
Mechoacan.

"Murder, no !—at least I hope not," replied he of Temejuatlan, "But he will fleece you, if you fall into his hands.
He would not, I verily believe, let the Pope himself pass by
scatheless, if he could lay his clutches on him."

These communications did not tend to allay our traveller's
fears, yet, on the next day, he continued his journey, carefully conforming to his friend's instructions. It was well he
did so, for he had not proceeded fifteen leagues, when, in the
middle of a thick palmar, (id est, a grove of palm trees,) his
caravan was assaulted by a large gang of ragged ruffians,
who rushed upon them, with the national cry of "*viva nuestra
señora de Guadelupe y mueran los Gachupines.*"*

---

* Long live the Virgin of Guadelupe and death to the Spaniards.

Not perceiving, at first, the mysterious abacus, in the hands of the guide; they were beginning to beat the muleteers and to pillage their loads; when he of the talismanic truncheon rushed in among them, flourishing his stick and calling out, "Look here, gentlemen, look here!—*We*, also, are for the Virgin of Guadelupe." Whereupon the marauders immediately stopped, and taking off their hats, respectfully inquired who occupied the coach. Upon being informed that it was a padre and a friend of the parish priest of Temejuatlan, they begged his pardon, kissed his hand, and even escorted him a little distance, till he emerged from the woods.

The next day, at noon, they crossed the limits of that parish, and entered a territory under a different jurisdiction where it was expected the mysterious cane would lose its virtue; still they met, every now and then, some solitary ranchero, who would pull off his hat at the sight of it, and cross himself.

Aware that they were now within the district over which Padre Torres claimed a sort of right, from its being frequently scoured by his troops, they sought, by a circuitous route, to escape, if possible, his marauding parties; but the country became more broken, as they proceeded, and consequently retarded their progress. Frequently, their road lay in some of the many deep ravines by which the plains are intersected, when the carriage was slowly dragged along over the shingles, brought down from the mountains by the winter torrents, which rendered its motion irregular and exceedingly painful to father Letinez. At times, too, those ravines, winding down steep descents, and bordered, on either hand, by high banks, in the form of perpendicular cliffs, precluded all possibility of flight, or of defence, in case our travellers should be attacked. This was a melancholy prospect which they were afraid to see realized at every moment, nor were their anticipations without just foundation; for, at a short turn of one of these ravines, known by the name of *los Berendos*, along the narrow bed of which they had been marching for about two hours, without having reached the place of egress, they were assailed by a party of troops belonging to the formidable corps of father Torres.

A gun was fired as a signal, and immediately the precipitous banks, above their heads, were seen crowned by armed men, some with muskets, some with lances; but most of them with no better weapons than long sticks, at the extremity of which they had fastened their daggers. Their sudden appearance was accompanied by the well known cry of "Death to the Spaniards." In vain did the guide of the travelling party ride up and down, flourishing his Temejuatlan stick ; the assailants paid no attention to it, and insisted that the travellers should throw down their arms, and surrender themselves prisoners, in order to be dealt with according to father Torres' discretion.

At the sight of their obduracy, the guide began to expostulate, with tears. " For the love of God, Señores," said he, " and of the Virgin, do not offer any indignity to the only brother of the Count of Letinez. He is a priest, Señores, and we are his servants."

He was interrupted by some of the marauders, who had let themselves down the steep banks, and now, in a rough manner, forced him and his fellow servants, to alight from their mules. After taking possession of the animals and binding the men with cords, they took Padre Letinez out of the coach. However, upon seeing, round his neck, the black stock , edged with blue, the distinctive mark of the clerical order, in Mexico, they felt ashamed of their rudeness, and abstained from offering him any insult. This did not prevent them from insisting upon carrying him to the place where their chief resided. In vain did father Letinez persuade them to permit him to continue his journey ; they were deaf to his voice, and, although, upon his earnest request, they unloosed his men, still they marched them all, with their mules and baggage, towards a range of high conical hills, called los Remedios, which towered aloft, at the distance of fifteen, or sixteen leagues to the eastward.

It was on the summit of the highest of these mountains that their chief, surrounded by barbaric luxury, held a kind of royal court. Our travellers did not reach the entrance of the deep glen, that gave access to it, till the afternoon of the ensuing day ; and they were astonished to see the natural strength of the place, which made it impregnable to all the forces the Spaniards could, at that period, bring against it. Immense precipices surrounded it on every side, and rendered an approach impossible, except by following the bed of a torrent, which wound round the base of a steep hill, commanded by perpendicular rocks, whence a handful of men could have easily arrested the progress of a whole army. The bed of the torrent itself was fortified with intrenchments, and even, after clearing all those obstacles and external works of defence, one encountered, before reaching the high level plain, on the summit, a ravine, more than twenty feet broad, which entirely precluded all access beyond, and could be crossed only by means of a drawbridge. On the other side of the *barranco*, the top of the mountain was perfectly level and produced excellent grass, and in sufficient quantity to maintain a stock of cattle for provisions, in case of a siege ; while there was also a sufficient supply of water, from a deep well. There, Padre Torres, the ecclesiastical chieftain, had established his head quarters, whence he directed the movements of no less than seven thousand men.

# CHAPTER VIII.

When Liberty south of the Tropic strays,
She runs a muck !—throws off her robes and cap,
And makes herself a perfect fright.
                                        *Anonymous.*

THE dreaded clergyman, who, from the summit of this
mountain, like an eagle from his eyry, domineered over the
surrounding plains, had, by the insurgents, been raised to the
dignity of *Mariscal de Campo*, and had divided the considerable extent of country under his command into districts, at
the head of which it was a singular feature of his policy, to
place none but men whose gross ignorance was likely to
make them always subservient to his own will.   He was not
unskilful in the arts necessary to ingratiate himself into the
favorable opinion of those officers, and, as long as they conformed to his instructions, he did not care for their conduct.
Thus, sure of impunity, provided they should not contradict
the orders, or stand against the interests of their chief, these
commandants became petty tyrants in their districts, and made
no scruple of pillaging the friends, as well as the enemies of
the independence of their country.   Many of the patriots,
therefore, dreaded falling into their hands, as much as into
those of the royalists, and it was not without great terror that
father Letinez saw himself about being presented to the strange
and capricious being whom circumstances had rendered
master of his fate.

In the centre of the plain to which the drawbridge gave
access was a collection of huts, towards which our good ecclesiastic was obliged to march on foot, for he had been forced to leave his coach at the entrance of the glen, below, and
his horses, on the other side of the ravine.

As he drew near to that species of village, he could distinguish a house, or, rather, cabin of more elegant construction than the rest, and soon after, hear two or three cracked

female voices, singing a curious ditty, in praise of the war-like achievements of the chieftain.

From time to time, the melody already mentioned, was interrupted by loud peals of laughter, which seemed to proceed from a very strong pair of lungs. It was the Mariscal de Campo, himself, listening to the rehearsal of his own exploits, and manifesting his heartfelt satisfaction by these noisy cachinnations.

Our traveller, being introduced into the presence of this personage, was no less surprised than disappointed, when, instead of receiving him, at least, with the common marks of civility, Padre Torres did not even vouchsafe to rise from the bed upon which he was stretched at lazy length. There he lay, surrounded by military officers and women, some of whom employed themselves in fanning him, while others administered the most fulsome flattery, which he would interrupt, every now and then, by exclaiming, " I am the chief of all the world."

" Alas, for the independence of my country !" thought father Letinez, within himself, " if it must be achieved by such men as these." He was, nevertheless, very cautious not to manifest his disgust by any outward sign, and stood at a respectful distance, awaiting his interrogatory.

The mighty chieftain, after listening to some information, whispered into his ears by the officer who had headed the capturing party, vouchsafed at last to address father Letinez in the following words : " So, I find that you are travelling northward, with a large retinue, and a splendid coach !—And where may you be going ?—Towards Monterey, probably,—with some message for Arredondo : the Gachupines must pay you well, man, to enable you to keep such a state ; whilst we, here, who are fighting for liberty, think ourselves happy, if we can get a *mesteño*, or a broken down mule, to ride."[15]

" May it please your Excellency," replied father Letinez, "I have no relation with Arredondo—neither am I opposed to the independence of my country. On the contrary, I do all I can for its accomplishment."

" You do all you can !" exclaimed Torres, fixing sternly his eyes upon Padre Letinez.

" Yes, sir," replied the other ; " all I can do, in reason—and all that a man of my character ought to do."

" In reason !" shouted Torres, incensed by the allusion to his own military exploits, included in the above answer. " That is the cant,—that is the word under the shelter of which the partizans of Spain seek to conceal their treachery.—But it will not serve you here, I tell you. We must have patriotism."

" Father," returned Señor de Letinez, who, though constitutionally timid, had a proper sense of his dignity, and was not disposed to suffer himself to be insulted, " I am a Mexican and a clergyman, as well as yourself, and as you are now at the head of a large share of the forces who are fighting for the liberties of your country, it is your duty to protect and not to oppress a peaceable fellow-citizen. My life is in your hands, no doubt ; but remember that the tree of liberty never throve, where it was besprinkled with the blood of grey-headed and innocent priests."

Here a murmur of approbation was heard among the bystanders, and Señor de Letinez, somewhat encouraged by it, continued, " I can refer you to the parish priest of Temejuatlan, who is one of the secret leaders of the partizans, in the bajio. I am a friend of his. This puts me above suspicion. I am now bound on a journey to the state of Durango, in the success of which, the welfare and honor of our family are deeply concerned ; and it would be an irretrievable misfortune for us, were I prevented from continuing my route. Therefore, I hope you will not detain me,—and in order to prove that I am well affected to your cause, I will give towards the equipment of your soldiers, the sum of one thousand dollars. I will leave you an order upon my brother, at Pascuaro, and it will be paid at sight."

" Umph !" replied Padre Torres, " it is a great way hence to Pascuaro, and who knows whether your brother would honor the order ?—We want money, sure enough ; but letting you go is not the means of providing for our necessities. I cannot take upon myself to decide in an affair of so much importance. It must be referred to *Congress*, and they will decree what they please. I am not free to decide by myself."

" Is there a Congress, hereabouts ?" inquired father Letinez. " And where do they sit ?—I will go myself and lay my case before them."

" Yes, there is a Congress," replied Torres, in a tone of

peculiar asperity, " the general Congress, for the liberty of Anahuac !—The supreme government of the country ! Have you never heard of it ? They hold their sittings at Jauxilla, twenty leagues from this place. But you are not to leave los Remedios without permission. I will send them a statement of your case, and you must await their resolution."

At these words, Señor de Letinez lost patience, and forgetting his timidity, broke forth into a volley of objurgations, which stunned Padre Torres, declaring that he would set out, and daring the chieftain's myrmidons to lay their hands on him, in order to prevent his departure. None of them, in fact, dared to do so, being prevented by respect for his ecclesiastical character ; but, alas ! his servants did not enjoy the same privilege, and these were soon secured, so that, although father Letinez was left free, and might roam at large, yet he found no body to wait upon him, and was, in consequence, as much a prisoner, as if he had been confined in irons.

He went about complaining of the treatment he received, till Padre Torres began, at last, to fear, lest he should make upon his soldiers an impression unfavorable to his authority. To pacify him, he sent him a soothing message, informing him he had despatched one of his officers to Jauxilla, and that he would soon be informed of the resolution of Congress, which he had no doubt, would prove favorable to the continuation of his journey. Upon receiving this intelligence, father Letinez determined to wait with patience. Nothing definitive, however, was known, till the afternoon of the following day, when, the officer who had been despatched to Jauxilla returned with the news that Congress were coming to los Remedios, in order to have an interview with padre Torres. This was exceedingly surprising to our traveller, who could hardly believe it possible that a legislative assembly should so far forget their dignity, as to condescend to wait upon one of their officers, instead of obliging him to wait upon them ; but he did not know what kind of an assembly that Congress was, nor of what they were capable.

Towards sunset, they arrived, sure enough—the whole of Congress, on three horses !—That sovereign assembly consisted of a President and two members, whose names have been immortalized in Mexican history. At the entrance of

9*

the village, they were received with military honors, by the ragged garrison, and Padre Torres vouchsafed to rise from his bed of repose, to invite them into his own house, where an extraordinary session was immediately opened.

They sat with closed doors, and after a quarter of an hour, no less a personage than a general of brigade was despatched to summon father Letinez to their presence. This officer condoled with the good clergyman, upon the treatment he had experienced ; and, out of reverence for his character, condescended to communicate a slight hint of what had been resolved in Congress, in relation to him, and moreover imparted some advice, which he assured him, would prove, if followed, exceedingly advantageous.

"What a pity !" said he, "What a scandal, to treat a reverend gentleman, like you, in the way they have done ! An ancient professor of philosophy ! The light of the university of Guadalaxara, at its most brilliant period ! But, Padre, you know what Tully says, 'inter leges silent arma,' no,—It is 'inter arma silent leges,' I should say. The fact is, reverend father, that we are hard pushed for money, and though his Excellency and the General Congress are inclined to treat you with all possible lenity, yet they dare not dismiss you without—ransom—I mean without something to stop the clamors of our men, who have not received one single *ochavo* for three months past. It is merely to prevent their murmurs :—you understand me, Padre. But what you have offered is not enough for one month's pay for the garrison of this fortress. Now, should you make it three thousand, instead of one, it would, perhaps, suffice for immediate relief, and terminate the grumblings of our soldiers, for, as to us, no portion of it will enter our pockets, much less those of the members of the sovereign Congress, who, God bless them, exercise their functions gratis, and out of mere zeal for liberty. There is another little thing, also, which would help you greatly, but I hardly dare to hint it, unless you would promise me strict secrecy."

"And what is it ?" interrupted father Letinez. "You may rely upon my discretion."

"Why," resumed the other, "Padre Torres went down, last night, to the entrance of the glen, to look at your coach, and was greatly pleased with it. He has nothing to ride in, but a poor gig, which is somewhat out of repair, and he says it is a shame for a Mariscal de Campo to make use of so paltry a kind of chariot. I think he would be glad to effect an exchange, and, no doubt, would cover the trifling difference, to make odds meet."

" Our family coach! He wants to swindle me out of that, also," exclaimed father Letinez, incensed.

" Well," resumed the officer, " you can do as you please, I only give you friendly advice, and show you how to make a protector of the Padre. But have a care how you join the name of father Torres with that odious word, swindler. Happily no one has heard you, besides myself. May Heaven keep your reverence from harm, but many a man has been shot here, for much less."

They had, by this time, got to the door of the chieftain's house, and our traveller was soon admitted before the General Congress. Padre Torres was sitting at the head of the table, having on his right hand the president of the sovereign assemby ; on his left, the two members who composed that legislative body, and the secretary, opposite to him, at the other extremity. There were cigaritos on the table, and a bottle of brandy, with glasses, which showed that those worthies did not perform their work *dry lipped.* Father Letinez was invited to sit down, after which the president imparted to him the resolution they had taken, in the following words.

" His Excellency, our Mariscal de Campo, has informed us of the offer you have made for the equipment of the brave soldiers who are fighting for the liberty of Anahuac. As we do not suppose you are a disaffected person, nor can, in any wise, be dangerous to our cause, we have agreed to accept your proposal, yet, at the same time, to remonstrate with you, on the small amount to which you have limited your offers ; inviting you in the name of your country (de la Patria) to make it three thousand. Your bleeding country demands this little sacrifice, and the most Holy Virgin of Guadelupe, our patroness, will not fail to reward you, and prosper your journey, if you show yourself liberal towards her cause. You agree to it, Padre—Don't you ? You may send as many of your servants as you please to Pascuaro, to fetch the silver, and, in the mean time, remain here yourself, as hostage. In the interval, we will take good care of you. You shall not want a little drop of paxarette, for your dinner, and you will say mass for the troops, in the absence of father Torres, and as soon as the money arrives, you will be at liberty to continue your route."

To this Señor de Letinez answered that he could, on no account, consent to prolong his stay, because the object he had in view in the journey he had undertaken, was urgent, and a delay might cause its failure. They had, therefore, nothing to expect from him, unless he should be permitted immediately to continue his route. This was his firm and unalterable determination.

Neither the Congress nor the Mariscal de Campo had expected to find so stern a firmness in their unwilling guest, and they were not a little perplexed by his dogged resolution. They thought, however, that it would be proper to take some time for reflection, previous to liberating so important a prisoner ; and, remanding him for the present, they gave him to understand that he would be summoned again, the ensuing morning, to appear in their presence. There was a secret reason prompting their accession to his terms, of which father Letinez could not be informed, and that had been the real motive of the Congress' coming down from Jauxilla, to consult with Padre Torres.

Some time previous, the celebrated Spanish chief, Mina, had gained a considerable victory over the royalists, at San Juan de los Llanos, and all the party of the patriots were anxious that Torres and his troops should co-operate with him, and that Mina, as a man of greater military talents, should act as generalissimo ; doubting not, but, under so skilful a chief, the Mexican cause would prosper. Padre Torres did not relish a plan by which he was to be reduced to act a secondary part, and had, hitherto, opposed it, but solely by secret manœuvres and intrigues, without openly showing his disinclination. His party and the very commandants he had placed at the head of the various districts under his jurisdiction, became, however, so clamorous, that he was obliged to sacrifice his private feelings and appoint an interview with the Spanish general, at the fort of Sombrero. The day was at hand, and Torres was to leave los Remedios on the following Tuesday. Taking with him his principal officers, he feared lest, during his absence, father

Letinez should avail himself of the influence of his sacerdotal character, to obtain his release and that of his servants, which was not at all improbable, considering the great reverence the insurgents entertained for their native clergy. Torres would, in that case, be deprived of his prey. On the other hand, he dared not confine the Padre in prison—the only effectual means to prevent his escape—for it would have been an abominable scandal for his whole party, and might have proved dangerous to the stability of his own authority. Torres resolved, therefore, to accept the draft, and liberate his brother clergyman, and it was for him the easiest thing in the world to obtain the sanction of his Congress.

On the following morning, it was, of course, announced to father Letinez that, upon his signing the draft, he would be allowed to depart. He very joyfully availed himself of the permission, thus unexpectedly obtained, and to his unspeakable comfort, after a few hours' bustle, on the part of his servants, saw himself at the head of his caravan, on his way to Phelipa. The provisions which had been so liberally made for his journey, were, nevertheless, sadly diminished ; and when they stopped, at night, the steward had a long and woful account to impart of the felonious abstraction of whole boxes of chocolate and delicate *fiambres*, of which the officers of los Remedios had been guilty.

## CHAPTER IX.

Prostrate shall lie the honors of your house,
And dread extinction o'ertake your name,
Unless this tender scion's growth retrieve
Your waning hopes.

*The Feudal Baron.*

WE will pass over the inconvenience which resulted to
father Letinez, from the scarcity of his travelling provisions,
as well as from the fatigues he underwent, during the remainder of his journey, and, at one single bound, transfer our
reader to Phelipa, that he may witness the first interview
between the Mechoacan clergyman and Don Fernando de
Larribal.

It happened, that, when father Letinez alighted from his
coach, before Don Fernando's house, there was no one at
home, save the house-keeper, who was not a little bewildered
at the sight of his numerous retinue.   Her first thoughts
were about the slender stock in her larder, which the new
comers were likely to leave in a desolate state, should the
parish priest, as was his wont, insist upon entertaining the
servants, as well as their master.   This did not, however,
prevent her from showing a proper degree of civility to the
strange ecclesiastic, whom she introduced into the grand sala,
and begged to consider himself at home, till the return of her
master, who had gone to a neighboring village.

Father Letinez availed himself of the house-keeper's lo-
quacity, to inquire about the state of Mr. Faring's child, and
no sooner did he manifest a desire to see him, than, glad of
an opportunity to oblige a visiter, who had condescended to
enter into conversation with her, the old woman summoned
Tio Pedro, who was working in the huerta, and ordered him
to fetch the infant.   Tio Pedro did not set out upon his errand so briskly, but that he found time to take a peep at
father Letinez, his grand carriage, his numerous servants and

the splendid trappings of his mules. He was not a little puzzled to imagine what kind of a visiter he might be, for he had never seen so much magnificence in all his life, nor so much gilding as the stranger's coach displayed, except at the altar of St. Matthew, the patron saint of the parish! " Even the Bishop of Durango, (God bless his most illustrious Lordship,) was not attended by so great a number of servants, when travelling through his diocese, to give confirmation! Nor were they so richly dressed, nor had they such handsome mules!" He went, nevertheless, to acquit himself of his errand, and shortly afterwards returned with the nurse and child.

As soon as father Letinez saw the little babe, there was a burst of feeling, which he tried in vain to master. He took him into his arms, and burst into tears. A thousand tender recollections of his niece, who had been so dutiful to him, and whom he had so tenderly loved, rushed upon his mind. All her fondness and respect towards her father and himself were brought back to his memory, and the idea that she had died far from her family, in a state of distress, and, perhaps, in consequence of the ecclesiastical persecution which she had suffered, made him experience such a pang of anguish as he had never felt before. Yet, there was a consolation, though Maria del Carmen was dead, there was a remnant left of the ancient and noble house of Letinez. The beautiful and sweet looking infant, who was now innocently smiling upon him!

In this child were now centred all his brother's hopes, as well as his own. Upon this babe, depended the consolation of their old age; but he was still in the hands of strangers, and it was doubtful whether he would succeed in obtaining his release from the parish priest of Phelipa. Since Señor de Letinez had entered the state of Durango, he had acquired a better knowledge of the situation of the northern provinces, and convinced himself that, should Don Fernando de Larribal resist his entreaties, there was but little chance of using forcible means, because the Spanish power was yet unshaken in those parts, and the officers of Ferdinand VII. could not fail to side with one of their own countrymen, in the determination of any legal claim against the best of Mexican creoles. He plainly perceived, therefore, that the attainment of his object, depended entirely on the generosity of the Spanish priest;

and, fully convinced of the inutility of other measures, resolved to appeal to his feelings, in the hope that this mode of proceeding would be conducive to success.

He was not mistaken:—Don Fernando de Larribal was endowed with a noble, elevated soul, and incapable of being bullied into any concession, through timidity. All the Biscayan energy and spirit of independence, burned in his bosom ; yet he was compassionate to excess, and unable to resist supplications for relief of any distress, which it was in his power to remove. The sensibility of his mind was so exquisite, as to degenerate into a kind of weakness, and to this foible did father Letinez, in the end, owe the ultimate success of the suit he had come to urge.

When the parish priest returned home, he was not a little surprised to behold the splendid vehicle in his court-yard ; but, upon entering his parlor and perceiving the strange clergyman, who still held the child in his arms, he immediately understood who he was, and the purport of his visit.

Advancing towards him, therefore, he said, with a cold, yet civil air, " I need not, I suppose, fear being mistaken in saluting my guest, as Señor de Letinez. No one else could take such an interest in *this* infant. But I can tell him, in one single word, and in order to prevent all necessity of further explanation, that, if his object be to separate me from my charge, his intention will be frustrated. I received him from his father, to whom alone I am accountable ; and to him alone am I bound to deliver the child. I am sorry to be obliged thus to appear rude with a reverend guest, but it is better fully to understand each other at the outset. Where no expectations are raised, no disappointment is felt.

Father Letinez was confounded by this address. With an admirable presence of mind, nevertheless, and a nice tact of good breeding, which was an indirect reproof of his host's bluntness, he replied : " My dear Sir, I am so much delighted to see my grand nephew—the only remaining scion of our house—in such good health, and to become acquainted with the noble-hearted man to whom our family is so much indebted, that I do not feel inclined to grumble at any resolution he may have taken, much less to quarrel with him, should he even deprive us of what we conceive to be our just rights. Let us, therefore," added he, tenderly embracing Don Fernando, "make this pledge of friendship, the first step to our future acquaintance."

The parish priest of Phelipa, who, to quick feelings, united nice powers of discrimination ; felt rebuked, and somewhat abashed on receiving the embraces of Señor de Letinez. Thus the latter had already obtained some advantage, which he was very careful not to lose. He turned the conversation on his niece, and the various circumstances that had attended her death, which he wished to hear detailed by Don Fernando personally.

After hearing from his host, the melancholy story, he did not fail to tender him anew his thanks, and there was in his language a certain warmth and unction, which manifested that his heart sincerely felt what his lips expressed. His powers of conversation were of the first order, and Don Fernando could not help thinking he had seldom seen a man of such a pleasing address. He, nevertheless, kept on the reserve, being rather dubious as to the stranger's views, and was incessantly on the watch, in order to seize upon any expression which might afford him the least chance of entering into protestations against resigning his young ward to the family of Letinez. His precautions were, however, vain ; for the Mechoacan clergyman, who did not lack a certain knowledge of the human heart, and had

—————————"Skill
To rule and warp the human will."

abstained, during the rest of the day, from broaching anew the subject, and thought proper to study the temper of his host, before treading again upon such delicate ground.

Having announced to Don Fernando his intention of prolonging his stay at Phelipa, during some days, he rented a house for the use of his servants, and though the parish priest strongly insisted upon entertaining the whole party, father Letinez would by no means consent to impose such a burthen upon a man who made so benevolent a use of his income. He did accept his hospitality for himself, but his servants kept house apart, at his expense, under the direction of one of their number, who acted as steward.

Having, thus, temporarily become a member of Don Fernando's family, father Letinez insisted upon assisting him in his ministerial duties. He preached repeatedly in the parish church, and spoke with so much eloquence, that all the parishioners, as well as the parish priest, himself, were delighted. There was no talk, through the whole country, but of the famous Padre, from Mechoacan, who was so pathetic in the pulpit, that he could almost have drawn tears from a rock ! Father Letinez was, moreover, generous, and as he had plenty of money at his disposal, his charities were more extensive even than those of the parish priest, so that all the inhabitants of Phelipa, rich and poor, sang his praises. With any other clergyman, besides Don Fernando, so much popularity, so rapidly acquired by a stranger, might have begotten jealousy and envy ; but that worthy man was so entirely guiltless of those vile passions, that he became more attached to his guest, in proportion as the latter recommended himself more extensively to the public, and loved him, as much for the advantage he thought his parishioners derived from his labors, as he himself admired his talents.

When father Letinez saw that he had made a deep impression on the public mind, he proposed to his host to give to his parishioners a course of religious exercises, such as are delivered in the house of St. Philip of Neri, in the city of Mexico.([16]) We must here, for the information of our Protestant readers, state that those exercises, which are calculated to produce what is, in the United States, denominated a revival of religion, were originally devised by St. Ignatius of Loyola, the founder of the Jesuits, and that they are, on a reduced scale, similar to what is, in the Wesleyan economy, supposed to constitute the process of conversion. Wesley, probably, borrowed his plan from St. Ignatius' book of Exercises, but he had the great merit of enlarging the scale, and was thereby enabled strongly to affect large masses of hearers. Thus, what was done by the Jesuits, in their *professed houses*, with a dwarfish apparatus, and reduced means, which could be brought to bear only upon a few scores of people, at a time, was, by the patriarch of Methodism, attempted in broad plains, and in the green wood, which enabled him to electrify thousands at once, and give the widest sweep to supernal grace.

Such were the spiritual exercises, the benefit of which father Letinez was desirous to impart to the parishioners of Phelipa.

We must do him the justice to say, he was urged by no fanatical or knavish object ; yet we cannot but confess, he was, in some measure, moved by selfish considerations ; for, while he expected that these exercises would be the means of conveying spiritual grace to many obdurate sinners, he flattered himself, also, that they would procure for him the mastery of Don Fernando's conscience. He had, in a few days, become thoroughly acquainted with his host's character, and found him to be a man of religious scruples, exceedingly fearful of the judgments of God, and, in a word, one, over whom a ghostly director might exercise the greatest authority. Upon this knowledge he formed his plan of action, which, though it savored a little of *finesse*, had nothing criminal in its nature, since he wished to obtain that mastery, merely for a purpose, not only lawful, but even, according to his notion, a matter of strict justice.

The exercises to which we allude consist of a series of prayers, familiar exhortations and sermons, digested in a methodical order, and calculated to work a strong commotion in the soul, leading her on from the tremendous paroxysm of the fear of death and hell, to a desire of forgiveness, and a tormenting anxiety about the uncertainty of its attainment. From that state, the smitten sinner is led to the perspective of hope—reconciliation is presented as within his reach, and then comes the master stroke of justification, which, among Methodists is wrought instantaneously, but among Roman Catholics is attained by means of confession and absolution. It was to this father Letinez trusted. " Let me but once see you kneeling at my feet, in quality of a penitent, my dear Don Fernando," thought he within himself, " and I will make you accede to my own notions of justice." The method he took to compass his purpose, was uncommon, but sure, and the only one he could possibly employ, or think of, in the circumstances in which he found himself placed.

It was, therefore, announced from the pulpit of the parish church of Phelipa, that exercises similar to those of the Professa, in Mexico, would be given to the public, and that all who felt inclined, for the benefit of their conscience, to avail themselves of the opportunity, should give in their names.

There were no less than two hundred applicants, and one of them was the parish priest himself, who thought proper to set this good example to his parishioners. A kind of prospectus, containing the order of the exercises, and the rules of conduct to be observed by the applicants, was distributed, and the first sermon preached, in which the Mechoacan clergyman so far surpassed himself, that there was not a dry eye among the audience. So auspicious a beginning was followed by the most flattering results; for in less than five days, one hundred and fifty persons entered themselves on the penitent list, and took father Letinez for their confessor. The parish priest was in the number, and thus his guest had the satisfaction of seeing his efforts crowned with complete success. When sitting in the secret tribunal, as an interposer between God and his penitent host, he might assume a tone of authority, which he could not possibly avail himself of elsewhere, nor was there any appeal from the decisions he gave as a spiritual judge. As the task, however, had a spice of selfishness, we must do him the justice to say, that, in his admonitions to Don Fernando, he reasoned the case with him upon its intrinsic merits, abstractedly from all personal interest, begging him, at the same time, to consult skilful divines, in case he should doubt the correctness of his own decision. In fact, the reasons he gave were irresistible. " By detaining the child," said he, " you expose him to lose his grandfather's fortune, for, in the present distracted state of Mexico, when it is impossible to foresee what party will ultimately triumph or, what political measures will, after the end of the contest, be adopted by the victors, with respect to the conquered; it is not improbable that the boy may, if unknown in the country, at the time of the Count's demise, be deprived of the family estate, or be impeded, by insuperable obstacles, from obtaining possession of his property, should it once fall into the hands of collaterals, or, what were worse, of government.

" Moreover, though his grandfather is, at present, well disposed towards him, yet he may feel so much offended at your refusal, which he will probably ascribe to his son-in-law's instructions, as to conceive some idea of revenge. I have already mentioned collaterals. There are several branches of our family now seeking to worm themselves into my brother's favor, and nothing but the little boy's presence is able to counteract their secret machinations. Will you, for the gratification of your own individual feelings, detain him, and, by so doing, expose him to the loss of so brilliant a fortune? You may despise wealth for yourself. It is heroical—but you have no right to despise it in behalf of others, who cannot exercise their own judgment. Were the infant exposed to any spiritual danger, from the fear of an heretical education, you might be justifiable in his detention, but in his grandfather's house, and under my superintendence, you cannot possibly have the least motive of fear."

In a word, the reasons which Señor de Letinez gave to the parish priest, delivered with all the authority of a ghostly director, triumphed over the latter's repugnancy, and he consented to a separation; whereupon he received absolution, and on the following morning the religious exercises were concluded.

It was, nevertheless, with the deepest sorrow that Don Fernando saw himself about to be deprived of his charge. Separated by the broad Atlantic, from his relations,—placed in the midst of a nation, that was now learning to execrate the Spanish name, which they had so long held in veneration,—without any bosom friend,—he had already become passionately attached to the child of the foreigner, whom chance had thrown upon his protection, and had made a thousand visionary plans of future happiness, founded on the gratitude of the boy, whom he intended to bring up with all the tenderness of a father. To be now obliged to part with him was the most cruel stroke that could be inflicted. He resigned himself, nevertheless, since it was the will of God, and two days after the conclusion of the religious exercises, father Letinez departed, with the little boy and his nurse, who was by the hope of a large reward, induced to follow him to Mechoacan.

With him, we will take leave of the honest parish priest of Phelipa, who, though conscious that he had acted up to his duty, in relinquishing all claims over the child, felt, every now and then, something like rancor against father Letinez, and personal vexation, as though he had suffered himself to be outwitted.

**10\***

## CHAPTER X.

When great Columbus came from swarthy Spain,
On his frail vessel borne, across the main,
Civilization's cheering torch reveal'd
To arts and sciences a wider field,
And nations yet unborn high fate design'd
T' adorn with brighter glories human kind.—
Then liberty did mark her place of rest
In these wide spreading regions of the west,
And bid revive the scenes of Greece and Rome,
So long eclips'd, beneath the feudal gloom
Which o'er European climes, with fatal sway,
Reign'd uncontroll'd.—In vain, to bar the way,
You send your legions, it is Heaven's behest
We execute.
                                        *The Texian, a Poem.*

FATHER Letinez arrived at Pascuaro, with his grand-
nephew, in perfect good health.   The old Count's satisfaction
at the sight of the child was inexpressible, and the transports
of joy with which the latter was received by the servants, un-
bounded.   Formerly attached to his mother, even to a degree
of enthusiasm seldom felt by those of the Indian race, they
now transferred a portion of that love to her son.
  It is not, however, our intention to follow our hero, through
the protracted period of infancy and youth, nor to describe
every petty incident connected with his education.   Be it
sufficient to inform the reader that he was brought up, in the
most careful manner imaginable, under the immediate superintendence of father Letinez, who, though rather too
much addicted to metaphysical studies, was really a man of
literary taste, considerable erudition, and great tact and experience in the management of youth.   He taught his grand
nephew the ancient languages, himself, together with Spanish literature, philosophy and rhetoric ; and procured him
the best masters Mexico could afford for French and English,
as well as Mathematics.   Corporeal accomplishments were

no less attended to. The young gentleman could draw, fence and dance, so that it was his uncle's boast that he was a *Caballero perfecto*.

During the period of his youth, his father paid him several visits, from the United States, and felt under strong temptation to carry him away ; but he was so closely watched, in consequence of the Count's suspicious disposition, that he saw abduction was impossible ; yet he found means to create in his son's bosom a strong attachment towards himself, and a romantic idea of the improvement to be derived from extensive travels abroad. He thus laid the foundation for the execution of a design, which he carefully concealed from his father-in-law.

These things being premised, we will, dear reader, suppose eighteen years to have elapsed, and present our hero, a second time, under the form of a tall, handsome young man, mounted on a superb horse, and heading a troop of cavalry, under the command of General Urrea. The corps to which he belonged was winding down a long steep hill, on the eastern side of the rancho de la Manteca, a few leagues after having crossed the river del Capadero. These troops were the flower of the Mexican army. The common soldiers, clad in fine uniforms, of red and blue, had on their heads, brazen helmets of antique form, which shone in the sun, like burnished gold ; and they bore in their hands long lances, adorned with party-colored streamers, after the fashion of the ancient knights. They were preceded by a choice band of music, consisting of the finest looking men imaginable, in a brilliant scarlet uniform, with red and white plumes in their caps ; who, every now and then, made the echos resound with warlike melody.

These warriors were going to fight the battles of their country, against men, whom they had been taught to consider as a horde of treacherous foreigners—mortal enemies to their religion and independence—the insidious colonists of Texas, who had, not only set at defiance the popular chief that the Mexican nation had placed at their head ; but even carried their ingratitude so far as to declare themselves independent, and attempt to deprive of the most fertile portion of their territory the people who had so generously cherished them in their bosom.

The gallant army intrusted with the care of wiping off this stain from the national escutcheon was marching in two divisions towards what was imagined would prove an easy conquest. The northern corps, being under the command of the chief magistrate of the nation, in person ; and the southern, under the conduct of Urrea, a courageous and skilful officer. Though Captain Letinez (for our hero bore his grandfather's name) did not, properly speaking, belong to the staff, yet the vast influence and wealth of his family, and his gallant bearing, together with his intelligence, so far superior to that of his brother officers, had rendered him a special favorite with the general, who frequently honored him with his conversation.

They were riding together, surrounded by several officers, a little in advance of the first regiment of lancers, when they were overtaken by a courier, who appeared to have been riding with great speed. He brought important despatches for the general, and while the latter was perusing them, the messenger, interrogated by some of the military, informed them that he had been sent from Mier, a town of some importance, on the right bank of the Rio Bravo, eighty leagues above its mouth. That place had been invaded by a party favorable to the Texian cause, aided by a large swarm of Indians, who were spreading desolation on the left bank of the river, and the object of his mission was to implore a speedy succor.

When the general had made himself acquainted with the contents of the despatches, commanding a halt, he summoned a council of officers, and confirming the tidings which the messenger had already imparted, added many other particulars, that had been concealed from the bearer of the news.

One of the principal federalists of the state of Durango, who, at the time of the downfall of the ex-vice-President, Farias, succeeded in making his escape into Texas, had, it seems, assembled a little band of adventurers and formed the plan of penetrating into the heart of the *Provincias internas*, in order to re-establish the constitution of 1824. His force amounted in all to ninety men, and with so small a number, he, now, found himself within reach of Santa Anna's army, which was marching from Saltillo, eight thousand strong, for the purpose of invading Texas. The bold fellow, who had thus taken possession of the town of Mier—though he could not possibly dream of resisting the Mexican forces—yet maintained his ground and issued proclamations, lording it over the district of country immediately adjacent, and endeavoring to excite a rising of the people.

Some of the magistrates of that parish, annoyed by his measures, had despatched this express to beg a speedy succor, which general Urrea granted on the spot ; and, in order to furnish our hero with an opportunity of distinguishing himself, he selected him, to command the expedition. By his order, therefore, Captain Letinez, placing himself at the head of a hundred lances, proceeded towards Mier.

Our hero expected to enter the place unperceived, under cover of night, and thus to surprise the Texian force ; but their commander had, somehow, or other, been apprised of his approach, and had time to cross the Rio Bravo. He kept the ferry boat, on the left side of the river, as was natural, after his passage ; so that it became impossible for our hero to continue the pursuit, until some means of crossing over should be devised. In the meanwhile, the Mexican force could, from the right bank, perceive their enemies' fires on the opposite side, and when day had dawned, were tantalized with their gestures of contempt and provocation. The sight so much enraged Captain Letinez's soldiers, that several of them requested permission to swim the river, upon their horses, in order to chastise the insolence of the Texians ; but their commander, considering it as fool-hardy, refused his consent.

In order to surprise the invaders, he had recourse to stratagem, and leaving thirty of his men on the river bank, with a certain number of the citizens of Mier, disguised in soldier's uniforms, he gave orders to amuse the enemy by making a show of building a raft. In the meantime, he led the remainder of his troop to a place six miles up the river, where he was informed the channel was very narrow, and could be easily crossed by swimming. This piece of intelligence proving correct, he succeeded, the next day, in crossing over, with all his force, by sun-rise. As soon as the soldiers had dried their equipments, (which took but little time,) he set forward on his march, his guide having promised to conduct him within two hundred yards of the enemy, unperceived. Captain Letinez ordered his men to ride slowly till within sight of the Texians, when all the bugles were to sound, and a simultaneous rush was to be made. As it was difficult to wield the lance with effect, in the thicket of prickly pear, (nopalera,) in the centre of which the enemy was encamped, the Mexicans were directed to lay aside that weapon, and to depend on the *lasso*, every soldier selecting his man and abstaining from firing his pistols, except in case he should miss entangling his foe in the fatal noose.

We must state, in praise of Captain Letinez, that it was with repugnance he gave orders to use the lasso. He considered it as a mode of warfare hardly worthy of a civilized nation ; but his aim was rather to frighten the invaders, than to use them barbarously, for he gave strict commands to his soldiers to grant quarter, and by no means to drag their victims to any distance, whereby their limbs might be seriously injured, or lacerated. He knew that by this mildness he was disobeying general orders, but was, nevertheless, determined not to swerve from the rules of civilized warfare, be the consequences what they might.

The Mexicans rode so slowly that the sun had passed the meridian, when they reached the skirts of the Texians' camp. Around it they formed, in a semicircle—facing the river— each man holding the coiled rope in his hand, and waiting in the greatest silence, for the signal of attack. The Texians, according to their custom, were unconscious of the impending danger. They had sent out no scouts,—placed no videttes—and quite unmindful of contingencies, they were cracking their jokes, more noisily than wittily ; when, all at once, the Mexican bugles sounded a blast, and their enemies rushed on them with the rapidity of lightning. It was all over in a few seconds. About thirty men were caught, like wild animals ; some by the neck, others, by an arm, or leg, and dragged through the thicket of overgrown prickly pear, with all the impetuosity of a Mexican steed. Then arose the most piteous cries and calls for mercy !—Limbs and faces were lacerated by thorns,—clothes, torn to pieces— hats and swords, strewed about the ground, and the earth, in many places, streaked with blood ! Several of the Texians were seriously injured. Some had lost an eye, others had dislocated an arm, or broken a leg, and others had fainted, through sheer fright ; when Captain Letinez gave, at last, the signal for putting an end to the bloody race. Of those who were not taken prisoners at the onset, five were killed by the discharge of fire-arms, and the chief, with six privates only, succeeded in making his escape, while the remainder surrendered at discretion.

On alighting, to take care of the wounded, the victors beheld the most melancholy, and, at the same time, the most ludicrous spectacle it is possible to imagine. Many of the Texians were so ignorant of the manners and peculiarities of the Mexican race, that, although they still felt the fatal noose round their body, they were at a loss to understand by what means they had been captured, and much less could they account for the extraordinary violence with which they had been dragged about.

There was a hale, vigorous Kentuckian, who had suffered no serious injury, but whose superfine blue cloth coat was literally torn into shreds. When he got upon his legs again, and was free from the noose, he lifted one of the skirts from the ground, and raised it on high, with an expression of comical horror ! There he stood, like Habackuck Mucklewrath, in old Mortality, denouncing anathemas against his foes. " By the living Jingo," exclaimed he, " I could never have thought it ! A fine spot of work !—curse the fellows, for mean, cowardly wretches ! If they are scarce of gunpowder, can they not come forward and make use of their fists, like men of spirit ? I had rather be *gouged*, than noosed like a pig. I wonder what these cannibals will do next ?"

A little further, a Yankee adventurer, instead of idly venting his ill humor in exclamations and curses, was examining a little package containing rings, breast-pins and other articles of jewelry, of that kind of thrice refined gold which pedlars generally deal in. His budget of *notions* had been crushed in the fray, but with the thrift peculiar to the race from which he was descended, he had already set about mending some of his nicknacks, that happened to be less damaged than the rest.

The most ludicrous circumstance in this scene of confusion, was the strange fancy which entered the mind of a negro slave, who had followed his master from the river Brazos to the borders of Mexico. He took the assailants for demons,

who had thus triumphed by supernatural art.   In that thought,
he entreated one of the Texians to read a pocket bible, which
he carried about him, in order to break the spell.   But when,
upon further examination, he found that the complexion of
most of the Mexican soldiers was nearly as dark as his own,
he changed his opinion, and began to think they were runaway slaves, fighting for their liberty.

Aware that there exists, in Louisiana, many settlements of
negroes, who, after flying from their masters, live independent,
in the unexplored recesses of the swamps, with which that
country abounds, he supposed such to be the kind of assailants by whom the party to which he belonged had been so
roughly handled.   Entranced by the prospect of liberty, now
dawning upon him, he addressed himself, in raptures, to a
common soldier, and  heartily shaking him by the hand, exclaimed, "Thankee ye, thankee ye, my good feller!   Me
free man, now!   Oh, if me only had my Sally with me and
the childer!   Poor, dear childer!   But me go and show you
how to steal them, my good feller.   But white Massa, here,
alive!" added he, in surprise ; happening to cast his eyes
upon his master, whom he had believed dead, and who, at
that moment, approached him.   " You no kill him.   He not
so bad a Massa, neither!   Give plenty *vittles*, and no workee
on the Sabbath.   And his Missus!—Oh, she a very good
Missus!   Give blanket and shoes for winter, and take good
care of my Sally, when she sick.   Lets us go to meeting also,
when the Rev. Zerobbabel Windhowl comes round; while
Massa, he not so willing ; ' bekase,' says he, ' them things of
the gospel and 'tother world spoil niggers and open their eyes
too much.'   He not love the abolition, Massa, and he thinkee
that there be a little abolition in the gospel; but he say 'twas
put there in the times of the old Romans, for white folks,
and when there was no niggers in America.   For all that,
not kill Massa, my good feller ; for Missus she cry too much
if he be killed."

Captain Letinez, who understood English perfectly well,
and spoke it fluently, could not help smiling, upon hearing
the negro's address ;  and, drawing near, assured him that he
might consider his liberty as secure, and even could rely upon
a special protection, in  Mexico, if he would settle in the
country.

The negro felt his joy somewhat abated, upon perceiving that he who addressed him, and acted as chief of the capturing party was a white man, and could not help manifesting the fear it inspired, saying, " How be this, Massa ? You white man, I declare ! As white as my young Missus, God bless her, who was the most beautifulest soul 1 ever seed ! And you, commander of these niggers ?"

" Why, they are not negroes," replied Señor de Letinez. " They are Mexicans, as well as myself. I am their captain, and we have taken you prisoners, and that is all. But you have nothing to fear. *You*, in particular, shall be immediately put at liberty, provided you promise not to return to Texas."

" Return to Texas !" exclaimed the black, " you may trust me for that, there is no danger of it, Massa. But you, Mexican and them Mexican, also ; and yet you be a white man, and them is niggers—or, at best, mulattoes. How is that ?"

" Why, you blockhead," replied the captain, a little nettled ; " They are not negroes, they are Indians. You take too much liberty. Remember that, although I have been thus idly parleying with you, it was out of pure philanthropy, and there is a certain distance between us."

The poor negro's apprehensions were by no means allayed by being informed that his captors were Indians, for he could not suppose that Indians were susceptible of civilization, and he wished himself once more in the cotton fields, on the banks of the Brazos. The captain, however, anxious to continue the pursuit of the savages, who had spread devastation on the left bank of the Rio Bravo, crossed over to the town of Mier, with his prisoners, whom he left there, under the guard of the citizens of the place, with strict injunctions to take care of the wounded. After this, he re-crossed the river with all his force, in search of a large body of Comanches, who, he had been informed, were scouring the plains, on both sides of the river San Anton, and spreading desolation far and wide.

The Comanches, one of the most remarkable tribes of North America, are the best horsemen in the world, being as far superior to the Mexicans in the art of riding, as these are to the western nations of Europe. It was, therefore, no easy matter for Captain Letinez to overtake them, in case they should happen to receive intelligence of the pursuit. This was an expedition which he undertook upon his own responsibility, and merely to appease the complaints of the inhabitants of Mier and Camargo, whose flocks had been carried away by these marauders.

He travelled with his party till he came to the river Nueces, a sluggish stream, which derives its name from the immense quantity of peccon trees found on its banks. The country, extending hence to the Rio Bravo, is a level plain, producing fine grass and endless thickets of prickly pear of a gigantic size ; but there is no timber of any account, except on the immediate banks of the streams, where flourish groves of tall saplings, the lines of which meander with the water courses, and seldom exceed a mile in breadth. About fifty leagues above the mouth of the Nueces, a large creek, called Rio Frio, disembogues into it, from the east, after fertilizing a bolder and more romantic district, somewhat similar in its features, to the central parts of Kentucky. Ledges of fine granite intersect and diversify the plains, stretching across the water courses in every direction, damming up the streams in the form of petty lakes, and affording excellent localities for the establishment of mills. This district, being better watered, is well wooded, abundant in game, and the favorite haunt of the Lipanes and Carankaways, the latter of whom have the reputation of being cannibals.

In these fastnesses did Captain Letinez suppose that the party he was in pursuit of had probably taken shelter, and he resolved to ferret them out, in order to recover, if possible, the booty they had carried away.

Those he wished to overtake, however, eluded his pursuit, but he had the satisfaction of encountering another company of Comanches, who had been on a pillaging expedition towards the Trinidad, and had come into those deserts to conceal their plunder from the rest of their tribe, who would not probably have suffered them to enjoy so much booty undisturbed.

When Captain Letinez came up with them, he found them encamped on the banks of a rivulet—quite unconscious of danger—so that he was nearly upon them before they could put themselves in a posture of defence. On perceiving the Mexican troops, however, they quickly mounted their horses, and prepared to resist their invaders ; but the first discharge of fire-arms so much thinned their ranks, that they abandoned their booty and fled.

They were not pursued, so eager were Captain Letinez's men to seize upon the plunder thus fortuitously obtained.—Besides a considerable number of horses and horned cattle, they found, in the enemy's camp, various articles of furniture, which the Indians had stolen from the American settlers, on the waters of the Trinidad ; and the Mexican soldiers very little acquainted with the tools of modern husbandry, or the refinements of Northern luxury, viewed with the utmost surprise many things of which they could not understand the use.

There was a fellow who imagined that he had made a prize of immense value, in a log chain, for he had never seen so much iron together in his life ; and actually hung it round his neck and declared that he would carry it to Mier,—a distance of two hundred and fifty miles,—a feat which he accomplished, on foot.*

Another, having opened a bandbox, and found in it a lady's bonnet, adorned with a wreath of artificial flowers, was unable to discover for what use it was intended ; whereupon, having consulted some of his fellow soldiers, one of them expressed the opinion, that it was a Texian cap of Liberty, and intended, by the rebels, to be used as a military standard. It was, of course, considered as a very honorable spoil, and the fellow who owned it resolved to offer it to the church of Mier, to be hung up, in the sanctuary, by way of *spolia opima.* In the meantime, it was placed on the point of a lance, as an object of derision, and many a jest, at the expense of the Texian republic, was elicited at the sight.

A third one, having got hold of a pocket book, found in it some bank notes, and imagined that they were pictures of saints, with printed indulgences—mistaking English for Latin—whereby he was greatly edified, supposing, from this circumstance, that all the Texians were not heathens, or Jews, as he had been led to believe ; but that there were some *Christians* among them. The poor fellow was, however, wofully undeceived, when he returned to Mier, for there those pictures were found to be worth ten dollars a piece ;

* A fact.

but he had already exchanged them, with a fellow soldier, for a silver medal and a pen-knife, and they were now sold to an Italian merchant, for their full value.

But what attracted the attention of the men, and principally of the captain, was a vehicle, closely covered with buffalo robes, which the Indians made their utmost efforts to carry off; but were obliged to abandon. Towards it Señor de Letinez, accompanied by his officers, rode, with all possible speed, and was the first to tear down the skins by which the interior of the barouche, for such it proved, was concealed ; when a melancholy spectacle presented itself to his view.— It was a young lady of extraordinary beauty, strongly bound to the carriage with cords.

## CHAPTER XI.

What seemed fair in all the world, seemed now,
Mean, or in her summed up, in her contain'd
And in her looks, which from that time infus'd
Sweetness into my heart, unfelt before,
And into all things from her air inspired
The spirit of love and amorous delight.
*Paradise lost, Book VIII.*

How reluctant soever we may be to shock our readers'
feelings by the exhibition of a scene of inhumanity practised
upon an innocent and interesting female, still the truth of
our story forces us to lay before them the sufferings of one
who, in the sequel, is to play a conspicuous part. We beg,
therefore, that it be not attributed to the desire of producing
an effect; because, far from aiming at the species of interest,
which results from the description of physical pain, we are,
on the contrary, persuaded it evinces literary merit but of
the lowest order, in the writer who is obliged to have recourse to this means to move human sensibilities. Indeed,
we are so averse to such a kind of literary *charlatanisme*,
that, had it been possible for us to continue the narrative of
our hero's adventures, without adverting to the misfortunes
of this female, and the cruel treatment inflicted upon her by
her Indian captors, we would gladly have availed ourselves of
the chance. Were we to omit it, however, we would be unable to render our narrative intelligible; but we will soften
the picture, as much as the general connexion of events will
permit.

The young lady whom Captain Letinez found in the vehicle
was so far exhausted, that, although judging, from the report
of musketry, there had been a conflict, and she had probably
changed masters, she was unable to manifest her feelings,
except by some faint moans. Her deliverers found her reclining on the back seat of the carriage. The dreadful state
of debility to which she was reduced preventing her from re-

11*

taining an upright position, her head was drooping on her left shoulder, her arms were forcibly outstretched, and her hands tied to the sides of the barouche. Her wrists were swollen and bleeding from the chafing of the ropes. Her habiliment, which had originally been costly and elegant, was soiled, and she seemed, from weakness, entirely incapable of motion; yet so regular and beautiful were her features, that it was impossible to behold her without admiration.

When the ropes with which she had been bound were cut away, and she was lifted out of the carriage, the captain was shocked with horror at the sight, and there was no one, even among the rough and uncultivated Mexican troopers, there present, who did not vent his indignation against the barbarians, who had treated fragile beauty with so much cruelty.

Our hero immediately directed some of his soldiers to erect a kind of tent, with their blankets, in order to shelter her from the burning rays of the sun; and, as soon as it was ready, placed her under it, on a pallet made of the buffalo robes which had served for her previous concealment. This posture, more favorable to repose, and the administration of some cordials soon restored her to the use of speech, and the first words she uttered were expressive of gratitude towards those who had effected her deliverance.

She expressed herself in English, and as the captain was the only one present who understood that language, this necessarily obliged him to remain in close attendance upon the fair captive. She had no idea of being indebted for her rescue to an advanced party of the Mexican army; but imagined she had been recaptured by a company of Texians, sent in pursuit of the Indians. Her father was a wealthy cotton planter, living on the waters of the Trinidad, whose farm had been pillaged and house burnt by a party of Comanches. The invaders had suffered all the inmates to escape, except her, whom they had carried away, in the manner already related; and, although now she beheld around her many dusky faces, she supposed them to be friendly Tankaways, who had assisted in her deliverance. Addressing herself, therefore, to the captain, she inquired with much solicitude about her father, to which our hero replied, in good English, but with an accent that betrayed his foreign extraction, " I am sorry that I am unable to give you any information respecting your father :

I have not the honor of his acquaintance, neither did we, indeed, perceive any white man among the Comanches."

"It is not probable that he is with them," interrupted the captive. "They would hardly have brought him so far. I have reason to trust he escaped, when our house was burned, and, as I supposed you came from the Brazos, I hoped you might inform me of his subsequent fate; but you are not a Texian! Tell me to whom am I indebted for my deliverance, and to what part of the country have I been conveyed? nine days have elapsed since I have been allowed to behold the light of the sun. Where am I, now, and into whose hands have I fallen?"

"Madam," replied the captain, "rest assured that you are in perfect safety. We are Christians, well acquainted with the honorable treatment due to your sex and rank, and such as will do all in our power to alleviate your sufferings. It will, perhaps, be repugnant to your delicacy to travel with a company of soldiers, but, as their captain, I pledge my honor that you shall be treated as respectfully as if we were united by the ties of fraternity. I only wish your recent sufferings may not incapacitate you for bearing the fatigues of the march, for we cannot remain here longer than to-morrow morning. My force is small—we might be surprised. Feeble as you are, you cannot possibly ride in the barouche. If you have no objection, a covered hand-litter shall be constructed by my soldiers, and by this means you can be carried more comfortably."

"Alas! Sir," answered the young lady, with tears, "my dependence is entirely upon you, and I confide in your honor. Great God, am I forlorn and abandoned, in the hands of utter strangers—and these strangers soldiers!—Oh, thou, father of Heaven, be my protector!—Young gentleman," added she, suddenly addressing the captain with a fervor which manifested how great was her apprehension; "the profession you have embraced hardens the heart, and inures it to profligacy—yet there is *that* in your countenance which gives better hopes :—do not deceive them. I beseech you, by all that is sacred, to protect me and restore me to my father. . . . Oh, my father—what anxiety must he suffer on my account!—Am I doomed never to see him again?"

"Madam," replied the captain, "your suspicions are un-

just ; yet I forgive them :—they are but too natural in your
situation. I will take immediate measures to inform your
father of your rescue and present state of safety ; nevertheless, the small party under my command cannot venture into the heart of Texas. Were the Trinidad nearer, I would
send a flag of truce, but present circumstances render it
impracticable. Duty compels me to return to Mier. I see
no alternative for you. You shall be escorted to Matamoros,
in all honor and safety, and there, embark for New-Orleans.
Nothing shall be done without your concurrence, but it
would be utter madness in you, to prefer perishing in this
desert. Can you doubt the sincerity of a Mexican officer, who
protests, in the face of Heaven, that he would rather forfeit
his existence, than permit the least insult to misfortune ?"

The mention of " Matamoros" and " a Mexican officer,"
augmented the fair captive's distress and redoubled her tears.
The captain much moved, endeavoured to console her by
repeated assurances ; but, seeing his efforts were unavailable, he thought it would, perhaps, be better to leave her to
the aid of reflection, during some hours. In the interval, he
went to hasten the necessary preparations for marching back
to Mier.

After a tolerable long absence, he returned to the young
lady's tent, and found her more resigned. She assented to
the proposed measures, on condition that the captain himself
should constantly watch over her safety. The next morning,
therefore, the party began their march. It was opened by
twenty men, on horse-back, with their lances couched, in
case of surprise. To these succeeded the litter, borne by
four men, and immediately behind it, Captain Letinez, followed by the rest of his soldiers, in close column, to guard
against an attack on the rear.

Their fears proved groundless. Their march was, nevertheless, interrupted by a flag of truce, despatched by the
chief of the defeated Indian party, charged with a petition
of a most singular nature. It was no less than a request
that the Mexicans should exchange the white lady they
had taken, for a number of horses and mules, of which
the Indians had rendered themselves masters in their various marauding expeditions, through the states of Chihuahua
and Durango. The warrior who commanded the party of

Comanches, one of the principal men of the nation, had become so great an admirer of his captive's charms, that he had resolved to take her for his wife, and, lest his tribe should grumble at his choice—as well as to interest them in the success of his scheme—he had given out that it had been revealed to him in a dream, that, from this white female's marriage with him, would spring up a famous warrior, who was to avenge upon the Mexicans all the injuries the Indian race had received, and re-conquer the country through which their forefathers roamed, as far as the Huasteca.*

As this worthy united the prophetical character to that of warlike chief, his desires were implicitly submitted to by the whole tribe, who thought the future glory of their race intimately connected with their fulfilment; and they were, now, ready to sacrifice all their booty, in order to repossess themselves of her who was destined to be the mother of the great chieftain. That an Indian be susceptible of such a sentiment as love may be questioned by some of our readers; but we will answer, that beauty—like omnipotence—works in a thousand wonderful ways; and if it has been supposed capable of softening the wild beasts of the forests, it involves, we are sure, no absurdity, to suppose it able to soften the heart of an Indian.

Be our readers' opinion what it may, the fact is that Shawky-my-atty-mawck, whose name, being interpreted, signifies, *the hearts of nine panthers;* (the warlike chief to whom we allude) had, at the sight of this young lady, suddenly experienced a sentiment, hitherto unknown to him—which prompted him to rescue her from the flames, when her father's house, on the waters of the Trinidad, was destroyed; and induced him carefully to convey her away, in the family barouche. He treated her, to be sure, in a manner which, to a civilized man, must appear barbarous; but he had no idea of being cruel. It was merely to prevent her escape, and so far from intending being harsh to her, her captor, had, on the contrary, a notion that he was too indulgent.

* The *Huastecapan* of Montezuma's empire—where the Mexican Indians placed their paradise—is the most fertile district in Mexico, and probably in the world. It is somewhat hilly, borders on the Rio Panuco, and is partly included in the state of Vera Cruz. It produces almost spontaneously the banana and other tropical fruits.

An Indian warrior's idea of love, whenever he happens to experience it, is very different from the sentiment which a white man entertains for that passion. The former looks upon it as a weakness which *unmans* him, and is, therefore, extremely careful to conceal his flame. The extravagance of the Indian chief's attachment for this white damsel would have entirely ruined his character, in the estimation of the warriors whom he commanded, had he not subtly brought his spiritual influence to favor his plan, and rendered it thereby, an *affair of state*, in which the whole tribe were interested.

The proposal of the flag of truce, as it may be supposed, was indignantly rejected by Captain Letinez, who was, however, too well bred, to afflict the young lady, by informing her of the purport of the message. After this strange incident, nothing of importance occurred to disturb the security of their march ; and they entered Mier, on the eleventh day after leaving the Rio Frio.

On his arrival there, our hero was informed that General Urrea had pursued his way towards Matamoros, and left orders for him to follow with all possible speed ; but the noble-hearted young man found himself greatly embarrassed by his fair prize, for whom he began to experience sentiments of tenderness, which he had never, hitherto, entertained for the fair sex. To leave her in Mier, among utter strangers—without a protector—appeared unnatural. To induce her to travel in his company was exposing her reputation, by giving her the appearance of a "*light o' love.*" His perplexity was so great that he resolved to consult the parish priest of the place —an elderly man, who enjoyed a reputation for prudence and benevolence. This clergyman, after hearing an exposition of the case, was clearly of opinion that the young lady, having a vehicle of her own, might, without any breach of propriety, continue her journey towards Matamoros, in the wake of the military, provided she were accompanied by some respectable female, who would appear in the character of her protectress.

It very luckily happened that the same Italian merchant, of whom I have already made mention, was on the point of setting out for the same place, with his wife, an aged matron, for whose respectability the priest was willing to vouch, and these people would, probably, be delighted with the idea of travelling in a carriage. Besides that this way of journeying, being rather uncommon, in those parts, is supposed to confer a certain degree of consequence on those who can afford the expense ; our merchant and his wife would enjoy the benefit of a military escort, by keeping within sight of the lancers, whom Captain Letinez commanded, and the latter would be enabled to watch over their safety, without appearing to take in their welfare, a higher interest, than might be ascribed to common courtesy.

In this manner, the clergyman thought Miss Quinton (such was the young lady's name) might reach the sea-coast without exciting suspicion, or the captain's benevolence being exposed to misconstruction. The plan devised by the old man being plausible and of easy execution, it was, of course, followed. The old Italian's wife, on the recommendation of the parish priest, undertook to act as chaperon for the *Señorita Americana*, and they all set out under the escort of the lancers.

It was peculiarly lucky for the Italian, thus to travel under a military safe-guard ; for a portion of the road, west of Matamoros, may be accounted the most perilous on the face of the earth. It is literally lined with monuments of lately committed murders.

> " For wheresoe'er the shrieking victim hath
> Pour'd forth his blood, beneath th' assassin's knife,
> Some hand erects a cross of mould'ring lath,
> And grove and glen with thousand such are rife
> Throughout this purple land, where law secures not life."

The poor merchant shuddered, as he went along, at the sight of so many crosses, and hugged his bags of dollars, doubting not but, had it not been for Captain Letinez's protection, he would have shared the same fate, as had been the lot of so many unfortunate wayfarers before him, and will continue to be of future travellers, until a better race introduce a better administration of justice.

## CHAPTER XII.

I ask no pledge to make me blest
   In gazing when alone ;
Nor one memorial for a breast
   Whose thoughts are all thy own.
                        *Byron.*

AT Matamoros, our young lady continued the guest of the Italian merchant, who, intending to remain two or three weeks in the place, immediately upon his arrival, rented a house, and furnished it in a temporary fashion. Though this seaport be now a city of seventeen thousand inhabitants, among whom is found a considerable number of foreigners, yet it is one of the blessed results of the Mexican system of civilization, that it does not possess a single hotel, inn, or boarding-house, where a bed can be got. Every new comer should he have no acquaintance willing to give him hospitality, must, as soon as he arrives, rent a room, or go to lodge under the canopy of heaven, in a public square, situate at the north-west extremity of the city, and appropriated to that hospitable destination, by the munificence of the *Ayuntamiento.* As for beds or furniture, they are not easily found for sale, so that ignorant, or imprudent foreigners, who neglect bringing them along, are in no enviable situation.

In such a state of things, it would have been truly unfortunate for our young lady, to be abandoned to her own exertions, in order to procure the absolute necessaries of life. She clung, therefore, to the Italian merchant's wife, with all the affection of one who feels grateful for past benefits, and for whom the price of present protection is enhanced by the prospect of future deprivation.

The Mier lady, under whose matronly authority she enjoyed, in a strange place, a degree of security, which she could not, otherwise, have obtained, was far from being a woman of education, refinement, or elegance of manners, but she was motherly, good-hearted, and of unimpeachable moral character. She had already contracted a great affection for the young " Americana," as she called her, and being childless, entertained the notion of adopting her, and waited but for a favorable opportunity, in order to propose it to her husband. For some days succeeding her arrival, her multifarious occupations rendered her too busy to think about the matter. She had to instruct a female cook in the particular manner in which she wished her Indian corn to be ground for her tortillas. A filtering machine was indispensably requisite to clarify the river water before she could use it ; a cooking hearth must be constructed out of doors, for a French fire-place, as she called it, was her aversion, and she was affected in a peculiar manner at the sight of houses adorned with chimneys, a fashion that had already been introduced into Matamoros, from the north, and which she, on that account, was inclined to look upon as somewhat allied to heresy.

But when, at last, all those bustling cares were over, her imagination recurred to her favorite plan, and to revolve the means of insuring success. Her ward, if we may designate her by this title, was already restored to perfect health. The joy of being freed from her pursuers, the Indians, and the hope of being soon restored to her father had wrought wonders, and her face became the very picture of health and animation. Captain Letinez visited her two or three times a day, under pretence of serving as interpreter between her and the old matron, but conscious to himself that another sentiment was his prime mover. Though he had never seen so handsome a woman, yet it was not mere physical beauty which attracted him. It was, rather, her graceful and dignified demeanor, equally free from prudery and coquetish airs, her sprightly conversation and well informed mind,—

> " —————————— those graceful acts,
> Those thousand decencies, that daily flowed,
> From all her words and actions,"

and her superior wit tempered by prudence, which commanded his admiration. The merchant's wife, proud of having a man of Señor de Letinez's rank as a visiter, encouraged him, and bethought herself of making use of his influence, to further the accomplishment of her scheme. She perceived he was in love, and supposed that by fanning his flame, of the honorable nature of which she entertained no doubt, she would be most likely to succeed in her views. It became, therefore, her object to engage the captain in many little parties of pleasure, where she expected her *protégée* to shine conspicuously. One night, he was invited to escort them to a *tertulia*, where the young Americana had been requested to display her musical talents on the piano. The next day, he was in requisition to give them an airing, in the carriage, after the siesta, for the Señorita was languid. He accompanied them to church, or in their shopping excursions, and was often invited to partake of chocolate with them ; to all which calls and invitations the young man, as may be supposed, was exceedingly punctual. In a word, the old merchant's wife, though untutored, and actuated merely by female instinct, was as perfect in her manœuvres as if she had been an English marchioness, with half a dozen daughters to dispose of.

The young captain's personal beauty, with his mental and physical accomplishments, rendered him as conspicuous, in his own sex, as the fair stranger proved in her's, and it was not improbable that the impression made upon his heart might be reciprocated. True love, however, is never presumptuous. It rather blushes and trembles, in presence of the beloved object, and Captain Letinez, who was endowed with all the delicacy which a refined education can impart, was impressed with a profound respect for the woman whom he loved. Still, his flame was betrayed by thousand nameless circumstances—manifestations which escape even the most discreet—and the young lady, also, began to be sensible of his merit, as her involuntary blushes would sometimes proclaim.

When the old matron supposed things sufficiently matured to render a discovery of her views expedient, she, in a confidential conversation, broke the matter to the captain. " Now, Señor de Letinez," said she, " what do you think of our Americana ? Is it not a pity to suffer one so fair and interesting to return to Texas, to be, probably, driven back into the United States, with her kindred, when our triumphant troops will chase away the rebels ?—How much it afflicts me, that so rare a beauty should be a vessel of heresy !—Does it not behove us, who enjoy a knowledge of the Christian religion, to teach the true doctrine to these poor stray children ?—Oh, how much I wish I could get her baptized and made a Christian !—To you, captain, I will communicate an idea, which God, our Lord, and the Virgin of Guadelupe, have inspired me with :—it is that I and my husband should adopt her. We have no children, captain, and are amply provided with worldly goods. What better use can we make of our fortune, than in gaining a precious soul to the church ?—I know that my husband is attached to his relations, who never paid any attention to him, when he was poor and needy, and would not, now, give the parings of their nails to relieve him, if he were in distress ; and, I am afraid, on account of that foolish family attachment, he will oppose my ideas. Therefore, I want you to use your influ- ence over his mind and hint it to him ; for he has a great regard for you. We are both old, captain,—that is to say, my husband, at least ; and he may slip off, when least ex- pected. Now, what will become of me, in my widowhood,— without any affectionate person about me,—for I am passed all thoughts of marrying again, and my relations hate me, on account of my husband. But here is this pobre Ameri- canita, who, I am sure, loves me, and has so wound herself round my heart, that I cannot think of parting with her."

Gladly would the captain have lent his aid to the further- ance of any scheme tending to obtain the young lady's con- sent to remaining in Mexico ; but he had sufficient tact to understand that neither the town of Mier, nor the city of Matamoros afforded a state of society to which a female of her breeding could possibly conform ; much less did he sup- pose that she would renounce the thought of returning to her father, in order to throw herself into the old woman's arms. Her continuance in Matamoros, he knew, was occasioned only by the absence of the vessels accustomed to trade to New- Orleans, and, notwithstanding all her gratitude towards her benefactress, she was as anxious as ever to leave the country.

Had the captain been unprincipled, he might have thought the present circumstances would afford him a fair chance of playing off his stratagems, in favor of his passion ; but he was too generous and honorable, even to conceive such a thought. He, therefore, answered the merchant's wife, that he judged her plan impracticable, and that, notwithstanding her husband might be brought to consent to the measure, he was sure the young lady would not accept her offers ! " At all events," added he, " it is but prudent to ascertain her sentiments before you hazard a proposal to your husband."

This was a difficulty which had not occurred to the old woman's mind, for she was as shallow, as good natured. She agreed, however, to the expediency of the captain's suggestion, and it was arranged between them that she should have an explanation with Miss Quinton—Señor de Letinez acting as interpreter.

The result was such as our hero had anticipated. The young lady answered she could not possibly think of remaining among strangers, and that, how strongly soever gratitude might attach her to those who had so generously extended their protection to her, still she could not act so unnatural a part, as to renounce her father and kindred. From thence she took occasion to beseech the captain to do all in his power to accelerate her departure, for she knew what grief her absence and the uncertainty of her fate must cause to her family.

Our hero promised to comply with her wishes, and thinking this a favorable opportunity for declaring his sentiments, assured her that he could never be happy, if deprived of the hope of being, at some future period, blessed with her hand. " I know, Madam," said he, " that, in your present situation, it may be considered worse than uncourteous, in me, to press my suit, and that my declaration may expose me to the suspicion of indelicacy ; but the idea of your leaving this country without being informed of the profound impression which your charms, your accomplishments and your noble mind, have made on me, would be beyond endurance. Forgive my boldness—I am prompted by an irresistible sentiment. A new existence dawned upon me, from the first moment I beheld you ;—I am no longer master of my heart :—it is bound to you in an irrevocable manner, and from your lips, I await the sentence of my happiness, or misery."

The young lady, thus addressed, far from manifesting a surprise which she did not feel ; replied with dignity and composure, " For having saved me from the greatest calamity, I will always feel the most fervent and lively gratitude towards you, and *this* is, for the present, all I can impart. You are, yourself, aware that my dependence upon you does not permit me to receive a declaration of the nature of the one you have avowed. Act generously to the last, and abstain from a renewal of your suit, while I am still under your protection. I demand it of you; and your acquiescence will strengthen your claims to my gratitude. In so short an acquaintance as ours, the character cannot be sufficiently developed to enable one party to form a correct estimate of the congeniality and disposition of the other. Moreover, there is such a difference between us, in point of religion, political feeling, and prejudices of education, as would, perhaps, render a union a source of misery. I am a Protestant, and my father belongs to Texas. Texas has declared herself, and now the die is cast. With her, he will stand, or fall. Your duty to your country obliges you to fight against the cause he has embraced! See under what auspices our promises would be exchanged, were I so weak as to listen to your protestations!"

" Deprive me not of hope, Madam," replied the captain. " Let me still enjoy the consolation of hope, I beseech you. The difference of country is no objection—virtue belongs to every country. As for your religion,—I have already told you that my father is a Protestant. I shall never love him the less, on that account, though I will faithfully adhere to my own creed. As for the present war with Texas—one short campaign, Madam, and it will return under the obedience of Mexico. We will, then, both belong to the same country."

" Return to the obedience of Mexico!" replied she, with a vivacity which surprised her lover, " Never, sir; never! You know not the mettle of those you are going to attack. But cease your importunities. Under present circumstances, I cannot listen to them with the dignity that becomes an American maiden. Your heart is endowed with sufficient nobleness to understand *this*. Obey its nobler feelings and be deaf to the selfishness of passion. I will hear no more of it, and *by my dependence upon you*, I conjure you to be silent."

" Yes! I understand you—and am worthy of understanding you:—thou noble-minded woman!" answered he, im-

12*

printing a kiss upon her hand, (which she withdrew with the rapidity of lightning, but not in anger.)  " My heart is worthy of you, and you shall be obeyed."

Their dialogue, the meaning of which, though it was held within the old woman's hearing, had, from her ignorance of the English language, remained a perfect blank to her ; was, here, interrupted by her exclaiming, "*Ave Maria, purissima!* The little dove will be a Countess, yet.  But lo ! how she takes the least trifle to heart !  One would have thought from the haste with which she withdrew her hand, that a snake was crawling upon it.  But what does she say ?  What does she answer to your suit, captain ?  It seems you have been more earnest in pleading for yourself than for me."

"Indeed, Madam," replied Señor de Letinez, " I have not been more successful in urging my own petition than yours. The young lady is determined to go, and we must engage her passage in the first vessel that will happen to sail from the Brazo de Santiago."

At this information, the Mier lady set up a pitiful lamentation.  "*Y me dejas, querida alma mia!*" exclaimed she, adding many other honeyed expressions, which the captain did not stay to interpret.  He went out to inquire from one of the principal merchants of the place, whether there was any vessel shortly expected to leave the port, for New Orleans ; but he was stopped by an officer of artillery, who knowing his intimacy with the Mier merchant, wished to complain of an affront the latter had offered to the corps to which he belonged.  The long and short of the story was, that the merchant during his morning ramble, had visited the park of artillery, and upon discovering that the bombs, and even the canister shot were made of copper ;* had enjoyed a hearty laugh at the expense of the officers, and, thereby, wounded the sensibility of the troop. " Would you believe it, Letinez," said this worthy artillerist, " he has, in bitter irony, told us that no civilized nation would commit such a blunder, as we could have iron balls manufactured in any quantity, at the works, near Durango, or at the Amilpas mines, not far from Mexico, for

---

* Founded on fact.  That copper was carried from Chihuahua, to Mexico, there cast, and sent to the seat of war, all the way on mules.

the tenth part of the cost of the copper ones, or, even, that we could exchange these, here, at the sea-port, for eight times their number of iron ones, which would answer as well to kill the Texians. *Voto a Dios !* I could not help being indignant, particularly when he added, by way of taunt, ' Your enemies will be much obliged to you, for such an unexampled generosity ! Blessed are the towns which you will bombard ! Oh ! that one of your battles might be fought on land of mine ! It would enrich me !' I have a great mind to call him out, for I understand he has served ; but there is, I think, an excommunication fulminated by the Council of Trent, against duelling, and *that* staggers me. I ·vould not like to die excommunicated."

" Never mind the excommunication and the duel, my dear fellow," replied Captain Letinez. " The man is right enough. It is an unpardonable oversight in our government, but our republic is still young, and she will learn wisdom from misfortune. You would be very foolish to fight for such a thing. But come along with me, and help me to make preparations for a trip to the Brazo de Santiago."

" How ? Are you going to sea ?" exclaimed the artillery officer. " Some secret commission ! Eh ! Bound for Texas, incognito ?"

" Not I, indeed," returned Letinez ; "I am only to accompany a young lady, who is going to New Orleans."

" What !" interrupted the artillerist. " Not that jewel, you rescued from the hands of the Comanches, I hope."

" Even the same," sadly resumed our hero.

" Is it possible you let her escape, young and beautiful, as she is !" exclaimed the other. " But I understand how it is. She is unwilling to be baptized, and become a Christian ! That is an insuperable barrier, indeed. What a pity, nevertheless. It must be confessed that those women of the northern people are handsomer than ours, and somewhat better bred. What complexions ! what features ! But, then, they are no better than animals, you know, being unbaptized ! A Christian cannot possibly think of such creatures, as long as they remain obstinate."

" Abominable block head !" thought Letinez, within himself. By this time, however, he had reached the counting room of one of the principal importing merchants of the town, who informed him that a fine schooner, with decent accommodations for female passengers, had just arrived at the mouth of the river, and would in ten days, at latest, be ready to sail again for New Orleans.

He sadly went to impart the intelligence to the young lady, who immediately began to make her preparations, and when the time of her departure had come, was escorted by Captain Letinez, the Mier merchant and his wife, to the place of embarkation. Many were the tears of the latter, when the separation took place, but though our hero tried to stifle his grief, he felt it more acutely than any of them. We will, now take leave of the Mexican party, in order to follow the young lady, in her navigation, the doleful narrative of which will become the subject of the following chapter.

# CHAPTER XIII.

Bland hospitality, with generous hand,
Will give relief—a virtue chiefly found
Where needed most, in newly settled lands,
Or in the desert.

*The Pilgrim, a Poem.*

THOUGH the Rio Bravo is the largest river in the Mexican republic, yet the bar, at its mouth, prevents vessels of a certain size from entering it, and even those which do not draw so much water as to be unable to succeed in it, have, sometimes to wait four, or five days, for high tides, and to ride at anchor, in sight of the port. The same may be said of the various bays by which the coast of Texas is indented. When strong southerly winds prevail, they cause a great flow of the sea into the lagunes, which raises the water on the bars, at their mouths, thus enabling ships of larger burthen to cross them ; while, at other seasons, they are sure to perish, should they attempt it. In a word, there is no coast, in the whole world, where the depth of water is so variable, and where nautical art can place so little reliance on preceding soundings and experience.

This, which has been the cause of numerous shipwrecks, proved detrimental to the voyage of the schooner upon which our fair traveller was embarked. Hardly had they lost sight of land, when there arose a furious south wind, that drove her with irresistible fury, towards the narrow sandy island, which extends, from the Brazo de Santiago, near the mouth of the Rio Bravo, to St. Bernard's bay. That long strip of sand is intersected by three principal passes, whereof the middle one, called *Corpus Christi*, is nearly opposite the mouth of the river Nueces and not far from Live oak point, where a smart little town has lately sprung up.

The captain of the schooner, despairing of his ability to ride the gale, sought to put his vessel in security, by enter-

ing the above pass ; but it unfortunately happened, that, having no pilot, and being himself but imperfectly acquainted
with the entrance, he managed his vessel so unskilfully, that
she stuck fast on the bar, and the storm increasing, it was
evident she would go to pieces. In that emergency, no
other resource remained but to take to the long boat, and if
the crew and passengers could cross the bar in safety, they
would, afterwards, easily reach the coast of the main land.

The captain succeeded, after infinite fatigues, in landing
all his people, consisting of ten persons, among whom were
three females, at a point about fifteen miles distant from St.
Patricio, a little colony of Irish people, on the left bank of
the river Nueces. This village had been founded five or six
years previous, and promised to become an interesting settlement, because its original inhabitants were tolerably or-
derly. They had for pastor an Irish Dominican friar, and
their magistrates were selected from among themselves, and
though they lived under the allegiance of the Mexican government, they hardly felt the hand of their civil rulers, and
rather bore the appearance of an unknown, independent community, " the world forgetting and by the world forgot."

Our poor shipwrecked people had no other resource, after
the loss of their vessel, than to take shelter in this village,
where they were well treated by the inhabitants. The Alcalde exercised his prudence in billeting the new comers, according to the rules of propriety, and he assigned our young
lady, to a widow woman of great respectability of character,
who was no less remarkable for her physical than for her
moral qualifications, being a figure about five feet ten inches,
with a rotundity of corpulency quite proportionate to such a
height.

This notable female did not lack a certain coarse dignity,
with which she tempered her coarse hospitality, and as she
took the young lady's hand, in order to *pilot her home*, as she
quaintly expressed it ; (for she had been sent for, by the
mayor, and the scene passed in his office) said, with a strong
Irish accent, but a look of great benevolence ; " Well now,
come, my swate young ladhy—sure Mr. Smartclutch, the
Alcalde (that is his honor, the mayor of the town, honey—
as we would call the loike of him in ould Ireland—for, may
be, you don't know what an Alcalde is, in this counthry)

could do no betther than to place you with me. He is a considerate man and well maning—I must say *that* for him! And you may thank him, my swate jewel, bekase you fall into good hands. There is plenthy to ate, in my house—which is not the case every where, in this town, honey : for, do you see, praties have failed, this year, and this is not a good counthry for praties, no how—save for the swate ones, that the Mexican people call *camotes*. And you shall have plenthy of milk, chaze and butther; and don't be afraid of them Texians—they are not going to hurt the loike of you! They were here, in great force, the other day, and rampaged about, but, in the end, did no damage, bekase there was nothing to pillage in our chapel. They could not do, here, as they did in Goliad, where they took the picthures of the saints out of the church, and picked out their eyes, for sporth—with their daggers—cutthing the blessed vestments into shreds—and their officer men took all the goold lace, to make epaulets out of. Och! murdher! To hare and see the loike of it! And then they took the grand crucifix, from off the althar—that is the image of our Saviour, honey, that was painthed all over with goold—and picked out its eyes—then put an old hat on its head, and fired at it, for their diversion. The unhappy wretches, who cry out, Liberty of conscience! Liberty of conscience! and then to fire upon our Saviour, honey! The captain who was here swore that they would clare the counthry of praste-craft and swaipe all superstition away from the land. Och, for his swaiping! That was a lucky job for him,—the ill-favored, foul-mouthed blackguard, heretic and villain thief! He took all the silver chalices and the golden pix of the church of Labahia,—and the candlesticks that were on the althar, besides the precious stones, around the remonstrance, honey! As good as twenty-seven pounds of silver, together with pearls, topazes and rubies! No wondher that he was so fond of handling that broom of his, that swept such trash. But och! some judgment will fall on them, and God forgie me for saying so. The Mexican Gineral will soon be here, with his lancers, and give them another kind of swaiping, I trow. But you need not fare anything, my jewel : though I am a lone woman, I will defend you. Never fare, St. Patrick will protect his own!"

Her monologue lasted till she reached her house, which

was nothing but a log cabin, divided into two apartments, by a partition of reeds ; but remarkable for its cleanliness, and two small windows with glazed sashes—the greatest piece of luxury in the whole village.

They had no sooner entered it, than the old woman resumed her speech. " Now, honey," said she, " you must be almost spenth with hunger. Rest yourself, after changing your clothes, while I cook some thing good for you to ate. There are some clane clothes which used to belong to my daughter, that was,—but now she is dead and is with God, I hope. They will be somewhat too large for you, for she was a stout crathur of her years, but mane while, I will wash your own, honey, and iron them too,—they shall be ready to-morrow. So, now, get into that inner room and do as I tell you, while I fry some eggs for you, bekase to day is Fridhay. And we will have some batther cakes and fresh butther. Och, there goes a swate crathur."

The sweet creature stood in need of rest, indeed, and of course, gladly followed her kind hostess' direction, while the latter went to borrow some tea and sugar, for she was out of those commodities. She found none except at the parsonage, and even there, she could not get it, without entering into a long explanation with the priest's house-keeper,—a very singular woman, half nun and half servant,—who manifested her surprise at her neighbor's request, and was particularly inquisitive about the motives which prompted her to so extraordinary an expenditure.

This woman enjoying a great authority over her master's mind, was accustomed to take upon herself a great state with the females of the village, and, in some instances, to act as the priest's deputy ; which had procured for her the malicious nickname of the *priestess*. Puckering up her lips and majestically throwing back her head, she exclaimed ; " How, now, Mistress Jordan, something very strange must have taken place in your house, that you should want to buy tea and sugar !—Why, woman, I have not known you to get these articles during the last eight months,—when you bought some, you know, for your daughter's wake ; because you said it would come cheaper than brandy. Sure, when I got the milk cow from you, father Supplegrowl wanted to pay you in coffee and sugar, but you insisted upon getting the silver."

" Och! bless your swate face, Miss Troy, the loike of it is not for me," answered Mrs. Jordan. " You know how I love milk, best, or even butther milk, but the Alcalde has given me one of those poor shipwrecked crathures, that got strand-hed at Loive oack pint, and she seems such a delicate ladhy, that I could do no less than to get her some tay,—I will pay you in butther,—you know that father Supplegrowl loikes my butther, above all things, Miss Troy."

" Ah, ah," resumed the priest's housekeeper," is it for the like of them you put yourself to such an expense ? I thought you were more careful,—however, I will let you have half a pound, but you must furnish me with all the butter I shall want in passion week, which is shortly coming on, you know."

" Och! never fare, Miss Troy. You shall be satisfied," replied Mrs. Jordan, " and father Supplegrowl also,—I will bring you such butther !—As yellow as the purest goold, and so swate, that you will hardly fale it melting in your mouth. Let me alone for churning! Many is the woman who is come from ould Donegal, Miss Troy, but this I dare say, that no one can bate Peggy Jordan, in making butther, or spinning flax ; though it is but little of the latther I can get here to spin, unless I should go out through the prairie, to pull the wild, yellow bloomed flax, which Mr. Gallberry says is the same as grows in New-Zealand,* and makes betther thread than that of ould Ireland.—Sorrow upon him for saying so."

" New-Zealand !—May be it is New-Holland, he means ; he, he, he !" interrupted Miss Troy, laughing at her own jest, which was meant as a cutting sarcasm against Mr. Iso-celes Gallberry, the principal mathematician of the town of St. Patricio, who was no favorite of hers, nor of father Sup-plegrowl, by whom he had been excommunicated, five or six times, and anathematised from the altar, with *bell, book* and *candle light.* " But how long, Mrs. Jordan, are you going to keep this young *lady*, as you call her. Take care, perhaps she is only a *girl !*"

* We beg leave to state that Mr. Gallberry was mistaken in his as-sertion. The species of flax to which Mrs. Jordan alludes, is a variety of the *Linum Sativum ;* whereas that of New-Zealand is the *Phormium tenax.* The species found wild in Texas seldom rises above seven or eight inches.

"She is a ladhy, I warrant you," replied Mrs. Jordan, "but dare heart! I don't know how long she will stay with me, I am sure. She is welcome to stay as long as it shall plase God, and till she can hare from her own people, who live in the east of Texas, somewhere about the Trinidad."

"Ah, it will be sometime before she hears from them," resumed the housekeeper. "The Mexican general will soon be here, and will slash the Texians, I warrant you. Your young lady will have very little chance to return to her parents. She may be a burthen on your hands for a long time to come."

"Well, well," replied honest Mrs. Jordan, "she may be a burthen as long as it shall plase God. I say again I will not dhrive her away, as long as I have a mouthful to divide with her. Sure, Miss Troy, you have read a grate dale, and are a larned woman, seeing that you have all them books of father Supplegrowl undher your hand,—save the Latin ones, out of which he says mass—but you never saw, nor read that any one became poorer, by giving some help to a forlorn, shipwrecked crathur. But, Lord! It is getting late, and I am here, chatthering like a magpie, and the swate young crathur is so hungry.—So, Miss Troy, give me the tay and sugar, if you plase, and let me go."

Having received the provisions of which she stood in need, for the comfort of her guest, Mrs. Jordan returned to her cabin, which she soon made to reek with the steam of a savoury dish of fried eggs and onions, and having laid the table with a degree of neatness one could hardly have expected under so humble a roof, awoke the young lady to invite her to partake of her good cheer. "Come, now, to ate a mouthfull," said she, "here are new-laid eggs and fresh butther, honey, of my own churning. The eggs would have been betther, had I put in them some rashers of bacon, to make them more richer.—And, may be, you would have aten the mate—being that, as you come from the Trinidad, you will not keep Fridhays in lent; but father Supplegrowl would have found it out and read my name from the althar. And besides, honey, I have no bacon, being as how I sold the five hams that remained to ould Hardgrasp. But come along and ate something."

Her fair guest sat down, but ate very sparingly, for her

heart was too full ; and as soon as her light meal was over, she inquired of her hostess, whether there was any means to get herself conveyed as far as Matagorda, where her father had some acquaintances, who would not refuse to furnish her with the means of continuing her journey by land ; or taking a passage for New-Orleans, where she had relations.

To her inquiries the old woman answered that she was not herself acquainted with the state of the roads, in the present circumstances, but did not think any one in the village could be prevailed upon to undertake it. She added, however, that she would inquire from the Alcalde, who, being better in. formed, would be able to give the best advice.

At her return, she brought the unwelcome news, that there was no possibility of travelling in an easterly direction ; as all the roads, from Goliad, up to the north, were scoured by bands of volunteers, or marauders, and nobody would run the risk of being fired upon by their picquets. She added that General Urrea was momentarily expected, and that the Alcalde was of opinion some action of consequence would take place between St. Patricio and Goliad.

This was sad news for our young lady. To find herself, thus, in the midst of war—far from her kindred and natural protectors—with no other dependence than what could be placed in a lonely woman, entirely unknown to her ; made her shudder, and she could not refrain from tears.

This did not fail to excite the sympathy of her hostess, who endeavored to console her, saying, with her characteristic kindness, " well, now, honey—you need not take on, so !— Them Mexican soldiers will not hurt you. They will pro- tect the loike of us, here. The Alcalde and Mr. Gallberry have been writing to the Ginral, under-handedly,—and the latther made a trip to Matamoros to settle every thing—and then there is father Supplegrowl, our *clargy*, who will spake a kind word for the town, honey, and for his own people, who belong to the true church. Them Mexicans have a great reverence for the clargy, you know. So, so, don't take it so much to heart."

In that doleful occupation—of grief, manifested by tears, on one side ; and well meant, but awkward consolation, on the other—they spent the five following days ; and the sixth morning opened a new scene, which we will endeavor to portray in the next chapter.

## CHAPTER XIV.

Hail, precious drops, which first, in Freedom's cause,
Crimson'd the soil!—To our adoptive country
You were a blissful dew.

*The Texian, a Poem.*

On the twenty-sixth of February, precisely three days after Santa Anna had taken possession of the city of Bexar, the inhabitants of St. Patricio were startled from their beds, by a tremendous report of musquetry, followed by distressing cries, which proceeded from some Texians who had been surprised by Urrea. There were three houses, in the village, where they slept, after a carousal, quite unconcerned and without videttes (for they thought it, not only ridiculous, but even derogatory to their character to take against their enemies any of the precautions used in time of war) so that it was easy for the Mexicans to pounce upon them unperceived. Besides those who got killed, and some who escaped ; twenty one were made prisoners. All the inhabitants of the village, as may be supposed, rose up in a moment, but as many of them were indiscreetly looking out of their windows, or even venturing into the streets ; certain well meaning officers of the Mexican army ran about, exhorting them to keep quietly within their doors, lest their soldiers, in the first pride and confusion of success, should misuse them.

One of those who thus ventured out was our valiant Irish amazon, who stationed herself on the threshold of her cabin, holding in her hands an axe which she brandished with great resolution, ready to defend the entrance of her premises. Her grey hair escaped, in long elf locks, from under a red flannel night cap, too small for her head, and a sheet, which she had hastily thrown over her shoulders, by way of shawl, fluttered in the wind, so that her appearance was somewhat ominous and bordered on the supernatural. Some dragoons, who had come upon her, unawares, were so startled by such an apparition, that they actually drew back in terror, repeatedly crossing themselves. *" Valga me Dios!"* exclaimed their leader ; *" que es eso ?—Una alma de la otra vida !"*—Yet, ashamed of his cowardly movement, he was no sooner at a reasonable distance, than he stopped, and after an adjuration, in order to dispel the charm (if charm there was) he commanded his men to make ready to fire. Mrs. Jordan, who understood but too well the meaning of their preparations, was frightened out of her courage and began to scream and call aloud for help in the Irish language, which she used in the extacy of her fear, without reflecting that it was unintelligible to the dragoons. Happily for her, at that moment, a young officer, mounted on a superb charger, approached, and after having investigated the matter, commanded the dragoons to retire. He than addressed the old woman to give her assurance of protection, and exhorted her to keep herself within her walls. He had hardly exchanged a few words with her, when Miss Quinton, who had risen, and was already dressed, recognized our hero's voice.

In her present confusion, when she thought the village was actually being sacked, she could not help calling upon him for protection, though, in any other circumstance, she would have rather chosen to remain exposed to the greatest inconvenience, than to press herself, in this manner, upon her lover's observation. " Oh, Captain Letinez," exclaimed she, " it is heaven itself that sends you hither. For God's sake, do not leave this poor woman without protection." She could not get so far as to implore protection for herself, but, though she had no time to reflect upon the wording of her petition, yet it was the instinct of true love, which, at that instant, directed her tongue, and such a reticence was more significative than she was aware of.

" Heavens !" exclaimed the captain, " is it your voice I hear, Miss Quinton ?—Is it possible you are in this place ?— And by what strange chance did you come to St. Patricio ?" At the same time, alighting from his horse, and giving the reins to a soldier who was in attendance ; he entered the cabin,—the old woman courtesying, as he crossed her threshold, and shouldering her axe, in imitation of a soldier presenting arms. Before he had time to present his respects to the young lady, the old matron opened her battery of congratulations.

13*

" Sure honey," said she ; " you need not have been so much afraid, knowing you had such an acquaintance in the army of them people. Being as how his honor, this here captain, is your friend, you should not have so much taken it to heart. Och, captain! your honor ! had you but seen the swate crathur crying and wailing from share fright, it would have melted your heart. It would have made a four year ould cry !"

Señor de Letinez paid but little attention to the old lady's address, and altogether engrossed by Miss Quinton's presence, said to her, in a tone of deep respect, " What happiness for me to meet with you again, under circumstances which enable me to render you new services ! Oh ! be assured this is the greatest enjoyment I can possibly feel. This moment alone amply repays me for all the fatigues of the campaign, whether past or future."

" Captain Letinez," replied Miss Quinton, in a tone, in which melancholy and playfulness were blended, " there would be something peculiarly improper, in urging your suit in this place, and at this time, when we are altogether in the power of the military. I hope, therefore, you will not be less generous *here*, than you were at Matamoros, and continue faithful to the promises you then made."

" Any thing to please you, Miss Quinton," replied the captain, " and to obtain your esteem. Yet, let me hope, that when this unnatural war is over, and all parties are reconciled, you will receive my addresses with more indulgence. Sorry as I am for the accident which brought you hither, still I cannot help giving thanks to heaven for meeting with you again, and finding the opportunity of making a new tender of my services. All I am afraid of is, that I shall not long enjoy the pleasure of your company, for, I believe, we are to march towards Goliad, in two or three days."

" What a pity," returned the young lady, " that this unhappy contest cannot be terminated by pacific measures, and that so fair a country as this should be crimsoned by so much human blood ! My father, I am afraid, will be among the foremost, and, God knows, whether his courage will not carry him too far."

To this the captain would have replied by words of consolation, but he was interrupted by a sergeant, who came to inform him that he was wanted by the general. He, of course, took his leave of the young lady, but not without earnestly recommending her to the care of her hostess, and promising to send a guard of soldiers, to protect the house against any attempt at pilfering, on the part of the military.

He wished to afford Miss Quinton pecuniary aid, but dared not offer it himself, for fear of wounding her sensibility. In order, therefore, to relieve her, he had no sooner waited on the general, than he went to the parish priest's, and begged him to take charge of a sum of money, with instructions to give it to the old woman at whose house Miss Quinton lodged, for the young lady's benefit; but to preserve the strictest secrecy as to the giver, and rather let her believe that it proceeded from Mistress Jordan's generosity, in order that her suspicions might not fall upon him.

This clergyman, whom we have already introduced to our reader, under his own euphonic name of Supplegrowl, was not devoid of information, but was sadly deficient in common sense. He had travelled over a great part of the world, without finding any place fit for him, and had, as his last resource, established himself in St. Patricio. With his superiors, he was awkwardly cringing, but with his inferiors, or those whom he thought so, exceedingly haughty, and he had, besides, the unfortunate knack of mistaking any mark of respect paid to him by unknown persons, for a token of inferiority, and a willing acknowledgment of it on their part. As he had lived for a number of years, secluded from any thing like polished society, lording it over a number of Irish people, who used to tremble at the very sight of him; his self-conceit had so far got the better of what little judgment nature had originally given him, that it bordered on folly, and had he exhibited his spiritual freaks in any other country but the Texian wilderness, he would have been in no little danger of visiting a mad-house.

When Captain Letinez, with all imaginable politeness, laid his request before him, our hollow brained friar conceived the idea that this species of charity was a cloak for some mystery,—being probably intended to conceal some amorous intrigue—and his delicacy, which, for one of his order, was rather squeamish, took the alarm. He began to moralize in broken Spanish, with Señor de Letinez, and in a harsh

style, and consequential air, represented to him the wickedness of military men; and, moreover, manifested his indignation at the idea of our hero having sought to make him a
*go-between*.

The captain, whose love for Miss Quinton, was as pure as
disinterested, felt roused to anger by the suspicions of father
Supplegrowl, and treated him so cavalierly, that the clergyman resolved to be revenged, and, for such purpose, had recourse to his spiritual weapons. Miscalculating the influence
of his order, in Mexico—and as lofty as if he lived in the
days of Gregory VII.—he bore himself with the greatest
haughtiness. But he had reckoned without his host; for,
notwithstanding the respect which is still, externally paid, in
that country, to religious ceremonies, the high classes really
entertain very little veneration for the clergy, whom it is even
becoming a mark of *bon ton* to treat cavalierly. Father Supplegrowl found it so, much to his disappointment, as well as
the great diversion of Urrea's staff.

The young officer had no sooner left the clergyman's
house, than the latter, full of holy wrath, trudged to the general's to inform him that the majesty of the church having
been offended in his person, it became his painful duty to
punish the guilty, and that, of course, he would, on the following Sunday, proceed to the solemn excommunication of
Captain Letinez. " I am," said he, in a doleful canting tone,
" very sorry to be thus obliged to cut off a guilty soul and
deliver it up to Sathanas; but it is *in interitum carnis*, General, as St. Paul has it, and to the building up of the spirit.
A door of entrance is always left to the repentant sinner, and
as soon as the captain aforesaid will come to throw himself
at my feet, I will be ready to receive him, as a tender father
receiveth a penitent son, and reconcile him to the church.
Do not believe that, in acting thus, I am carried away by my
resentment against the culprit, for having insulted me. No,
it is out of pure zeal for Christian discipline, and merely for
the discharge of my duty, I thus use the spiritual sword of
St. Peter."

This address, as may be imagined, surprised Urrea, as
well as the superior officers, who surrounded him. Some
thought father Supplegrowl was mad—others, quite indignant
at his impertinence, were for driving him out with ignominy;

but one, who was a wag, after winking to his comrades, feigned to be frightened by his threats, and began to excuse Captain Letinez, and sue for mercy in his behalf.

Father Supplegrowl did not fail to imagine, from this, that his menaces had produced the desired effect and to suppose that showing himself inexorable would tend to enhance his dignity. He, of course, resisted these feigned applications for mercy ; until the wag, at last, bethought himself, in order to prolong the farce, to remind him that, before excommunication, three canonical *monitions*, on three different days, were required by the ecclesiastical law, and requested the clergyman to go through this form, in order to give his friend time to repent and offer satisfaction.

This was a request which father Supplegrowl could not refuse. In consequence, he consented, though with a bad grace, to go through the formality, and prepared to make the first monition *instanter*. The captain, however, was not present to receive the spiritual summons ; but the wag, who was carrying on the joke, having given the wink to his comrades, and the general, not unwilling to be amused, having granted his consent, by a cunning smile ; he undertook to bring the culprit in presence of his ecclesiastical judge, and immediately went out to look for him.

He soon met with the captain, but found some difficulty in engaging him to act his part in this strange frolic. By dint of importunity, however, he prevailed, and the culprit soon appeared before the assembled officers and father Supplegrowl.

As soon as the latter perceived him at the door, he opened upon him, at the highest pitch of his voice, like a public crier, in the streets ; and thundered out his admonition, in broken Spanish, which we will translate into English. " In the name of the most Holy and undivided Trinity, I, an unworthy brother of the Dominican order, make known unto thee, Ambrosio de Letinez, before me corporally present, that, having received from thee, an insult, I have, as ecclesiastical judge of this parish, declared and decreed, that thou shalt be cut off from the bosom of the Holy, Catholic, Apostolic and Roman Church, by the sword of the greater excommunication ; unless thou come to resipiscence, by publicly asking pardon of me ; and this thou shalt do, by appearing at the door of the church and kneeling, bareheaded, before me, holding in thy hand a waxen torch (and take notice it must be lighted) without sword on thy side, or gloves on thy hands,—and this doing, thou shalt save thy own soul."

After delivering this elegant formula of canonical elo- quence, father Supplegrowl bolted right off, with the greatest precipitation, for fear the captain should manifest his repen- tance on the spot, and prevent him from hurling his spiritual thunderbolts. The whole company were so much taken by surprise, that it was sometime before they could recover themselves sufficiently to enjoy the joke. They did so, at last, and after a hearty laugh, wishing to improve the occa- sion of diverting themselves—so unexpectedly offered—in- sisted upon Captain Letinez going through the repenting scene, in order to quizz the padre, but he absolutely refused, because he thought it would be carrying mockery too far, and bordering on sacrilege.

This was hardly over, when another Irish figure, quite as original in his kind, as father Supplegrowl, presented himself, " *craving*" an interview with the general, in order to lay be- fore him a plan for the campaign, which, he said, he would permit him to use " *whole, or in part*," just as his Excel- lency would " most vouchsafe to think fit." As Urrea was not acquainted with the English language, our hero was re- quested to serve as interpreter.

The communications which this new applicant had to make were prefaced by a long tale of the many subjects of disgust he had received from the government of the United States, whereby he had been induced to leave " *that nation*"—which, it was evident, from his tone and manner, he considered as a tremendous misfortune inflicted upon them. Among the grievances he enumerated were the pamphlets daily publish- ed against the Catholic Church, and the burning of the Ursu- line nunnery in Boston ; whereby the chartered rights of Roman Catholics had been so grossly violated, that he as- sured the general they would all emigrate to Texas, as soon as the Mexicans should effect the conquest. He had himself come *ahead*, to help by his advice, for he possessed consi- derable experience in the art of war, having served under Wellington, in Spain ; and he doubted not of Santa Anna's ultimate success, because the Mexicans were the children

" of the true church, with which Christ had promised to be, until the end of the world—and that the gates of hell should not prevail against it," &c. &c.

After such a preamble, of which we have given only the substance to our readers, sparing them the infliction of many texts of Scripture, as well as long complaints against the Orangemen of Ireland, he proceeded to unfold his military plan. It was much of a piece with the one that Buonaparte, in his memoirs, attributes to General Cartaux, at the siege of Toulon, id est, " to march in three divisions, fight the enemies and *beat them.*" But the most curi ous particular of his communication was the drawing of a pontoon of his invention, for crossing rivers. The boats were to be anchored sideways, as well as up stream, and he had provided a kind of wooden grate to stop the drift wood! It was evident the man had seen a bridge of boats, somewhere, but had not well understood its use, for some of his ideas were predicated on the supposition of its being stationary. Though Urrea could not penetrate all the absurdity of the plan, thus offered to his acceptance, yet he was amazed at the man's assurance, and inquired what grade he had occupied in Wellington's army, to which our Irishman answered, drawing himself up to his full height, that he had been a Sergeant.

Upon hearing this, a smile was exchanged by the officers who were present, and the General could not help telling them, " I am afraid these people take us for such fools, as to fancy any thing will go down with us. We are too ready to give credit to foreigners for superior information, and this induces them to believe that the meanest among them can instruct us. Only think of a petty Sergeant of an European army drawing up a plan for a campaign, for soldiers he has never seen and whose language is unknown to him!—Santa Maria! It requires the greatest patience to stand it."

Though Urrea expressed himself in this wise, he did not give the man to understand what he thought of his plan, and far from manifesting the contempt he entertained for his ideas, he, on the contrary, gave him hopes that he would examine them more carefully, when at leisure, and excused himself from so doing, at the present moment, under the pretence of a pressure of business. It often happens that the concealing of an unpleasant truth, for fear of giving pain to those whom it may concern, is a real art of cruelty, and, by a necessary recoil, exposes the weak minded man, who thus indulges his cowardice at the expense of his sincerity to considerable vexation. It is what befell General Urrea, in this instance. For not having had the resolution to tell the Irishman what he thought of his plan, he induced him to conceive hopes of causing them to be admitted, made him lose five months in useless attendance, and brought upon himself the infliction of thirty, or forty importunate visits and prosing explanations ; for, the ex-sergeant was one of the most awful bores ever sent forth by the river Shannon.

The defect here alluded to, which proceeds from mental debility, is generally prevalent among the Mexican gentry, who have got a notion that it is a part of true politeness. They are excessive in demonstrations of cordiality and offers of service, even where they do not feel the least interest, and will frequently insist with obstreperous violence, upon the acceptance of favors, which they have not the remotest idea of conferring.

Urrea made but a short stay at San Patricio, for, seeing with what carelessness and ignorance the portion of the Texian forces opposed to him acted, when on the defensive, he rightly judged that it would be easy to pursue his advantage. He had left the main body of his troops, with all his infantry, eight days' march behind, and had advanced only with one hundred men. Of these, he took forty eight with him, leaving the remainder to garrison the village, and went in pursuit of Dr. Grant, and his men, who were amusing themselves in collecting horses, and had scattered themselves about, for that interesting purpose, at the very time they knew their enemy was advancing upon them in great force.

Dr. Grant was a gentleman distinguished for his literary acquirements, who, for a number of years, had superintended a manufacturing establishment, attempted on a gigantic scale, in the town of Parras, state of Cohahuila, by an eminent English banker. His employer had already spent immense sums in the undertaking, without realizing one single penny, and he began to suspect that this want of success was owing to the Doctor's mismanagement. Pretty certain of being superseded, the latter embraced the opportunity of leaving his stewardship with some *eclat,* and threw himself headlong into the party politics which, at that time, divided the inhabitants of the north of Mexico, into two factions. When Texas declared herself independent, his name and standing naturally gave him a certain weight in the western parts, and he was appointed to command a small body of troops, which was to act between St. Patricio and Goliad. He was, nevertheless, soon ferretted out, by Urrea, who had some secret spies among the Irish of St. Patricio, and in six days' time, the Mexican general returned in triumph to that village Dr. Grant and his adventurers having paid the forfeit of their folly ; but, in the meantime, an event had occurred which filled our hero's heart with grief.

The general to whom he had been especially recommended, and who, in consequence, wished to afford him occasions of distinguishing himself, took him along when he went in pursuit of Dr. Grant ; and the summons was so sudden and unexpected, that our hero had barely time to take leave of Miss Quinton, but without making any disposition to insure her safety during his absence.

Immediately after his return, his first care was to visit old Mrs. Jordan's house, but judge of his surprise, when he heard that Miss Quinton was gone, and that her father had sent for her. " Gone to her father's !" exclaimed he, in the utmost amazement. " It is impossible ! Her father did not know where she was ; moreover, she could not have gone in that direction, without meeting with some of our scouts. No—This is an awkward invention ! An idle tale, set up to delude me ! But tell me where she is, for I will know. She cannot have fled from me ! Perhaps, she is the victim of some infamous plot, to bring her into danger. Woman, you are a party to it—but do not dally with me, or play false, for you shall dearly rue it. By all that is sacred in heaven and upon earth, if you have betrayed her, I will be revenged. Tell me, at once, where is she ; or by the living God," continued he, with increased violence, and drawing his sword, " you might as well dally with the honor of my mother."

The old woman, in spite of her masculine character, was frightened, and trembling like a leaf, replied, " Sure, Captain, I don't know ! I don't know where she is. For heaven's sake, sir ! Though I were at this blessed moment, to appare before God and St. Patrick, I could not tell you any more, your honor. You have it in your power to kill a poor lone woman, but my innocent blood will be upon your head, and upon *her whom you love.* I know she loves you also, but if you take away my life, she will execrate you. She will look upon you as a monster."

Fear sometimes renders the rudest people eloquent, and the old woman uttered these words with so much warmth, that the captain, ashamed of his own violence, put back his sword into its scabbard, and looked greatly confused ; while Mrs. Jordan, reassured by these pacific signs, resumed her familiar gossipping style. " Two days afther you were gone," said she, " there came three men, ridhing upon three horses, and ladhing a fourth one, that was a mare, by the bridhle, with a sidhe-saddle on her back for a woman to ridhe. They alighted before my house, and inquired if a young ladhy, precisely of the description of Miss Quinton, was not lodged with me. I told them she was, your honor. ' Well, then,' says one of the men, ' we have a letther for her from her father.' Thereupon, Miss Quinton, who heard the whole conversation from within, came out to spake with the men, and when she read the letther, ' This is not my father's handwrithing,' said she. ' No, Madham,' says the man. It was he that was spokesman, all the while, your honor, ' And so,' says he, ' your father could not writhe, bekase he was sick a-bed ; but he made the docthor that tendhs him writhe the letther in his name, and he sent us to pilot you home, which we will do in all safethy, for we know all the bye-roadhs and secret paths, and are not afeard of the Indians, and we have got a pass from the Mexican gin-ral.' ' But how did my father know that I was here ?' says Miss Quinton, for she was wary and prudent, your honor. ' Och, Madham !' says the other, ' he was informed of it, and the story of your shipwreck, by one of the men, who was a sailor in the Lively Sally, when she was wrecked in Corpus Christi bay. It was Jim Rapeseed, who was the second mate. You remember him, no doubt. He procured a horse from a Mexican ranchero, and rodhe, in seven days, to Mr. Pierson's plantation, where your father is now staying. The old gentleman is very low, Madham, not expected to live, and is incessantly inquiring whether you are arrived.'

"Thereupon the young ladhy began to wape, your honor, at the idhea of her father's dying, and she said she would go with the men. Dare soul! I told her how dangerous it was to venthure out, through them prairies and woodhs; but all would not do. She said she could not bear the idhea of her father's dying and her being absent. Happily for the dare crathur, I had half a keg of hard crackers and two good chazes, which I gave her,—though the men said she should want for nothing, in the way. They took the chazes, for all that. Bad luck to them! They will do Miss Quinton but little good, I am afeard."

"And did she go in company with men she was not acquainted with?" exclaimed Captain Letinez, with the bitterest sorrow painted on his countenance. "An unprotected female. All alone! Good God! what an imprudence!"

"Och, your honor, I told her it was a monsthrous cruel thing thus to travel that long route, on horseback; but she would not be advised, and said neither dangers, nor fatigue should detain her. She kept waping and sobbing and saying she must see her father, before his death; and see him she would. But, sure, captain, she is in no dhanger from them men. They all spake English, your honor. I will warrant you they are Americans. The loike of them is not going to injure a lone woman! 'Tis not as with Mexicans, captain; but, may be, you don't know the difference."

"Tut, tut;—do not tell me about your Americans," interrupted the captain; "a parcel of robbers and outlaws!— Oh, heavens! whither have they carried her? But this must be some deeply laid scheme of villany. I must to the general, beg a company of soldiers, and instantly go in pursuit of the wretches."

So saying, he left Mrs. Jordan's house with precipitation, but had not proceeded a hundred yards, when he was met by father Supplegrowl, who had been on the look out for him, in order to pounce upon him with his second *canonical admonition*. During the few days of the captain's absence, he had been on thorns, for fear he should pass into another parish, and thus elude his jurisdiction. As soon, therefore, as he was informed of his return, he hastened to execute what he termed "a painful duty." He could not have selected a more inauspicious moment, the captain being wrought up to the highest pitch of exasperation, and breathing nothing but vengeance against the villains who had carried off Miss Quinton.

Father Supplegrowl, therefore, had no sooner drawn near, and begun to utter the above quoted formula, " In the name of the most Holy and undivided Trinity ;" &c. than Captain Letinez, seizing him by the collar of his coat, and giving him a vigorous shake; exclaimed, " Father Supplegrowl, father Supplefool,—I am not now in humor to carry on a joke. I would be sorry to strike a clergyman ; but, henceforth, take care how you cross my path." So saying, he pushed him off with so much violence that he sent him reeling to twelve paces distance.

From what our reader has been told, touching this friar's temper, he might be inclined to think that after being thus handled by our hero, he would have displayed against him all the terrors of the *canon law ;* but the fact is that he cooled off, as if by enchantment. Father Supplegrowl was a spiritual bully, and, for such people, there is an anodyne virtue in the *argumentum baculinum*, which nothing else can supply. He peaceably withdrew to his own house, and, in token of forgiveness, indited a letter to the General, by which he begged him to act as mediator, between the captain and himself.

In the meantime, our hero, having obtained a sufficient number of soldiers from General Urrea, began the pursuit of the wretches, who had deceived Miss Quinton. He engaged three rancheros, from the vicinity—a class of people so skilful in tracing, by the prints of the horses' feet, the direction of any one who has preceded them on a road, that, in some cases, their success appears almost supernatural. These skilful *pilots*, after carefully examining the shape of the horse-shoes, the marks of which were still perceivable about Mrs. Jordan's premises ; declared they were not of Mexican manufacture, and the animals were, probably, strangers to that part of the country.

The foot prints led them to about twenty leagues east of San Patricio, where they bivouacked the first night, near a large marsh, which those they were in pursuit of seemed to have crossed. There they were afraid to lose the *scent ;* but one of the party, being of opinion that this had been done by way of stratagem, the whole company spread themselves about, following the banks of the *laguna*, and looking for the *track*, which they found again, and in such a spot, as was an evidence of design on the part of the fugitives.

The latter, after wading through the marsh, the distance of half a league, had retraced their steps, and taken a westerly direction; crossing a frightful thicket of prickly pear, by which both horses and riders must have suffered cruelly. Captain Letinez's heart bled within himself, when, upon an inspection of the road they had held, he saw to what sufferings Miss Quinton must have been exposed, and the desire of avenging her wrongs was a new incitement to hasten his march.

The guides led briskly on—animated by the promise of a considerable reward, in case they should make any discovery;—but when they reached the river Nueces again, the captain began to despair of success, and told them they must be mistaken. They still insisted that they were on the track and that those they were in pursuit of had certainly crossed the river.

14*

## CHAPTER XV.

The best of passions once profaned
To foulest deeds, resistless, will impel
The human heart.
                    *The Vestal, a poem.*

How repugnant soever our hero might be to believe his guides, knowing he was now near St. Patricio, he thought it prudent to accompany them, until they should give up the undertaking of their own accord. They all crossed the river, therefore, and following its right bank, down the stream, soon arrived at Lepantitlan. This was a fort the Mexican government had built, about two miles from St. Patricio, in order to protect the colonists, and of which the Texians had taken possession, at the same time they occupied the Irish village. Before the gate, which was closed—though the fort seemed abandoned—the guides stopped ; declaring that the young lady must be secreted within. The assertion appeared extravagant, and Captain Letinez was on the point of giving up the search in despair ; but the *rancheros* were so positive, that he, at last, consented to demand admittance. In consequence, they repeatedly knocked at the gate, but received no answer. He knew that the place, after having been retaken upon the Texians, had not been garrisoned by Urrea ; of course, he could not account for the portal being so scrupulously locked inside.

Seeing, after repeated efforts, that nobody heeded their summons, they forced the entrance, and the guides had no sooner crossed the threshold, than they declared they could discover the same marks by which they had been, till then, directed. This considerably raised the hopes of our hero, who, now, began to visit the buildings. A strong log house, of large dimensions, which had been used as barracks, was in a sad state of dilapidation ; yet it seemed, from the relics of a late carousal, to have been the resort of some convivial party. This discovery increased the ardor of the search, and soon after, one of the rancheros espied a man softly stealing over the palisade ; whereupon he raised the hue and cry, and started in pursuit of the fugitive.

The fellow was, nevertheless, too nimble for his pursuer, and, at one single leap, from the top of the stockade, cleared the ditch that ran round the fort, and made for the thick grove, on the margin of the river ; where he succeeded in concealing himself, before the captain's men could come round by the gate, and intercept his flight. Some of the party continued the chase, while others, among whom was our hero, returned to the fort, to pursue their researches. They tried to enter a small building, which had been used as a powder magazine ; but found it locked. As they shook the door, they were startled by hearing some faint moans, proceeding from the interior ; whereupon, one of the rancheros exclaimed, " *Aqui esta, aqui la tenemos !*" (here she is) " *Animo, señores !* we have succeeded."

Captain Letinez, nearly delirious with joy, called out to Miss Quinton, from whom he was sure the wailing moans proceeded ; that it was himself, who had traced her to her place of imprisonment, and come to set her free, and begged her not to be frightened, if they should break open the door. An exclamation of joy, followed by loud sobs, informed him that those good tidings had reached her ears. He found, however, considerable difficulty in effecting his purpose. The door was strong, covered with thick plates of iron, and studded with large nails. In vain they tried to raise it off its hinges, by means of a long lever ; or to break it, by repeated knocks, with a large beam of timber : their efforts proved useless, and after an hour's severe labor, it still remained fast on its hinges, and precluded all entrance. The young lady, from within, encouraged them, with a faint voice, and suggested the idea of getting in, by the roof, in case they should not be able to break open the door.

" By the Virgin *de los Dolores*, she is right," exclaimed one of the rancheros ; " and it is a shame for us, not to have thought of it. The roof is strongly terraced ; but, for all that, I will soon dig a hole through it. Here, Juan Dolos, let me climb on thy shoulders, man :—now, hand me that sharp ebony handspike, and let one or two more get up here to help me."

No sooner said than done. In less than half an hour, a portion of the roof was off,—yet, as the young lady would not consent to be lifted up through this sky-hole, they continued their work till they had made a gap in the wall,—which was no difficult task—the stones, though massy, being badly cemented, and, of course, easily removed, when once the superstratum of the roof was thrown down.

At last, Miss Quinton came out of her prison, but almost fainting, and nearly as weak as when she was first rescued from the hands of the Comanches. The first words she uttered were addressed to her lover, " Blame me not, Captain Letinez," said she, " I was unworthily deceived. Alas, I was made to believe that my father was dying! I was told he earnestly desired to see me and had sent for me. Could I, then, listen to pusillanimous suspicions and remain unconcerned ?"

" I know it," replied the captain, " Mrs. Jordan has given me a faithful account. But tell me, my dear Miss Quinton, who was the author of this infamous deception ?—I need not inquire about the vile motives by which he was impelled."

" Indeed, captain," returned Miss Quinton, " the man is a Mexican, to all certainty, and an officer of high rank, if I may judge by his military costume, but I do not know his name. After leaving St. Patricio, I was made to travel two days, till we came to a large marsh, through which we waded. Then crossing the most frightful thicket of prickly pear, I ever saw, in two days more, we reached this place, which my guide made me believe was a Texian fort, and that we should remain here, till a carriage should come for me. In about three hours' time, there arrived, instead of a carriage, the officer already mentioned. He spoke English very imperfectly, but sufficiently to make the vilest proposals ; confessing that he was the author of my abduction, and that I was in the hands of persons entirely devoted to him. I treated him with all the contempt and execration he deserved, and irritated to the last degree by my reproaches, he caused me to be shut up in the loathsome dungeon whence you have just freed me. Since I have been imprisoned in it, he has himself come twice to bring me food, and has renewed his efforts to shake my resolution."

" It must then be some one of the principal officers of the southern division of the army," resumed the captain, " for you are here in the old fort of Lepantitlan, about three quarters of a league from St. Patricio. But where could he previously have seen you, and who are the men of whose help he has availed himself to execute his execrable purpose ?—Mrs. Jordan told me they spoke English perfectly well, and she took them for Texians."

" The wretched man must have seen me, at the chapel, in San Patricio—on the Sunday when I accompanied Mrs. Jordan to mass," replied Miss Quinton. " As for the agents of his villany, two of them, if I can judge from their pronunciation, are Scotchmen, and the third one struck me as having some of the peculiarities of the colored race of Louisiana. At all events, he knows French and speaks it as Creoles do, —but where my persecutor found them passes my comprehension."

" Oh," returned the captain, " there are so many adventurers following our army, in order to partake of the spoils, in case of success, that it is not difficult to account for his finding such vile tools, quite at hand. But what are we to do, now, that you are free ?—It is difficult, or rather impossible, to provide against the snares of a powerful and secret enemy, and by returning to San Patricio, you will be exposed to new persecutions. Could I be continually present, to watch over your safety, there would be no great danger ; but we are shortly to march towards Labahia, and the Irish village will be left unprotected. Resolve, Miss Quinton,—what are we to do ?"

" Alas !" said she, " I see no alternative. Surely, you do not wish me to follow your army ?"

" Dear Miss Quinton," resumed the captain, " I am aware it would look improper, if we were in ordinary circumstances, but reflect that necessity has no law. There are some of our officers' wives, who are women of virtue, standing, and good breeding, and have female servants with them. Might you not, without any great breach of propriety, travel in company with some of them, until we reach the Brazos ; when a flag of truce shall be sent to the enemy, and you shall be conveyed to your friends, in all honor and safety."

" Indeed," returned Miss Quinton, " I cannot do so ! the

ladies you speak of may be very honorable, but their ways
and customs differ so much from what I have been used to,
that I cannot help thinking they border upon licentiousness.
I do not, however, condemn them. Every country has its
peculiar sense of propriety. But familiarity with them I
would consider like a committing of my own principles. Better for me to return to my good-natured hostess, and wait
until the campaign is more advanced."

" Well, then," said the captain, " since such is your resolution, we may begin our march for St. Patricio, immediately. We have found here, a side-saddle, probably the
same on which you rode, when you left the village, and if
you feel yourself sufficiently strong to ride, we will leave
this wretched abode."

Miss Quinton having given her consent, every thing was
quickly made ready, and they set out for St. Patricio. The
three men who had gone in pursuit of the young lady's jailer,
returned as the rest of the party were leaving the fort, and
informed them, that the villain, after leading them a race of
two miles up the river, had, at length, escaped, by swimming
over to the opposite side, and mounting a horse, which, it
seems, was ready at that place, having been left hobbled, in
case he were wanted. Sadly did Captain Letinez regret
that they had not taken him, for he had expected to discover by his means the author of the outrage against Miss
Quinton.

In about three quarters of an hour, they got to the Irish
village, where old Mrs. Jordan was delighted to see Miss
Quinton in the middle of the cavalcade, which stopped before her door. " Och, och !" did she exclaim, " what a blessing, honey, that you are found again. By my troth, my
jewel, the dare captain would have gone beside himself, I
think ! But you are welcome home, for I declare to goodh-
ness, I have been in the fidgets, ever since you went away.
Them prairies are so dangerous to travel through ! They
are full of *painters*, honey. And the sarpents ! The rattle-
snakes, black vipers, and mocasins, besides the scorpions,
that crape about the grass, and are so apt to get among the
bed clothes at night ! And the tarentulas ! Och, we have
none of them things in ould Ireland, blessed be St. Patrick
for it ! Ah, faith, he fixed them crathures ! With his crook

he drove them all into the say ! But alight, honey, you must be fatigued and hungry. And how did you like· the two chazes I gave you, and the crackers ? But I dare say you hardly tasted them, and them monsthrous crathures who carried you off, ate the best share of them."

Miss Quinton was soon established again in the little room which she had previously occupied, and her lover obtained leave from General Urrea, to place a guard of two soldiers at the old woman's door, in order to watch over the young lady's safety. He also, made his utmost efforts to discover who could have been guilty of her abduction, but the general showed a considerable degree of unwillingness to favor his researches. " It can be no other," said he, " than some one of the superior officers, and if discovered, it might be dangerous to attempt punishing him. During a campaign as arduous as the one we have undertaken, it is impossible to prevent every misdemeanor of the kind. It is one of the sad consequences of war, that many acts of licentiousness, which, in time of peace, would be severely punished, must be suffered to pass by unnoticed."

This was but a poor satisfaction for Captain Letinez; but, as he had no means of obtaining redress, he was obliged to put up with it. About a week after this occurrence, General Urrea began his march towards Labahia, otherwise called Goliad. There was, on his way, a considerable settlement of foreigners, chiefly Irish, at a village bearing the quaint name of *Mission del Refugio;* of which a party of Texians, commanded by one Captain King, had taken possession, and whence the Mexican commander judged it necessary to dislodge them. For that purpose, he detached a portion of his troops, who fell in with Captain King's men, about ten miles below the village, whither he had sent a division of the small corps under his command, and drove them back towards the Mission. King and his men fought with various success, until the whole of the Mexican army having come up, many of the Texians, seeing their retreat cut off, surrendered as prisoners of war, and others were so lucky as to make their escape. Among the latter was Coloned Ward, who fortified himself in the church of the village, and defended himself throughout the day, until Urrea at nightfall, having begun to batter the building with a piece of artillery ; the besieged surrendered, as the former had done.

Some of them, however, refusing to trust their foes, made their escape, while those who became prisoners of war had no reason to anticipate what a dreadful fate was reserved for them, as they were treated with a kind of carelessness unusual in border warfare.

After taking the Mission, the forces which had been on that service advanced, full of animation, towards Goliad, which, Fanning—whose conduct was, throughout the contest, wavering and imprudent—resolved to abandon. The next day, at an early hour, he began his ill-starred retreat. The sick and baggage were piled up in Mexican carts, drawn by oxen, as well as the cannon, and many of the drivers, not understanding English ; or, more probably, inclined to favor the Mexican cause, managed the animals in such a manner, that they ran about, in the utmost confusion. The march being thus retarded, Urrea had time to come up with Fanning, and found him in the middle of a plain, intrenched behind some wagons.

The Texian commander had neither knowledge to fight, nor discretion to retreat, for there was a large wood, at a short distance, on his rear, in which it would have been easy for him to fortify himself in an inexpugnable manner. He neglected altogether the chances of escape which this might have afforded, and yet did not avail himself of his superiority in point of numbers and artillery, to make his resistance good.

Urrea, on the other hand, showed very little less indiscretion and fool hardiness, for he advanced to the attack of Fanning's intrenched camp, with so scanty a supply of ammunition, that, shortly after dusk, his soldiers were obliged to suspend their fire for want of cartridges. He had left his *materiel* a great distance behind, and had the Texians attacked him, at this critical moment, and improved the occasion, his total discomfiture would have been the inevitable result. But Fanning kept himself quiet, within his camp, while the Mexican, commanding his soldiers to lie flat on the ground, amused the Texians by feigned demonstrations, which he made with his music and drums, in various directions, round their intrenchments, thus gaining time to send for his ammunition and two pieces of cannon.

Having suffered the precious occasion to escape, Fanning, when attacked, the following morning, by all the troops of Urrea, surrendered with a facility which could be atoned for only by the fortitude and sang froid with which he met a barbarous and unjust death.

As it is not, however, our object to expatiate, in this place, on the horrors of the violation of Fanning's capitulation, we beg to be excused, if we cursorily run over the surrender of his corps, to return to Captain Letinez's private affairs. When he saw the Texians capitulating, though possessing every means of resistance, he could not help, in his heart, accusing them of cowardice. He knew the orders to refuse quarter to every one taken with arms in his hands were peremptory, but he had not the least suspicion they would be enforced against such as surrendered, and, in consequence, put themselves out of that category—much less could he anticipate that a solemn capitulation, granted and signed with due reflection, would be violated in a manner which has no precedent in modern warfare. Of course, he felt no uneasiness about the prisoners' fate, and availed himself of his knowledge of the English language, to mix among them, and become acquainted with their officers. He chiefly remarked a middle aged man, of good appearance—though seemingly oppressed by sorrow—whom he heard some one call by the name of Major Quinton. It immediately occurred to him that he might be a relation of the young lady to whom he had become attached in the manner already related, and he soon discovered that he was her father. Drawing near to him, therefore, he introduced himself with that proper degree of civility, which a courteous victor never forgets with a vanquished enemy, and said, " I rejoice, sir, that it is in my power to alleviate the chagrin you must naturally feel, in finding yourself a prisoner, by imparting to you the most happy news."

" Alas, sir !" sadly returned the major, " what happy news can you announce to a man who has lost all. Property and child ! All is gone, and now, I am myself a prisoner."

" But, sir," resumed the captain, "it is about your daughter."

"My daughter!—What of her?—Oh, do you know any thing about her?—For God's sake, tell me immediately," replied the major, taking hold of Captain Letinez's hands, and pressing them to his bosom, with an ardor which brought tears to his eyes. "Do you know where she is?"

"She is safe and in good health," returned the captain; "but be master of yourself—moderate your excitement. Miss Quinton is not far from this place, yet I doubt whether I should communicate what you seem, in your present state, hardly able to bear."

"Able to bear!" resumed the major; "oh, for the sake of humanity, tell me all. Uncertainty is beyond my powers of endurance. Proceed, young gentleman, proceed,—in the name of heaven!—where is my daughter?--where is my child?"

"Well, sir," replied our hero, "Miss Quinton, as I have already told you, is in a place of safety. Having casually fallen in with the party of Comanches who were carrying her off, I had the happiness of becoming the instrument of her deliverance." Thereupon, he gave the major a brief history of the young lady's journey to Matamoros, of her embarcation and subsequent shipwreck, as well as of her landing at San Patricio; which, in order not to go twice over the same tale, we will abstain from repeating. Be it sufficient to state that the father, delighted at the idea that his daughter was safe, and not far from him, manifested to Captain Letinez, his gratitude, by the most lively and sincere expressions.

The latter, anxious to show to the major all the civility in his power, and desirous he should be treated with more indulgence than the other prisoners, went to the general and begged permission to take him immediately to his tent; laying before Urrea, in a candid manner, the motives by which he was actuated. But, notwithstanding the great influence he possessed over the general's mind, he found no small difficulty in obtaining leave. Urrea believed, or affected to believe, that it might displease the commander-in-chief. The captain, nevertheless, was so importunate that he carried his point, and Major Quinton found in his tent the refreshments he stood so much in need of, and part of his own clothes and linen, which had been pillaged by the lancers, but which Señor de Letinez had redeemed at his own expense.

Several other officers availed themselves of the example
set them by our hero, to show civilities to certain prisoners,
with whom they happened to have been previously acquainted.
The most moving instance was that of a young lieutenant of
*cazadores*, who found, among the Texians, a dear friend, with
whom he had received his education at a Catholic college, in
the west of the United States. This officer was named Marinez. He had no sooner cast his eyes upon young Brashears,
than he rushed towards him and tenderly locking him in his
arms, exclaimed, in his native language, " oh, my dear friend!
Is it possible we have been arrayed in arms against each
other, and I have been exposed to the danger of piercing the
bosom of the man who saved my life! Cursed be war, with
the arts and ambition of politicians! Hadst thou perished, I
would not have survived thee, my Brashears; but now thou
art safe. With thee I will divide the bread I eat and the
narrow tent under which I sleep. Dost thou remember the
day when thou savedst my life, by exposing thine, when I
was on the point of being drowned in the Ohio river? Oh,
what happiness, to meet with thee again!" While Marinez
was thus addressing his friend, he could not refrain from
tears, and though this flow of gratitude was rather a strange
spectacle for the Texians, and seemed to them to border on
the ridiculous ; the Mexicans manifested by their looks, that
they respected the feelings by which it was prompted, though
evinced towards an heretic ; for (to do them justice) in spite
of the many vices that sully their character, they reverence
and practise the virtue of gratitude to a degree which might
put to the blush nations far more advanced than they in the
path of civilization.

After receiving the necessary permission from his superior
officers, Marinez led away his friend, and along with him
another young man, of the name of Duval, from whom Brashears refused to be separated, and treated them with all the
tenderness the strongest friendship can inspire.

We do not, however, intend to dwell on the interest which
might be derived from this episode, but return in haste to our
main story, in order to show to our readers Major Quinton,
in Captain Letinez's tent, in close deliberation with him, on
the practicability of sending for his daughter. " And she
is in St. Patricio, you say, Captain ;—only seventy miles

from this place ?" did he exclaim. " We must send for her immediately, unless you can obtain leave for me to go to St. Patricio. I must see her, and relieve the painful anxiety which she must feel on my account."

" It would be impossible to obtain leave for you to go," resumed Señor de Letinez. " From our General's present temper, the mere proposal would appear to him fraught with absurdity. Nothing remains, therefore, but to send for Miss Quinton. She will not refuse to come, when informed that you are here. Captain Alvarez, a friend of mine, has a gig for the use of his lady :—I will obtain the loan of it, and I do not despair to prevail on Mrs. Alvarez herself, to go for your daughter. I know she took a great interest in her, and she is obliging, even to a degree bordering on enthusiasm. Write a letter for Miss Quinton, while I am going to bespeak my friend's gig, and you will soon have the pleasure of embracing her."

" Well, my dear friend," replied the Major, " I am going to write." Thereupon the captain leaving him, went out to look for Alvarez ; but, in the meantime, certain deliberations of dreadful import were going on, among the principal officers of Urrea's corps.

## CHAPTER XVI.

If the assassination
Could trammel upon the consequences and catch,
With surcease, success; that but this blow
Might be the be-all and the end-all here,
But here, upon this bank and shoal of time,—
We'd jump the life to come. But in these cases,
We still have judgment here ; that we but teach
Bloody instructions, which being taught, return
To plague the inventor: this even-handed justice
Commends the ingredients of our poisoned chalices
To our own lips.
*Macbeth, Act I. Scene VII.*

UNDER a large marquee, seven officers of high rank were sitting, in various attitudes, upon trunks containing the general's baggage, while he lay himself half reclined on his camp-bed, smoking a cigarrito. Though apparently in a mood of great listlessness, there was a sombre look spread over his countenance, which indicated that highly unpleasant thoughts occupied his mind. " By the Virgin *de los Remedios*,([17]) exclaimed he, addressing a middle aged man, who was sitting at the foot of the bed, " all this embarrassment arises from your having granted them such advantageous terms."

" Indeed," replied the officer, thus addressed, " I cannot be blamed, without your excellency participating in it ; for you saw the articles and approved of them. I acted only as your deputy."

" Oh, I saw the articles !—To be sure, I did," resumed Urrea. " But my intention was merely to take *the birds in*, (agarrar los pajaros,)—I wanted to prevent the effusion of Mexican blood. Those devils were so curiously intrenched with a row of wagons, that our cavalry could not open a way to itself :—You know, we tried it,—and to be thundering at them, from afar, with our artillery, was a lengthy work and

15*

a great waste of gunpowder. Besides, I did not like to expose ourselves to the chances which might have turned up in favor of the confounded rascals, had we refused them terms, and rendered them desperate. But now, what are we to do ?—Major Farialega, have you seen Fanning, and informed him of what I said ?"

" I have had an interview with him," answered Farialega. " He maintains his right to be treated like a prisoner of war, according to the uses and laws of civilized nations, and says, that, whatever be the point of view under which the Mexican government looks upon the Texians, a capitulation is like a solemn treaty, and that the terms granted them cannot be violated, without a breach of faith, which will leave an everlasting stigma upon any Mexican general who shall be guilty of such an enormity."

"*Voto a dios !*" exclaimed Urrea, interrupting him, " a solemn treaty with a parcel of rebels, and ungrateful colonists !—They are no nation and have no right to be treated like one."

" Certainly, they are no nation," replied Farialega, " but still, they are men."

" Men ! confound them," returned Urrea, " a parcel of heretics, who want to introduce Protestantism into the republic !—If they were Christians, they might have some plea, but, as things are . . . . . . However, gentlemen, let every one of you openly say what he thinks. I have convoked you, in order to get your advice. You, Colonel Bebe-Sangre, what is your opinion ?"

" Oh, my opinion is soon expressed, and my advice soon given," said Bebe-Sangre. " They are rebels, taken with arms in their hands, and the Señor Presidente's orders are express. The sooner they are made away with, the better. Provisions are growing scarce with us, and what is the use of allowing them to consume a portion of them to no purpose ?"

" And you, Don Prudente Mira-lejos," interrupted Urrea, " what do you say ?"

" For my part," answered the officer thus appealed to, "if I am free to express what I think, I must say this appears a weighty affair, which should be viewed in all its bearings. If we treat our prisoners in the manner Señor Bebe-Sangre seems to wish, we expose ourselves to retaliation, in case any misfortune befall our army. Gentlemen may consider the success we have obtained with too partial an eye. In my poor judgment, it is not decisive. I have had some acquaintance with the Anglo-Americans. They are cold and apathetic, but, by no means, cowardly. It always takes two, or three defeats to put them in motion and warm their blood. They lose ground in the beginning of every war, but triumph in the end. You may be sure that, after our two victories, we are in greater danger than ever. As to this Fanning, you are undoubtedly aware he is no deacon of his trade, otherwise he would have remained in the fort of Goliad, and sustained a siege. It would have taken us at least six weeks to force him to surrender."

" Well, now, hush, Miralejos !" interrupted Urrea. " Did I not consider thee as more crazy than Fanning, I would be angry with thee. Two victories brought us into greater danger than we were in before ! *Santo Dios !* What art thou saying, man ? Thinkest thou we are in the season of Carnes tollendas (shrove-tide) to play the buffoon ?"

" May it please your Excellency, I am rather afraid we are near passion-week," replied Miralejos, with some asperity.

" Gentlemen," resumed the general, " our consultation will never come to an end, if it degenerate into an altercation, and the two bottles of choice Burgundy, which are cooling for us in the *jarro,** will lose their relish, if we drink them after exciting feelings of bitterness amongst us. Come, Milagros, tell us what you think. You, who are my aid-de-camp, will be of my opinion, I know."

In spite of this broad hint, Milagros took the liberty of differing from his general. " I could not think," said he, " of putting them to death, according to the President's orders, even if they had surrendered at discretion, but that was not the case. They laid down their arms on certain specified conditions, and if we violate them, we trample upon our military honor—we defile our glory. There is but one line of conduct for me—it is the line of duty ! Here, however, expediency persuades us to the same course ; for if we treat

* Earthen jar.

them mildly, and keep faith with them, it will induce others to surrender, and Texas will soon be clear of them."

" You have perfectly well expressed my sentiments," said Colonel Mascaña, addressing Milagros, " and since the general left it to the majority, I believe his Excellency may now be satisfied."

" So I am, gentlemen," interrupted Urrea, with a forced smile ; " I am quite satisfied that you are nearly all for throwing the responsibility upon me in the eyes of the world. You know the President's orders strictly forbid giving quarter to any of the rebels taken arms in hand, and still you are afraid to vote for their execution. But if you wash your hands of it, so do I. Urrea is something of a fox, I assure you. I will not act by myself in this business.—Now the consultation is over, gentlemen ; but let us have the wine. Here, boy—Pedro ! Bring drinking glasses, and the two bottles of Burgundy which are in the jarro. I drink to you, gentlemen of the staff. By the Holy Cross of Queretaro,([18]) this is excellent ! What a taste ! It is superior to the best champaign I ever sipped. Well, thanks to Fanning's officers ! They have taken good care to provide for us. Won't you take a bit of this Bologna saussage ? Won't you taste these French *sardines*, or this *patè de trufles ?* Long live Texas, I say ! We found no such dainties after the battle of Zacatecas,([19]) though our President found *ore* enough, and indemnified himself tolerably well for the advances he had made, in order to buy over the partizans of poor Farias."

The wine was drunk, and the officers who had assisted at this strange consultation departed, except an intimate counsellor of the general, with whom he held the following dialogue. " I am sadly disappointed. This cursed consultation, to which you advised me to have recourse, does not turn out as well as we expected. Had they all voted like Bebe-Sangre, they would have taken the odium of the job off my shoulders ; but now, what shall we do ? The articles of Fanning's capitulation, or surrender, or whatever it may be called, are public ; and *I* was the fool who published them, and sent a copy to Matamoros ! On the other hand, Santa Anna's orders are too strict to be trifled with. I know his temper. One might as well dally with an African hyena, as to attempt soothing his mind. It were as much as my head is worth, or, at least, my post. By the Virgin of Guadelupe, I am well nigh bewildered! What am I to do?"

"I will tell you," replied the other, "send a courier to Santa Anna, to consult him. You know, beforehand, what will be his answer; but you can be absent when the messenger returns."

"An admirable idea!" exclaimed Urrea. "This is well contrived. It extricates me from all my difficulties. But whom shall we find to execute the job?—It is a cursed dirty piece of work!"

"Whom shall we find, you ask?" replied the other, "why, you have forty, fifty persons, who will gladly undertake it. But I think Garrafon deserves the preference. He will do it without flinching, I warrant you."

This being settled, Urrea's *ame damnée*, (as the French call it,) departed, leaving him to write his despatches to Santa Anna, who was then at San Antonio de Bexar, the principal inland town in Texas, of which he had taken possession as early as the end of February, and that has always been the point most coveted by the Mexicans.

While these things were going on in the general's tent, our hero was looking for captain Alvarez; a man whose name deserves to live for ever, in the heart of every Texian, for having, at his own imminent peril, and against the general feeling of his countrymen; saved about one hundred prisoners, who were taken after Fanning's surrender, and who, by his heroical exertions and those of his noble-minded lady, escaped being massacred. In the midst of the confusion and bustle incident to such times and circumstances, captain Alvarez was not easily found; but when, at last, our hero lighted upon him, and begged him to lend him his gig, Alvarez answered—"My dear friend, I am sorry to refuse you, but really, my wife is on the point of being confined, and I am obliged to send her to some place where she may enjoy more quiet, than is to be found in a military camp."

"Why," replied Letinez, "I did not suppose that Mrs. Alvarez was so near her term. I had thought of begging her to go along with the gig, in order to bring hither a young lady, whose father turns out to be an officer of rank among the prisoners, and is ardently desirous of seeing her. She was carried off by the Comanches, and I had the happiness

to rescue her. Now, she is at St. Patricio, without a protector, and probably in great danger. Along with her father, she
would be safe. Alvarez, you must not refuse me. I know
your lady is more humane than you; I will speak with her."

"Hey day!" replied Alvarez, " what an heroical squire of
distressed damsels you are become! *Tandem homo factus es!*"

"Hush, for God's sake," returned our hero, " nothing of
*that*. The lady I am speaking of is a woman of rank, education, and unblemished character. The slightest joke at
her expense might seriously hurt me. It might blast all my
hopes."

" Oh, sits the wind in that quarter!" exclaimed Alvarez.
" Real love, matrimony, and all that!—Well, well,—I am
no spoiler of fair play. Go to my wife: I dare say she will
undertake the expedition. Were she sure to be seized by
the pains of *accouchement*, even in the midst of a nopalera,
she would go; for females are wonderfully heroical, when it
is question of alleviating the sorrows of one of their sex."

Having thus obtained his friend's consent, our hero went
to the lady, who, after much supplication, suffered herself to
be persuaded to oblige him. She took half a day to make
her preparations, and, at last, set out for St. Patricio, escorted by a corporal and two soldiers belonging to her husband's
company, and provided with ample credentials from Major
Quinton and Captain Letinez. The latter was anxious to
go along with her, but having received strict orders from the
general, to hold himself in readiness for an expedition towards the Guadelupe([20]) river, he could not follow the bent
of his inclination.

Soon after Mrs. Alvarez's departure, Urrea began his
march eastward; leaving the prisoners and a large body of
troops to guard them, under the command of Colonel Garrafon; with instructions to receive and open all despatches
which might arrive from Bexar, directed to him, and execute
whatever orders they might contain. Our hero, quite unsus-
picious of what was to happen—for none, besides the superior officers, had been intrusted with the secret—left Major
Quinton in possession of his tent, and directed his servant to
wait upon him with all possible attention. He, also, earnestly recommended him to Captain Alvarez and some other
friends, and set out quite unconcerned, not doubting, but, at

his return, he would enjoy the satisfaction of seeing both father and daughter happy in the company of each other.

While our hero is marching at the head of his troop, towards the Guadelupe river, we will transfer the scene to San Patricio, in order to make our readers acquainted with the interview between Miss Quinton and Captain Alvarez's lady. The latter, not understanding English, had no sooner got to the Irish village, than she repaired to the priest's house, in order to beg him to accompany her to Mrs. Jordan's, and act as interpreter. The clergyman, rendered wiser, or, at least, more condescending, by his preceding altercation with Señor de Letinez, dared not refuse the favor, and both were soon in presence of the young lady.

Mrs. Alvarez, who had previously had a slight acquaintance with her, introduced herself with graceful politeness, and father Supplegrowl addressed Miss Quinton, saying; " it gives me the greatest pleasure, Madam, to be the interpreter of the happy news which this lady brings you. Your father is alive and in good health. It is true, he is in the number of the prisoners who were taken on the other side of Goliad ; but, being, now, under the care of Captain Letinez, there is no doubt but every attention will be paid to him. However, the letters this lady brings will inform you, more in detail, of these particularities."

Upon hearing that her father was alive, Miss Quinton, who had already heard of the skirmishes, or battles, as they were called, fought against the Texians, and who had feared the worst, was seized with universal tremor, and, in spite of all her efforts to master her emotion, shed tears of joy. She raised her eyes up to heaven, while her tears were trickling down her face, and seemed for a moment, absorbed in mental prayer ; after which, she read her father's letter with comparative composure.

As soon as she had done perusing it, Mrs. Jordan, who, already anticipated her departure and felt chagrined at the idea of losing her company, told her, " Now, honey, you will be for laving the ould woman, I am afeard. But, mind me, though I am glad that you have found your father safe and sound, yet I do not know how I shall be able to live without you, afther being accustomed to the loike. Och, dare ! you were to me loike my own daughther, who died last fall ;—

save that you could not work in the pratie garden, as she
did ; for she was a stout crathur of her years :—God be
marciful to her sowl, and the blessed St. Patrick !  And now
I will be alone,—all alone ; with nobody about the house to
kape me company—baring the brindled cow—her that is so
tame, you know.  Och, och, but this a sad hour for Peggy
Jordan.   It is, indeed, honey !"

"I must go to rejoin my father," said Miss Quinton ; "yet,
my dear Mrs. Jordan, I hope to see you again, before long.
Trust me, I will never forget the kindness with which I have
been treated under your hospitable roof.   I wish it were, at
this time, in my power to offer you a just remuneration for it,
but what I cannot do *now*, I hope to be shortly able to effect."

"The dare !" exclaimed Mrs. Jordan.   "Do you spake
of recompense to me !—Is it money you mane, honey ?—I
want none from you, I am sure ; but if you would do the
poor Irish widow a favor, there is a thing she could mention
which would be quite asy for you."

"It is granted, ere it is named," returned Miss Quinton,
"what is it ?—It shall be done immediately."

"I will tell you in your ear," resumed Mrs. Jordan, "for
it is not for every body's hearing."   Thereupon, she whispered to her guest : "Be kind to young Captain Letinez.
He is a good lad, and well favored and loves you dearer
than the very drops of his heart.   The poor crathur wept
when he found you gone,—when them monsthrous chates
carried you off to Lepantitlan.—Yes, he wept for love !—
Now, only think !  A man loike him, to wape !—An officer !
—you will brake his heart, if you don't have him."   Upon
hearing this request, Miss Quinton colored up to her ears,
and gently pushed her hostess from her, interrupting her, at
the same time, by informing Señora Alvarez that she was
ready to set out.

Miss Quinton's baggage was limited to few articles, and
very little time sufficed to pack them up in a small trunk ;
after which, she set out with Mrs. Alvarez, accompanied by
their military retinue ; Mrs. Jordan pursuing them, about
one hundred yards, at a hard trot, to shower upon them her
parting blessing, and vowing, that, as soon as she should
have milked her cows, she would go to the chapel to say a
pair of beads in behalf of the dare, swate crathur.

# CHAPTER XVII.

My conscience hath a thousand several tongues,
And every tongue brings in a several tale,
And every tale condemns me for a villain.
Perjury, perjury, in the highest degree ;
Murder, stern murder, in the direst degree,
Throng to the bar, crying all—guilty ! guilty !
—— Methought, the souls of all that I had murdered,
Came to my tent : and every one did threat
To-morrow's vengeance on the head of Richard.
                              *Richard III.*, *Act* 5.

OUR female travellers proceeded towards Labahia, with
great rapidity, and were already within three miles of the
place, when they stopped, to take some refreshment, under a
wide-spreading poplar, or cotton-tree, as some would call it.
It was on Palm Sunday morning, and Mrs. Alvarez, in allusion to the religious solemnity of the day,—which is one of
peculiar sanctity among the Roman Catholics,—tore a green
bough from the tree under which they were sitting, and gave
the young lady, partly by signs, and partly in broken English, to understand, that palms were consecrated, on that
holy-day, in sign of spiritual joy, and carried about in procession ; and then, in playful mood, twined a verdant crown,
which she placed on her companion's head, signifying that
she found some coincidence between the festival of the day,
and her present situation.

The sentiments which, in her disjointed mode of utterance,
she sought to express, might, if translated into correct language, have amounted to this : " After so many difficulties
and dangers, from which Divine Providence has delivered
you, you are, at last, going to meet your father, therefore
you should rejoice in God and give him your thanks." Miss
Quinton, who understood her meaning, could not help being
moved, and in a silent and impressive manner, pressed to her
bosom the hand which had been just crowning her ; when,

at that moment, both were startled by the noise of some horse-men, who were approaching at a swift rate. The ladies arose in surprise, which was soon changed into consterna-tion, upon Mrs. Alvarez recognizing her husband's favorite servant, and Miss Quinton, that of captain Letinez, with the greatest terror depicted on their countenance. The informa-tion which the new-comers hurriedly communicated increased their alarm. "For God's sake, Madam," said captain Alva-rez's servant, "mount and ride—ride on, as fast as you can : It is for life or death. They are going to shoot the prisoners ! They have marched them all out, under pretence of embark-ing them for Louisiana ; but it was merely in order that none of them should remain concealed. Captain Letinez is ab-sent, and my master has done all he could to save the life of the Texian major, who is his friend ; but he can obtain noth-ing. The latter begs to see his daughter before he dies. Only one hour is granted him.—Oh, ride on,—ride on, for Heaven's sake !"

Happily for Miss Quinton, her fortitude did not abandon her. Without shedding a tear, or making any useless la-mentations, she was soon seated in the gig. Nature, how-ever, could not long withstand the shock given to her feelings, and in less than a minute after resuming their march, she fainted away, on Mrs. Alvarez's bosom. The latter did not think proper to stop, while the old major's life was in jeopar-dy ; but, though she abated nothing of the rapidity of her march, she so successfully exerted herself with her smelling bottle, that Miss Quinton recovered her senses, just as they approached the place, whither the first lot of prisoners had been led to suffer death.

Several companies of soldiers had formed into a hollow square, in the centre of which, the Texian commander was made to sit on a low stool ; while the Mexican colonel who presided at the execution, addressed him with a degree of asperity, highly unbecoming. The address being concluded, Fanning took out his watch and a purse of gold, which he distributed to some suttlers' wives, who happened to be near the place. In the meantime, one of the soldiers appointed to shoot him, impelled by his blood-thirsty impatience, came up, and put his hand on his breast, in order to lay his bosom bare ; but Fanning, guessing at his intention, anticipated his purpose, by opening his coat and vest. Then pointing to his heart, without uttering a single word, he looked upon his executioners, with a magnanimity, of which they cannot, to this day, speak without admiration.—Now the hour of his death had come. The Mexican colonel raised his sword on high, the drums beat, the guards who attended formed into two parallel lines, the spectators, like a mighty wave receding from the foot of a cliff, with a sudden recoil, withdrew from the fatal spot, and the word was given.—There Fanning welters in his blood !—Four bullets, with fatal aim, are lodged in his heart, and, while his limbs are yet palpitating, and the muscles of his face quivering ; his executioners rush forward to divide the spoils. His clothes become an object of contention among them, and they

" Hold o'er the dead their carnival,
  Gorging and growling o'er carcass and limb."

But what was Miss Quinton doing, during this horrid scene ? She had espied her father, in the midst of a knot of prisoners, surrounded by dragoons, who kept their arms levelled at them, and in spite of all her efforts, tears and supplications, had not been able to open to herself a passage , but when Fanning fell, there was a remissness of attention on their part, and Miss Quinton taking advantage of it, crept through their ranks, and flew towards her father. She threw herself on his neck, crying out, " Father, father ! I will die with you—No ball will reach your bosom, but after having pierced mine. Oh, Heavens ! must we meet, after so long a separation, merely to die in each other's embrace ?"

Señora Alvarez had, in the meantime, sought out the commanding officer, and thrown herself at his feet, which she embraced, beseeching him to spare Major Quinton. " See, yonder, colonel," did she say, " his daughter holds him locked in her arms : you cannot reach his breast without slaughtering her.—Will you shed the blood of so innocent and beautiful a creature ? Will the most heroical filial piety ever seen, meet with no better recompence from a Mexican officer than cold blooded murder ? Have mercy, colonel— as you will, one day, wish for mercy yourself, in the presence of the everlasting God.—Oh ! have mercy, and spare him, or plunge your dagger in my bosom, and trample me under your feet."

"Women are the devil," brutally interrupted Garrafon. "This one would, now, make me weep, I believe! There-upon, Alvarez himself coming up, he called out to him: "Here, captain—Here, Alvarez—govern this wife of yours, man. She won't let me go about my duty."

"Oh! noble colonel," interrupted Alvarez: "I join my prayers to hers! I call again upon you to spare this man. Unless you do, his daughter will die along with him, and she is my friend Letinez's promised bride. He will not survive the loss!—Save him, oh! save him!—Here, I kneel to you!—I, who never knelt to man before." And suiting the action to the speech, he sank upon one knee, before Garrafon, and taking one of his hands, pressed it to his lips, and bedewed it with his tears.

"You are all mad," replied the colonel, "and make me as mad as yourselves!—By Heaven, I venture my post, and perhaps my life!—But rise up, Alvarez,—I cannot bear to see thee shedding tears. Take the man out, with his daugh-ter,—and, hark thee, carry him to the hospital and let him turn physician. Be sure to let him know the necessity of this measure!—The major must be dead and buried,—that is, shot and dead!—Hey, you take my meaning."

Thereupon, drawing near to the double line of dragoons, that surrounded the prisoners, he commanded them to open a passage for Alvarez, who immediately led away Major Quinton, thus suddenly transformed into a physician, without his own concurrence or knowledge, and soon installed him in his new employ, giving him brief instructions on the part he was to act.

They were interrupted in their conversation, by the firing of the soldiers, who continued their murderous day's work. The unfortunate prisoners were shot by fifty and sixty at a time, and those whom the musket missed, or only crip-pled, were, afterwards, despatched with the bayonet and lance.

In the second lot, were ten or twelve Catholic Irishmen, from St. Patricio, who called for a priest, but were not per-mitted to enjoy the consolation. There was a clergyman of their church, within a short distance, who might have been sent for :—A short respite was sufficient ; but their cries were not listened to. It was, according to the belief of their executioners, consigning them to the everlasting flames of hell, and yet it was done ! The cries and prayers of those unhappy men, who died, unshriven and unabsolved, melted even the rough Mexican troopers, yet the awful work went on, until the whole number of prisoners, amounting to five hundred and twenty, had been sacrificed !—Seven or eight only were saved, chiefly under the plea of being physicians, and two or three escaped by flight.

In the last lot, came two Baptist preachers, who went on exhorting their comrades. When they had reached the place where they were to suffer, the eldest called upon his companions to join him in prayer. Not one refused. Even many of the Mexicans, though unable to understand his language, fell on their knees, in imitation of the Texians.

Then, with an enthusiasm of which it is impossible for any one who was not an eye-witness to form an idea, the elder called upon God, saying : " We return unto thee, O Almighty being, who, from high Heaven, directest all things for thy greatest glory. This body, which thou gavest us, is now falling a sacrifice, because we have asserted the rights of freemen, and the liberty of thy Holy Gospel ; but, oh ! vouchsafe, thou, to receive our spirit unto thy bosom, and grant true freedom to this land which has drunk the blood of our companions in arms. Deliver it from the dark-ness that overshadows it, and inspire the people with repen-tance for their deeds of cruelty. *Thy* martyrs we are ; but lay it not to their charge. Let not our death be visited upon them. *We*, who bleed beneath their knife, beg it of thee !— Enlighten that obdurate priesthood, who have thirsted for our blood !"

Here, he was interrupted by the voice of the commander, who, in a rage, called out : " *Fuego, fuego ! Acabad con el-los.*" But yet, as the bullets whistled, and his companions fell around him, the preacher lifted up, towards heaven, his arms, now reddened with gore, and cried : " We come unto thee,—we come, O Lord !—O God of Heaven, look down upon us.—In thee we die !" He had no time to continue, for, one of the dragoons, running up to him, cleft his head at one single stroke, and was followed by his comrades, who

**16\***

frightfully hacked the dying and the dead, and soon achieved what their guns had left unfinished.

The work of destruction was now nearly over, and Garrafon's soldiers fell to rifling the pockets of the dead and stripping their bodies naked. He was himself, with an unmoved eye, surveying the frightful havoc ; and pointing, here and there, with his sword, to such of the Texians, as, by their groans or convulsive movements, showed that life had not yet departed, in order to get them despatched ; when an an Irish woman, whose only son had followed the party of the Texians, arrived from St. Patricio. As soon as she had heard of his being taken, she had abandoned every thing and set out on foot ; so that, when she reached the field of slaughter, she was nearly in a state of exhaustion. The horrible spectacle, however, seemed to act upon her as a stimulus, and she appeared to recover vigor at the sight. She paused and slowly turned round, several times—eyeing the field of blood, with awful composure—then made the sign of the cross—but, suddenly seized with a paroxysm of grief, she clapped her hands, and called aloud, with a dismal shriek ; " *Yesa ! Yesa ! Mavourneen !*"—No one answered to her call, and, in utter despair, she knelt down and began to examine the bodies of the dead.

The wildness of her manner appalled all the bystanders, so that the work of spoliation was partially suspended and a group of anxious spectators formed round her, intently looking on, while she proceeded in her examination. The fourth corpse she happened to lay her hands on was that of her son, —a youth of seventeen years of age and the only child she had. As soon as she recognized it, a convulsive shuddering came over her ; but, struggling to master her emotion, she anxiously bent over him and began to wipe the blood from his face. At that moment, the Mexican commander came up to rebuke the loiterers. At the sound of his voice, no longer mistress to contain herself, she called upon him by name ; " Come here, Garrafon !—come, and look at him !—My only child ! You have murdered him !—Slay me, also.—Monster," added she, taking, in the hollow of her hand, some of the blood that lay in puddles, at her feet, and casting it upon the murderous wretch ; " I mark thee with the blood of my son. It shall be upon thee as long as thou

livest, and may every drop of it burn to thy heart's core, until hell shall claim its own"—But we draw the curtain upon
this frightful scene. Be it sufficient to say that she was im-
molated upon the body of the son whose loss she deplored,
and this last act of savage cruelty filled the measure of horror.

In that indiscriminate slaughter, perished also young
Brashears and Duval, whom Marinez, the officer we have
already honorably mentioned, had promised to protect. He
would have saved their lives, had he been present, but care
had been taken to send him upon a remote expedition and
when he returned he found his friend already dead.

Dear unfortunate young men ! May the tear which bedews
this page prove to your manes how beloved you were by one
who had trod the same academic groves with you, and while
your bones are bleaching on the grassy plain of Goliad, may
these few lines, consecrated to your memory, convey to the
heart of every one who reads them, sentiments of detestation
for the act of cruelty of which you were the victims. May
the execration of the civilized world for ever pursue the man
of blood who consigned you to an untimely death, and blast
his name with infamy. You were cut off in the bloom of
youth,—amidst thousand curses, and your agonizing groans
were heard with derision by your murderers.—The wild dog
gnawed your heart and lapped your blood, and cannibals
danced over your mangled limbs, still your memory shall be
honored by a whole nation, and your name shall be a signal
for deeds of worth, to generations yet unborn,—still the remembrance of your death will nerve your fellow citizens to
fight for that freedom in the defence of which you fell. Land
of Kentucky, country of my youth, these have extended thy
moral empire ! They have concurred to found a new home
in the south for thy numerous progeny. Oh, forget them
not in thy records of fame.

> " —Egregias animas, quæ sanguine nobis
> Hanc patriam peperere suo, decorate supremis
> Muneribus."*

*\* Virgil.*

# NOTES TO VOLUME I.

Note 1, *page* 10.—*The Sierra Madre* may be considered as a continuation of the Andes of Peru, which, in the states of Mexico and Puebla divide themselves into two large chains—the western one running due north, at the average distance of one hundred leagues from the Pacific ocean, and the eastern chain following the sinuosities of the gulf of Mexico, at the same respective distance, till it is lost, in the state of Cohahuila, in the immense plains watered by the Rio Bravo. The highest peaks are found in the vicinity of Mexico, and in the state of Puebla, at the junction of the two chains, and are the Ixtacihuatl, (white woman,) and the great volcano of Popocateptl, which is 6083 "varas Mexicanas" above the level of the sea. (The Spanish vara is thirty two and a half inches English.) The limits of vegetation are at 1852 varas above the city of Mexico, and 4541 above the ocean. The *ribes odoratum*, a species of blackberry, is the last plant found on the sides of the mountain."

Note 2, *page* 11.—There are in the Mexican republic two universities, one in Guadalaxara and the other, in the city of Mexico, itself. Besides these, there is a college in every Episcopal city, maintained out of a contribution raised on the secular clergy. The city of Mexico anciently boasted seven seminaries of learning. In three of them a good literary education might be got, but the exact sciences, except chemistry, were rather neglected. The *seminario* possessed a good library—thirteen professors, who were secular priests, and 260 lay students, with about 20 ecclesiastical ones. *San Juan de Leteran* had seven professors and about eighty students. The other seminaries were trifling and not worth mentioning. In all the great colleges, the king maintained a number of bursars, who, after their education was terminated, became the objects of the special patronage of government. Frequently, too, some rich bachelor would adopt some promising young man, from among them, and make him his heir. None but Spaniards by birth were thus favored.

Note 3, *page* 13.—Don Vasco de Quiroga civilized the Indians of his extensive diocese, and instructed them, not only in the Christian religion, but in all the neccessary arts, and to this day, the Tarascos and other nations of Mechoacan call him *Tata Don Vasco*, and cherish his memory with deep veneration. His tomb, or rather shrine, is in the beautiful island of Tzintzontzan, in the middle of the lake of Pascuaro. It has been the lot of that Bishopric to have a succession of prelates who were men of genius. The present Bishop, Don Juan Guetano Portugal, is the only man of superior talents in the Mexican Church. He has reformed his clergy and set them on a somewhat more respectable footing than they are elsewhere. His predecessor, Senor de San Miguel, of whom Humboldt makes very honorable mention, originated the plan for the general and final enfranchisement of the Indians, and it is upon the rules he laid down, that the various state legislatures have acted since the revolution.

Note 4, *page* 13.—The Virgin of Guadelupe, which is a very coarse and ill executed painting, on a rude fabric of pita thread, was found by a pious Indian, of the name of Juan Diego, on the spot, where, in the reign of Montezuma, had stood the temple of the goddess Tonantzin. At the same time, a supernatural being, supposed to be the Virgin, appeared to this individual, commanding him to go to the Archbishop of Mexico, and direct him, by her order, to build a church on that spot, in honor of the aforesaid image. As Diego required some sign to prove to the Archbishop the truth of his mission, the mysterious being gave him a handkerchief full of fresh roses, which was a miraculous proof, it being then a season when roses are not in bloom.

The image was first placed in an hermitage, where now stand the houses of the servants and sacristan. It was, afterwards, translated to a chapel, which forms the vestry-room of the old church. In the month of November, 1622, a third church was dedicated, on the spot where had stood the first hermitage, and the present fabric was begun in 1695.

In 1750, it was erected into a collegiate, with a number of prebendaries, and a prelate who enjoys the title of Abbot. The capital for the dotation of the chapter was of $533,882, left by Don Andrew Palencia. The Spanish government took the money and bound itself to pay the interest to the chapter, at the rate of five per cent., out of the king's share of the tithes of the dioceses of Puebla and Mexico. The votive offerings, in wax candles alone, amount to a prodigious sum, and there is no sacrifice which the Indians and Creoles are not ready to make for this image, which is for them, a type of their nationality, and with which they suppose the honor of their race intimately connected.

The present church was dedicated on the tenth of June, 1709. The building alone, without the sanctuary and sacristy, cost $490,000, which were collected by voluntary offerings. The silver gilt throne upon which the miraculous image is placed weighs 1628 pounds, and behind the painting is a plate of the same metal, of one hundred weight. The principal tabernacle cost $19,000. The effigy of the Virgin is clearly seen at a distance, but, when the spectator is close to it, nothing can he distinguished. This singularity is accounted a standing miracle. It is owing to the image being painted on a very *hirsute* fabric, but it would be highly imprudent to account to the Mexicans, in this natural manner, for this singular appearance.

NOTE 5, *page* 17.—*Vino mescal* is a kind of brandy, with a strong empyreumatic taste, distilled from the fermented juice of the *Agave Americana*, large plantations of which exist in the states of Puebla and Mexico, some of them so important as to afford an annual income of seventy or eighty thousand dollars. The singular plant which furnishes this liquor flowers but once, and dies immediately after, but if the stem, which is to support the bunch of flowers, be cut, before it begins to mount, the plant gives out, during three months, a sweetish liquid, which, being fermented into a kind of small beer, is used under the name of *pulque*, as the general beverage, in the southern provinces of Mexico, and this being distilled constitutes the *vino mescal*. The pulque is generally supposed to be a very wholesome drink, but its smell is unpleasant.

NOTE 6, *page* 21.—Pascuaro, situated on the banks of the lake to which it gives its name, at an elevation of six thousand feet above the level of the sea, has a population of seven or eight thousand souls. Here was the seat of a large Indian kingdom, quite independent from the empire of Montezuma, when the Spaniards entered the country.

NOTE 7, *page* 23.—Tzintzontzan, or Huitzitzilla, was the Athens of Mechoacan, before the conquest. The Indians of these parts were more advanced than the Aztecs, in certain branches of knowledge, and, to this day, some of them cultivate astronomy with success. The population of the town amounts only to fifteen hundred souls.

NOTE 8, *page* 24.—Valladolid, the metropolis of the department of Morelia, and a Bishop's see, is situated in a delightful climate, in latitude 19 deg. 45 min., about five thousand feet above the level of the sea. This city is embellished with a splendid aqueduct which cost the late Bishop one hundred thousand dollars. The population amounts to twenty thousand souls.

NOTE 9, *page* 36.—Catorce, or la *purisima conception* de *Alamos de Catorce*, is a mining town, among the richest in Mexico, known only since the year 1773, when its veins of silver were discovered by Sebastian Coronado, and Antonio de Zepeda. At one time, this place produced five millions of dollars annually. The mining operations are now, in a great measure, suspended, in consequence of the unsettled state of the country; but the mines are far from being exhausted. Some of the works are on the most magnificent scale. The *socabon grande*, in particular, which is roofed over with wrought stone, is large enough for a loaded wagon to drive from one extremity to the other, and can vie with the *cloaca Maxima* of ancient Rome.

NOTE 10, *page* 49.—The Mexican Jesuits. Charles III. held, in 1767, a secret extraordinary council, composed of the Marquis de Roda, secretary of state, the Count of Aranda, president of the council of Castille, the Count of Florida blanca, the Count of Campomanes, the Archbishops of Burgos and Saragossa, and the Bishops of Tarrazona, Albarrazin and Orihuela, in which the expulsion of the Jesuits, from all the Spanish dominions, was unanimously resolved, but the secret was so strictly kept, that the Jesuits never suspected it. On the night of the 24th of June, in the same year, under the Viceroy, Marquis of Croix, the Mexican Jesuits received intimation of the decree of expulsion, and all the professed members of the institute were embarked for the Pope's dominions. Their church, in Mexico, was given to the Philipini, and their extensive landed possessions were sold for the benefit of the crown. In the colonies, they had done much more good and less harm than in Europe. To them the Indians of California owe the degree of civilization they enjoy and the country, at large, what little literature it possesses. Among the old Mexican Jesuits who have left a reputation, may be mentioned Alegre, Abad, Campoy and Clavigero. A strange phenomenon attended their expulsion. On the eve of their departure, it snowed in the streets of Mexico. This was looked upon as a miracle.

NOTE 11, *page* 59.—The Mexican inquisition. This dreadful tribunal existed in Mexico till 1815, and the last *auto da fe*, was held upon Morelos, himself a priest, and the most talented of the insurgent generals. The following are authentic accounts of several Autos da Fe celebrated by the Mexican inquisition.

It was solemnly established on the 11th of November, 1571, and three years afterwards, it held its first *auto*, in which sixty-three culprits appeared, five of whom were burned. From the last mentioned date, to 1604, it held publicly nine *autos* more.

On the 16th of April, 1646, and the 30th of March, 1648, there were two others, in the ·first whereof appeared fifty penitents, and in the second, twenty eight, nearly all accused of Judaism. But it was on the 11th of April, 1649, that was held the most famous ever seen in Mexico. An immense scaffold was constructed in the public square *del Volador*, and the ceremony was graced with the presence of all the corporations and persons of rank in the city. The sermon was preached by a Bishop of Cuba, on the text " *Peace be with you.*" In this auto there were a Lutheran, thirty-nine persons guilty of Judaism, and seventy-seven statues representing culprits, who had either fled or died. Of the Jews twelve were burned, although *they had recanted.* The only favor showed them, on that account, was to strangle them before throwing them into the flames. Among them were six women. An old Castilian, of the name of Thomas Treviño de Sobremonte, a wealthy merchant who could never be brought to recant, was burned alive, in the plazuela de San Diego. The culprits who were not burned were condemned to the confiscation of their property, whipping and exile. Ten years afterwards, there was another *act of faith*, celebrated in the great square. The Viceroy Duque of Albuquerque, was present. This auto was graced by twenty-nine culprits and a statue representing an absent. Two men were strangled and four burned alive. Among the latter was an Irishman, of the name of Lamport. The remainder were condemned to confiscation, whipping and exile.

Upon examining the records of that abominable tribunal, one does not know what most to wonder at,—its horrid cruelty, or extravagant puerility. A distinguished physician, of the name of Santa Maria, was ordered to be taken into custody, for having advised giving a patient who was recovering from a fainting fit, a cup of broth, in preference to extreme unction. A poor woman was taken up for having washed a statue of St. Anthony of Padua in brine, in order to obtain rain, after a long drought. Another, for having made a little dragon of black felt, to keep rats out of her garret. But the most melancholy case of all, perhaps, was that of a baptized Indian, who received thirty-nine lashes for having said that, in spite of all that St. Francis and St. Dominic had done, the moon was still the wife of the Sun, and brought forth a star every month !

NOTE 12, *page* 82.—The civil year, among the old Mexicans, was divided into eighteen months, of twenty days each, and five intercallary days, called *Nemonteni*—something like the *sans culotides* of the French revolutionary calendar. We give here the correspondence of that system with the Gregorian.

| | | |
|---|---|---|
| 1st day of the month Titit Itzcalli . | 9 January. |
| " Itzcalli Xochilhuitl . . . | 29 January. |
| " Xilomanalitzli . . . | 18 February. |
| " Tlacaxipehualitzli . . . | 10 March. |
| " Tozoztontli . . . . | 30 March. |
| " Hueytozotli . . . . | 19 April. |
| " Toxcatl . . . . . | 9 May. |
| " Etzalqualitzli . . . . | 29 May. |
| " Tecuihuiltontli . . . . | 19 June. |
| " Hueytecuiltontli . . . . | 8 July. |
| " Micailhuitontli . . . . | 28 July. |
| " Heymixcaithuilt . . . . | 17 August.[1] |
| " Ochpanitzli . . . . | 6 September. |
| " Patch . . . . . | 26 September. |
| " Hueypactli . . . . | 16 October. |
| " Quecholli . . . . | 5 November. |
| " Panquetzaliztli . . . . | 25 November. |
| " Atemoztli . . . . | 15 December. |

The grand cycle of years for the Mexicans consisted of fifty two, as ours does of one hundred ; but they never reckoned them by odd numbers. They knew that the solar revolution exceeded their civil year by six hours, and after the termination of each cycle of years, they intercallated thirteen days, before beginning again the first month of the following cycle. Every fifth day was a market day.

Independently of this manner of reckoning time, they had another, which was purely lunar, and constituted their religious year. How the old Mexicans had come by so improved a manner of regulating their civil year, is a mystery, that shall never perhaps be cleared up ; but it was not certainly of their own invention, and denotes a people far more advanced in civilization than they were.

NOTE 13, *page* 91.—The atmosphere is so dry in Mexico, on the table land, that it is indispensable to water the wheels of carriages, every day, otherwise they would shrink and fall to pieces. The wheels of Mexican carriages are exceedingly clumsy, but very solid and better able to resist the atmosphere of the country, than the more elegant ones imported from the United States.

NOTE 14, *page* 94.—Hidalgo, parish priest of Dolores, was the first who raised the standard of rebellion, or independence, against the Spanish government on the 16th of September, 1810. He owed a grudge to the King of Spain, by whose order an extensive vineyard he had planted, near the town of which he was pastor, had been destroyed. It was, in great measure, in order to avenge that injury, he entered the first conspiracy with Allende,

Abasolo and others. Some of the latter were practical military men, but, as Hidalgo's popularity, on account of his ecclesiastical character, was of more importance, he was declared generalissimo, and, in a few weeks, raised a body of more than seventy thousand men, badly armed, indeed, but so fanatically devoted to the cause thay had espoused, that, in many instances, they ran up to the cannons' mouth, and, in their ignorance, crammed their hats into them to stop the balls. At their head, Hidalgo advanced as far as the city of Mexico, which he would have taken, had not his heart failed him. After this, he was repeatedly defeated, taken, at Bajan, while on his way to the United States, degraded from the priesthood, and shot at Chihuahua.

NOTE 15, *page* 99.—*Mesteno*, which the inhabitants of Texas have anglicised into Mustang, is the designation of the wild horse, immense flocks of which are found in the *Haciendas* of the Northern States.

NOTE 16, *page* 110.—St. Philip of Neri established a society of priests, who are bound together by no vows, and can leave the institute whenever they please. They contrive, nevertheless, to stick together very closely. Their principal avocations consists in instructing the ignorant, by preaching, cathechising, and giving spiritual exercises. When the Jesuits were suppressed, their churches and houses were mostly given to the Philipini. Among those buildings was the *Professa*, one of the most sumptuous edifices in Mexico, and upon which the Jesuits had spent more than a million of dollars.

NOTE 17, *page* 182.—The *Virgin de los Remedios* is, next to that of Guadelupe, the Madona who enjoys the greatest reputation, in New Spain, although she labors under the disadvantage of being *Gachupina*, id est, imported from Europe. It is a small statue which one of the soldiers of Cortez carried about with him, as a safeguard. When that general was obliged to effect that disastrous retreat, distinguished in history, under the name of *Noche triste*, during which so many of his soldiers were taken and offered in sacrifice to Vitzliputzli ; the owner of this little Madona succeeded in making his escape, and having fled up the mountain, dropped the image, which was picked up by his pursuers and treated with great honor. They constructed for it a little shrine, under a nopal, decked it with flowers and burnt perfumes before it. The Spaniards, at their return, finding the virgin had been treated so handsomely by their enemies, looked upon it as a miracle, and thought it incumbent upon them not to be behind hand. In process of time, a splendid church was built for that statue, on the spot in which it had been found—

some miles distant from the city—whence she is, in times of drought, inundations and other public calamities, brought to the Cathedral of Mexico, in procession. As late as 1836, under the government of chief-justice Corro, this Madona was brought down from her sanctuary, with an extraordinary display of magnificence, and when, at a later period, her jewels were stolen, that theft was looked upon as a *national calamity.*

NOTE 18, *page 178.*—*The Holy Cross* of Queretaro is a convent of Missionaries, of considerable celebrity, called *Cruciferos,* from the name of their principal church. This establishment, as well as that of Guadelupe, six miles from Zacatecas, has furnished a great number of zealous preachers, who have propagated a knowledge of the Christian religion and civilization, among the northern Indians, as far as Taos. Many of those friars were men of no despicable attainments, in literature and the exact sciences, and have written works that throw great light upon the History of the Northern tribes. Humboldt, in his political essay on New Spain, and in other works, frequently quotes the *Cronica Serafica* of the cruciferos, besides which, he availed himself of several manuscripts written by members of this fraternity, and preserved in the convent of Santa Cruz. These two establishments had kept up their respectability and usefulness till the political dissensions which have desolated the Mexican republic. They were unexceptionable in point of morality, and the most prejudiced man could not visit them, without being edified. They were a proof that Convents might do much good, and be a blessing to mankind, if their members were made strictly to observe their rules.

Queretaro was one of the largest cities in New-Spain, having had, at one time, a population of fifty thousand inhabitants. It owed its flourishing condition to the manufacture of woolen and cotton goods. The introduction of the power-loom in other parts of the Mexican republic has ruined its trade, and the population has dwindled down to twenty thousand. The Departamento of which it is the capital, is one of the smallest of the republic, but well cultivated.

NOTE 19, *page 176.*—*Zacatecas,* the metropolis of a Departamento, or state, of the same name, is a large and magnificent city, of about forty thousand souls population, situate in a mountainous district abounding in silver mines. The town is built in a deep *barranco,* or ravine, and the streets are very irregular ; but the splendor of several of the edifices is astonishing. At the distance of twelve miles from Zacatecas, is found the city of Fresnillo, another mining town of great importance, boasting a population of twenty four thousand inhabitants. Its mines were abandoned for several years, after the exile of the Spaniards; but, of late, the works have been re-established on an improved plan, and immense profits realized.

All the region, north of this state, to the Bolson of Mapimi, possesses immense deposits of precious ore, the half of which has not, probably, been yet discovered. The richest mine ever known was found in this district. It was the *black vein* of Sombrerete, out of which the family of Fagoaga netted seven millions of dollars, in half a year. Most of the ores of these parts can be wrought without the use of mercury, a circumstance which renders the miners less dependant on foreign countries, and increases their profits. Were improved machinery introduced in all the places where there is a sufficiency of water and fuel, the product of those mines would be greatly increased, and the agricultural interest of the fertile district at the mouth of the river Nasas, and of part of Cohahuila, greatly promoted.

Since the revolution, three great impediments to the development of the mining enterprise of the country have been removed : first, the duty on silver, which, under the Spanish domination, amounted to seven per cent., has been reduced to three ; secondly, quicksilver, indispensable for amalgation with certain qualities of ores, has been made duty free ; and thirdly, several mints have been established in the northern states, such as Zacatecas, Durango, &c. Independently of these changes, an immense quantity of foreign capital was introduced ; but, on the other hand, the mining industry of the country received a fatal blow by the exile of the Spaniards, who were the principal owners of the mines, and carried away more than one hundred and forty millions of dollars.

The foreign mining companies in Mexico have nearly all proved unprofitable speculations. The first was established by British capitalists, in 1823. Others soon followed, till they amounted to ten :—seven English, two American, and one German. They have spent twelve millions of dollars, in draining old mines ; introducing expensive machinery, which, in nine cases out of ten, has proved useless for want of fuel ; and importing miners from England, who are far less useful than the Indians. In consequence of so much mismanagement, these companies have sunk an immense capital and totally failed in their expectations. The German association has been the only one that has met with success, owing to the judicious manner in which it has been conducted. In spite of all these discouraging failures, the mines of Mexico are far from being exhausted, and should the country be blessed again with peace and a stable government, it might annually produce as much bullion as it did before the revolution. In the single mint of Zacatecas, they coined fifty four millions of dollars, from 1810 to 1827, though in the midst of civil war, and since that period, some new mines have been discovered in the north, which are amazingly rich. At *Sorrillo*, on the borders of Durango and Chihuahua, a vein of silver ore, on the side of a mountain, was laid bare by a tornado, nine years ago, and it bids fair to rival the famous *veta rica* of Potosi. In consequence of this discovery, a town of twenty thousand souls has already grown on that spot, and is increasing every day. The attention of skilful miners has been lately directed, in a special manner, to the northwest, and they have ascertained that the greatest mineral wealth extends in that direction, far beyond Sonora, and that the ores are richer than those of the south.

It is a great mistake to believe that the labor of the mines is compulsory. That system, which was known in Peru under the name of *Mita*, was never introduced in Mexico. The miners hire themselves to the owners of mines, like other free laborers, and are paid in proportion to the quantity of work they perform. Sometimes they work on shares ; the common rate, in that case, being to give the Indian miners the half of the ore they extract. They prefer this mode of being paid to any other, because it affords them a chance of great profit, and frequently, too, greater facility for pilfering.

NOTE 20, *page* 178.—The Guadelupe river takes its source in the highlands, between the district of Bexar and the territory anciently allotted to Milam's new grant ; then passes between Austin's second grant, and the region that formed the department of Bexar ; next, through the western half of de Witt's grant, and the eastern half of de Leon's, and lastly, mingles its waters with the river San Antonio, ten miles from the northwestern head of the Bay of Espiritu Santo. Its course is, in all, two hundred and fifty miles, and its waters are limpid and wholesome.

The principal branches of this stream, as we ascend it, are on the east. The Techocote, Peach, San Marcos, remarkable for the romantic scenery of its banks, which remind the traveller of the stupendous marble cliffs on the Kentucky river, Cedro and Piedras. On the west are the Colete, Cuchillo, Carizo, Fuente and Sabinas. There are good waterfalls for mill seats, on the head branches, but hardly any on the main stream, since, for uniformity of current and depth of water, it surpasses all the other rivers of Texas.

The Rio San Antonio, which joins the Guadelupe, as we have already said, twelve miles from Espiritu Santo Bay, flows over a rocky bottom, with a clear translucent stream, until it meets the Medina, twenty five miles below Bexar. The Medina, which is really the main trunk, heads in the south-east corner of Wood-burry and Co's grant, and crosses the western half of the county of Bexar, and the territory anciently allotted to de Leon's grant; having a course of two hundred miles, before it joins the river Guadelupe. Were it not for the shallow bay, at its mouth, it would bear vessels of considerable importance, one hundred and twenty miles up, to its junction with the San Antonio. The river Guadelupe labors under the same disadvantage; neverthe-less steamboats of a light draught of water ascended it as far as Victoria, which greatly favors the commerce of that place, and renders it the emporium of the west. The land on both banks of the Guadelupe consists of a good prairie soil, with rich wood-lands, but somewhat subject to inundations. On this river is also situated the town of Gonzales, anciently the capital of de Witt's colony, nearly one hundred miles from the northwest head of Matagorda Bay. This town is built between two large prairies of exuberant fertility, the northwest and southeast bor-ders of which are beautifully variagated by groves of live oak, post oak and honey locust, with knolls of the finest building stones; the whole abundantly watered by fine springs. For salubrity of climate, fertility of soil, and beauty of scenery, it is surpassed by no other locality in Texas, Bexar only excepted.

The second great river, as we advance eastwardly, which is the largest in the republic, and divides its territory into two nearly equal portions, is the *Colorado*, which rises in Cameron's second grant, in the northwest, and disembogues into Matagorda bay, after a southeast course of four hundred and fifty miles.

Its principal branches, as we ascend it on the east, are Cum-ming, Duty, Rabb, Pine, Honey, Hunting, Bear, Petcon, Wiss-hauca and Pasigono. On the west, are Jennings', Ralls', Scull, Williams', Buckner, Pine, Bonillo, Garapatos, Piederuales, San Josè, Almagro, San Saba, and Piedra Pinta, which last stream is celebrated among the Indian tribes that inhabit Texas, for its *enchanted rocks*, which they suppose to be the abode of certain genii of the same nature as the fairies of the old hemisphere.

The Colorado is very rapid, and its bed is crossed in many places by ledges of calcareous rocks, rendering its navigation difficult in dry seasons. In moderate stages of water, however, vessels of one hundred tons burthen can ascend it to its falls, about one hundred and fifty miles from its mouth. Its banks are steep and high, and although the water sometimes rises thirty feet, they are seldom overflowed. The hilly district through which the upper half of the Colorado flows, and from which it receives its principal branches, creates so many falls and of such consequence, as are seldom met with in other coun-tries, never being obstructed by overflows at any season of the year. The bed of this river is crossed by veins of stone coal, not far from Bastrop.

Near the mouth of the Colorado, we find Matagorda, a port of entry, the population of which amounts now to about seven hundred souls. When the raft, at the mouth of the river, will be removed, its commerce cannot fail to become important, as it will then become the emporium of all the country bordering on this stream.

Seventy miles north by west from Matagorda, we find Bastrop, on the east side of the Colorado, between Austin's first colony and his second one, and not far from the latter, the city of Austin, now the capital of the republic, in the centre of a rich district of country, and with natural facilities for commerce seldom enjoyed by inland towns.

The next important river, as we advance eastwardly, is the Brazos, on the banks of which, towards its mouth, are the richest and most dense settlements in the republic. It heads in the desert prairies of the northwestern part of Texas and in Cameron's first grant, running a course of five hundred miles. Its principal tributaries on the east are Buffalo, Pond, Walnut, Navasoto, Little Brazos, Tahuacaro, Noland, Red Fork, Tierras Blancas, Incoque, Tosohunova, and Timpisaracha. On the west are Varner, Big, Palmeto, Caney, Cedar, Yegua, Clampit, San Andres, Bosque, Cedral and Palo Pinto. Its western branch crosses a salt lake, situated in latitude 33 deg. and in longitude 23 deg. 20 min.

Around this lake, the land is impregnated with chloride of sodium and nitrate of potassa, which, in the dry season, when the waters of the lake are evaporated, incrust the superficies of the ground in prodigious quantity. But when the rains are abundant, the overflowing of this lake renders the whole river Brazos brackish, and its waters retain that taste until a rise in the fresh water branches neutralizes this brackishness. This river is navigable by steamboats five hundred miles, during the best part of the year, and were it not for the bar, at the entrance, ships drawing sixteen feet water could ascend as far as Columbia, fifty miles from its mouth.

On this river are found San Felipe de Austin, in latitude 29 deg. 50 min. and longitude 19 deg. 5 min. This town, one of the oldest in Texas, contains a population of one thousand souls, and is situated on the northeast side of a rich prairie.

The second town is Columbia, which, throughout the whole season, commands the trade of one of the most fertile districts in the republic, already famous for its fine cotton, and no less adapted to the production of sugar.

Brazoria, twelve miles below Columbia, on the same side of

the Brazos, has been of considerable consequence, but is now fast going to decay.

The river Trinidad, which comes next, heads in the northeast of Texas, near the Red river of Louisiana, in Cameron's first grant, passing through Filisola's grant, the western half of Burnet's and the western division of Whelin's, and entering Galveston Bay, after a course of three hundred miles. Its principal branches on the east are Turtle, Self, Big Cushate, Walnut, Hurricane and Big Prairie. On the west, Oak, Bidais, Bear and Triad. Its current is gentle, smooth and uninterupted by falls, which gives peculiar facilities for steamboat navigation. On the Trinidad are found the towns of Crocket, a thriving village, not far from the forks of the river. Liberty, beautifully situated, on the east side of the stream, thirty miles from its mouth, and eighty from the Sabine, and Anahuac, located on a high prairie bluff, southeast of Galveston Bay, opposite the mouths of the Trinidad. Galveston, on the island of the same name, the principal sea-port of the republic, is situated nearly at the mouth of the Bay, and boasts a population of about three thousand souls, with a commerce that increases every day.

The Rio Neches rises in the northern part of Burnet's grant, passes through the northeast corner of Whelin's, through the centre of Zavala's and empties itself into the Sabine lake, entering it by its northwest corner. Its principal tributaries are, on the east, the Ayish Bayou, Atoyac, Angelina, Nana and Big Salt. On the west, are Charles, Big Alabama, Pine, and San Pedro. The Neches is the largest tributary of the Sabine lake, and navigable at all times, for such craft as can cross that inlet of the sea, one hundred miles inland.

The Sabine, which divides Texas from Louisiana, heads in the eastern parts of the republic, between Milam's first grant and Filisola's, and, after a course of one hundred and fifty miles, enters the lake of the same name. It is, at certain seasons of the year, navigable for steamboats, up to Gaines' ferry, on the road from Natchitoches to San Augustine. It has more uniformity in the depth of its water than any other river in Texas, and seldom overflows its banks.

Of the secondary rivers, none, at present, claims much attention, except, perhaps the San Jacinto, which, after a course of seventy-five miles, through the eastern part of Austin's first grant, mingles its waters with those of Bayou Buffalo, and disembogues into an arm of Galveston Bay. The banks of this stream are deep, and its tributaries few ; therefore it is seldom overflows, but when southerly winds prevail, the waters of the bay back its current for some distance, and communicate to it a brackish taste. Bayou Buffalo rises also in the eastern parts of Austin's first grant and has a course of forty miles. It is deep, with a slow current, and though very narrow, is navigable for steamboats, which go as far as the city of Houston. This place, the commerce of which is increasing with great rapidity, boasts a population of nearly five thousand souls. It is very sickly, in the summer, and the yellow fever has already manifested its fatal influence there, for several successive years, yet the fertility of the surrounding district of country is such, that its growth has been unchecked.

The other minor streams are the Navedad, on the western side of Austin's first grant, with a course of one hundred and twenty miles, meandering through an undulated country and joining the la Baca, fifteen miles from Matagorda Bay. It is navigable to the junction, for all vessels which can ascend the upper side of that Bay.

The la Baca is a beautiful stream, though narrow . often shallow, but never dry, and seventy-five miles in length.

The St. Bernard, which anciently gave its name to a bay, on this coast, supposed to have been the same as that of Matagorda, rises in Austin's first grant, half way between the waters of the Brazos and Colorado, and after a course of one hundred miles, enters the gulf of Mexico, twelve miles west of the Brazos.

Cane creek is sixty miles in length and heads near the Colorado, on its eastern side. It passes within less than a mile of the northeast corner of Matagorda Bay, before entering the gulf. During two thirds of the year, it is navigable, thirty miles inland, for boats drawing four feet water.

The Aransasu rises in [the southeast point of M'Mullen's grant, and the southwestern part of what formed the department of Bexar. Vessels of such draught as can enter the northeast prong of Aransasu Bay can ascend this river about ten miles. At its entrance into the bay, we find the town of Refugio, now improving rapidly, and seven miles below, Copano, that, before the declaration of independence, was the port through which a lucrative smuggling trade was carried on, between Texas and the regions bordering on the Rio Bravo.

# AMBROSIO DE LETINEZ,

## THE FIRST TEXIAN NOVEL,

EMBRACING

## A DESCRIPTION OF THE COUNTRIES BORDERING ON THE RIO BRAVO,

WITH

## INCIDENTS OF THE WAR OF INDEPENDENCE.

### BY A. T. MYRTHE.

"The fourteenth century pitted against the nineteenth."
DON DIEGO DEL CHILE.

### VOL. II.

PUBLISHED BY CHARLES FRANCIS & Co., 252 BROADWAY.

GEORGE W. WOOD & CO., PRINTERS, 45 GOLD ST.

## 1842.

# AMBROSIO DE LETINEZ.

## CHAPTER I.

Nero is an angler in the lake of darkness.
*King Lear*, Act III.

The march of Urrea's division through the south-west portion of Texas was like the passage of an army of Cossacks. Every thing of a movable nature was pillaged. Flocks of horned cattle, of which that country contained, at the time of the invasion, a quantity sufficient to support the Mexican army, five or six years, were, every night, slaughtered in wanton prodigality,—a fat bullock being sometimes killed, for the sake of a favorite piece of meat, for which some of the officers happened. to have a craving, and the rest of the carcass being left to rot, without benefitting any body. Forgetting that, sooner or later, they would be obliged to return the same way, and miss, then, the provisions they were *now* wasting, they proceeded destroying every thing they could not use and laying the country bare.

In proportion as they advanced eastwardly and drew nearer to the American settlements, they found articles with the use of which they were totally unacquainted, and that *piqued* their curiosity, no less than they awakened their avarice. At the Mission del Refugio, even before reaching Goliad, they happened to see some frame houses, belonging to Irish settlers, with glass windows and painted Venetian blinds, and as window-glass is an exceedingly rare article, in Mexico, this struck the minds of the common soldiers as the ne plus ultra of magnificence. But when they reached Victoria, on the Guadelupe river, their expectations rose still higher, at the sight of some brick buildings two stories in height, and their covetousness was excited by the opening of some large stores full of merchandise.

The general, however, and his officers took care to have the picking of the choicest, and the common soldiers—though possessed of the best will in the world—obtained but indifferent gleanings after them ; being obliged to content themselves with coarse, frail, or unwieldy articles.  To them was abandoned the iron and crockery ware, as well as most of the glass furniture, and with such goods as these, they loaded their wives and the sumpter-mules which they secretly appropriated to themselves.  The immense number of women who followed the army, in fact, diminished the necessity of beasts of burden.  Every one of them immediately upon getting what she considered a valuable lot, would return to Matamoros—sometimes, on horseback—sometimes, in an ox-cart—but more frequently, on foot ; tottering under the load she carried.

Then also the desertions became more frequent.  Some men shaved their upper lip, and put on female apparel—the costume of Mexican women, which admits of a shawl being partly drawn over the face, favoring the deception, and the style of features being nearly as coarse in one sex as in the other.  Thus, dozens of tender couples, in disguise, would pass through the outposts, in the character of females, returning from a rag fair, and loaded with trumpery.  One man was seen with a load of smoothing irons, walking with an elastic step and a radiant countenance, as though he had been carrying away all the riches of Louisiana, while his wife groaned under a burden of crockery ware, exclusively consisting of tea-pots.  Another had loaded the massive feet of a billiard-table, upon a mule he had stolen, and put a parcel of empty bottles on the top to complete his cargo.  But the most ludicrous spectacle was afforded by a corporal who carried on his back a large Yankee clock, the weights of which dangled down to the calves of his legs, against which they thumped at every step he took.  Sorely vexed, the poor man cursed the weights, but durst not throw them away, in the idea that it was indispensable to keep the clock continually going, and that by stopping her, she would be spoiled for ever.  The smartest, however, at this kind of work was Urrea himself, who, though acting on a larger scale, fell sometimes into no less ludicrous mistakes.

After crossing the Guadelupe river, and pillaging the town of Victoria, he resolved to wait awhile for the troops he had left behind at Goliad. Whilst waiting for them, he sent his scouts about to sweep the country, and one of these soon returned with the strange information, that he had found a breed of hornless cows, which, he had been assured, gave an immense quantity of milk. As the general had never before heard of this breed of cattle, he was rather dubious of the truth of the information, and one of his officers warned him against the artifices of those Jews, the *colonists*, who, most probably, had dealings with Sathanas, and might have contrived this, in order to entrap him. Being, however, what the Spaniards denominate *un espiritu fuerte*, (anglice, an unbeliever,) Urrea made it a point to see with his own eyes, and commanded some of the above-mentioned cows to be brought into his presence. The cows came, and after he had examined their heads, and convinced himself that there was no deception in the case, he was delighted with this *phenomenon* in natural history, as he termed it, and seized upon forty of these highly privileged animals, which he sent, under an escort, to stock a hacienda he owned, in the state of Sonora.

The country about the Guadelupe river is the most fertile it is possible to imagine ; but being somewhat swampy, it is inferior in point of salubrity, to the district about Bexar, and the river San Anton, which may be considered as destined to become the paradise of North America. To the most salubrious climate, it unites the most enchanting scenery, consisting of an elegant mixture of hill and dale, watered by large springs, which furnish abundant supplies for irrigation. The temperature is such, that winters are hardly felt, and two yearly crops of Indian corn are the regular tribute of husbandry. The sugar cane lasts eight years, and a certain species of cotton, three ; their product being superior in quality to what is grown in Louisiana. To all these advantages, is to be added the facility of raising cattle, the wild grass being so excellent and abundant, that they multiply without any care on the part of the owner. And then the fruits ! From the orange and *chirimoya*, of southern climes, to the apple and pear of northern regions ; the immense variety of Pomona's gifts embellishes this land, and enriches the husbandman. The most delightful districts of the south of France, with all the wealth and refinement which ages of civilization have accumulated, do not deserve to be compared with this blessed spot, such as it is even now, when its natural resources have hardly begun to be developed : nor could the island of Calypso herself, in the fabled description of Fenelon, enter into competition.

It was of such a land as this, the poet of the seasons dreamt, when he exclaimed :

> " Bear me, Pomona, to thy citron groves
> To where the lemon and the piercing lime,
> With the deep orange, glowing thro' the green,
> Their lighter glories blend. Lay me reclined
> Beneath the spreading tamarind that shakes,
> Fanned by the breeze, its fever cooling fruit.
> Deep in the night the massy locust sheds
> Quench my hot limbs ; or lead me through the maze,
> Embowering endless, of the Indian fig ;
> Or, thrown at gayer ease, on some fair brow,
> Let me behold, by breezy murmurs cooled,
> Broad o'er my head, the verdant cedar wave,
> And high palmetos lift their graceful shade.
> Or, stretched amidst those orchards of the sun,
> Give me to drain the cocoa's milky bowl,
> And from the palm to draw its freshening wine !
> More bounteous far, than all the frantic juice
> Which Bacchus pours."

Through the southern part of this district, did Urrea's troops spread themselves, rioting in wild exultation, and the mass of plunder they had accumulated, by the time they reached the Rio Colorado, was so considerable, that the general's share alone loaded eleven wagons. This rich booty he was careful to send betimes to the state of Durango, and what could not be appropriated to the decoration of his own house was sold on advantageous terms. He, nevertheless, met with some singular disappointments in his attempts at removing objects which he considered as valuable, and one of these, in particular, is so ludicrous, that we cannot resist the temptation of relating it.

A little marauding party, consisting of five soldiers, having strayed to some distance, up a creek, called " La Reser-

vada," rejoined the main body in great alarm, bearing upon
their shoulders one of their companions, sadly wounded with
a gash which had penetrated the frontal bone, and inflicted
considerable damage upon his nose. Being questioned upon
the cause of this accident, they described a monstrous piece
of machinery, which, they shrewdly conjectured, had been
set up by the colonists, for the express purpose of injuring
the Mexican army. They represented it as an enormous
knife, of solid steel, moving perpendicularly, with the swift-
ness of lightning, and connected with various wheels, the
whole so complicated, that they had not been able to discover the principle of motion! "The machine, Señor," said
the corporal who commanded the party, "was at rest when
we entered the lofty shed under which it is erected. We
proceeded to examine every corner, thinking some of the
rebels might be concealed in some nook, or other; when,
suddenly, upon Juan Ferdajo pushing aside a piece of wood,
which dangled from the roof, the machine was put in motion,
and at a most tremendous rate! Wheels began to whirl, levers to creak, iron chains to drag ponderous logs, and the
knife that I told you of, to saw up and down, with such a
velocity, that the eye could hardly follow its motion. We
fled for our lives—I mean we *retreated*—thinking it might
be some stratagem of the enemy; but Pedro Tifos had
drawn too close to the treacherous *knife* to make his escape
unhurt, and it wounded him in the way your Excellency beholds. The poor fellow followed us about a hundred yards,
calling for help, and crying out that he was losing all his
blood; whereupon, seeing that we were not pursued, I turned back to take him up. Now, it is my firm belief, that
this *invention* was contrived by those heretics—those infer-
nal Jews—in order to cut us off. And they deal in the black
art, for, how could they otherwise have invented such a
thing? Oh! what a pity we have no chaplain with us! Had
we but one of the Franciscans of Zacatecas, he could, in an
instant, dispel this *brujeria*, (witchcraft.) He could give the
foulest devil his due, and send him a packing with all his heretical wheels and levers, and it would cost him no more trouble, than four or five words out of his ritual book, with, may
be, the matter of three or four drops of holy water! But
so it is, we are poorly provided. There is but one padre

for so large an army, and the Señor Presidente keeps him wholly to himself."

Urrea was not superstitious ; of course, he feared not the supernatural powers attributed to the Texians ; yet, from the strange description he heard, he conceived some dread of an ambush, or some other stratagem, and resolved to go himself a reconnoitering, at the head of four hundred chosen men.

His orders were immediately issued, and the party were soon on their march. They approached the place in the greatest silence, with their arms ready, and upon drawing near, were startled by the noise of the machine, at the sight of which, not a few of the soldiers crossed themselves, and exclaimed ; "*Valga me Dios!*" and "*Ave Maria Purissima!*" But they were immediately disturbed in their devotional feelings, by a broad peal of laughter, which proceeded from a Hungarian—a lieutenant in the regiment of Tampico. This officer, being questioned upon the cause of this scandalous cachinnation, could not help answering, that their present expedition reminded him of the adventure of Don Quixotte and the fulling-mills ; for, what they beheld was neither more nor less than a *Saw-mill!*

Upon receiving this information, Urrea, though mortified, acted like a gentleman, and joined in the laughter ; but though he, thus, in good taste, gave vent to his mirth, he did not lose sight of his interest ; and after having examined the machine, seen it work, and admired its ingenuity, resolved to send it to his own farm, in the state of Sonora. The execution of this order, however, found insuperable difficulties in the unwieldiness of the pieces of which the mill consisted, and the general was forced, much to his sorrow, to renounce his project.

The Mexican commander continued his march towards the Brazos, without meeting with any considerable difficulty ; but, before reaching Brazoria, finding himself under the necessity of sending a trusty officer to Santa Anna, in order to communicate to him certain alterations he wished to make in the plan of operations which had been sketched out for his division, he selected our hero, as the most intelligent person he could find.

Young Captain Letinez, therefore, came into contact with

the President of the Republic ; and though the latter was accustomed to browbeat and treat with brutality any one of his
inferiors who ventured upon opposing his plans, yet the young
officer behaved with so much independence, and argued in
favor of Urrea's ideas, with so much force of reasoning and
perspicuity, that he carried his point, and the general-in-chief
assented to the proposed alterations.

While Captain Letinez was vindicating the correctness of
Urrea's views, with the President of the Republic, he knew
so well how to temper his resistance, by demonstrations of
respect, and his military frankness was so well set off by
gentlemanly courtesy, as could not fail to charm one, who,
though not well bred himself, was, nevertheless, peculiarly
pleased with elegance of manners in his inferiors ; and the
young man's information appeared so important to the general-in-chief, that he became desirous of securing his immediate attendance about his person. Captain Letinez, therefore, received an official order to join the main body of the
army, and was appointed aid-de-camp to the President,
whilst another officer was despatched to carry an answer
back to Urrea, who had, by this time, crossed the Brazos, a
little below Cartwright's plantation.

Our hero being, by such an unforeseen series of events, prevented from hearing any thing about Miss Quinton and her
father, or providing for their welfare in person, had no other
resource than to write to Alvarez and several other friends,
in order to recommend his *protégées* to their attention ; and
he doubted not that, from their attachment to him, they would
comply with his request.

It is not our intention to follow him through the various
military movements in which he participated. The fool-
hardiness of Santa Anna, who, after having seen one thousand
of his soldiers killed at the taking of the Alamo, by a garrison
of two hundred backwoodsmen, still persisted in the notion
that the Texians were inferior in bravery and intelligence to
the peasantry of his own country, prompted him to rush headlong with his vanguard, into the very snare prepared for him ;
and the fatal twenty-first of April taught him the difference
between the two races.

It was on the sixteenth of April that our hero joined Santa
Anna, who was, then, some leagues west of New Washing-

ton,—entirely bewildered, but still, in order to encourage his troops, keeping up an appearance of design. The Mexican commander, without any positive information about the number of the enemy, or their resources ; without the least knowledge of Houston's abilities and talents, or the least acquaintance with the nature of the country, through which his course lay ; had left the main body of his army, with all his *materiel* sixty miles behind, under the command of Filisola, one of his personal enemies ; and had pushed ahead, at a venture, with twelve hundred men, in search of Houston. His movements were not unlike those of a giddy boy, playing at blind man's buff—who is sorely afraid to knock his head against a post, but yet, in order to disguise his fears, talks loud and makes as much noise as he can. On the other hand, General Houston, who did not know the amount of force with which Santa Anna was advancing, thought it prudent to keep under cover of the woods, until he should draw the Mexicans into a proper field of battle, where he would venture less, by an attack, than in an open naked plain. Military genius, in this instance, served Houston, as well as a long experience of the art of war could have done.

On the nineteenth, Santa Anna sent our hero, with one Captain Barragan, and a considerable body of dragoons, to a point on the Lynchburgh road, ten miles distant from New Washington, in order to watch the approach of Houston, and the next day, early in the morning, Captain Letinez rode post haste, to inform him that the Texians had just arrived at Lynchburgh. In spite of the swaggering rodomontades of Santa Anna, this piece of intelligence was very unwelcome ; and his first measure was to send to Filisola, for a speedy reinforcement of his best troops. These were immediately despatched, under the command of General Cos, the same who had, in the beginning of the war, surrendered the fort of Bexar, and been *paroled* and was, now, bearing arms, in violation of an express article of his capitulation. He made a forced march, and arrived on the morning of the twenty-first, between nine and ten o'clock ; but his troops were so far exhausted, that it was found indispensable to grant some refreshment to the soldiers. Soon afterwards, Don Miguel de Aguirre, the commander of the escort, despatched to protect the mules which were bringing ammunition, insisting upon the same privilege being extended to his men, and that their horses, also, should be permitted to drink, (for they had not been watered for twenty-four hours) Santa Anna availed himself of this delay, to take—a nap! He found himself under some lofty trees, the dense foliage of which produced a cool shade,—the ground was carpeted by the most delicate blue grass,—he had just taken a copious breakfast and all concurred to render the temptation irresistible. But oh! the fatal nap! Well might he say, like Lafontaine's ass:

> " ——l'occasion, l'herbe tendre et, je pense,
> Quelque *diable* aussi me poussant!"

Never was poor sleeper awakened in a more unpleasant manner! The Texian general, who was not to be caught asleep, had perceived the arrival of Cos' reinforcement, and *that* determined him to precipitate the attack, lest the enemy's strength should continue to increase. He gave the word, and his men, advancing, surprised the Mexicans. One of their wings drove away three companies, which had been posted in a wood, to cover Santa Anna's right; and from among the trees, the Texian marksmen kept up such a well directed fire, as quickly threw the Mexicans into confusion. The rest of Houston's infantry attacked their enemy in front, with two pieces of cannon and in spite of General Castrillon's efforts, to re-establish order, the latter were in complete discomfiture, in less than forty-five minutes. The rout was entire and left nothing to desire to the Texians.

The action of San Jacinto has been sufficiently celebrated to render a detailed description of it, in this book, a work of supererogation; but it is not likely that its results have been justly estimated by any one not intimately acquainted with Mexico. What that battle made Texas, it will remain, at least, for ages to come. In less than an hour, a country larger than France and Italy was lost to the Mexican republic, and an opening made for the Anglo-American race, to the immense mineral wealth of Chihuahua and Sonora, the far greater part of which is yet unexplored.([1])

The Texians, after the first heat of battle was over, generously gave quarter to the vanquished,—though they would have been justifiable by the laws of war in retaliating upon them,—and it was to this merciful conduct, on their part, our hero was indebted for the prolongation of his life. When he beheld the whole Mexican vanguard, thrown into sudden disorder, he and some other officers tried in vain to rally their men. Having seen one of their own captains killed by his soldiers, whom he attempted, by blows, to force against the enemy, they became convinced that the defeat was irretrievable, and thought they had nothing better to do than to follow the stream of those who fled.

After a ride of about four miles, with his enemies in full pursuit, our hero found his further retreat impeded by a deep and broad creek, the bridge over which had been burned by the Texians. The main body of the Mexican army, under command of Filisola, lay only eighteen leagues distant, and he fancied the fortunes of the Mexicans might still be retrieved ; for that corps consisted of about five thousand men, with a well appointed park of artillery ; but the impediment in his way served only to render these considerations more tantalizing. The banks of the creek were so high and precipitous as to render it impossible for him to urge his horse into the stream. After repeated attempts had been foiled, perceiving that the jaded animal refused the perilous leap, and seeing his pursuers ready to overtake him, he alighted and with much difficulty succeeded in concealing himself in a thicket of dwarf pines.

In the meantime, his pursuers had drawn near, and judging, from the difficulty with which they knew an attempt to cross the creek, at that place, would be attended, that the fugitive would endeavor to conceal himself on the left bank ; they began a rigorous search through the grove which skirted the margin of the stream. As if to favor our hero's efforts for concealment, night set in, very dark, and while the Texians were running up and down, and shouting to each other, he crept, unperceived, through the grass, and contrived to reach the verge of the perpendicular bank, from whence he could obtain an imperfect glimpse of the water below.

There he lay, shrouded in darkness, hardly daring to draw his breath, and expecting, every moment, to be discovered by his pursuers ; when, to his surprise, he heard whispers seemingly proceeding from a recess, in the cliff, a few feet below the spot where he lay concealed.

He lent an anxious ear and his surmises were confirmed.

There were voices—human voices—carrying on, though in stifled whispers, an earnest conversation. He bent his head farther over the stream, to catch the sounds, and a ray of hope lighted up in his bosom, when he heard the accents of his own language.

"I tell thee, Pablo," said one of those who carried on the conversation, "that Don Ambrosio has been shot. I saw him fall from his horse, as he was riding through the ranks, cheering our men, when the battle began."

"And I assure thee, Juan," replied the other, "thou wert mistaken. It was General Castrillon, whom thou sawest fall, while galloping to and fro, to re-establish order among our soldiers; when the new recruits, brought by General Cos, had thrown every thing into confusion. Don Ambrosio was too prudent to expose himself to such a danger. As soon as he got a horse, he fled for dear life, as well as the best of us."

"I would what thou sayest were true, and that we could fall in with him," replied Juan. "If he be not dead, he cannot have crossed the creek, and will never cross it, without being shown the ford. It was a lucky hit of thine, to discover this crossing-place, the other day, when the passage of the bridge was encumbered by the artillery and tumbrils.—But why should we wait any longer? As soon as the noise of these Texian bloodhounds ceases, and we think they have withdrawn from the margin of the creek, we must drop into the water. We will be more secure on the opposite bank."

"It is my intention so to do," resumed Pablo. "But I must precede thee."

"Why, as to that, I will not deny thee the privilege, thou knowest; for I am not acquainted with the spot, and must be led by thee. There is little danger of my running away, and leaving thee in the lurch."

Here, the two individuals that had been holding this conversation, who, as the reader may have inferred were Mexican soldiers, just escaped from the field of battle, were interrupted by Captain Letinez, himself, calling to them, from above: "Hist! hist! If you are Mexicans, for God's sake, show me a passage to your hiding place,—and how to cross the creek. It shall make your fortune."

"*Santo cielo!*" exclaimed one of the soldiers; "we are discovered. Whence comes this voice, and whose can it be?"

"I am a Mexican officer,—Ambrosio de Letinez," interrupted our hero. "For the sake of heaven, refuse me not
your assistance !—Without it, I must perish."

"Oh, if you are one of us," replied Pablo, "we will do
every thing in our power to save you. Perhaps, we shall not
be able to effect our escape ; but we will, at least, bring you
down to our place of concealment ; whence we can reach
the water and cross the river without danger. Remain where
you are : I am coming up, to guide you hither." So saying,
the trooper left his hiding hole, and ascended, until he reached Captain Letinez, whom he safely conducted to his place
of concealment.

Once there, the fugitives, after a short deliberation, made
immediate disposition for crossing the creek. The place had
previously been surveyed by Pablo, and though the night was
dark, he entertained no fears of missing the ford. He, therefore, fearlessly plunged into the stream, and though, at first,
stunned, soon got upon his legs and proceeded a few yards,
with the water up to his breast. His companions imitated
his example, and holding each other by the hand, they toiled
through the mud and oozy slime, until they reached the western bank. Having, with infinite difficulty, scrambled up,
through the thick tangled mass of reeds and bushes, which,
almost every where, in the eastern division of Texas, skirt
water-courses, they set about drying their clothes,—a task
which brought to the continuation of their march a delay, they
had the greatest reason to regret. However, they succeeded,
and resumed their way towards the west ; but in constant
danger of falling into the hands of the Texians, several parties of whom had already crossed the creek, and were scouring prairie and thicket, in the eager expectation of capturing
Santa Anna.

A few leagues from the creek, they reached a house,
abandoned by its inhabitants, and the day beginning now to
dawn, they thought it prudent to enter the lonely habitation,
for the purpose of concealment. Every thing about the premises bore the marks of the ravages which the Mexican soldiery had committed on their march, a few days previous.
The doors were battered down, the windows dashed into
pieces, the furniture defaced, and several articles of clothing
scattered about the apartments. The two soldiers would

have thought this a fine opportunity for pillaging, and would most gratefully have thanked their stars, for being allowed to *glean* in such a field, though the harvest had been reaped by others, had not Captain Letinez rebuked them, and represented the utter impossibility of carrying off their plunder, and the danger it would create, by retarding their march. Each of them, nevertheless, availed himself of the opportunity, in order to exchange his soiled uniform for fresh garments, which, besides the comfort of cleanliness, added something of probability to the slight chance they had of passing undiscovered through the disseminated batallions of the Texians. This might indeed have been relied on, had it been in their power to alter their speech, with as much facility as their outward appearance.

Entirely disregarding this important consideration, and trusting too far to their present disguise, the two soldiers had no sooner put on their new equipment, than they manifested a desire to continue their flight. Such a measure was strongly opposed by our hero, but it was in vain he represented to them the fool-hardiness of the undertaking, and exhorted them to wait until the first heat of the pursuit on the part of the Texians should have abated—clearly proving to them that their chances of escape would then be multiplied—they turned a deaf ear to his expostulations, and resolved to continue their flight forthwith; leaving him to shift for himself, in the best way he could.

After their departure, the prudence of Captain Letinez suggested the precaution of concealing the Mexican regimentals, which he and his companions had exchanged for American dresses, lest they should, in case of any unexpected visit, betray the presence of a stranger on the premises. He next took a survey of the house. A large staircase, though greatly damaged, gave access to an upper story, divided into several rooms. Along the east front of the house, ran a wide balcony, screened from the rays of the sun, by several large trees, the branches of which projected over it. Two of those trees chanced to be a bastard species of ebony, sometimes met with in those regions of Texas, and the foliage of which is so dense, as to be impervious to the glance of the eye, no less than to the rays of the sun.

Our hero was just finishing his survey, when he was alarmed by the report of musquetry, at a distance, and presently descried, through one of the windows, a party of Texians, on horseback, rapidly advancing towards the house. How could he escape their search ?—Flight was impossible, for they were mounted.—Concealment in any of the apartments would afford but a short respite.—What should he do ?—Should he go to meet them and surrender ? But would they grant quarter ?—He could judge of their disposition, merely from what the practice of his countrymen rendered probable, and the cruelties which Santa Anna had exercised, during his advance through the heart of Texas, made him look upon bitter retaliation as certain, now that the Texians were triumphant. There was no time for reflection, however, as the unwelcome visiters were fast approaching, and no other place of concealment offering itself, he sprang up from the balcony, into one of the ebony trees, the dense foliage and heavy boughs of which would, he thought, screen him from observation, without preventing him from noticing what might take place about the premises.

Leaving our hero to solace himself in the cool retreat where he has effected a lodgment, we hasten to meet our Texian friends, as they alight before the house. One of the new comers is the owner of the plantation, returning to take possession of his property, accompanied by a lady of an exceedingly interesting appearance, and by five negroes.

There is such an evident disparity between the age of the gentleman and that of his fair charge, that she can hardly be his wife, and it is no less plain, from the tender, yet authoritative tone, in which he addresses her, that she must be connected with him by some close tie.

The company have alighted, and are casting their eyes around, to view the havoc made by the invaders.

" As I lib, Massa," exclaims a negro wench, her eyes almost starting from their sockets, and looking the very picture of horror, " If them Mexican dragoons has not tore up Miss Nancy's shrubbery by the roots !—And look yonder !—Oh ! gemini.—It is the head of the white cow, stuck on the corner of the garden paling !"

While the black dairy-maid is pronouncing a funeral oration over her favorite, a shrill exclamation arises from the precincts of the parlor. It proceeds from the pipe of another sable damsel, who is horrified at the sight of her young lady's wardrobe ; the articles of which, she beholds in a most woful plight, scattered about, and miserably soiled. While these discoveries are going on in the house, the owner of the plantation, accompanied by his negroes, is visiting the stables and out-buildings, and finds that the same ravages have been committed in every part of the premises.

During the absence of the old gentleman, the young lady, with the help of the negro women, had busied herself in restoring things to order ; but the whole establishment made but a sorry appearance, so that, on his return, the farmer held a consultation with all concerned, as to the best and most effectual means of remedying the deficiencies.

It was, at length, concluded that he should go back to the camp, with two of the men, to procure a wagon and horses, and return as soon as possible with furniture and provisions. The remaining negro man was to see what cattle was left alive in the prairie, and the two black women to stay with their young mistress, and try to make every thing comfortable. " You are in no manner of danger," said the old gentleman, as the young lady looked fearfully around. " There does not remain a Mexican under arms, within a dozen miles. The plain is alive with our men, moving in every direction, and if Santa Anna is not yet taken, he must be more cunning than a fox."

Before the return of their master to Houston's camp, the servants had to prepare a hurried meal, which though indifferent, was eaten with a hearty appetite. It was served on a table, consisting of planks hastily nailed on two trestles, that were the only articles on which the invaders had not vented their rage, and the cloth was laid precisely under the tree, in the foliage of which our hero was ensconced.

Poor as was the banquet and unsavory as were the fumes that ascended from the table, they sufficed to tantalize the Mexican, who from the lap of the ebony tree, could descry most of what was passing below. Having tasted no food for about thirty hours, he felt the keenest appetite, but had no prospect of finding an opportunity to satisfy its cravings, without endangering his life. He saw that the house was taken possession of by its owner, and it was a matter of

2*

doubt whether he should find an opportunity for reaching *terra firma*, without being discovered ; and discovery, in his ignorance of the American character, he considered as certain death. He was, therefore, a prey to the most gloomy apprehensions, while the triumphant laugh and jest came up from below.

The Texians' breakfast was, at last, concluded. The farmer, accompanied by two of his negroes, set out for Houston's camp, the remaining black man took up his march across the broad expanse of the prairie, in search of his master's stray cattle ; and the young lady, sending the two negro women to a spring at some distance, remained alone in the house.

This unexpected turn of affairs somewhat relieved the anxiety of mind under which our hero labored. He, *now*, began to hope that escape was not impossible. While the coast was clear, might he not descend from his place of concealment and leave the premises ?—There was no fear of detection, and he might pursue his flight so briskly, as to be beyond the reach of the negroes, when they should return. But the debility to which he was reduced by his protracted fasting made him doubt whether his strength was adequate to the task he proposed. He could not, however, devise any means of procuring food, without alarming the young lady.

From these desponding thoughts he was roused by her voice :—she was singing. Her accents were melodious and evidently proceeded from a great proficient in the art. He lent an attentive ear and recognized the tune. He knew the verses also ! The song was in his own language !—It was one of the finest pieces of Melendez Valdez—the Spanish Pindar—hardly equalled by any lyric poet of modern Europe.

Inferring from this that the young lady was familiar with Spanish, our hero's resolution of throwing himself upon her mercy, was strengthened, and he proceeded to immediate execution, though, not without some misgivings. Having contrived to reach again the gallery, without noise, he softly descended the staircase that led to the parlor, and, presenting himself before the fair vocalist, addressed her in Spanish, saying ; " Señora, I am one of those who, yesterday, escaped from the battle field of San Jacintho. My life is in your hands : I am so faint for want of food, that I can proceed no further. Will you grant protection to one who has saved many of your countrymen, and who, now, thinks less of his humiliation, in being enabled to apply for mercy, to that compassion so congenial to the female heart ?"

The young lady, thus taken by surprise, could not restrain her emotion. At the first appearance of the Mexican, an exclamation escaped her ; but she had too much natural intrepidity to give way to fear, and the address of the stranger was so elegantly worded,—his tone, so moving,—and the vein of chivalric gallantry, with which he threw himself upon her generosity, so flattering,—that she could not help being interested. Happily the negro women had not heard her cry for help, and now she listened, with absorbing interest, to the romantic history of his escape from the field of battle, and his concealment in the ebony-tree, and as she chanced to be well acquainted with the Spanish language, she lost none of the peculiar charm, which the elegant and winning manner of our hero lent to his narrative.

The interest felt by our young lady in the story of her Mexican guest did not, however, cause her to forget the duties of hospitality. As soon as he had concluded, she invited him to partake of a repast, which, in other circumstances, might have been styled a sorry one ; but under the present distress, was most welcome. Time passed on, and the young lady began to be perplexed, as to the manner of disposing of Captain Letinez ; or, rather, as to what course she should advise him to pursue ; when further reflection on that subject was precluded by the return of the black women from the spring. They approached the house, unperceived, and no sooner heard the foreign accents of Don Ambrosio, than they threw down their water buckets, and ran off, screaming at the top of their lungs,—" The enemy ! the enemy !—They have killed Missus !—They'll burn the house !"

Away they went, with might and main, taking the way to Houston's Camp, and accompanying every step, with a new ejaculation of terror, or a new scream for help. They might have run and screamed a long time in vain, had not, as we have said, most of the Texian soldiery been, at that time, scattered through the prairies, in pursuit of the Mexicans, who had escaped from the field of battle. About two miles distant from the house, a party of those troops came across the black women, whose flight had been so rapid, that they were almost dead with fatigue. The exaggerated ac- count which they gave induced the Texians to believe that some of the Mexican fugitives were making head, and they immediately fired their muskets, as a signal for their com- rades, who might chance to be within hearing distance, to join them. The report of musquetry soon brought a large reinforcement to their aid, and, marshalling themselves in close column, they proceeded towards the house, guided by the two black women, who, as they went, bemoaned, now, the murder of their young mistress,—now, the death of the white cow,—now, the loss of the provisions.

In the meanwhile, our hero had made his escape. After taking leave of the young lady and protesting that he would always remember, with the most heart-felt gratitude, the favor he had received from her, he directed his march west- wardly, at an accelerated pace, and had the good fortune to encounter no interruption for about half an hour. As he was entering a little thicket of locust-trees, however, his happy star deserted him. A company of Texians were in ambus- cade in the grove, and though the captain, upon being chal- lenged, answered in good English, the circumstance of his being unarmed betrayed him. It was of no use to persist in a feint, and he declared his name and condition. Now, he enjoyed an immense advantage in speaking the language of his captors ; and a Texian officer of rank, prejudiced in his favor, by his noble mien, and elegant manner of expressing himself, took him under his protection, and exercised with military frankness, such rites of hospitality as his own desti- tute condition left in his power.

Great was the surprise of the victors, to see among their prisoners, a number of officers of gentlemanly appearance and good breeding, for, judging from the excesses their army had committed, on its passage, they thought them so many monsters, insatiable with human blood. The fact is, how- ever, that, Mexicans are, in general, remarkable for their mildness and suavity of manners. They are indeed suscep- tible of sudden mental exaltation, and while under the empire of political phrenzy, they will sometimes forget their charac- ter, but they cannot be called a cruel, much less, a ferocious race.—It is true, the number of assassinations, by highway robbers, is considerable ; but we make bold to assert, that any portion of Europe, suddenly placed under the empire of the same political circumstances as Mexico, would soon present a greater number of crimes.

In the parts of the old world most distinguished for morality and intelligence,—Scotland, for example,—murder and theft have been, within the memory of man, of more frequent occurrence, than they are, at this day, in Mexico.   Yet, how soon was a wholesome reformation introduced into that country, by the exercise of a vigorous gospel ministry and a strict execution of the criminal law.   Would not the same take place in the land of Anahuac, by a proper administration of justice ?   We have no doubt it would, for, we repeat it, the people are docile, and easily receive impressions from their civil rulers.   In fact, instead of being astonished at the sight of the immorality which the poor Mexicans exhibit, we should rather be surprised that they have not fallen into utter confusion and absolute barbarism.—Moral instruction is almost null in the country.   The priests are in too small a number to discharge even the mechanical duties of their religion,— hardly sufficient for the administration of baptism, marriage and the celebration of masses and funeral rites ; so that, even if they would, they have no time to instruct the people. Their parishes are too large,—averaging, at least, sixty miles, in diameter, which prevents most of the peasantry from repairing to church above once, or twice a year.

The mass of the clergy, moreover, are grossly ignorant, most of the vicars, or laboring priests, hardly understanding the Latin of their breviary ; and where an exception occurs, either in point of knowledge, or morality, (which is more frequently the case, among parish priests, than is supposed abroad,) the subject thus distinguished generally lacks that zeal for proselytism, and *esprit de corps* which render the Roman Catholic clergy in Europe, so efficient.

With this capital defect, of absolute ignorance in the people, is combined a complete perversion of justice in the tribunals of the country.   In civil affairs, the magistrates are as accessible to bribery, as Turkish Cadis ; and in the cognizance of crimes, as nobody pays them, to be severe ; they, of course, give way to the mildness of human nature, and almost always suffer the guilty to escape.

In the organization of the courts of *primera instancia*, (common pleas,) all the rules of common sense seem to have been set at defiance. Every parish is governed by three or four Alcaldes, who concentrate in their body all kinds of power, save spiritual jurisdiction, and are obliged incessantly to labor in the administration of justice, or the management of municipal concerns, without any emoluments, from fees of office, or the public treasury ; so that these charges would become ruinous to the incumbents and intolerable burthens, were it not for the bribes the latter receive. This causes all honest men to shun them, and whenever such individuals happen to be elected, (which is not a case absolutely without example,) they must be forced to accept by the fear of heavy fines. There is no country where the profession of the law is so much despised.—The Alcaldes act, generally, without any other rule than their individual notions of right and wrong, and concentrating in their hands powers which are, every where else, carefully kept separate, they incessantly fall into the adoption of arbitrary measures.

Add to this, that the clergy and military* are not amenable, even in civil causes, before the common judges of the land, which insures them impunity, in any thing they may attempt against common citizens, and you can form an idea of the confusion prevailing in this country.—Ignorance, in the mass of the people—a general system of bribery, in the administration of justice—impunity, in criminal cases—and the foolish privileges of the soldiery and clergy have done much to demoralize the nation ; yet it is wonderful they have not had more fatal results.

---

* There is a *juez ecclesiastico* (spiritual judge) in every parish, who is, almost always, the parish priest himself. Other clergymen can be sued before him, but he can himself be sued only before the *provisor*. Those ecclesiastical judges, however, if a suit is brought before them, are sure to cast the *lay* plaintiff. Every incumbent of a parish has the fee simple of his cure, of which he cannot be deprived by any vote of the people, how enormous soever be the subject of complaint against him. The *cures* are given *ad concursum ;* but there, also, bribery avails the unworthy.—The military are amenable only to their superiors, were it even for debt ; and many *civilians*, by being graduados, have acquired the same privilege, though they never bore arms. These exemptions are styled *fueros.*

## CHAPTER II.

I have consider'd well his loss of time ;
And how he cannot be a perfect man,
Not being try'd and tutor'd in the world :
Experience is by industry achiev'd
And perfected by the swift course of time.
*Two Gentlemen of Verona, Act. I.*

Our hero, now brought into contact with a foreign race, and a people of dissimilar modes of life and religion, had new chances of enlarging the sphere of his ideas upon civil government and human nature. He saw, with his own eyes, a moral phenomenon, which had never, till then, taken place in christendom, and will not probably happen a second time. A handfull of backwoodsmen, without previous organization, without pecuniary means, or any connecting band among themselves, save the tie of language ; springing up into a nation, with the rapidity of lightning. A people of twenty five thousand souls, at most, resisting one of eight millions, and, by means of that coolness and indomitable spirit of free-dom, inseparable from the genius of English civilization, making their resistance good ! His mind was not mature enough, nor his experience of the world sufficiently enlarged, to enable him justly to estimate the causes which had pro-duced so strange a result. Neither would his patriotic feel-ings have permitted him to allow them their just weight, had he been clear sighted enough to discover them ; but yet he was eager to study the Texians, supposing that he would see in them a sample of the Anglo-Americans, whom, he was, on account of his father, rather inclined to esteem. The man-ner in which he proceeded in his examination partook, in a singular degree, of the prejudices created in his mind by his education.

He, first, directed his attention to their religious tenets ; for, this is a subject, which, with a Mexican—whether pious or im-

pious—is always uppermost. Catholicity, in Mexico, en-
grosses, by its multifarious ceremonies, a fourth part of the
people's time ; so that it is not surprising thinking persons,
there, should be so prone to attribute to it more influence
than we would naturally suppose, in forming the character of
a nation. But captain Letinez could not realize among the
Texians any thing bearing the semblance of worship. He
perceived no images in their tents—no beads about their
necks !—They never made the sign of the cross—neither
had they any thing like a religious service, on Sundays !—so
that, although convinced such a mass of people could not be
kept together without the band of religion, he was at a loss
to guess of what description it might be.

The notions he had conceived of Christianity (which will
appear singular to some of our readers) were, that, no matter how its speculative tenets might be modified by human
passions, there should be, at least, something external, fixed
and formal. In Mexico, Catholicity, though of a more plastic nature than is generally supposed by Protestants, has put
on the inflexibility of the ancient religion of the Aztecs.
The barrenness of imagination, and propensity to servile imitation, which are the distinguishing characteristics of the people, have, probably, had a considerable influence in bringing
about this result ; but, whatever may have been the cause,
the ceremonial of the church, there, admits of fewer local
differences, than in any other Catholic country. In the dominions of the Pope himself the ritual is not so rigid and exact !
Throughout the vast extent of Mexico, not the least deviation has ever been permitted from the religious forms settled
at the time of the conquest. From the frontiers of Guate-
mala, to Santa Fé, the churches are, every where, built upon
the same plan,—the same number of bells is suspended in
every steeple,—the statues of the Holy Family are carved in
the same posture and with the same inflexible rigidity of features. Nay, so much importance is attached to this uniformity, that the least deviation from it would be considered as an
act of impiety. This great importance attached to mere rites
has had the tendency to elevate the accessory above the principal, and to induce the people to view Catholicity, merely as
a series of ceremonies, digested so as to retrace the historical part of Christianity, in the course of the year, and adapt-

ed to the various seasons—a very false and perverted idea of the Roman Catholic system.

With views on the subject of religion, such as the state we have been describing is likely to inspire, our hero could not help wondering at the total want of formality on this important subject, among the Texians; and, though afraid to give offence, he inquired from his host, in what Protestantism consisted.

His entertainer happened to be a well educated man, of a philosophical turn of mind, no ways hampered by blind adherence to any particular creed; and, in order to enlighten our Mexican on this point, answered that the Protestant religion consisted chiefly in opposing Popery. "Catholicity," said he, "is like a figure dressed up for winter, with cloak, and cape, and lining of fur. Protestantism is like a young fellow, in his summer dishabille. It may be called Christianity in *round about*. Our creed sits upon us as light as summer air: it is of a most plastic nature, suffering itself to be moulded into any form or shape. There is but one point in it that can be considered as immutable, and in which we all agree.—It is to *protest!* Hence comes our name. To be serious with you, my dear friend," continued he, "we are divided into so many petty schisms and parties, that the whole is well nigh reduced to an impalpable powder—having lost all original leaven and savor. It will be necessary that some strong genius arise, to knead that dust, and fashion it into a new shape. Such an event is not probably far distant: North America is prepared for it, but he must be an original and powerful mind, indeed, who will undertake the *moral* conquest of such a people.* As for us, here, in Texas, you may be sure we are in no ways particular about religion, as far as yet; however, think not that we deny the necessary articles which constitute the basis of all religions—such as the existence of the Supreme Being, the spirituality of the soul, and a future state of rewards and punishments. We hold fast that indispensable *substratum*, without which,

---

* Peut etre sommes nous a la veille d'un develloppement du Christianisme qui rassemblera dans le meme foyer, tous les rayons épars et nous fera trouver dans la religion plus que la morale, plus que le bonheur, plus que la philosophie, plus que le sentiment meme.—*De l'Allemagne*, by *Madame de Stael.*

not even a civil government could be carried on. I must also say—how harsh soever it may sound in your ears, and deprecating all ideas of offending you—that we are purer in morals than your people. There are no highway robberies among us, nor thefts, except what proceed from negroes. Whenever we feel tempted to wrong our fellow-citizens, we go about it in a peaceable manner, and under cover of law ! The party attacked is in no bodily fear : he can foresee, and take his measures ! In point of chastity also, the most important and influential qualification of northern nations, we are infinitely superior to you.—Lust, with us, is both shameful and hateful.—With your people, it is a matter of indifference. This is the chief curse of southern countries—the leprosy, which unnerves body and mind. It is *this* which caused the Roman empire to sink under the assaults of the Northern barbarians—notwithstanding all the science, policy and refinement of the *Queen of the Earth*, she saw herself struck as with a moral consumption by this vice, and all her strength was swept away by a deluge from the North. A mighty *wave* is again starting from the same point, and it will sweep even to the equator. The southern races must be renovated, and a new vigor infused into them, and the United States are the *officina gentium* for the New Continent. Your country cannot withstand the shock, nor your people resist. How should they ? Who is there able to rouse them, to concentrate, and direct their efforts ? — Your priests ?—Are they not sunk into gross immorality and ignorance ?—What will a sacrilegious priesthood, loaded with concubines and bastards, do for you ?—Are they not polluted to their heart's core ?—Have they not introduced a pestilent distinction between morality and religion ?—It is not so with us.—Christianity is for us, one and the same thing with morality, or, at least, we never attempt to separate them. There are, undoubtedly, hypocrites among us also, but I would say, comparatively few ;—and they know that they are cheats and condemned. They cannot trust in outward rites, as possessing any value of themselves, in order to lay a ' deceitful unction' to their souls. Your religion, I know, possesses in itself all the rules of morality, with the most efficient means for spiritually enforcing the practice of virtue ; and those who assert the contrary, utter an abominable calumny ; but the kings of Spain *modified it* for the use of their colonies, and your statesmen are not likely to succeed in purifying it. Catholicity, with you, receives a strange hue from your system of civilization, which is, in the main, too much akin to the Morisco."

Captain Letinez, who was not endowed with a great stock of patience, could bear no more, without retaliating upon his entertainer, and interrupted him, exclaiming, " And how does it happen that so moral and chaste a people as your Anglo-saxon race, have so many mulattoes among them ? You may travel the whole extent of Mexico, without meeting with half the number of individuals of mongrel breed, though marriages between the different *castas*, among us, are neither prohibited by law, nor stigmatised by public opinion.—And your slavery !—What have you to say to *that ?*—How can you reconcile it with the first article of your Declaration of Independence ?—How dare you utter the word liberty ?"

" Ah, ah !" replied the Texian, " You think, no doubt, you have me, now, but I am not in the least embarrassed to answer you. I can prove by good arguments that negro slavery is, not only a justifiable, but even a praise-worthy institution, and tending to the perfection of civil society.—The blacks were made by nature purposedly to be hewers of wood and drawers of water for the white race.—If you desire scripture authority, I can quote the curse of Noah, against one of his sons and his posterity, and nothing prevents us from supposing that our negroes are descended from Ham, you know.—In this case, we do no more than fulfilling the scripture. And really, if we consider well the matter, it is a kind of obligation incumbent upon us !—Do you crave philosophical proofs ?—Dissect a black man, and you will find the internal structure of his body somewhat different from ours.—It is about the lumbary regions, anatomists say ! Does not this make my assertion good, and prove that black men were intended by nature to serve us as playthings ?—If you want metaphysical arguments, we will show that negroes are inferior to us in judgment, and though it is pretended that this deficiency is compensated by a superior warmth of fancy, nothing obliges us to acknowledge the truth of such an assertion."

" Are you in earnest," interrupted the Mexican, " when

you bring forward such arguments, or are you jesting? It sounds in my ears like a bitter irony against the right of slavery."

"Jesting!" said the other, "upon my word, it is far from my thoughts. These are the reasons and arguments all the south uses against the northern philanthropists, and we cannot conceive what right they have to meddle in our family concerns, and aim at subverting a *patriarchal institution*, which unites together, by the bands of a domestic compact, the lower and higher species, and makes brute force the useful instrument of superior intelligence."

"They have the right of nature," exclaimed Señor de Letinez, "and the order of the Almighty Creator, who has so constituted the heart of man that it is shocked at the idea of injustice and cruelty inflicted upon his fellow man. Mankind are bound together by *feeling*, and when I seek to relieve the pains of others, it is my own I assuage.* Each individual is personally concerned in the welfare of the whole, and a general law of responsibility pervades intellectual nature.—Your pettifoggers of the law, and sophistical writers on diplomacy may seek to obscure this truth, but it rises, in our mind, more powerful than all their endeavors to stifle it. Did you ever read the famous passage of Sheridan's speech, on the trial of Warren Hastings, without feeling your heart thrilled and your bosom warmed?—Is it not from *this* sentiment it derives its matchless force?"

The Texian, not a little surprised at hearing his guest quoting Sheridan, exclaimed, "whew! has this kind of stuff crept into Mexico, also?—But beware of bombast, beware of fanaticism!—You are too smart a young man to deal in nonsense.—Besides, I must tell you, *querido mio*, that this species of sublimity is somewhat dangerous, here.—Our planters might be tempted to handle you without gloves, were you to express yourself before them in such a manner. So, you must be discreet; the time is not yet come to make a parade of philanthropy. In the meanwhile we will do better to converse about something else."

In conformity with his entertainer's wish, they turned the

---

* The ideas of Señor de Letinez are highly blameable, no doubt, but he speaks according to the prejudices of his countrymen.

conversation on another topic—the progress of the mechanical arts in the United States—and our hero was lost in amaze, when the great revolution introduced into the civilized world, by the application of steam to machinery was explained to him. Steamers, locomotive engines, and power looms were the subject of his wonder! He had, indeed, before, heard of these things, but had no idea that they were applied on so extensive a scale, to the purpose of social life. He had been under a vague impression that these inventions were, rather, philosophical playthings, calculated to show forth the ingenuity of their authors, but not to become popular ; —much less had he suspected that they were destined to change, one day, the face of Christendom, and increase the comforts of mankind to such a degree, that, before long, we will see a common laborer, among the descendants of the Celtic race, partaking of more enjoyments, than the wealthiest nobleman did, five hundred years ago, in the most powerful monarchies of Europe.

Now, that his curiosity was awakened, he bitterly lamented having lost his liberty, for he anxiously desired to travel through the countries where those prodigies are met with at every step. But though a prisoner, along with his fellow soldiers, he found the rigors of his captivity softened by his love of reading and the interest which he created in the breast of his captor.

Filisola, having agreed to obey the instructions that Santa Anna, after falling into the hands of the Texians had sent him ; the latter abstained from avenging on their prisoners, the massacre of Goliad, while the old Italian fox appeared to grant, as a favor, and in order to save the President's life, a retreat, which necessity imperiously demanded, and without which, his army would have been entirely lost.

A portion of the Texian forces followed Filisola, in his march, through swamps and thickets, while the rest of Houston's troops were dismissed,—a part of the prisoners being previously secured in various *depots*, and some being disseminated among the farmers, in order to be supported with more facility. Under this new arrangement, it was not difficult for the gentleman who had been our hero's captor to obtain leave to take him to his farm, situated a few leagues west of the Sabine river.

3*

Once there, Captain Letinez had a greater facility for studying the domestic habits and modes of life, of the Anglo-Americans ; things which, though seldom descanted upon, by writers on morality, or legislation, have a far greater influence on the political existence of nations, than is generally supposed. He saw, in the Texian yeomanry, a bold, undaunted race, of an outward bearing, bordering on the profane, which might have been easily mistaken for ferocity ; yet, at bottom, humane, hospitable and generous. He was peculiarly struck with the noble liberty with which, even in the more refined circles, the sexes converse together ; whilst, in his own country, the least communication between them is looked upon as suspicious, and sufficient to ruin the character of the most respectable female. The process of husbandry, also, appeared to him to have attained a high degree of improvement. He admired the American plough, and wondered that the Mexicans were still content to put up with the rude *Aratrum* of barbarous ages. The extent to which female in-door industry is carried, excited no less his attention, being not a little surprised to see the spinning wheel and common loom in operation in every family, whereas, in Mexico, the like is found only in large factories : the weaving process being carried on, among the poor farmers, by a rough, portative instrument, similar to the one used by the wild Arabs, in the great desert of Zahara, as described by Captain Riley—while the good wives' method of spinning has not even yet reached the dignity of the distaff.*

We will not pursue those details, relatively to the remarks which our hero passed on the more advanced state of civilization enjoyed by the Anglo-Americans,—whether political, moral, economical, or religious,—fearing even that what we have said should appear irrelevant, in such a work as this :

---

* There were, before the war of independence, very important manufactures of woolens, in the city of Queretaro, and of cotton cloth, in Puebla. The latter have increased and are now numerous, both in that State, and in the valley of Mexico ; but the woolen factories of Queretaro are gone to decay. Cotton factories, with improved modern machinery, flourish also in the *departamentos* of Morelia and Durango. The Indians make excellent workmen in these new establishments, and work at a cheaper rate than the whites, in the United States or England.

the greater number of our readers being, probably, rather inclined to look in a novel, for emotions and amusement, than for instruction. Nevertheless, as usefulness is the main object we have in view, we beg to be excused for having introduced into our story so many details, hitherto hardly ever mentioned by novelists. Mexico is behind hand by, at least, three centuries, in politics, religion and civil economy. It is now, by a series of strange circumstances, brought to wrestle against all the weight of modern civilization, and the glare of modern lights. The portraiture of the contest cannot fail being interesting to the reflecting mind ; and, though we are far from believing ourselves adequate to the task, we may perhaps deserve the praise of having " *started the game*."

# CHAPTER III.

O Libertad preciosa
No comparada al oro
Ni al bien mayor de la espaciosa tierra !
*Lope de Vega.*

WITH a sufficient share of tranquillity and comfort our
hero would have spent his time, on his friend's plantation,—
every day's occurrence having the charm and zest of novelty,
and his pursuit after knowledge being diversified by bodily
exercises most fitted to his age, such as hunting, fishing and
riding,—had not his heart been preyed upon by gloomy and
distressing thoughts. The uncertainty of Miss Quinton's fate,
incessantly occupied his mind, and the ignorance in which he
was of the movements of the southern division of the Mexican
army, since he had himself joined Santa Anna, made him fear
the worst for the dear object of his affection.

He had heard, from the Texians, the history of the massacre at Goliad, and though he believed it exaggerated, yet he
dreaded lest Major Quinton's life should have been sacrificed ;
in which case, he doubted not, the young lady would not survive him. Even should the major and his daughter's life
have been spared, in what situation could they find themselves,
in the midst of an army, forced to retreat, in confusion,
through a ruined and deserted country, where, at the time of
their triumphal advance, the necessaries of life were doled
out to the soldiers, with a sparing hand ? To think that
Miss Quinton, so delicately brought up, should, after having
already experienced such heavy calamities, be exposed to fatigues and deprivations of every description, and, perhaps, to
the horrors of famine, in the midst of a disorganized army—
where the bands of discipline could no longer restrain the
licentiousness of the soldiery, and where unprincipled officers
might be tempted to take advantage of the general disorder,
to insult her—was for him the bitterest torment he had ever

felt. Every day his grief grew more intense, and its ravages became visible on his countenance. In vain did his friend try to dissipate his sorrow ; his efforts proved unavailing. At last, Providence offered him the facility of regaining his liberty, when he the least expected it.

On a plantation adjoining that of his captor, there lived a wealthy physician, who had, among his servants, a quarteroon, of so fair a complexion, that, in many a country, he might have easily passed for a white man. This slave was rather a favorite with his master, who employed him chiefly in hunting, in order to provide game for his larder. Our hero had frequently met him in the woods, and, by chance, exchanged a few words, but never paid any serious attention to him, until his curiosity was awakened by the following circumstance.

One day, he found the quarteroon, reclined at the foot of a tree, fast asleep, with his gun by his side, and a book on his knees. Not a little surprised that one of his condition should know how to read, our hero, without awaking the sleeper, gently took up the volume ; but his astonishment increased, when he found it was Milton's Paradise Lost ! While he was looking for a favorite passage, the slave awoke, and seeing Captain Letinez with his book in his hand, started up, in dismay, exclaiming, with an air of supplication, " For God's sake, sir, do not betray me."

" Betray you ! " replied the Mexican, " and for what?— But I understand how it is !—You have stolen the book ?"

" Oh no, sir.—Not so bad as that, neither," resumed the quarteroon. " The book is my lawful property ; but I meant to beseech you to keep secret the discovery you have just made—that I know how to read. Were it to become known to the planters in this vicinity, they would cause my master to get rid of me, and I might incur the risk of being sent back to Louisiana. I hope, sir, you will not refuse to listen to my prayer. Being yourself acquainted with misfortune, you will bear a compassionate heart."

Captain Letinez thought, within himself, this was a pretty close hit at the famous verse of Virgil :

" Non ignara mali, miseris sucurrere disco ;"

and he was moved by the eloquence of the sentiment expressed by the slave, still more than by his tone of supplication, to condescend to promise secrecy, which his suppliant thought of so much importance to himself.

The latter thanked him, with the truest effusion of grati- tude, for what he considered as an act of extraordinary con- descension, and both began to converse on literary subjects, with which the quarteroon was tolerably well acquainted. He possessed a small collection of English classics, that he kept carefully concealed, and in the reading of which he fre- quently indulged, for his hunting rambles gave him many oc- casions of doing so, unperceived. Sometimes, also, during the frequent absences from home, which the exercise of the medical profession imposed upon his master, he would ven- ture upon borrowing a volume from his library.

In the stolen enjoyment of this mental luxury, our hero had it in his power to assist the slave, and he made no scru- ple to lend him, from time to time, all the interesting works he could obtain. Thus, they frequently met, and pity, on the one hand, and gratitude, on the other, soon gave to their intimacy the charms of friendship.

We are afraid that, by this avowal, we shall, in the opin- ion of many of our southern readers, ruin the character of our gallant captain, and that he will, from henceforth, be considered as a degraded being—if many have not already turned away from him in disgust. Indeed, we have reflect- ed a long time, whether it would not be better for us, to sup- press altogether this portion of his history, than to present the *scandalous spectacle* of a white man befriending a quarteroon,—or, which is worse, suffering himself to be be- friended by him. But some of the most important events which follow, being intimately connected with, and depend- ent upon the acquaintance that our hero contracted with this poor slave, the suppression would have maimed our history, and, perhaps, rendered the latter part unintelligible. It is, therefore, through mere necessity we proceed to state some of the principal events which resulted from their close inti- macy.

Captain Letinez, happening, during a conversation he had with Flambeau, (such was the quarteroon's name,) to learn that his master had been one of the officers who were present at the taking of Bexar, at the time of Cos's capitulation, and that he had himself accompanied him in that expedition, asked him many questions on the nature of the intervening country,—the difficulties of crossing the rivers—the possibility of procuring food, in the prairies—and was so minute in his inquiries and so precise in noting down every item of information which the slave communicated, that it awakened suspicions in the latter's mind.    " Excuse me, sir," said he, when the captain had made an end of his inquiries,—" It is your kindness which renders me presumptuous.—From your queries, I am led to suspect that you have a mind to escape back to Mexico, but beware how you undertake it, without a guide, for, if you do, you will surely find your death in the wilderness.    Could you get the company of some one, acquainted with the country, the undertaking would be comparatively easy, but all alone, and unaware of the dangers that strew your path, you will certainly perish with hunger, should you escape being killed by the Indians, or retaken by the Texians."

" Alas," replied our hero, " there may be much truth in what you say, but where am I to find a trusty companion ? And how could I, with security, reveal my secret to any one here, besides yourself!—However, I am no longer able to withstand the torture of mind I am now enduring."

" Why, sir," resumed the slave, " the confidence you have reposed in me would be but ill repaid, were I not to place the same trust in you.    I, also, long to be liberated from my present state of servitude, and if you will accept of my services, as *pilot*, I promise to take you, with safety, as far as Bexar.    Beyond that place, I am not acquainted with the country, and am told it is, for the space of sixty leagues, a complete wilderness and scarce of water.    It is what has, hitherto, prevented me from abandoning my master."

Captain Letinez was delighted with the quarteroon's proposal, yet he did not accept his offers immediately, but took time for reflection.    After having long considered the subject, he held new communications with the slave, and it was settled between them, that they would effect their escape in company.    Flambeau bound himself to act as pilot, in the way, and find provisions for the journey, and the captain became security, that, once arrived on the Mexican territory, he would be admitted to the enjoyment of all the rights of a freeman. The captain was highly blameable, to be sure, but the desire of freeing himself from captivity may, to a certain extent, palliate his crime, in the eyes of our southern readers.

The quarteroon took half a week to make his preparations. He pounded a quantity of dry venison and mixed it with suet, in the form of *pemican*,—a composition well known, in Canada, among the *coureurs des bois*, as affording the most sustenance in the smallest compass ; and he provided, besides, a quantity of ammunition, in order to procure game, during their march. The captain bought a small keg of crackers and a runlet of old whiskey, and their necessary clothes being made up into two bundles, with some favorite volumes, belonging to the quarteroon, the whole cargo was slung, in proper equipoise, upon a mule which Flambeau took from his master's pasture grounds, and one fine moonlight night, in the end of July, they took their departure in a westerly direction.

They walked on foot, the mule having as much as she could do to carry their effects, but the hope of succeeding in their undertaking made them bear the fatigue with cheerfulness. The slave having assured his travelling companion that he was well acquainted with the way, and that the fear of the Indians would prevent his master from pursuing him to any great distance, their dread of being overtaken diminished as they advanced. Still, they were not remiss, but pushed on at a brisk pace, in order to get out of reach ; but, on the ensuing evening, their mule being sadly tired, they were obliged to stop, in order to give her time to rest.

With a rare degree of sagacity, the quarteroon selected, for their encamping place, a secret nook, in a bend, formed by a muddy creek, with precipitous banks, where it would have been a thing next to a miracle, for any one sent in their pursuit, to discover them. He would not, however, permit Captain Letinez to light a fire, lest it should betray their place of concealment, and, of course, they had, at supper, nothing but pemican and dry crackers, while the mule feasted, far more luxuriously, on muskit grass.

As they had long to wait before sleeping time, Captain Letinez begged the slave to relate the history of his life, and how he had become possessed of literary knowledge,—a favor the latter granted readily—and as his narrative may give an insight into the manners of several classes, seldom, if ever described, in American literature, we hope our readers will be pleased to find here Flambeau's recital, as delivered by himself.

VOL. II.                    4

# CHAPTER IV.

Can Genius dwell beneath a sable skin ?
Faith ! they say Terence was a blackamoor,
And yet he wrote a classic work !
*The New Lollard.*

" I was born," said Flambeau, beginning his history with
great composure, " in the city of New Orleans, of a mulatto woman, who belonged to a female tobacconist of celebrity,
and the first years of my infancy were spent in the *labora-
tory* of that distinguished artist.   The reputation of our mistress's snuff was so great, that she was obliged to keep a
number of negroes incessantly occupied in the manufacture
of this precious commodity.   She was even forced to in-
trust some of them with the preparation of the liquid, from
which her tobacco derived the peculiar pungency to which
it owed its great fame, and she, her wealth ; for she would
not have been equal to the task of preparing the vast quantity of *sauce* consumed in her manufactory.   The slaves intrusted with a knowledge of that important receipt, were
strictly cautioned against divulging it, because it was on the
exclusive possession of it, our mistress's monopoly of the
pungent powder depended.   The revealing of it would have
seriously affected her fortune, and, in order the more effec-
tually to guard against it, she had threatened the severest
punishment against a breach of confidence.   In spite of her
jealous caution, and the incessant watchfulness she exercised,
there started up a rival establishment in the city, the master
of which pretended to be in possession of our receipt, and
as his snuff was equal, if not superior to ours, our mistress
suspected that some of her servants had sold her secret.
After long surmises, her suspicions settled on my mother, in
consequence of which, she made her undergo a series of ill-
treatments that well nigh ruined her health.   In the end,
Madame Racletole, (such was the name of our mistress,)

fearing lest my mother should die on her hands, caused her to be sold at public auction ; but she was kind enough not to separate me from her, and both together, we were knocked down to a clergyman of the name of Grifagno, at the low price of three hundred and ninety-five dollars, which was no slender mortification to my mother, for, in the pride of her heart, she had expected to fetch, at least, seven or eight hundred.

" Our new master treated his slaves with humanity, and seeing my mother's health very weak, he employed her in a light occupation, well suited to her situation ; and which, at the same time, enabled her to make a little money for herself. He had been one of a numerous company of clergymen who, shortly after the transfer of Louisiana to the United States, settled in that province, in quality of missionaries, and as, at the epoch of their arrival, religious books were scarce in the country, he undertook to furnish a supply, which he imported from Europe. To disseminate them more rapidly, he had several negro women, who hawked them about the streets, and to whom, in order to stimulate them to exert themselves to the utmost, he allowed a per centage, on the profits they made. My mother, upon her earnest supplication, was permitted to share in the labors of these *revendeuses*, as the French style them, and being gifted with an insinuating address, and a flippant tongue, she met with great success. The per centage she received soon amounted to something considerable for a woman who had never before had ten dollars in her possession ; but that breath of good fortune served only to sharpen her appetite, and created in her an enlarged spirit of speculation. She ventured upon acquiring a stock in trade for herself, individually. At first, she limited herself to some pictures of Saints, and small engravings on pious subjects ; but finding, among quarteroons and free people of color, a rapid sale for these articles, she soon enlarged her store of holy wares, many of which had never before been an object of speculation in the city of New Orleans. She sold rosaries of every description—blessed rings of St. Birgitta, which preserved the wearers from lightning and sudden death—pious medals, both silver and pinchbeck—exorcised baby-shirts, for children afflicted with worms, and thousand other things, which it would be too tedious to mention. It is certain that, in the selection of articles best suited to that market, my mother showed considerable discernment ; and I will even say, some powers of invention, and she might be considered as having opened a new branch of trade.

" She obtained the reward of her ingenuity and made money fast. It was a curious spectacle to see her going out, in the morning, with a load of trumpery, to commence her rambles through the city. A huge basket, full of little books and religious tracts, in one hand, and a large bundle of pictures of saints, flaming in red and gold, in the other ; grosses of beads of every color, dangling from her neck, and her fingers garnished with blessed rings, up to her nails. She looked like a walking repository ! In proportion as her stock increased, she became less able to do without help, and as I was, by this time, grown to some size, she took me in partnership, and allotted me a little basket, proportioned to my strength.

" I was not a little proud of my new avocation, and imitating my mother's insinuating cant, I quickly acquired the nack for recommending our goods to our humble customers. I soon grew fond of the chinking of picayunes ; but my greatest delight was, at night, when our perambulations were terminated, to hand to my mother two, or three handsfull of sixpence, out of my little pocket ; when my diligence was rewarded by some tender caress. I was, however, destined to be deprived of those endearments, at an early period, and though it was in a manner which my mother thought a first step in the ladder of fortune, and a presage of happiness, yet in reality, I have found it exactly the reverse. To the change which then took place in my condition, I am indebted for the acquisition of the art of reading and writing ; and this, afterwards, led to further acquaintance with literature, which, to one fast bound to slavery, as I was, proved a curse, rather than a blessing. And yet, let me not curse knowledge !— Bitter, hitherto, have I found its fruits ; but who knows what Providence has in store for me ?

" My advancement consisted in being taken into the house of Abbate Grifagno, as his body servant. This gentleman lived with several other clergymen, who kept house together and formed but one family. In this house I became first acquainted with luxury and good cheer. The dwelling of those clergymen was small, but the apartments were decorated with the costliest furniture, and their reverences kept a table which might bear a comparison with the best in the city. The most refined delicacies from foreign parts were our daily fare, and the most precious wines from France and Spain, our common beverage. Liking well my new situation, I sought to render my service as acceptable as possible, and as I soon perceived that Abbate Grifagno and his brother clergymen, were fond of having their wishes anticipated, and their particular comforts attended to, without being put to the trouble of commanding, I watched every little opportunity of flattering this foible, and insinuating myself into their good graces. A house servant has a thousand chances of administering this innocent species of flattery, which often terminates by procuring him a kind of authority over his own master. I had no difficulty in succeeding with mine and his coadjutors ; for, to tell the truth, though they were not very pious priests, nor even very honest men, they had a kind heart and were free from prejudices against the colored race. They soon grew fond of me and treated me with a degree of familiarity, which, after it had passed into a confirmed habit, encouraged me to sue for favors of the greatest importance. The principal one was to be taught to read and write, and this I asked by my mother's suggestion.

" They made no difficulty to grant my petition—yet, as it was a delicate thing, which might render them obnoxious to their parishioners, they enjoined the strictest secrecy upon me, and gave me my lessons with the greatest mystery. Under their tuition I learned to spell in less than two months, and seeing my progress, they took a certain relish for the task, which they had undertaken, at first, merely, in a spirit of frolic. I was not loth in availing myself of their good will, and in fifteen months I could read and write correctly the French and Italian languages, and had acquired some knowledge of grammar.

" One of the gentlemen possessed a considerable library, and as I had a good deal of time at my disposal, I indulged in promiscuous reading to an extent which soon filled my head with the most incoherent materials. His collection of books consisted of the most heterogeneous medley it is pos-

4*

sible to imagine. His shelves were furnished, in front, with volumes on divinity, canon law, sermons and lives of Saints, but there were lurking behind those orthodox works, small rows of fashionable novels, plays and light poetry, which were more to his taste, than the musty Latin of the fathers. Out of such multifarious materials, I stuffed myself, at random, with what I could get and understand,—now, reading the life of a Saint, and next, a comedy of Goldoni,—to-day, a sermon of Massillon, and to-morrow, a canto of the Orlando Furioso. As I grew learned, I began to grow vain, and fancied that I was destined to make a figure in the world. I found out, in the course of my reading, that Terence, a Latin poet, had been a Mulatto slave, like myself; and had, nevertheless, by dint of genius, risen to fame and wealth, and lived in habits of intimacy with the great Scipio. *This* inflamed my imagination. I expected to find some Scipio, also, who, discovering my talents, would be proud of patronizing me, but I was far from my reckoning. Louisiana is not a country favorable to black geniuses, and I was daily and hourly reminded of the lowness of my condition, as well as of the impossibility of my ever passing the barrier that separated me from freemen.

"Every morning, I had to wait upon my master, in the church, while he said mass, heard confessions, or performed other duties. During those long spells of leisure, I loitered in the sacristy, and found myself exposed to the insults of the *singing boys*, who took care, by continual taunts, to remind me of my low birth and servile condition. I had drawn their hatred upon me by answering mass better than they, and pronouncing Latin more fluently ! Their sense of inferiority was so galling to them, that they made serious complaints of my knowledge, as if it had been a nuisance ; and, in fact, obliged my master to part with me. The report having been spread, that Abbate Grifagno kept a learned quarteroon, for his body servant,—who could answer mass as well as a white boy, and was even suspected of knowing Latin ;—his reverence became alarmed for the consequences, which might have been fatal to his popularity. He was indeed loth to part with me, yet, at last, he made up his mind and sent me to an auctioneer, to be sold for whatever I might fetch. I was not, it seems, a very marketable article, for the auctioneer kept me eight days on his hands. Every time he set me up, a whisper ran through the crowd, which frightened every chapman.—At last, however, an old lady, who exercised the very lucrative profession of fortune-teller, bought me for two hundred dollars.

" When I got to the house of my new mistress, I was not a little surprised to find my mother, an inmate of the family. She had prevailed upon the fortune-teller to buy her, at a high price, by persuading her that she would prove useful to her in the exercise of her profession ; and in reality she became of infinite help to the old lady, and was the means of doubling, at least, the number of her customers.

" Our new mistress was not one of those vulgar fortune-tellers, who go about, from door to door, teasing people to dupe them.—She was a lady, to all intents and purposes ! She kept her coach, a well furnished house, and was often visited by persons of distinction—generally Creole ladies, and even, sometimes, by gentlemen. She had practised her art more than twenty-five years, and, during the Spanish domination, had been twice arrested by order of the inquisition of the Havana, to be tried for witchcraft ! How she was able to free herself from the clutches of the Holy Office was never known; but that circumstance had increased her reputation. She practised by means of cards, considering palmistry as proper only for gypsies. From that circumstance, she had acquired the French nickname of *Madame Coupe-carte*. We lived well in her house, and had but light work to perform. Our labors were altogether of an intellectual kind. My mother had, by her frequent rambles through the city, become acquainted with the house servants of most of the French and Spanish families of distinction ; and, as she was a shrewd gossip, had, by their means, been informed of an infinite number of secrets, the knowledge of which was of much value to Mrs. Coupe-carte. She acted as a kind of prompter to Madame, and by whispering the names of unknown visiters, as well as giving timely hints, in relation to the circumstances about which they consulted her, enabled her to acquit herself in a more masterly manner.

" Madame Coupe-carte had curious principles of divination, in which she herself partly believed. She was exactly in the case of Sancho Panza, who ended by believing what

he had himself invented about Dulcinea, when he saw his
master giving credence to it.   Each card had a certain meaning, which, though rather vague, when considered by itself,
became better defined, when taken in connection with that of
other cards, that happened to turn up in the course of the
game.   Thus, for example, if a young lady whose lover was
absent wished to be informed of the actual state of his heart,
and a spade was the first card to turn up, it portended a speedy receipt of intelligence from him ;  but, if the next card
happened to be a *queen of hearts*, it became indicative of unpleasant news—for, that queen represented a rival, whose
arts were on the point of decoying her lover away from his
plighted faith.   If any coquette, who had cast her eyes upon
some rich bachelor, to entrap him into a matrimonial connexion, came to inquire the result of her machinations, provided
an *ace* of hearts were followed by a ten, or eight of diamonds,
she was sure of success, no less than of realizing a fortune
by the match ;  and should chance, shortly afterwards, bring
up a *knave*, it was a sure sign of a speedy widowhood, when
she would be sought in marriage, by some handsome young
man, endowed with all the qualities which can render a husband commendable.

" You must take notice that Madame's predictions were always favorable to the desires of the persons who came to
consult her, except, sometimes, in love affairs, when she
thought, that, by inflaming a sentiment of jealousy, she would
create a craving for protracted consultations.—Then, she was
the woman to sort her customers, and serve them to their
heart's content!—She could spin out such tales as would have
put to shame the authors of the Arabian Nights' Entertain-
ments.   As long as she felt that her female visiters had any
money in their pockets, she would keep their curiosity on tip-
toe ;  but when their purse was exhausted, the cards would
suddenly lose their virtue, for they ceased to give an insight
into futurity, if they were not crossed with silver, in the beginning of each game.   So, the principles of her art were
settled in such a manner, that she could, in no wise, be
balked of her fees.

" I spent my time very merrily in Mrs. Coupe-carte's
house, but it was decreed that my felicity should be of short
duration.   Our mistress fell into a lingering disease, and in

that state, the thought of Eternity made a deep impression on her mind. She had several conversations with a zealous clergyman, who, by his exhortations, prevailed upon her to renounce her art, and reconcile herself with the church. As her property had been acquired in an unlawful manner, she could not consistently with the principles of religion, retain it in her possession. She was, therefore, ordered to make restitution, by employing it in pious works. Part of it went to an orphan asylum, and part was employed in repairing an old church, under the direction of her ghostly father. I expected to be sold again, but was saved the mortification, by being given to an ecclesiastic, who, in consideration, was to pray for the souls of those whom I had helped to deceive. I was, in fact, sold for five hundred masses! There was something of retributive justice in this, since the value of my person was exchanged for spiritual merits, applicable to such as I had contributed to dupe! As for my mother, having been the special accomplice of Mrs. Coupe-carte's wickedness, in the art of divination, she was treated with great severity. Like Lafontaine's ass, in the fable of " *Les animaux malades de la peste,*" the principal guilt fell upon her :

> " ————————sa pecadille
> fut jugée un cas pendable !"

She was sent to a cotton plantation, to work out her salvation, in the fields, with the hoe and mattock. She soon found means, however, of bettering her condition, but of that more anon.

" My new master had no sooner got me, than he sent me to the upper country, to a college in which he had an interest. Behold me, now, in a seminary of learning, in the midst of men who spoke Greek and Latin from morning till night!—Where Mathematics and Philosophy were all the rage,—and where literature was not only an occupation, but even a passion ! The gentlemen who conducted it were all ecclesiastics, and lived together, forming but one family with their boarders, who were numerous, and generally belonging to families of distinction. The name of this seminary of learning was 'Scratchnoodle College.' It had had many ups and downs in the world, and when I entered it, it was just beginning to recover from one of those spells of ill-luck, to which similar institutions are nowhere more subject than in the south-west of the United States. The means to which the Scratchnoodle Faculty had had recourse, in order to recover their popularity, was ingenious. They had started a literary periodical, to be published monthly, in their name, and in which they professed to give none but *original pieces;* but Heaven knows what kind of originality it was! All their tricks were not known to me, yet I saw enough to be convinced that they hardly ever came up to their promises.

" The editor was a certain Abbé du Plagiat, a Frenchman, by birth ; but who, having long resided in America, had become thoroughly acquainted with the customs, habits and literature of the country. His knowledge of several of the principal languages of Europe, gave him the facility of pilfering from foreign authors what he thought would be acceptable to American readers. He was exceedingly venturesome in these *forays,* as he facetiously termed his plagiarisms ; yet one precaution, which he never omitted, proved sufficient to prevent a discovery of his disingenuity. Upon borrowing any article from a foreign writer, he never failed to alter the beginning and the end, and change the order of the paragraphs,—interlarding the piece with thoughts of his own, which he was careful to italicise. He once compared himself, in an unrestrained conversation with a literary friend, who was in the secret, to a haberdasher, who is in the habit of buying stolen clothes, but immediately unsews them, cuts the cloth again upon a new pattern, and sews it up a second time. ' The newly cut coat,' said Abbe du Plagiat, ' when ironed, and properly trimmed, can never be considered the same as the old one, nor shall such a prudent thief ever be caught *in the manner !*'

" The reverend gentleman's confidence in his own skill was never disappointed, and, sure enough, he was never caught with the manner, though *never without it.* He had acquired a little fame, as a writer, and now, by means of his periodical, he contrived to patch up the reputation of Scratchnoodle College. The public were induced to believe that the faculty consisted of eminent men, and, in consequence, the number of scholars increased apace.

" I became especially acquainted with his reverence, on

account of my having been appointed to wait upon him in the library, where he had his editorial chair. It was I who made the fires, in the stoves—swept the room—brought water and went on errands. These menial occupations, far from preventing me from improving in knowledge, on the contrary, multiplied the occasions of instruction. Abbé du Plagiat had a coadjutor, in his editorial labors, and these two worthies held frequent conferences, on literary subjects, and, sometimes, sharp controversies and disputations ; to which, without appearing to notice, or even to understand what they said, I, nevertheless, listened with attention. This served to teach me the elements of criticism, and the manner of appreciating literary beauties, according to their just value ; while, from their corrections, I caught some insight in the art of composition. I cannot but confess that I improved greatly, while an attendant upon Monsieur de Plagiat.

" To render this clergyman full justice, though sadly addicted to literary theft, he was not entirely devoid of invention and could sometimes be original. It was particularly in satire he excelled. His post in the college being accounted lucrative as well as honorable, he was envied by other clergymen of his church, who were *out* on the mission and did all they could to embroil him with the bishop of the diocese, in regard to his theological tenets, which they represented as heretical. Those enemies of his he paid back in lampoons and pasquinadoes, that, every now and then, afforded a rich treat to the faculty. There was, in particular, an epigram he had made against three French Abbés, to whom he owed a grudge, and which always appeared to me to possess considerable merit. The remembrance of it has often afforded me a subject of laughter, and as you understand French, I have no doubt you will enjoy the wit of the thing, which is too good to be lost. The three priests who had incurred our poet's displeasure were called *Chabrat, Tuit* and *Dérigaud ;* and here is the way in which he gave them their due.

> " Savez vous rien de plus nigaud
> Que Chabrat, Tuit et Dérigaud ?
> Non, il n'est rien de plus petit
> Que Dérigaud, Chabrat et Tuit,
> Et je ne vois rien de plus plat
> Que Dérigaud Tuit et Chabrat."

"I was forced to enjoy Monsieur de Plagiat's wit by stealth, and not to seem to understand it, for a slave must be wholly illiterate; but, as stolen waters are the sweetest, I, perhaps, appreciated it the more on this account.

"Thus time rolled on, till the college, having reaped, from their periodical, all the benefit they expected, resolved to discontinue its publication. The editor was now to lose his post, and I a snug berth. Rather than be deprived of so powerful an auxiliary, however, the faculty offered him the professorship of chemistry, which he accepted, though he had never seen a full course of experiments,—nor even studied the science regularly. For my part, as my labors were no longer wanted in the library, I was sent to the kitchen to help the cook.—Oh, Jupiter, what a downfall was there!— From the theatre of literature and the seat of the muses, to pass into a vile and greasy kitchen!—Instead of listening to the sweet humming of the bees of Parnassus, to be employed in holding the handle of the frying pan, or in cutting up saussage meat!—My lot was painful, indeed, yet I was forced to submit.

> "And stooping down as he need's must,
>     Who cannot sit upright;"

I sought in my new avocation of scullion, to enlarge my knowledge of human nature. By studying the temper and character of my fellow servants, and the officers of the college who had the department of the kitchen and cellar, I made curious observations.

"The steward was a smart young man, who was not a priest, but could turn the penny as well as if he had been one. My lively disposition pleased him, and he selected me as his errand boy. This gave me an insight into the manner of carrying on the fiscal concerns of institutions of learning. The boys who boarded in the college had an allowance of pocket money, amounting to half a dollar a week, each, and our steward contrived to pocket nearly the whole of it. He kept a petty store of ginger-cakes, sugar-candy, and other sweet things, of which children are generally fond, and he frequently employed me in retailing them, at a little window, in the college-yard. He was a *protégé* of the treasurer of the institution who understood, still better than himself,

the proper method of fleecing the boys. His station gave
him an opportunity of knowing what parents were generous
and paid readily, and he, in consequence, made advances to
their children, from which he derived very considerable
profits.   It was he who furnished them with instruments of
music, books on literary subjects, and even sometimes, with
articles of jewelry!  The boys had surnamed him "Dr.
Swindlebrat," and he richly deserved the name.   You will
perhaps tell me, what did the president of the institution do,
all the while ?   Why did he not put a stop to those abuses ?
—Alas ! he had a finger in the pie : being a near relation of
Swindlebrat, they divided the booty.

" Abbé du Plagiat himself had no sooner been transferred
to the chemistry class, than he began to put together many
natural curiosities, which were, from far and near, presented
to this noted institution.   He arranged them in a scientific
order, in small wooden frames, and formed little geological
cabinets, as it were, which he found means to sell to the
undergraduates.   The gentleman had, also, a nice hand at
making artificial magnets, diminutive galvanic batteries, &c.,
&c., and from these various articles he contrived to reap a
handsome addition to his income.

" I could not but profit by such examples, and, as I had
no philosophical machines to sell—neither books, nor jewels,
—I sold my services to the boys who needed them, in order
to introduce into the house, in secrecy, wine, cordials, and
other articles, which were against the rules.—Poor thing !
It was the only kind of industry left me.—Truly, it did a
notable harm to the boys, and I was not without scruples of
conscience, but necessity forced me to it.   The college did
not keep me in clothes,—it was supposed that any cast off
rags would do for a scullion, and, had it not been for the
secret benefactions of the scholars, whose *pourvoyeur* I was,
I must have gone dressed like a scarecrow !

" This kitchen life was horridly disgusting to me, and at
the end of five months, I resolved to bid adieu to Scratchnoodle
College.   I was enabled to execute my purpose in the following wise.   There passed, through the little town of
Mountwrangling, in the immediate vicinity of which our
house was situated, two emissaries of the northern abolitionists, well acquainted with the existence of several secret

societies, established among colored people, in imitation of free-masonry among the whites. These men were in possession of the signs and pass-words of one of those societies to which I belonged, and had influence enough to cause our headmen to convene a numerous assembly of the members, to whom they made important communications. They had a boat on the Ohio river, before the plantation of a man who was in the secret, and this boat had been provided with hiding places for twenty persons. An opportunity was now offered to as many of us, for escaping from slavery, and we were promised that they would carry us to Philadelphia, with safety and despatch. Strange as it may appear, only few of the slaves to whom the proposal was made were willing to avail themselves of this occasion for regaining their liberty. Their masters had imbued them with an idea that the Northern abolitionists were Kidnappers, whose practice was to decoy negroes away, in order to sell them to the Spaniards, about whom the most frightful tales are propagated among Western negroes. They dreaded being entrapped and preferred remaining at home.

" For my part I was more venturesome, and with five intimate friends, set out that very night, and the next, reached the boat, into which we were admitted, (after one of the officers had come on shore to examine us,) and had no sooner got on deck, than we were accosted by a venerable personage, looking much like a clergyman, who shook hands with us, in a cordial manner.—Shaking hands with a white man was a thing so novel for me, that I was struck with awe by it.— The sensation I felt was actually painful! Presently we were invited down into the cabin, where I thought a substantial meal awaited us, but, instead of it, the same venerable personage called upon us to kneel down. ' Now, brethren,' said he, ' let us all give glory to God, for this great deliverance, that he hath wrought in your behalf, and let us lift up our voices to him, in psalms, and hymns and canticles, that the light of his countenance may shine upon us, and that he may perfect his gracious work, and bring you out of the land of Egypt, and deliver you from the hands of the Moabites and Amalekites !' Then, he gave out a hymn, in the singing of which he was joined by all the crew, who knelt, helter skelter, in the greatest confusion. This exercise lasted half an hour, during which we looked foolish enough.

" When it was over, we were invited to sit down, while the gentleman addressed us an exhortation, or sermon, the purport of which was to explain to us the great reformation introduced into the world by the establishment of the Temperance society. He railed against the use of brandy, wine, beer, rum and cordials, in a very edifying manner, while my companions,—five stout negroes, who had never in their lives tasted any of the *creature*—stared at him, with their large goggle eyes, without being able to understand his purpose. He ended his discourse by a request that we should take the pledge of the society, and sign our names to the engagement. This request, in our present circumstances, I considered as equivalent to an order, which it would have been dangerous to resist. I signed, therefore, but with a mental protestation against the violence done me, and a full reservation of my natural rights. As for my companions, not knowing how to sign, they made their marks without hesitation. This ceremony being over, there was another prayer, put up with great fervor, after which, the captain introduced us into our hiding places.

"There we remained five days, without daring to appear on deck, except in the night, and having nothing to eat but sea bread and molasses. In the meanwhile some of our liberators scoured the country ; but being unable to obtain any more recruits, in those parts, they were obliged, in order to complete their cargo, (as they termed it,) to stop at various other stations, on the left bank of the Ohio and Mississippi rivers. They met, however, but with indifferent success. The inhabitants of the southern states bordering on these two mighty streams are mortal foes to all schemes of philanthropy that tend to relieve them of their slaves, and the penalty with which they visit any intermeddling with them is no less than death—sometimes administered, even without the semblance of formality. Strict means are devised to render the plans of the abolitionists abortive. Rigorous patroles perambulate the woods, in the night ; spies are stationed in various places, along the rivers ; and visiters frequently examine the boats coming from the upper country, where abolitionism is known to be rife. All this prevented our gentlemen from venturing too far.

"In the meantime we were approaching Natchez, below which a vessel was waiting for us, to carry us to the north; and our liberators anxious to complete the full score of regenerated slaves—which, it seems, they were, by some secret contract, bound to do—resolved to visit the Devil's punch-bowl, a noted place of refuge for runaway negroes, not more than two miles distant from that city. The banks of the Mississippi, which are, there, above one hundred feet high, have, in consequence of some grand convulsion of nature, caved in, in the form of a vast amphitheatre, three quarters of a mile in diameter. Its steep sides, as well as central parts, are overgrown with lofty trees, vines and creepers of every species which that prolific climate produces; and cut up into so many deep ravines, gullies and intricate mazes, as to afford a secure and convenient shelter to fugitives. It forms, in reality, an unexplored and unexplorable labyrinth, to which slaves incessantly resort; and though the place is frequently visited by bodies of armed men, from Natchez, it is but seldom they succeed in capturing any of its inmates.

"Our gentlemen doubted not but they should get half a score of men, or so, out of that punch-bowl, provided they could find means to inform the runaways of their charitable intentions. But how were they to obtain a medium of communication?—They were prepared for this. In their philanthropic plan every thing had been provided for, and every contingency anticipated.—They had letters for a secret abolitionist, who lived in Natchez under the hill; which they despatched by a trusty messenger, while they stopped the boat, ten miles above that city, under pretence of making some repairs.

"Meantime four of our gentlemen went to visit the punch-bowl, each with a gun on his shoulder, under semblance of hunting; and, as I could easily pass for a white man, they did me the honor to request me to accompany them. We took an exact survey of the place, and in particular reconnoitered a knoll, situated nearly in the centre of the concavity, and crowned with lofty trees, so that there was not much danger of committing mistakes, the ensuing night. We were out till late in the afternoon, and at our return to the boat found an answer from the abolitionist, directing us how to proceed; and informing us that, for the present, we would get only three men and three boys. 'Every little helps,' said the gentleman in black; 'we will go, even for six souls. But we must be prudent. Every man shall carry a dark lantern, and we will proceed like Gideon going into the camp of the *Midianites*. Children, take some refreshment, and go to sleep till midnight, which is the hour appointed for setting out. In the meantime, I will prepare every thing according to instructions.'

"At midnight, our boat fell down the river, about seven miles, and landed us close to the punch-bowl; towards which we set out, in the greatest silence. With no little difficulty we made our way to the knoll above mentioned, where we crept into the thickest part of a tangled mass of creepers and vines. There we were no sooner securely ensconced, than our leader gave the signal agreed upon, which consisted in a low whistle of peculiar modulation. The sound was hardly out of his mouth, when a huge body slipped down a magnolia, against which I was leaning, and, lighting on my head, whispered, 'here I am, master.' At the same moment, similar acorns fell from several boughs of the same tree. By the time we were all huddled together, we opened our lanterns and immediately saw that we had a greater number of applicants than we wished. 'Why, what is this?' said our leader; 'we expected but six of you; and, here, you are twelve, or thirteen! How comes this?—There is some mistake.'

"'And there is no mistake at all, plase your honor,' answered one of the new comers, with a strong Irish accent; 'but it is me, and my five boys,—save one that is a girl—who wish to go to Philadelphia, and the devil a copper have we to pay our passage. I heard, by the merest chance in nature, how you were going to take them fellows, free gratis, for nothing; and Arrah, says I, if it lies only in having a black face, to get a free passage, I'll get one for me and the childer; or black paint will be scarce in Natchez.'—The man could not be refused.—He held a rope round our necks, and behaved with provoking freedom; yet his wit and humor served to soften the mortification of our leader in being thus outwitted. With this accession of numbers we returned to the boat, and unmooring it, we soon left Natchez behind us. Below a place called Fort Adams, we were transferred to the ship which awaited our coming.

"In five weeks we arrived at Philadelphia, where some charitable persons volunteered their services in our behalf. We were informed they were *friends*, and that by following their directions, we would find advantageous situations. A portly gentleman, in a snuff-colored coat, of a curious cut, and a broad-brimmed hat, took me home with him, and gave me some work, of which I acquitted myself to his satisfaction. Pleased with my diligence, he had, in the evening, a long conversation with me and became acquainted with my history; several passages of which appeared to him so diverting, that, more than once, he lost his gravity and indulged in peals of laughter, not much in accordance with the seriousness of his garb. 'Well, friend Flambeau,' said he, when I had made an end of my recital, 'thou hast, I see, too much education to make a drayman, or a common laborer.—Thou must take some profession bordering on the trade of a gentleman!—I see nothing better for thee than *shaving*. I am acquainted with an honest hair dresser, who keeps a fashionable shop in Second street. If thou hast no objection, I will speak to him, and I have no doubt, he will take thee, on my recommendation. He is a colored man, like thyself, and, on that account, will, probably, have more regard for thee.'

"I had nothing better to do than to agree to the proposal. I was, therefore, the next day, introduced to my new master; who treated me with great kindness and took particular pains to teach me his trade. In less than three months I could shave beards and trim hair to perfection. Our shop was nearly opposite to Christ's church—the Protestant cathedral —situated in the most populous part of the city, which especially abounds with inns, and houses of entertainment; so that we had an immense number of customers. Three journeymen, besides my master and myself, were hardly sufficient for the work.

"I had already been seven months in that shop, when, one day, (it was the seventeenth of September, I will always remember it,) a stranger entered, took a seat and put himself in a proper posture for being shaved. I had not noticed his features, having been, at the time of his entering the shop, busy in a remote corner; and now, at my master's bidding, I drew near, with my soap-suds, and hurriedly began to lather his face. I had just commenced to shave his upper lip, when upon looking at him more closely, I recognized him.—Merciful Heaven !—It was my master, Monsieur Grosjean, himself, just come from Louisiana !—Seized with sudden fear, and without knowing what I did, I fell on my knees before him, and began to sue for mercy.   He knew me immediately, and laying his hands on me, loudly called for help, although I made no resistance.   His cries caused a great concourse of people before our shop and set the police officers on the alert.   Abbé Grosjean availed himself of their presence to cause me to be conveyed before the proper authorities, and after some formalities had been undergone, I was lodged in jail.   He had all his papers in good order—his testimonials, certificates and warrants !—I found, nevertheless, some assistance.   Even pecuniary aid was procured me by some friends, so that a prolonged litigation ensued ; yet, in spite of my protracted resistance, Abbé Grosjean triumphed in the end, and I was adjudged to him as his property.

" It would be too painful to dwell upon this catastrophe. Be it sufficient to relate that I found in Abbé Grosjean a most cruel and revengeful master.   I was put in irons, conveyed again to Scratchnoodle College, and, at last, sent back to New Orleans.   As soon as I arrived in that city, my trespass being of the most grievous kind, I was put among the chain-gang ; and especially recommended to the care of the officers, as a '*grand mauvais sujet*,' who could read and write and was even suspected of understanding Latin.   This was the worst character that could be given of me.   Theft, or house-breaking would not have been half so bad !   The officers who watched over us acted in consequence, and they never punished me for any fault, either real or pretended, without an ironical compliment upon my acquirements and learning.

" There I would probably have continued the remainder of my life, had it not been for the interposition of Dr. Standifer, the master whose service I have just left.   He lay sick at a boarding-house, in the second municipality, when the building having taken fire in the night, the flames spread with so much rapidity, that it was with the greatest difficulty the inmates could make their escape in their night dress. The doctor was left behind, but the word being given out that a gentleman was in imminent danger, and a great reward being offered, I rushed through the smoke, and had the happiness to save him."

Here Flambeau was interrupted by the Mexican, who asked him whether slaves kept in the chain-gang were allowed to go to fires in the city of New Orleans.

"They are marched thither," interrupted Flambeau, "or, at least, they were, in my time, in order to work the fire-engines, which the whites of that city pretend is a labor too severe for them. But, to resume, the promised reward which I had so richly earned, was put into the hands of Monsieur Grosjean, my master, who, out of it, generously allowed me a pair of shoes! As I grumbled against his meanness, he caused me to receive thirty-nine lashes from the hand of the public whipper, the marks of which I still bear on my back, and will undoubtedly carry to my grave. This piece of injustice reached the ears of Dr. Standifer, and he rescued me from my painful situation, by buying me. He treated me with great kindness, and this milder mode of servitude did not fail to produce its effect upon my heart. Little by little I conceived a fondness for the family, yet my old desire for freedom lurked in my bosom, and when my master removed to this country, I hailed the transmigration as an event which might give me the facility of asserting my independence."

"And what became of your mother?" asked Señor de Letinez; "you promised to mention her again:—I expected something singular from that side, too."

"Ah!" replied Flambeau, "she did not long remain at work in the fields. She had fallen into the hands of certain French nuns, who kept a fashionable boarding school in the western part of Louisiana, and she found favor in the eyes of their chaplain, by going to confession every other day. She pretended to be entirely converted from the error of her ways, and as that clergyman was a great mystic and pretender to supernatural experiences in religion, my mother flattered this foible, aimed at extraordinary communications with the Paraclete, through her confessor's means; and, at last, really succeeded in persuading him that she was a saint, and had reached an intimate union with the Deity. In that quality she was taken into the house of her ghostly father, where her peculiar skill in the art of cookery, soon confirmed the idea of her sanctity beyond all doubts."

Our quarteroon's narrative being terminated, he and his companion tried to compose themselves to sleep ; but hardly had they shut their eyelids, when they were awakened by a noise at a distance. They lent an anxious ear to discover what it might be, and soon heard a boat, which was being rowed up the creek, on the bank of which they had encamped.

" We are discovered," whispered the Mexican. " There are men in pursuit of us !"

" Impossible," answered the quarteroon. " They would not pursue us in a boat :—listen,—I hear their voice. But, what can it be ?—They do not speak English !"

" No, by the Virgin," replied the Mexican, " they speak Spanish !"—From the conversation of the intruders, it soon appeared that they were Mexican prisoners of war, who, since their capture, had renounced their allegiance to their native country, and taken some land, which the Texian Government had given them. Their settlement was not far from the spot where our travellers had pitched their camp. Presently the new comers landed on the opposite side of the creek, lighted a fire and set about preparing their supper. While it was getting ready, they all joined in a grand chorus, to sing an ode which is a great favorite with the old Texian *rancheros* ; and the first specimen of poetry that country has produced. On that account, it will be, we suppose, an object of curiosity to our readers. It was composed by Don Diego Marin, Bishop of Monterey, when he visited Texas, in the beginning of the present century, and exhibits the enthusiasm of the poet, and the piety of the divine, happily blended together. Perhaps the quality of its author has contributed to render it so popular, in the west of Texas ; but the truth is, that, although composed by a Bishop, and a Spanish Bishop, to boot, the piece is very beautiful. Let our readers judge for themselves.

## TEXAS.

Oda del Ilmo. Señor, Don Diego Marin, Obispo que fue de Monterey.

Dios te salve, tierra de Texas,
Do Natura, con hermosuras
Antes no conocidas se mostrò:
    Aqui la mano divina
    Que todo lo ordena,
Con mas complacencia se parò.

El llano de tus Verdes prados,
De mil colores esmaltados,
Con la quietud del vasto mar
    Y horizonte imenso
    Se revela estenso
Quando se ve el Sol rayar.

Tu sierra Madre al Oriente
Opone su superba frente,
Y all pie de cada ramal
    Serpean reveladas
    En picos y canadas
Preciosas vetas de metal.

Las aguas frescas, cristalinas
Que bajando de tus colinas
Esparcen la fertilidad
    En tus huertas floridas,
    Yerran divididas
Y animan tu soledad.

Lugares llenos de encanto !
Que nunca visitò el llanto,
Ni cruel hambre ni dolor :
    El mismo zefiro,
    Que os visita ligero
Da un suspiro de Amor !

Entre mil naranjos floridos,
Que se desmayen mis sentidos.—
Quiero mis lores olvidar,
    E ya no Prelado,
    Dormirè sepultado
En atmosfera de Azaar.*

* Hail Texas, fruitful land, where Nature has revealed charms un-

Our travellers resolved not to stir from the place where they were concealed, till the intruders should have left their encampment. In that resolution they went to sleep, and when they awoke, the next morning, they saw no sign of the strangers.

known elsewhere. When the Almighty hand framed the globe of the earth, it lingered *here* with complacency.

The vast expanse of thy prairies, enamelled with thousand hues, stretches afar, unto the distant horizon, like an ocean of verdure.

Thy sierra Madre, from her lofty peaks, reflects the orient beam, long before the plains of Louisiana catch the first glimpse of day, while in her deep valleys, glittering veins of silver hardly perceive the noontide rays.

The crystalline waters, which rush from thy thousand hills, spread fertility in thy blooming orchards, and, divided into numberless streams, impart life and animation to thy fields.

O, abodes of enchantment, never hitherto visited by grief, or pain; the very zephyr that flutters over you, with silken wings, breathes a sigh of love.

There, amidst thousand orange-trees in bloom, may I forget myself away, and, casting off my importunate greatness, and the pride of science, let me slumber in an atmosphere of fragrance.

# CHAPTER V.

What is the matter? Have we devils, here? Do you put tricks upon us with savages and men of Inde? Ha! I have not escaped drowning, to be afeard now of your four legs.

          *Shakspeare.  The Tempest.*

RISING, the following morning, quite refreshed, the Mexican and the quarteroon pursued their journey with the same speed as before, and at last reached the Rio Colorado without accident. That river had been swelled by heavy rains, and it became for them a matter of difficulty to cross it; still the quarteroon succeeded by his industry in conveying the mule over to the right side. Then, with a hatchet he had purloined from his master, he cut down a number of saplings, which he bound together with withes, in the form of a raft; and upon it, our hero, who did not know how to swim, ventured himself, having previously seen the experiment tried, in ferrying over the baggage. Flambeau swam behind, to push it forward, while the captain, with a long pole, gave also some assistance, under his companion's directions. He was, however, so awkward, as to lose his equilibrium, and the consequence was that he fell into the river. The slave immediately plunged into the water and was fortunate enough to seize the Mexican by an arm, whereby he was enabled to bring him to the surface; when he got a new hold and contrived to elevate the drowning man, with his head up. At this critical moment, the Mexican made a convulsive movement and seized Flambeau round the neck, when both sank again. The quarteroon, however, by the exertion of great strength, succeeded in freeing himself from his grasp and again brought him manfully to the surface, when his right hand being now at liberty, he took hold of a log, that happened to be floating by; while, with his left, he still supported the captain, holding him by the hair of his head. The latter, in the end, grasped the log in his turn; and his companion, thus relieved from his encumbrance, was enabled, with comparative ease, to save his fellow traveller's life.

Having put the Rio Colorado between him and his master, the quarteroon relaxed something of the precautions he had hitherto taken, and told our hero that they should now remain a few days encamped where they were, in order to rest themselves from their fatigues, and refit from the effects of their ducking. The mule also was sadly jaded, and needed repose, so that all concurred to render a halt necessary.

Flambeau, who was extremely shifty, soon built a nice little booth, well deserving the name of cabin; and under its roof, secured his books and baggage. Then taking his rifle, he went out to look for game, while the captain remained at home to make a fire. Deer are so plentiful, in that part of Texas, that our hunter had no need to ramble to any great distance. Within three hundred yards from the place where they had established their abode, he killed a fat buck, which he had great difficulty in dragging home. Once there, however, the creature was soon hung by the hind legs, upon a bough of a neighboring tree, flayed and quartered, and the richest portion of the saddle, set on a wooden spit, before the fire.

While it was roasting, Flambeau, addressing his companion said, " Now, captain, we should have some fresh bread, to eat with our venison.—I am tired of these dry crackers."

"Fresh bread!" replied Señor de Letinez,—" Are you crazy, Flambeau?—Unless you have the gift of miracles and can change these stones into loaves, wishing for bread is rather a vapid jest."

" Well," resumed his companion, " I can give you something not much dissimilar to bread, with your meat. Is it possible that you have made the Texian campaign and are still so little acquainted with the natural resources of the country? There is, here, a plant, called *Topinamboux* by the French ; the root of which resembles the Irish potato, in taste and flavor. What say you to a dozen of them, nicely roasted under the embers ?"

" Ah!" returned the captain, " it would be a luxury, indeed, were it but true.—But, I dare say, you are only jesting. What pleasure can you find in tantalizing me in this fashion ?"

" Jesting !" exclaimed Flambeau : " well, I will convince

you ; and to make you the more ashamed of your incredulity, I will not only furnish you with bread ; but bring you, besides, a delicious dessert of fruit."

" And what kind of a dessert ?" inquired the captain.

" Peccons," replied the quarteroon.

" Oh, that is true !" returned the Mexican. " They are to be got here, by shiploads.—Well, go in quest of your topinamboux. The meat will soon be done ; and I long, in my turn, to show you an article of dessert, with which, I dare say, you are not acquainted."

Away went the quarteroon, armed with a large knife, to dig up the roots, and soon returned with fifteen of a large size, which he put under the embers. He brought also a handkerchief full of peccons ; and while he amused himself in cracking some of them, by the fire, watching the saddle of venison, his companion went in quest of another fruit, far superior to the peccon. It was the yellow *tuna*—the product of a variety of the cactus opuntia He found some and returned in triumph to the cabin, where the quarteroon was delighted with the taste of that production, hitherto unknown to him. The savor partakes of that of the peach and pear, and it is an extremely wholesome fruit. Our travellers were enabled to make not only a comfortable, but even a luxurious meal ; and having satiated their appetite, they conversed upon the amazing fertility of the soil of Texas, and the singularity of this portion of the new continent—by far the best of the whole—having remained unsettled, and almost unknown till the present time.

" The country about the Brazos," said Flambeau, " is unhealthy ; but less so than Louisiana. In the latter, the yellow fever displays its malignant influence in the summer and fall of the year. About the Brazos it has not yet made its appearance, still bilious attacks are frequent ; but *west* of the Guadelupe river, the salubrity of the climate is perfect, and fully equal to that of New-England and Canada ; while the fertility of the soil is superior to any thing the United States can boast. Two crops of Indian corn can be produced every year ! Cotton and the sugar cane need replanting only at long intervals ; the former lasting eight years, and the latter, three. Nearly all the fruits of northern climates, with many of those of tropical regions, succeed to perfection. There is a sufficiency of wholesome water and the most luxuriant range for cattle! Immense mineral wealth is also known to exist in the St. Sabas hills and other spurs of the Sierra Madre, particularly on the Rio Puerco. These are advantages sufficient to attract hither the half of the Anglo-Saxon race, and to turn the tide of emigration which is now pouring into the United States. Should the few Americans, already settled in the country, make their stand good, there will be, in less than a quarter of a century, such an influx from the north, as has not been seen, in the world, since the migrations of old, which overthrew the Roman empire. As soon as the Comanches, giving way, will permit the whites to work the mines, north of San Antonio, the immense profits will prove an irresistible attraction for the inhabitants of the upper counties of Louisiana, for those of Arkansas and Mississippi ; and I have no doubt, the mighty flood will sweep over the northern provinces of Mexico, till it reaches the Gulf of California."

"Now, heaven forbid," interrupted Captain Letinez, "that your anticipations should prove true."

"Indeed," resumed Flambeau, "I do not see how Mexico can escape it. They multiply much faster than any other race of people of whom we have any account, and they are far superior to your nation in mental power. There is but one means left Mexico to conjure the storm. It is to adopt, with all possible diligence, the modern improvements from which the Celtic race derive their superiority.—But are you prepared for it ?—Has the public mind among you that plasticity which renders the propagation of light easy and rapid ?—Is it not, on the contrary, too much cramped ?—Does not the genius of old Spain lie upon your nation like an incubus ?"

"I am afraid it is but too true," replied the Mexican, with a sigh. "The Spaniards have left us their laws and system of civilization, into which it will be an arduous task to introduce the necessary alterations. But, during their domination, there was, at least, something like system and method, which we seem entirely to have cast off, since our independence, and for want of it, I foresee nothing but political misfortunes for Mexico, during a long time to come."

"Really," replied the quarteroon, "the transition, from

absolute monarchy, to a republican form of government, was so violent and sudden, that nothing less than a state of anarchy could have been anticipated. It would have been better for you to admit, as had been at first designed, a prince of the Spanish branch of the house of Bourbon, to reign over you, and to content yourselves with a limited monarchy, which would have better suited your old habits and prejudices, and probably preserved you from the frequent revolutions and changes that have brought Mexico to its ruin."

" Had the introduction of monarchy been effected in proper time," replied Captain Letinez, " it might have been settled on a sure footing ; but now the chance of applying such a remedy to our political evils is passed. No scion of European growth would flourish in our land. Should any one ever ascend the throne, there, it must be one of Mexican birth and parentage."

Thus conversing on politics, religion and agriculture, and diversifying their conversation with hunting, reading and faring upon choice game, our two travellers spent four days, in a very comfortable mood, and perfectly rested themselves from their fatigues.

At last, the time appointed for the continuation of their journey arrived, but, before leaving their encampment, they held a consultation about the route which it was most prudent to pursue. Should they incline too much to the south, they were in danger of meeting with parties of Texians, either of those that had accompanied Filisola's army in their retreat, or others, who might be prowling about the country in the direction of Bexar. Should they incline too much to the north, they might fall into the hands of straggling parties of Comanches, or other Indians, scarcely less formidable than the Texians. Their perplexity was great, but, after long debates, they thought that steering a middle way would be most prudent. In consequence, they took a northwest course towards the Rio Bravo,—calculating upon leaving San Antonio somewhat on their left. The Captain had heard so much about the large mountain springs, which form the river San Anton, that he would by no means pass by without seeing them, and Flambeau was obliged to indulge him with the sight, but he conducted him to the spot during the night, in order to incur less danger of exposure. There, a vast body of water gushes out of four large pools, of unfathomable depth, and as clear as crystal, giving rise to a stream that would be navigable, were it not for the rapidity of its course. As our hero was lost in amaze, at the beauty of the scene, the quarteroon exclaimed. "Here is a place marked out by nature for one of the great cities of the globe. Water power enough to work as much machinery as Manchester boasts, a level road, from hence to the sea, the most fertile land, for hundreds of miles around, the most healthy and pleasant climate in North America, and the neighborhood of some rich mines of silver, all contributes to render this locality of paramount importance."

After satisfying their curiosity, they resumed their journey and soon crossed the river Medina. Having, now, as they supposed, passed the most exposed places, they bent their course towards the south, intending to strike the Rio Bravo, between Presidio del Rio Grande and Laredo. But, notwithstanding the prudence with which they shaped their route, they had the misfortune of encountering a party of Comanches, whom they especially dreaded. They were just emerging from a thick *nopalera*, when they descried two Indians, on horseback, coming towards them. It appeared that the latter had no design upon our travellers, for, as soon as they perceived them, they gave a loud whoop, in sign of surprise, and disappeared from the back of the animals on which they were mounted. The horses fled, retaking the way by which they had come, whilst there remained no vestige of the riders—nor could the poor quarteroon imagine by what legerdemain they had vanished. From the first moment he descried them, he had incessantly kept his eyes on them and he was sure they could not have alighted and fled, on foot, without being perceived, yet it seemed their horses were, now, running off, without their riders.

The captain diverted himself, for a while, in seeing him so much puzzled, but, at last, explained to him that the Comanches are the best riders of any people, ancient, or modern, that it is a very ordinary thing with them, in a flight, to lie in a horizontal position, on the side of their horse less exposed to the arrows of the enemy, and that they are enabled to continue a considerable time, in such a difficult posture, by putting one leg through a loop, depending from the saddle-

6*

bow, and provided for the purpose ; while they hold, by the horse's mane, with *one hand*, and find means to manage their shield, with *the other*.

" I have no doubt," continued he, " it is precisely the way in which these fellows are now effecting their retreat ; but I am afraid they are not the only ones of their nation, in this vicinity, and I wish we may not fall into the hands of some larger party. This neighborhood is one of their haunts, and the two who have just fled from us with so much precipitation are, probably, spies, sent about to make discoveries."

" And what, if we should encounter them ?" said Flambeau.

" It is not a thing to be trifled with," replied the Mexican. " They are irreconcilable enemies to my countrymen. But I have the facility of passing myself for an American. Should we encounter them, beware making any resistance, and let me manage every thing by myself. I have heard a great deal about their ways and customs, and am more likely to succeed, than you, in soothing them, or winning their favor."

The captain's forebodings proved but too true. They had hardly proceeded a league, when they saw themselves invested by a large party, consisting, at least, of two hundred men on horseback, many of whom were armed with lances, some, with rifles, but none of whom was without a bow and arrows. Instead of manifesting any fear, Señor de Letinez, on the contrary, drew towards the nearest group, with an air of confidence, bearing a buffalo robe, spread on high, which, according to the notions of those tribes, answers the purposes of a flag of truce ; and the Indians manifested their respect for this sign of peace, by stopping short. The captain was no sooner within speaking distance, than he began to harangue the Comanches, in English, for he supposed that, in so large a number, there would be some one acquainted with the language of the Americans, and able to translate the substance of his address, for the information of the others. He told them that he and his companion were Texians, sent, as spies, towards the Rio Grande, and that a considerable army of their countrymen was on its way, to lay waste all the towns on the banks of that river, after which the country would be abandoned to the Indians, its ancient and lawful possessors. He added that he was commissioned to propose an alliance between his people and the Comanches, in order to direct their simultaneous efforts against the Mexicans.

His expectation proved true. Several Indians understood English sufficiently well to seize the meaning of his address, the various items of which were translated by them and commented upon, for the information of their fellow citizens, or, rather companions in arms, whilst our hero waved his buffalo robe to and fro, with a gentle motion, and indicated by many accompanying gestures that he was a messenger of peace.

## CHAPTER VI.

Hospitality overdone
Is worse than none.
*Sardinian proverb.*

THE topics which Captain Letinez had treated, and the manner in which he had touched upon them, were highly gratify-
ing to the Comanches, who, by common consent, determined,
not only to abstain from doing any injury to our travellers,
but even to treat them with extraordinary honor. The chief
of the whole party now advanced towards the captain, and
shook hands with him, while one, who, it was supposed, acted
as interpreter general, gave him to understand they had resolved to exercise the rites of hospitality towards them with
the utmost magnificence, and, for that purpose, invited them
to repair to their place of residence, at the foot of the Sierra
of St. Sabas.

Such an invitation was far from agreeable to our hero,
who anxiously desired to get rid of those Indians, lest he
should be discovered; for their inveteracy against the descendants of the Spaniards is so great, that it is next to a miracle for any Mexican to escape from among them with his
life. The captain, however, by pretending that he was commissioned to propose a treaty between them and Texas had
entrapped himself. Such a commission necessarily required
that he should repair to their towns, in order to hold a talk,
and he could not, *now*, refuse, without rendering his veracity
suspected, and, perhaps, endangering his life.

On the other hand, it was a dreadful addition to the fatigue they had already undergone, (the nearest town of the
Comanches being nearly one hundred leagues distant,) no less
than a postponing of the so much wished for meeting with
Miss Quinton and her father; who, he had great reason to
believe, had followed Filisola's army to Matamoros. Pity
for the fate of the old major, and the state of suffering to

which the daughter was reduced, pleaded in his heart, with a voice almost as powerful as that of love, to make him desire a quick riddance of his present difficulties ; and it was less painful to venture exciting suspicions in the mind of the Comanches, than stifling the secret whispers of love and compassion united. He, therefore, intimated that, for the present, it was impossible for him to go so far north, because the errand on which he was sent, consisted in spying out the position of the Mexicans on the Rio Bravo, and the state of their affairs—that it was urgent on account of it should be immediately placed before the Texian authorities—but that, if they would agree, he would treat with them on the spot.

To this, however, the Comanches refused to accede. Not being invested with the necessary powers from the rest of their nation, they were, of course, unwilling to enter into any engagement by themselves. But though disappointed of their expectations, by the captain's false pretences, they lent a favorable ear to his petition for an escort as far as the Rio Bravo. He was afraid to meet with some other bands of Indians, who might be worse disposed than the present ones ; or, perhaps, some Carankaways, who are noted cannibals, and pride themselves upon a refined epicureism in anthropophagy, and he knew if once these Comanches plighted their faith to him he would be secure.

He obtained the object of his wishes, and no other remuneration was asked than the hatchet which Flambeau had purloined from his master, and the keg that had contained their whiskey ; but, which was then, much to their sorrow, quite empty. As there is between the Medina and the Rio Bravo a desert of fifty leagues, where provisions, and even water to drink, are scarce ; our travellers and the Indians who had undertaken to escort them, were under the necessity of preparing a certain quantity of jerked beef. For that purpose, they killed five beeves, (cattle, notwithstanding the great havoc made among them by Santa Anna, being still abundant,) and cutting the meat into thin slices, hung it up in the sun. The atmosphere in that country, is so dry, and the heat so powerful, that the meat thus prepared is soon cured, and proves, even in its raw state, pleasant to the taste and wholesome. The *pemican* had already given out, so that Flambeau was not a little rejoiced to see the *tassajo,* not quite so substantial, it is true, as the Canadian preparation, but nearly as agreeable to the palate.

It is no matter of surprise that the Comanches, who entertain a mortal hatred against the Mexicans, should have, thus, treated with distinction the two pretended Texian spies. These Indians felt a sympathy for them, and looked upon them as their natural allies against an inveterate foe. Had this been better known to Captain Letinez, he would have been less afraid of incurring suspicion by refusing to go to their towns. All the Indian tribes who inhabit Texas had, by this time, heard of the battle of San Jacinto, and felt a sort of reverential awe for the race who had won it. The new republic was, in their imagination, surrounded with a halo of glory ; and, had the Texians known how to cultivate that feeling—instead of suffering greedy and insidious land-hunters to alarm the Indians by ill timed surveys of their territory—they would now have the Comanches for allies. The latter were, at the time to which we refer, disposed to look upon every thing appertaining to Texas, with a special benignity ; and, in order to testify their high regard for the two pretended spies, they resolved, before dismissing them, to give them a grand feast, according to the custom of their nation, in the plain where they were assembled.

For that purpose the warriors divided themselves into various squads, say, fifteen or sixteen, and some went in search of game for the banquet, while the remainder employed themselves in building fire-places, for preparing their entertainment. The country is so productive of every kind of wild animals, considered as delicacies, in more civilized regions, that, in a short time, they were amply provided.([2]) One brought a fat buck—another, a couple of turkies—a third one, a dozen of those delicious thrushes, which are, in Louisiana, looked upon as the ne plus ultra of an epicure's desires. A boy killed a *pecari*, one of the most singular animals in nature, very abundant in the lowlands of Mexico, and the meat of which is but little inferior to that of the European wild boar ; while others repaired to a neighboring brook, for fish, which they easily caught by means of a *lariette*.*

* Lariette is the French word for lasso, which the Texians have adopted and anglicised. When used for the purpose of catching fish, it is of wire and placed in some narrow passage made by damming a brook.

All these articles, when prepared, though without any difference in the mode of cooking, afforded such a varied cheer, as would have made the mouth of a London alderman water ; and the keen wind which sweeps the plains of western Texas might be considered as giving them a new relish, by sharpening our travellers' appetite.

In spite of all those intrinsic and accidental recommendations, the captain shuddered, when informed, that, in order to do honor to the good intentions of his entertainers, he was obliged to partake of every meal which had been prepared, and Flambeau was no less shocked.

" Good God !" exclaimed the poor quarteroon, " how shall we be able to get through this tremendous job !—There are no fewer than twenty different boards spread out. It would require the gastric powers of a hyena to acquit one's self to these people's satisfaction. Oh ! had I but known this, betimes, I would have fasted so rigorously, as to be able, *now*, to come up to their most refined ideas of politeness ; but, after the four days we have enjoyed, on the banks of the Colorado, it will be impossible for us to do, here, any thing to justify our manhood. We will certainly offend our hosts and endanger our respectability."

Flambeau's lamentations were, however, unavailable, and the various parties being ready for the reception of their honored guests, it was, a second time, signified to them that they should perambulate the plain and partake of every meal prepared for them.

" *Oh ciel !*" exclaimed again the quarteroon, in the excess of his grief; " *ce n'est plus manger pour vivre, mais c'est manger pour mourir.*"

" *Santo Dios !*" echoed the Mexican. " *Ahora si, que he de reventar !*—Oh, my dear friend," added he, recommending himself to the quarteroon ; " do not fail to inform my relations of my fate, should I happen to die in this dreadful undertaking—in order that my family may cause masses to be said for the repose of my poor soul." But in the midst of their mutual condolences, the Indian who acted as master of the ceremonies, became urgent to usher them to the banquet. The first group had a quarter of a roasted buck, various pieces of which were served before our travellers, upon *maguey* leaves, instead of platters, and of which they ate sparingly, reserving their appetite to satisfy the numerous parties, who were impatiently watching their approach.

In a few minutes, they rose from their seats, and left their entertainers highly displeased with the abruptness of their departure. Passing on to a second board, they repeated the same manœuvre, and then passed on to a third, and to a fourth; until, at last, after having, by their sobriety—that looked like contempt for the feast—offended the half of the warriors there present, they were themselves ready to die of an indigestion.

In spite of the best will in the world to give universal satisfaction, they were obliged to leave about fifteen boards unvisited. In vain the kind hearted Comanches begged, complained, expostulated and tried to bully them into eating; a complete physical impossibility stood in the way of the accomplishment of their wishes; so that, after much teasing, they withdrew in high dudgeon.

It was represented to our two travellers, and in no very moderate language, that, had they gone up to the Indian towns, at the foot of the Sierra of St. Sabas, they would have been invited into every tent, to partake of a meal prepared for their reception; but that, as they could not comply with the wishes of their good friends, the latter had taken the pains of preparing for them a splendid banquet; and they had not, however, done to it the honor their entertainers had a right to expect, but rather left a part of it untouched, which was a slur thrown upon those who had prepared the feast.

The captain and Flambeau, thus teazed out of all patience, and driven to the last extremity, gave out, as a last awkward excuse, that they were suffering under sickness. This, they quickly found, was likely to involve them into still greater difficulties than those from which they sought to extricate themselves; for the Indians became urgent to treat them according to their notions of the medical art. Our travellers were, nevertheless, so happy as to make their refusal acceptable, under pretence that Indian medicines were not appropriate to the diseases of white men; and, in the end, succeeded in obtaining forgiveness from those whom their abstemiousness had so much displeased.

All matters being now pacified and all differences amicably adjusted, our hero and his friend took their departure from the field of feasting, and shaped their course towards the Rio Bravo, under the escort of thirty Indians, who brought with them a sufficiency of provisions for crossing the intervening wilderness. They suffered sometimes for want of water, but not so much as they had anticipated ; for, whenever they found none in the *charcos*, or pools, they generally obtained some by digging deep holes in the earth. A few times, however, they got nothing but what was impregnated with Epsom, or Glauber salts—chemical compounds exceedingly abundant in Mexico. During this march, our travellers familiarized themselves with the Comanches, and learned many interesting particulars concerning their nation. In physical qualifications they may compete with the most favored races, being tall, robust and well made. Their color is more glossy and lighter than that of the Indians who inhabit the United States, and their features approximate more to the Grecian model. Their agility and strength are extraordinary, and few white men could be found able to bend the bows which many of their warriors use. These weapons, principally made of the ribs of the buffalo, curiously spliced with splinters of elastic wood, will send an arrow through a bear, at a vast distance, and prove more dangerous, in the hands of the Comanches, than the musket, in ours.

As to their system of government, it is methodical and well defined. Forming a vast confederacy, which reaches from the borders of Bexar, to the mountains of Taos, they possess a great influence over several tribes extending westward, from the state of Missouri, to the foot of the Rocky Mountains, and particularly over the Pawnees, with whom they are connected by the tie of language and a common origin. Some of the northern sections of their nation are visited by Canadian *coureurs de bois*, from whom they have derived ideas of improvement. In many spots, they raise crops of Indian corn and employ in agricultural labors their captives, whom they treat much less cruelly than any other tribe of the aborigines. In a word, they are, at this time, in a state of progress, and will form to the agrandizement of Texas a more serious impediment than Mexico herself. To this may be added that the Jesuits of Missouri have conceived the idea of making establishments among them. Having already taken root in the Pawnee country, it will be easy for this order to extend themselves southward, and bright visions of a second Paraguay are now dancing before the eyes of the wise ones of the institute. Should they succeed, the Texians will find them a harder nut to crack, than any they have hitherto encountered.

Under the direction of their trusty guides, our travellers found, in the plants of the country, resources of which they had no previous idea. The largest kind of cactus melo-cactus, commonly called *viznaga*, when split in two, affords a substance, which, though filamentous, is not much inferior to an English turnip in taste, and the root* of the wild maguey, when the plant has reached its maturity, can be baked, and becomes highly nutritious and palatable. It is, indeed, a pretty severe labor to dig it up, but then a single one can furnish a meal for two or three persons. This district, therefore, is blessed with natural supplies which few others can boast, and our hero's experience was not a little improved by his communication with the Comanches.

In eleven days, they reached the Rio Bravo, where they dismissed their escort, intending to enter the Mexican territory, without any thing capable of exciting suspicion. They had struck the river a considerable distance below Presidio del Rio Grande, and were deliberating on the most ready means to cross it, when an unexpected facility offered itself. It was a large empty canoe, moored in a small cove, under some spreading sabinos. It might afford them not only a chance of crossing the stream, but even a convenient way for descending it as far as Matamoros, should they wish to escape the fatigues incident to a land journey. Flambeau proposed it to the captain, but the latter, still remembering his *ducking* in the Colorado, and the danger to which he had been exposed, made a wry face, and started several objections. The quarteroon, nevertheless, insisted with perseverance, and painted in such glowing colors, the ease and pleasantness with which a trip of that sort could be performed, on the smooth and meandering stream of the Bravo, that he conquered his companion's repugnance.

An impediment not so easily got over concerned the right

---

* The Agave Americana. The root, when baked, is called *quiote*. In the upper countries, towards the head waters of the Rio Bravo, it is called *Mescal*.

of ownership of the skiff. It was the property of another man, and by depriving him of it, they would commit an act of injustice ! To this difficulty, urged by the captain, the quarteroon replied, that they could easily indemnify the owner, by leaving a sum of money for him, in the hands of the parish priest of the first town they should come to, and informing him of such a disposition, by a letter left hanging on a bough of the cypress-tree, at the foot of which they had found the boat moored. The expedient appeared reasonable, and the plea of necessity seemed urgent enough to justify it. In fact, they were in such a case, for, how repugnant soever Señor de Letinez might feel, to trust himself to an element of which he was in special dread, the continuation of his journey, on foot, had become impossible, from soreness, and the district of country they were to cross did not offer the same resources to refit as are found in Texas. From the theatre of the mighty banquet which had caused them so much annoyance, our weary travellers had been swiftly conveyed to the banks of the Rio Bravo, on horses, lent them by the Comanches. But *now*, should they overlook the present convenience, they had before them the awful prospect of a journey of five hundred miles, to be performed on foot, through countries, not altogether desert, indeed, but mostly destitute of water, and exceedingly unsafe, on account of the great number of deserters, who had taken to the high ways, as the only means of support left them by the carelessness of government. This was more than sufficient to outweigh all the scruples Señor de Letinez might have felt at seizing on the canoe, and we hope it will be no less satisfactory to our reader's mind—particularly when he considers that our gallant hero made provision for reimbursing the owner its full value.

# CHAPTER VII.

This magnificent river, which now marks your western boundary, will soon become the main artery of your Republic.—*Sermon for the Anniversary of Texian Independence, by Antonio Agudo.*

THE resolution of trusting themselves upon the Rio Bravo being taken by our two travellers, the mule was unloaded and turned loose, their goods and provisions were transferred to the skiff, over the prow of which a little booth was constructed by Flambeau, with a few green boughs and a blanket, and, unmooring it, they began to descend the river. The quarteroon took upon himself the duties of pilot, and with a paddle in his hand, sometimes rowed, to accelerate their progress, or clear the eddies ; but, more frequently, contented himself with using his oar as a rudder, and sat motionless, merely directing the course of the canoe.

The Rio Bravo is at all times a rapid stream, but it was now a season of the year when, in consequence of the heavy rains, which fall at the foot of the mountains, it begins to rise ; so that the velocity of our travellers' progress relieved the want of excitement that would, otherwise, have resulted from the lack of personal exertion. At every turn and meander of the stream, a new scene presented itself. Here, were wide bottoms, indented by *bayous* extending far inland, as having, in past times, formed the bed of the river,—there, perpendicular banks, seventy or eighty feet in height, and crowned with magnificent evergreens. Whenever they landed, the quarteroon was amused, as well as instructed, at the sight of a multiplicity of plants growing wild, which he had, hitherto, considered as rarities, created by Providence for the ornament of conservatories, and the luxury of the rich, and for which he had, in consequence, entertained a kind of superstitious respect. As he brushed by, whole clusters of the mimosa sensitiva drooped and shut their leaves in vegetable convulsions, the ojasen shook its elegant

perfume, and the yellow-bloomed guisache embalmed the
air with odors equal to those of the blossoms of the grape
vine. In many places, they found the finer species of the
cocheneal insect, (coccus cacti sylvester,) at work, on the
mucilaginous leaves of its favorite opuntia, while every moist
spot glowed with the splendid flowerets of the red-bloomed
sauge, (salvia splendens) or dazzled their eyes with the
magnificent hues of gigantic dahlias and the variegated um-
bellæ of the asclepias curassavica. Not unfrequently, during the heat of the day, they would land, to enjoy their
siesta under some spreading ebony-tree, the thick foliage of
which, perfectly screened them from the rays of the sun,
while the sinsontle (mocking-bird,) lulled them asleep by its
mimickry ; and sometimes they would amuse themselves, in
looking, among the sand and shingles, in the shallow parts of
the stream, for a species of muscle, which produces pearls,
nearly as fine as those of California, and that have, indeed,
been more than once sold for such.*

Thus varied, their journey down the Rio Bravo proved
no less instructive than amusing, and it possessed, besides,
the invaluable advantage of affording them a perfect security,
for they were the first wayfarers who had travelled in such a
manner in that country, and it will be long, indeed, before
the robbers with whom it abounds be taught to consider the
greatest navigable river in the republic as a highway.

Near Revilla, they saw immense banks of stone coal, which
made Flambeau exclaim, in exultation, " Good Lord ! what
a resource for this country, where wood is so scarce ! What
a blessing has not Providence prepared for the population,
in order that they may navigate this fine river by steam, and
how ignorant, or apathetic must they be, to neglect availing
themselves of these advantages—especially as they have the
example of the North Americans before their eyes ! Now,
this is a continuation of the stone coal formation which pervades the northern parts of Texas, and it probably extends
further west. It is calculated to furnish immense facilities

---

* The *mytilus margaritiferus* is found in abundance in the Rio del
Norte and the rivers which fall into it, between the mouth of the Puerco
and Matamoros, and a little trade is carried on, in the adjoining provinces, in the pearls it produces. With the increase of the population, this
branch of commerce will probably become of greater importance.

for manufacturing purposes, in a country like this. When will the people open their eyes? And why do not the many foreigners settled among them enlighten them upon their true interests?"

"Why do not foreigners enlighten them on their interests?" interrupted the captain. "Ay, indeed!—The foreign merchants who thrive among them, are the first to conceal the light. A few years ago, a steamboat was started on the Rio Bravo, and it was immediately exclaimed against, by the American, Irish and French merchants of Matamoros, with as much bitterness as by the Mexican mule-drivers and ox-cart gentry. Even, at this day, if you want to stimulate them to a degree of excitement bordering on passion, you have but to maintain the *possibility* of establishing cotton factories in this country. Though there are, already, a good number in a flourishing condition, and some as far north as the state of Durango ; those foreign importers will not fail to cry out against it, as the greatest absurdity that can possibly enter the head of a reasonable creature. It is *statesmen* and *philosophers* who will enlighten us, if we are ever enlightened. As to merchants, they are, in general, mere routine men— heartless, and without elevation of mind ; and importers, in particular, are as great a clog to national industry, as the inquisitors of old were, to the development of science and philosophy."

Our travellers stopped a short time at Revilla to take in provisions, after which, continuing their voyage, they soon reached the town of Mier ; which had, a few months before, been the theatre of the captain's first exploits, and witnessed the dawn of his military career.

The Rio Bravo, notwithstanding its rapidity, describes so many sinuosities, that it took our travellers nine days to reach Camargo, a town of about seven thousand souls, at the mouth of the river San Juan, and seventy leagues distant from Matamoros, by water. There, Señor de Letinez resolved to leave his canoe, provided he should be able to procure mules and servants, to terminate his journey by land. Flambeau pleaded in vain in favor of the other mode of conveyance, as less fatiguing and more secure ; the captain was inexorable, thinking that he would become the laughing stock of his brother officers, if he should make his entrance into Matamoros by water ; and that the ridicule which would, in consequence, attach to him, might prove a stain to his military character. So unnatural does river navigation appear to Mexicans, in general !

" Excuse me, sir," said Flambeau, " I would be loth to offend you, to whom I owe so much ; but what you assert passes all belief. Your countrymen have not any religious scruples against navigation, like the Persians of old. Whence can such a strange feeling be derived ?"

" I am not offended at your doubting my assertion," replied our hero, " I could not believe it myself, were I not born a Mexican. Where that singular disposition originated I cannot say with certainty. For my part, I believe, it was inbred in the Indian race, on the *steppes* of great Tartary, where I wish they had all remained. Certain it is, that this hydrophobia-like disposition will keep our people in great dependence upon other nations, for ages to come. With eighteen hundred leagues of coast on the Pacific, we do not own one single vessel trading to the East Indies, though the Spaniards showed us the way, long ago ; and with an extension of six hundred leagues, on the gulf of Mexico, or the Atlantic, I question whether a Mexican vessel has yet appeared in the European seas. And as for our rivers, we have three of superior importance, that of Santiago, the river Mescala and the Rio Bravo ; but, for the advantage we derive from them, they might as well be dried up."(³)

## CHAPTER VIII.

'Tis torture and not mercy : heaven is here,
Where Juliet lives.
                                        *Romeo and Juliet.*

In Camargo, the captain found several cavalry officers of
his acquaintance, quartered in that place, with a number of
horses, for the convenience of pasturage. They welcomed
him with exultation, and congratulated him upon his escape;
for it had been reported that he had perished in the battle of
San Jacinto. From them he easily obtained mules, servants
and money, and soon resumed his route towards Matamoros,
impatient to hear what had happened to Miss Quinton, and
yet fearing to learn disastrous news.

Those who have never experienced love, when it rises pure
and unadulterated by any selfish motive, in a virgin heart,
can hardly form an idea of Captain Letinez's feelings, when
he approached that city. Though he had some reason to believe that Miss Quinton reciprocated his sentiments ; yet he
had no certainty of it, and this doubt was the source of
a cruel anxiety. He anticipated, also, a sad history of wo,
in the long series of sufferings she must have encountered, in
the midst of a demoralized soldiery, during Filisola's difficult
retreat. But, perhaps, even in this supposition, his thoughts
carried him too far ! He had no proofs that Major Quinton
had escaped the massacre of Goliad. His hopes of his safety
were founded only on the confidence he reposed in captain
Alvarez and others. He doubted not they had made all their
efforts to save him ; but, had those efforts been available
against the strict orders of Santa Anna ? And if the father
had perished, he was sure the daughter could not have survived. Now, the cruel doubt was going to be cleared up ;
but as he drew nearer to the city, the anxiety of his mind
grew more excruciating and wrought upon his body like an

agony of grief.   He felt dizzy—unable to support himself on horseback—and was obliged to alight, in order to rest himself, and give his feelings time to be calmed.

He laid himself down at the foot of a tree, and leaned on the quarteroon, who, not knowing the cause of this unexpected debility, attributed it to bodily exhaustion ; and expostulated with him on the imprudence of undertaking to terminate his journey on horseback, when he was so inadequate to the task.

The captain suffered him to murmur as much as he pleased, rather than discover the state of his mind ; for he was conscious that his feelings were above the comprehension of most men.   It was a fever of love, buoyed up by a virginity of heart, seldom found in the rougher sex ; but embittered by the most cruel uncertainty.   Since the day when he had rescued Miss Quinton from the hands of the Comanches—when that pale, fainting form lay, for a few moments, upon his bosom—beautiful beyond any thing he had ever dreamed of— the dear image had incessantly remained present to his imagination.   It had accompanied him in the field, as well as in the camp ; and supported him through the fatigues of war and the rigors of his captivity.   Why does he now tremble ? Why is his ardent desire of seeing her again mingled with an indescribable dread, the motive of which he hardly can, or dares define ?   Is it the mere surmise that, perhaps, she has died, which thus causes his torment ?—Is not there another thought, mixing its bitterness with this pang ?   Oh, the misery of his situation !—The object of his love has perhaps become unworthy of his aspirations.   A captive in the midst of a routed army—without a protector, among men accustomed to laugh at every kind of excess—how can she have escaped pollution ?   Oh God, avert the excruciating idea !—Heavens, distil your soothing balsam into that wounded heart, and let not the utmost of your rigor be poured upon a child of virtue !

Now, like Alp, before Corinth, he

> " Passed his hand athwart his face,
> Like one in dreary musing mood,
> Declining was his attitude ;
> His head was drooping on his breast,
> Fever'd, throbbing and opprest ;

> And o'er his brow, so downward bent,
> Oft his beating fingers went,
> Hurriedly as you may see
> Your own run o'er the ivory key,
> Ere the measur'd tone is taken
> By the chords you would awaken."

Now, with sudden exertion, he would rise, but remain root-
ed to the spot, listening to the mighty south wind, which
lowed and shook the gnarled boughs of the mesquites, as if
it could bring him news to calm the fever of his mind. Then,
his eyes, with a vacant stare, would follow the flight of the
pelican, which, from the highest verge of the sky, cleft the
air with the velocity of lightning, and plunged into the blue
pool at his feet, to seize upon his unsuspecting prey. Next,
his fingers would mechanically pluck a blossom from the adjoining bough, and scatter its leaves to the wind ; but from
nothing did his mind experience the least relief, and one single bitter, overpowering and crushing thought seemed to engross his attention.

The quarteroon endeavored to rouse him from that mu-
sing, which appeared to border on monomania ; but still, judging that it might proceed from some secret pain of the heart,
he essayed to probe the wound, and said to him : " Now,
sir, your soul is overburdened with some heavy weight :—
might I presume to solicit a share of your confidence ?—
God is my witness, it is not through vain curiosity, but only
through a desire of affording you consolation, I address you
this request. It is true, our acquaintance has been but short,
yet I have given proofs of the utmost devotion, and there is,
between kindred spirits, a communion of feelings !—If we
were in a country where the line of demarcation between
your race and mine is rigorously drawn, I would abstain
from urging my petition, but a perfect equality prevails here,
and you have been so kind to me, that I cannot suppose you
lack confidence in my probity. Oh ! disburden your heart,
and trust a man, who, notwithstanding the distance which
separates him from you, still dares call himself your friend."

" You are my friend, indeed," replied the captain, " neither will I, for one single moment, suffer an unnatural prejudice to control my feelings ; but I hardly know how to express the thoughts which engross my mind at this moment.

Confiding them even to an only brother would be excrucia-ting. Excuse me, then, dear Flambeau!—My heart is burst-ing, it is true ; yet, I am conscious there is no one fully able to understand me ; or enter into my grief."

"And why not?" replied the quarteroon. "Think not so meanly of one, whose lot it has been, indeed, to move in an humble sphere through life, but who is not altogether ig-norant of mental sensibility—that luxury of the soul—so apt to inflict on man exquisite pains ; but which is, nevertheless, the *seal of predestination* for great thoughts and noble deeds. I am able to understand you.—Why should I not ?—I have suffered so much myself !"

Señor de Letinez, notwithstanding his repugnance, was conquered by this ardent desire of sharing in his grief, and made the quarteroon participant of the state of his mind. The latter had not presumed too much on his powers of per-suasion and consolation. He assuaged the captain's anxiety, reanimated his hopes, and strengthened his confidence in himself. Thus restored, in great measure, to calm and for-titude, our hero proposed to continue his route, and had al-ready his foot in the stirrup, to mount his horse, when a band of robbers rushed upon him and his fellow traveller.

Flambeau and the captain were completely surprised, and in the utter impossibility of making use of their arms : of course, they were at the robbers' mercy. The latter were beginning to pillage their effects, and having discovered that Flambeau could not speak Spanish, began, with a volley of tremendous oaths, to curse him for an American, and even one of them proposed to kill him, when the captain recog-nized among them some of the troopers of his own company of horse.

"How, now ! Pedro Tormoya," cried he, taking a tone of authority, " Is it, thus, you welcome your captain, after he has been so happy as to make his escape from among the Texians !—You, who were one of my favorite soldiers !—and you also, Santiago Soliño ?—What in the world has oc-curred to induce you to take to this evil course ?—I could have sworn you were both men of honor !"

" *Y valga me Dios Señor Capitan !*" exclaimed Soliño and Tormoya, " who could have recognized you, under the strange garb which you wear ? But blessed be the Virgin of Guadelupe and St. Corolampio, that you have escaped from the hands of those heretics! Very sorry that we attacked you ;—very sorry, indeed!—It will give you a bad opinion of us ! But really, sir, we cannot help it. We must do it, or starve. We get only half a rial a day to procure victuals and all other necessaries, in a place, where, even a whole rial would not buy a sufficiency of bread for one man. Either the government makes no remittances, or they are absorbed by the generals. All the troops are perishing with want, and there is nothing now to be got in Matamoros. Half of the foreign merchants are gone."

"And who commanded the army, when you left it ?" interrupted Señor de Letinez.

" *Valga me Dios !*" replied Soliño, astonished at the query and crossing himself, " we have not left it ; we are not deserters.—God forbid we should be ! we can obtain leave of absence, every now and then. As our officers have little to give us, they are indulgent, but we do not make a bad use of their kindness and kill nobody. Even this fellow, here, a servant of yours, I suppose,"—added he, pointing to Flambeau ; " we would not have done him any harm, although we spoke so roughly about him."

" He is not my servent," said Captain Letinez. " He is my friend, and a *Christian* and I wish you to respect him as myself."

" Oh ! if he be a Christian, that is quite another thing," replied one of the robbers :—" so, all the Texians are not Jews, then, as our clergy say !"

This was, by the captain, translated to Flambeau, in order to convince him how important it was, in that country, to lean on the church for protection, and the quarteroon, wittily taking the hint, corroborated our hero's statement, and confirmed the robbers in the idea of his orthodoxy, by making the sign of the cross, which dispelled any doubt that might have been lurking in their mind, and delighted them so much, that two of them actually shook him cordially by the hand, in token of spiritual fellowship.

The captain inquired from Pedro Tormoya, who was endowed with intelligence above mediocrity, for news from the army, and the particulars of the disastrous retreat under Filisola, to which the other answered, that it would be rather a lengthy relation and tiresome to be listened to standing, (for they had all along retained that posture,) but that, if his worship had no objection, they might sit down, on the green sward, and he would recount all, *de pe a pa*, as it had occurred.

To this Señor de Letinez gave his assent, and after they had stretched themselves on the grass, Tormoya began his narrative, the thread of which he interrupted every now and then, in order to drop quaint reflections, of his own, on the conduct of the chiefs, or various accidents, which had had an untoward influence on the result of the campaign.

# CHAPTER IX.

The feast of Crispian :
He that outlives this day, and comes safe home,
Will stand a tip-toe, when this day is named,
And rouse him at the name of *Crispian*.
*King Henry V. Act IV.*

" SHORTLY after you left us," said the narrator, " we reached Brazoria, having crossed the river near the plantation of
a man of the name of Cartwright, who fled with all his family, but was so much disturbed in mind, that during a considerable space of time, he kept within sight of us, as though
we had been convoying him, with all his slaves and property.
This exceedingly diverted our officers and the amusement it
afforded was the cause that they let him escape scot-free.
Finding, however, that part of the country too low, we resolved to leave it, for, in case of a rise in the river, its banks,
we knew, would be overflowed, and our division could not
but perish.    You know what repugnance Mexicans feel for
water.    A single shower of rain dispirits us more than a
week's hunger and thirst.    Now, that cursed country of
Texas is nothing but a swamp—at least, along the sea-shore.
There is a river at every tenth league, and such rivers as
carry ships !    You may judge what a frightful prospect it
was for us, who, in all the table-land of Mexico, have no
larger stream than the Rio Nassas, and think a country well
watered, if there is a spring in forty miles.    We left Brazoria, therefore, with all possible haste and followed the left
bank of the stream, in order to reach an elevated spot, where
we would be safe against the fear of inundations.    But in
our march, we had a terrible fright.    We were first alarmed
by a horrid noise, repeated at short intervals, and with which
the woods rung to a vast distance.—It was like no earthly
sound that I ever heard before.—Some of our men, who were
from the state of Jalisco, declared it reminded them of the

hissings of the volcano of Colima, when heard from a distance, while a *Yucateco*, who had been at sea, maintained
that it was the blowing of a large fish of the whale kind.
All our corps came to a stand, and the men looked aghast,
not knowing whether to flee, or stand their ground. Presently, we saw a large machine, much bigger than a ship,
floating on the surface of the water, and coming towards us
with incredible velocity. On the prow was a large furnace,
from whence volumes of flame and smoke escaped, by two
big iron tubes, which towered aloft, like huge cannons, and
on either side was an enormous wheel, whirling round, as if
ten thousand spirits from the bottomless pit had been lodged
in it. These wheels were armed with flapboards, to put the
water in motion, and raise an artificial storm in the river,
as some of our officers conjectured, in order to prevent us
from recrossing to the other side. Upon that *abominable invention* drawing near, most of our troops were on the point of
breaking loose and running off, but the very terror it inspired prevented them! In fact, we were not sure it might not
overtake us by land, and we had no other resource than
prayer. So, we fell upon our knees and called upon the
Blessed Virgin of Guadelupe and Almighty God!—She delivered us from that horrid witchcraft, and we continued our
route, but sadly dispirited. How could it be otherwise ?—
without any priest amongst us, we were exposed to the wicked arts of those heretics and the powers of Hell !—Fighting
for our country, yet without absolution, or extreme unction,
in case of death ! And then, to be buried like dogs, without
either prayers, or *Suffragios*, from an ecclesiastic !—oh, sir,
but it was a disastrous prospect and awful anticipation !

" We were forced to continue our march, but, from that
moment, I augured badly of the expedition, and would to
God my forebodings had not been so well-founded ! Would
to God, Mexico had not received that deep humiliation, the
stain of which will prove so difficult to blot out.

" We had proceeded a considerable way towards bayou
Buffalo, when we heard the news of the disastrous defeat of
San Jacinto. Filisola now succeeded in command to Santa
Anna. We were all afraid lest the prisoners—among whom
was nearly the whole staff, comprising several of the most
distinguished generals—should be put to death by the rebels,

in order to avenge the massacre of Goliad, but Santa Anna had art enough to turn away the wrath of the Texians. It must be confessed, that, if he has the greatest knack in the world for falling into snares, he has also an admirable skill for getting out of them. His genius is a real paradox : such a blundering disposition was never before mingled with so much craftiness.—When, at Tampico, he so inconsiderately rushed into the clutches of Barradas ; did it not, in the end, turn to his greater glory, and did he not succeed in capturing his captor ? That very thing brought him to the presidential chair, and, I have no doubt, the affair of San Jacinto will, after all, turn to his profit and serve to his further elevation. He is a man whose fate it is to derive as great advantages from his defeats, as others do from their victories. He will, no doubt, find it difficult to get out of the hands of the Texians, but you will see that he will accomplish it, in the end, and rise again in Mexico. Though a prisoner, his instructions and orders were obeyed by Filisola. There was a grand council of superior officers held at the house of one Madama Paoli, where a retreat was agreed on, and where all the generals insisted upon Filisola retaining the command.

" The army, disorganized as it was, could not have continued on the offensive, and had the Texians known our situation, they might have easily destroyed us. Perhaps they were still afraid of us, after their victory, for I have, since, understood they had not above six hundred men, and, upon the whole, it was wisely done by Houston, to let us return, for it is certain this retreat has dispirited our nation as much as a complete annihilation of the army could have done. We are not the same in a foreign land as upon our own territory. When battling on the parent soil, against the Spaniards, we were incited by our native clergy, who had to avenge upon the Gachupines, the humiliation and contempt of two hundred years' duration—things which priests never forgive !—We prevailed by the weight of overwhelming masses, and, had the Spaniards been as numerous as we, it is very doubtful whether we could have succeeded. But none of these things can be brought to bear upon Texas. Our clergy would certainly be desirous that we should drive the heretics away, but none, among those who possess eloquence and can manage large masses, will take the trouble to come and inspire the minds of our soldiers; neither does the supreme government pay any attention to this powerful mover. If, after long murmurs, on the part of the army, they send us a chaplain, it is some foolish friar, who can hardly read the Latin of his breviary, and does nothing but bring religion into contempt. The race of preaching heroes seems extinct amongst us.—There are no longer any Moreloses, or Matamoroses!—Even father Belausaran seems to have turned a dolt, since they have put a mitre on his head. One would think that it has addled his brain!"

"But, my dear fellow, you are straying from the subject of your narration," interrupted the captain. "I long to hear the history of your retreat, and you lose yourself in useless reflections upon political subjects, which neither you nor I can amend."

"Ah, it is true, Sir," replied Tormoya, "it was my patriotism which carried me away.—But let us resume. As soon as the Texians had agreed to spare the life of the President and his companions in arms, we began our retreat. General Filisola offered again to cede the command to any one whom the other chiefs might elect, but all insisted upon his retaining it; yet, from that moment, Urrea commenced to undermine him, in his correspondence with the supreme government, and, at last, succeeded in obtaining his post.

"Our march was accompanied by every dismal circumstance that can be imagined—hunger, nakedness, violent rains and a complete *destitution of spiritual succors* for the sick and dying! The generals engrossed all the wagons and beasts of burden, to convey away the plunder they had seized, so that part of the necessary baggage was left behind. But it was particularly at a place called *Atascadito*, that we suffered beyond what I thought possible for humanity to bear. By a dreadful cold rain, we found ourselves in the middle of a swamp, through which the utmost progress of a day was only of three miles! There appeared no possible means of extricating the artillery, and our officers would have left it behind, had it not been for the unparalleled exertions of Don Pedro de Ampudia, commandant of that corps, who, by his indefatigable resolution, succeeded in saving all the guns, and prevented the soldiers from breaking the

8*

carriages to pieces, in order to get fire-wood to warm themselves.

" Our vanguard, under Urrea's command, preceded the main body, by five or six days' march, and, as they went, gleaned every thing which had escaped us, in the month of February ; so that, at our coming on, (for I had joined the main body,) we found nothing to pick up. We were followed by certain Texian commissioners, coming under the treaty, to claim some property taken from them, and particularly negroes, who had sought refuge in Matamoros. There was, also, a small body of observation, of theirs, who accompanied us part of the way, and even did us considerable service, by helping us out of some swamps, in which our artillery would have remained buried, had it not been for their assistance. This kindness, however, met but with a poor requital, for, no sooner did the commissioners reach Matamoros, than Urrea made them prisoners ; but this by the by.

" The troops which had been left to garrison Bexar had suffered, perhaps, more than the rest, so that, notwithstanding the earnest desire of our supreme government, at Mexico, and their strict orders that the place should not be abandoned, it became impossible to hold that post.

" Santa Anna had entered the city of Bexar on the twenty third of February, and after a considerable loss, before the walls of the Alamo, had taken that fortress by storm on the sixth of March, and now it was restored to the Texians, without firing a single gun. It is, perhaps, to a blunder, committed by Santa Anna, in the intoxication of success, after his entrance into the Alamo, that we owe all the disasters of our unlucky campaign. He had permitted a Texian lady,* who was found alive in the fort, after the slaughter was over, to withdraw in her gig, and it was by her means Houston got information of our arrival. But this act of foolish generosity on the part of our president was of a piece with the rest of his conduct. The title of *Vencedor del Alamo* turned his head, and he stopped at no extravagance. The troops that came from Bexar had such anecdotes to relate, concerning his many acts of profligate folly, that they stagger all belief, though too well attested to be called in question.

* Mrs. Dickinson.

" Many of the old inhabitants of that place followed the garrison and among them was a beautiful young woman, who, having, with the most persevering resolution, resisted Santa Anna's seductions, had been decoyed into a marriage by that monster. The chaplain of the army had been wicked enough to celebrate it, with all the accustomed formalities ; although he, as well as all the officers, knew that Santa Anna had a wife and children, in the state of Vera Cruz. The poor woman, in her simplicity, styled herself *Presidentess of the Republic*, and required to be treated with the respect due to her dignity. Out of compassion, nobody would undeceive her, and the state she affected, in the midst of poverty and rags, cast a hue of ridicule upon our retreat, which, in my opinion, seemed to render its gloom more disheartening.

"Before reaching the Rio Bravo, Urrea took the supreme command, and Filisola was obliged to repair to Mexico, in danger of being tried for *that* very retreat, which, though disastrous, was nevertheless, a proof of talent and generalship ; whereby he had, not only saved the president and his fellow prisoners' lives, but even rescued the army from destruction. No doubt, as it was a mortification for our national pride, he had to bear the odium ; and as he is a foreigner by birth, he found less sympathy. But I expect they will do him justice yet ; for, notwithstanding the outcry raised against him, it is certain our affairs have gone on much worse, since he has resigned the command.

" When we reached the river and were ready to cross over to Matamoros, we felt completely broken down, both in body and mind ; and since that time, desertions have become so numerous, that our army has dwindled down to two thousand men. In the meanwhile, Urrea is carrying on every thing with a high hand, in Matamoros, and seems determined to make hay while the sun shines. He has, by his own authority, displaced the collector of the custom-house, and given the office to one of his creatures, who *collects* in partnership with him.—This campaign will be worth to him a brilliant fortune."

Señor de Letinez had, all along, expected to hear some news of Miss Quinton and her father ; but his informer, it seems, had not noticed them ; for, even to his specific inquiries he could answer nothing satisfactory. He only happened to know that seven or eight of the colonists, taken at Go-. liad, had been saved, in quality of physicians, and two of them sent to Bexar, to attend the sick. Some of them, he added, were, *now*, at liberty in the city.—As to any young lady, he could not tell.—There were so many, young or old, who followed the army! The whole town of St. Patricio had come along with the troops, when the latter left Texas, in order to escape the wrath of the rebels, against whom they had borne arms, in the beginning of the campaign.— She might be among them! But he was not able to say.

Our hero, therefore, derived very little desirable informa- tion from Tormoya's confused account, and his anxiety about the fate of his fair one continued unrelieved. He could not, however, part from the robbers, without giving them a severe rebuke, for their wickedness; and the two who had belonged to his company were so sensible of their misconduct, that they asked his pardon and promised to change their lives.

## CHAPTER X.

Loved scenes, loved friends—long lost, around me rise,
And wake the melting thought, the tender tear !
That tear, that thought, which more than mirth
I prize.

*Mrs. Radcliffe.*

OUR travellers having resumed their route, soon entered
Matamoros, where the first scene which presented itself to
their view greatly surprised Flambeau, and excited his cen-
sure, as a ridiculous and unnatural thing. It was a procession, which he judged to be of a religious description, from a
number of clergymen in their canonicals, accompanying it ;
and holden for some joyful purpose, from the brilliant music
that played and the great number of rockets which were fired.
Yet they were carrying the corpse of an infant, and it was
the little creature's funeral obsequies they were thus solemn-
izing ! He asked the captain an explanation of this singularity and seeming contradiction ; to which our hero answered that the Mexicans, as Roman Catholics, not only believe
that infants, dying after baptism, are admitted to the immediate enjoyment of heavenly bliss ; but that they rigorously
follow up the consequences of this consoling dogma, and actually rejoice in their children's death, whenever they happen
to die under age. " This music and these rockets," said he,
" are a manifestation of gladness, on the part of the child's
parents ; because he is become a little angel, (angelito).
This will not be the only expression of joy. This night,
there will be a ball and carousal in their house, and how poor
soever they may be, they would not dare to omit these re-
joicings, which are, here, no less than tears and lamentations,
in other countries, accounted tokens of parental love."

" It is very strange," said the quarteroon, " that the strongest feeling of nature can be thus suspended, and the purest
passion of the human heart, counteracted, by a remote consequence of one of the minor dogmas of religion."

" Yet, perhaps, in this instance," resumed the captain, "it is of service. It affords, at least, a harmless consolation to the bereaved parents and dries up tears, which would flow to no purpose."

" Such is not my opinion of this singular practice of your countrymen," returned the quarteroon. " I would not speak against the religious dogma, upon which it is based. As a speculative tenet, it is consoling ; and I would not condemn the spiritual rejoicing of the church, at the death of the infant Christian ; because her joy is pure, grave and pious, and manifests itself by canticles of praise to the Most High. But to see rational creatures making the death of a poor innocent child an occasion of merriment—to see parents so far hardening their hearts, as to dance on the brink of their infant's grave—is shocking and worthy of barbarians."

" Well, you may be right, for aught I know," returned the captain ; " but beware how you express such an opinion to any body else, for it might give offence, and would be looked upon as downright impiety. Many other things you will see, which may appear strange and unnatural ; but be cautious how you manifest your feelings before the natives, for they are jealous of foreigners, and apt to suspect of Judaism, any one who gainsays their religious prejudices, and that may bring a man into great danger. My father, nineteen years ago, was stabbed for much less ; and, thank God, the dagger glanced along one of his ribs, otherwise I would not be here to tell the story."

" With these reflections, they passed by the funeral procession, and alighted before a fine house, in Sonora street, where the captain had been informed, in Camargo, that the *teniente* of his troop of horse, who had succeeded him, was lodged. The latter was delighted to see him, and received him with the utmost civility. He did not, however, permit his guest to rest himself, before he insisted upon his shaving and dressing, in order to pay a visit to the general-in-chief. *Dressing*, in 'the fashionable sense of the expression, was a thing entirely out of our hero's power ; for he found himself in that philosophical state of existence, when he might say, with the Grecian sage, " *omnia mecum porto.*" How humbling soever the situation, he freely confessed it to his friend ; who, immediately, placed at his disposal a suit of his own.

In this borrowed garb, therefore, our captain sallied forth, to pay his respects to Urrea. He felt inclined to go, first, in search of Miss Quinton and her father; but his friend, having represented to him that his first visit was strictly due to the general, he suffered himself to be led along, in hopes the interview would be of short duration, and fully resolved to spend the remainder of the day in his beloved one's company.

Urrea received him with transports of joy, and after inquiring the particulars of the battle of San Jacinto, and the state of affairs among the Texians, said to him, " Now, my dear fellow, although glad to see you, I confess your return embarrasses me. In your absence, your troop of horse has been given to your friend, here, who was once your lieutenant. We believed you dead, and he deserved promotion. We cannot make him retrograde to his former rank, yet you have suffered so much in your country's cause, that you cannot remain without a post, and I have none to give. What shall we do, in this case ? Will you accept of the rank of *colonel graduado?* It is honorable, and the fortune of your family enables you to dispense with the emoluments."

" Why, General," replied Captain Letinez, " do not put yourself to any trouble on my account. I will be glad to retire from the service, and by tendering my resignation of my own accord, I conceive I will smooth all difficulties."

" Resign !—No, indeed !" replied Urrea. " You shall not. You must accept my proposal. Think how glorious,—from a mere captain, to become, at once, a colonel !"

" There are so many *graduados,* sir !" resumed our captain.

" It is true," said Urrea, " we have an immense number: I dare say thirty or forty generals, and eighty or ninety colonels, without exercise ! But still it is accounted an honor, and will be especially so, in so young a man. Therefore, I insist upon it. I will immediately write to the secretary of war, and in the meanwhile, if you wish to go to Mechoacan, to visit your relations, I will give you leave of absence; and you may take your time for your return, for it will be long before we are ready for another campaign."

Our hero consented at last, rather to satisfy the general, and get rid of his importunities, than from any desire of elevation—and, having taken leave, proceeded to the *cuartel,* or barracks, where, he had been informed, several of the Texians were confined, in order to make inquiries concerning Major Quinton. These prisoners of war had been in great danger of being shot, by order of Santa Anna, but the French, American and Irish merchants of Matamoros had saved their lives,* by offering a large sum of money, and the Mexican ladies of the same place had, also, presented in their behalf a very eloquent petition; for which it is just to render to their humanity the meed of praise it deserves. But the lives which had been saved with so much difficulty were nigh being lost for want of food. The Mexicans gave their prisoners nothing to eat, and, had not the same men, who had already made such generous offers to save them from death, subscribed for their support, they would actually have been starved. Nor is it to be supposed that, in this instance, the Mexicans were impelled by any special hatred to the Texians, since it is in the same way they treat their own prisoners. As soon as a man is under lock and key, the government meddles no more with his bodily wants, but abandons him to the charity of the faithful! In desperate cases, only, and when hunger grows ravenous, they sometimes permit prisoners to go out, under the guard of a soldier, and *beg*, through the streets, when a portion of what he gets is bestowed upon his guard.

Captain Letinez did not find Major Quinton among the prisoners, but heard of his being in town, and was directed to his house. It was a little cabin, built of large unburnt bricks, called *adobes*, in the language of the country, and thatched with *tule*, a kind of rushes that grow in the swampy bottoms of the Rio Bravo, and are nearly incombustible. The thatch itself, by the effect of time, had been reduced to an earthy mass, now shrunk into consistency, and affording sustenance to a multiplicity of parasitic plants, which, being in full bloom, gave it the appearance of a *parterre*. Among them, various kinds of cacti, and young mimosas were remarkable, some with pink blossoms, and others with pale yellow ones. The captain was not a little amused by this singular appearance, but upon entering the edifice, he was shocked at the state of poverty which its interior exhibited.

* In half an hour, thirty thousand dollars were subscribed.

The only person he found in the house was an old female Indian servant, who acted as drudge to the family. This was no proof of easy circumstances in the owners, for servants are so cheap in that country, that almost every householder keeps three or four. The furniture consisted of a little cot, with coarse, though extremely clean bed clothes, a small table, four old chairs without backs, and a mattress rolled up in a corner, which, being spread at night on a rug carpet, served one of the inmates for bed. Some crockery ware upon a shelf, a few books on the mantel-piece, and two trunks completed the inventory.

The aged sybil who, for the moment, acted as housekeeper, being asked where was Major Quinton, answered with a kind of stutter, that he was culling fruit in the Huerta, and immediately opened a side-door, made of wattled reeds, giving access to a little court-yard, through which she marshalled our hero to the gate of the garden. It was rather a kind of orchard, full of fig, pomegranate and orange-trees, planted without any attention to symmetry. They were so thick, and their foliage was so dense, as to afford a coolness extremely pleasant in that southern climate ; and moreover produced a kind of artificial night upon the vision of one who, coming from the glare of the broad day-light, entered this deep shade.

The Indian beldame, having left our hero to grope his way as well as he could through this labyrinth in search of her master, hastily returned to the house, the door of which she had left opened ; so that Captain Letinez was at a loss which way to direct his steps, not knowing in what part of the garden the major might be found. His eyes having, nevertheless, in a few seconds, become used to the half light which rested on the empty space, under the verdant canopy that overshadowed his head, he distinguished at the extremity of the garden a little arbor, under which a female figure was in a sitting posture.

Thither he directed his steps, and had the inexpressible pleasure to find that it was Miss Quinton herself. She was so busy sewing, as not to notice his approach, and he stopped at a short distance to contemplate her ; while a variety of tender emotions rapidly succeeded each other in his mind. He had found her again—his beloved one !—the only woman he had ever loved, and whom he loved to adoration!—He had found her again, and under such circumstances, as rendered a union certain. Her father's life had been saved by his friend's exertions. Gratitude, he thought, would combine with love in Miss Quinton's heart, and in the intoxication of his hope, he was almost sure of her consent. She and her father had lost their fortune—they were now in want and poverty! He was almost pleased with it, for it would serve to prove the disinterested fervor of his affection. But she was pale!—Oh! how much she must have suffered in those scenes of war and desolation!—Yes, the weight of wo had sunk her eyes and diminished their lustre.—The tears of misfortune had furrowed her cheeks.—Perhaps some of those tears had been shed for him!—Yet, though suffering, how beautiful!—Even more interesting than when in the bloom of perfect health.

> " The rose that was upon her cheek
> Was mellowed by a tenderer streak."

He must advance, but lo! He trembles like a child! His knees can hardly support his tottering frame. He, the accomplished gentleman—who can acquit himself with so much grace and elegance, in the most polished circles and brightest companies—is now at a loss for words to hail the maid he loves. He feels that he is blushing at the thought of this interview. Blush on, dear youth—blush on! As Diogenes said, it is the color of virtue. She whom thou lovest cannot take offence at the embarrassment thou feelest.—Were thy heart less pure, thou wouldst be bolder.

The spell was at last broken by Major Quinton, who, till that moment, had remained busy, in a remote corner of the garden; but, having now finished his task, approached the place where his daughter was sitting, and was startled at the sight of a man standing so close to the arbor. He drew near with a threatening aspect, but, recognising him, threw himself in his arms, crying out, " oh, my dear friend—is it you?" He had no time to continue, when Miss Quinton raised her eyes from the work which had engrossed her attention—saw her lover—gave a scream of surprise—sprang up from her chair, but fell again upon it, in a deep swoon.

The captain and her father ran to her help, and after considerable efforts brought her to the use of her senses. The first manifestation she gave of her returning consciousness was by a flood of tears, which alleviated a little the fulness of her heart. Her lover was behind her chair, when she first recovered from that state, and missing him, she said, " oh, father, was it a dream, or has Captain Letinez really been here ?"

He could no longer control himself. " Yes, my dear Miss Quinton," said he, " I am here—your own Letinez, always faithful and true. Yes, my love,—I have returned, more worthy of you. I have learned, during my captivity, that you as much surpass your own countrywomen, in kindness of heart and generosity of disposition, as *they* surpass mine, in beauty and gracefulness ; and if I was thy lover, before," added he, kissing her hand with ardor, " I am now thy adorer !—Here is your father who will not refuse his consent to our mutual vows.—He will become *my* father, also, and I will glory in the adoption."

" Yes—I will," said the old man, embracing him, " and heaven is my witness, with what sincere joy !—I receive you as the greatest blessing God can bestow upon me. Had I selected a son-in-law among ten thousand, I could not have made a better choice. Yes, my children, you will be both happy, and crown my old age with gladness. Be not ashamed, my daughter," continued he, addressing Sophia, whose face was suffused with blushes, " be not ashamed to confess your virtuous flame, when you have your father's consent, and the approbation of your own conscience.—Consider yourselves as plighted to each other, and may the blessing of heaven attend you."

Miss Quinton, now a little composed, and feeling all the embarrassment of maidenly modesty, rose to withdraw ; but the captain, in an ecstasy of joy, at seeing the object of his ardent wishes obtained, and emboldened by the father's presence, could not help clasping her to his bosom, and stealing a kiss, as the earnest of future bliss.

> " Dear wedded love !
> Which men so seldom blameless prove ;
> A harmless pair, for once at least,
> Thy holy pleasures taste.

Now, walking hand in hand, they returned to the house, where the Major and the captain, in close colloquy, made their arrangements and took all the measures they thought necessary for the execution of their scheme. All parties being equally desirous to bring it to a happy issue, they did not anticipate any difficulty, chiefly as there was no matter of interest to be debated or settled. They were, however, destined to be crossed, by an unknown circumstance—which, how trifling soever it might have appeared, in any other country—is, in Mexico, a thing of the utmost importance, as the reader will see by the trouble it gave them.

## CHAPTER XI.

Heap up impediments to lawful things,
And then grant dispensation for an alms.
*Dr. Spunge.*

THE first thing our hero inquired of Major Quinton, after his transports were calmed, was the history of his escape from the massacre, with which our reader is already acquainted, and the details of his journey from Goliad to Matamoros, in which there was nothing peculiarly interesting. The few prisoners who had been saved from that horrid butchery had been sent, under an escort, to the Irish village, where Miss Quinton had found again her old acquaintance, honest Mrs. Jordan, and retaken possession of her little apartment, while her father and a few others were kept confined in an out-house, belonging to the Alcalde, who treated them, nevertheless, with humanity. They had, afterwards, followed the inhabitants of San Patricio, when the latter left their town, at the instigation of Urrea, who threatened, that, at his return, he would make no destinction between friend and foe, but would hang every man and burn every house. Since his arrival at Matamoros, Major Quinton, who had seen himself reduced to act the part of the *Medecin malgré lui;* had made several friends amongst the Mexican officers, and obtained permission to remain in a private house with his daughter. There he had maintained himself by tending his garden, while the young lady helped, also, by her skill in millinery.

The captain's curiosity being satisfied, the conversation naturally reverted to his intended marriage. Major Quinton had no idea of the many intricacies and formalities by which a matrimonial union is attended in Mexico. He supposed it would be as easy, as in the United States, where all that a man has to do, in most of the states, is to take out a license from the clerk of the court, and apply to a justice of the peace, who ties the knot in the twinkling of an eye. In Mex-

9*

ico, it is quite different. The canon law, there, regulates those matters, and it seems to have been the purpose of canonists to throw the greatest difficulties in the way of the most necessary thing in nature. They knew that people would marry, cost what it might, and, by their skilful ordinances, they have turned this into a capital source of revenue for the church.

In our hero's case, these difficulties were of a peculiar nature. First, the lady and gentleman, being natives of other dioceses than that of Monterey, in which Matamoros is situated, they were obliged to get their *fe de bautismo*, id est, their certificate of baptism. For this purpose, Captain Letinez must write to Mechoacan, and wait, at least, two months, before the important paper should arrive; while his bride would have, perhaps, to wait half a year, before she could get her papers, from Maryland, where she had been baptized in the Church of England.

" This difficulty once over, they had both to prove that they were *unmarried*, which was proving a negative, and might be considered by Anglo-Saxon metaphysicians as impossible ; but which is, nevertheless, strictly required by Mexican laws, and is done, every day, after some fashion or other, in the wise republic of Anahuac.

Thirdly, there was the article of religion. Miss Quinton being a Protestant, her marriage could not be solemnized without a special dispensation from the Pope, or the Bishop of Monterey—in case the jurisdiction of the latter should have been enlarged by the Holy See. All this would require time, expense and powerful friends.—Expenses the captain could afford—friends he had—but time was what he grudged. He thought proper, however, to explain all this to the Major, in order that his own sincerity might not be suspected, should not the marriage be accomplished as quickly as external circumstances might induce any one not acquainted with the laws of the country to think practicable.

This subject of conversation being exhausted, our hero took leave of the worthy Major, and returned to the house of his *quondam* lieutenant, where he soon began to receive the visits of his friends. As he was a general favorite in the army, and the history of his escape from among the Texians was so romantic, every one was curious to see him. One of the first who presented themselves was Captain Alvarez, whom Señor de Letinez embraced with real transports of joy, while some tears of gratitude, which he could not repress, bathed his cheeks and expressed to his friend, better than the choicest words could have done, the sincere acknowledgement of his heart, for having saved Major Quinton's life, and so efficiently protected the young lady to whom he was attached. Major Quinton had informed him of the noble and almost heroical manner in which Alvarez had stood forth, as the champion of humanity, and Captain Letinez thought he could never sufficiently acknowledge such a piece of service. " Alvarez," said he, " I will not fatigue you by long protestations of gratitude ; but had you saved my own life, I could not feel more than I do. From henceforth, all I have—my credit and that of my family— are at your disposal."

" Dear Don Ambrosio," answered his friend, " I did no more than humanity required. Would to God I had been able to save them all ! But, for Heaven's sake, let us drop that subject, and banish so painful a recollection from our minds. Let us rather talk about your marriage. Ah, lucky rogue ! You must have been born with a cawl upon your head—to light upon so much beauty and sense united ! It was your good angel, no doubt, who inspired you to go on that expedition against the Comanches ! We thought it the trick of a madcap, when we heard of it, but it will turn out a fortunate trick for you !—And now, when comes the wedding ?—The sponsalia ?—I hope you will give a ball, and the thing will be done with some *eclat*.—I want to open the dance with your bride.—By my *Santiguada*, it is my due !"

" So it is, indeed," replied Señor de Letinez, laughing, " and you shall dance as long as you please, but I am afraid, that, notwithstanding your impatience, we shall have sometime to wait, yet."

" Wait !" replied Alvarez, with surprise, " and for what— pray ?"

" Why," returned our hero, " I have to write to Mechoacan, for my certificate of baptism, and to get a dispensation of the publication of bans, both in my native parish and here ; and the young lady has to procure her *papers*, from Maryland—which is great ways off, in the north of the United States."

" Pooh, pooh !—wherefore all that ?" replied Alvarez. " Do not suppose that the padre, here, is so scrupulous.   No, not he—good man.   He will never require such things from you, provided you pay him a good round sum."

" Do you think," inquired the other, " that he will, to oblige me, violate those canons of discipline ?"

" Canons !" resumed Alvarez.    " He has spiked more canons than you or I ever saw fired.—What a babe you are ! You think every priest is like your grand-uncle, and that other good soul in Phelipa, of whom I have heard you speak so frequently !—Clergymen who are walking towards Heaven on tip-toe !   There are not many such in the Mexican church."

" But, then," objected Captain Letinez, " I do not want to render my marriage null and invalid."

" This will not affect it, in the least," answered his friend. —" It is an impediment, to be sure ;  but not one which breaks the bands of matrimony.   There is your *impedimentum dirimens*, and your *impedimentum impedins*.   The want of publication of bans, belongs to the latter category only.— You should know *this*, as you are now a courting gallant.— It is the priest's business to require it from you, but it is none of yours to make him mind it, if he be willing to overlook it."

" Well, really," replied our hero, " the thing had never struck my mind in this point of view.   I stand corrected by your superior knowledge of Divinity."

" So much the worse for you, then," said Alvarez,   " In a country like ours, where the canon law is part and parcel of the law of the land, every gentleman, particularly one who is in love, should be something of a canonist."

" Well," resumed Captain Letinez, " since you are so knowing, I will consult you upon another difficulty.   Miss Quinton is a Protestant, and will not change her religion, I know—neither do I intend proposing it to her.   Will *that* make any difficulty with this padre ?"

" Not the least—not the least," replied Alvarez ;  " only be liberal with him, and you will find him the most liberal man in the world.—*Ave Maria !*—He would marry a man of your condition to a Jewess, or Turkish woman, if you wished,

and never bogle at it. Foreigners accuse our clergy of illiberality, but they would reverse the judgment they pass on
them, were they all like Padre Rapiñez."

"If such be the case," said Señor de Letinez, "there will
be no difficulty with me, and I will come through, easily
enough!"

"You will—you shall," resumed his friend ; "and therefore, I hope the business will be soon over."

"Not so quick, either," observed our hero ; "for, although
there is no need of postponement, for the publication of bans,
and other formalities, yet I must write to my grandfather and
his brother.—It would be the basest ingratitude in me to marry without informing them of it, and asking their leave.—I
know their love for me will not permit them to refuse their
consent."

"As to this," said Alvarez, "it is a different thing !—
Certainly, it is your duty to write to them. I would be the
first to blame you, if you did not."

Thus enlightened by Captain Alvarez's superior information in canonical matters, and well assured of Padre Rapiñez's pliability of principle, our hero felt relieved from an
oppressive weight ; for, from what he knew of the history of
his father's marriage, he had imagined the difficulties he
would have to encounter would almost prove insuperable ; or,
at least, put so many delays in the way of the accomplishment of his wishes, that sometimes he felt tempted to despair.

Captain Alvarez was not the only one who took a lively
interest in his fate and future union with the worthy object of
his affection. A considerable number of his brother officers
congratulated him also on the acquisition of Miss Quinton's
hand, and it was in the midst of those friendly demonstrations,
that he directed to the old Count and the good clergyman, his
brother, a letter informing them of his engagement and asking their permission for his marriage.

There was another person to whom he was tenderly attached, and whom he wished it had been in his power to consult. It was his father. But he was at too great a distance.
Though Mr. Faring had never insisted on carrying his son
to the United States, for fear of exposing him to lose his
grandfather's fortune ; yet he had taken several trips to Me-

choacan, in order to visit him, and had made on the boy's mind an impression which time could not obliterate. The last of those visits had taken place about three years previous to the period of which we are now treating—when our hero was a lad of fifteen—and his father had then promised to return in four years and take him to travel. This plan would be now defeated by the young man's marriage ; but yet the latter complied with what filial piety required of him, by despatching a letter to Mr. Faring, at the same time that he wrote to his grandfather.

Our hero being now wholly engrossed by his matrimonial scheme, Flambeau, who had been accustomed to live with him in the greatest familiarity, saw himself somewhat neglected, and being exceedingly sensitive, resolved to leave the captain. In vain the latter expostulated with him, the quarteroon answered, in a melancholy manner, that he was too sensible of the distance which separated them, to expect familiarity, and that he could not resolve himself to live again as a menial. He had formed an acquaintance with some colored people, refugees, like himself, who carried on a little smuggling, between the mouth of the river and the city ; and he was inclined to try his luck among them. It was with great reluctance the captain parted from him ; but seeing it could not be helped, he took a servant to supply the deficiency.

## CHAPTER XII.

Grief boundeth where it falls,
Not with empty hollowness, but weight.
*Shakespeare, King Richard II. Act* 1.

WE will now leave our hero to carry on his courtship in the most approved manner known to a Mexican gallant, and beg our reader to transfer himself to the state of Mechoacan, in order to witness the scene that took place in the family of Letinez, upon their being informed of his captivity. The disaster of San Jacinto had been concealed as long as possible from the Mexican people, by their government ; and when it became, at last, necessary to publish it, they did so with every attenuating circumstance they could imagine, never acquainting the nation with the names of the prisoners. The Count of Letinez, therefore, who knew that his grandson was in General Urrea's division and was not informed that he had been transferred to the main body, under the president's immediate command, felt no anxiety about him. Having, nevertheless, remained a long time without receiving letters from him, after the return of the army to Matamoros, he wrote to Urrea, to whom the young man had been especially recommended, in order to know the cause of his long silence, and was informed of the doleful truth—that his grandson was a prisoner in Texas.

On the receipt of this intelligence, the old Count and the Abbate were well nigh overpowered with grief. Their child, —as both delighted to call our hero—was the only scion of their noble and ancient house—the object of all their affection—endowed with talents and qualifications which promised a new illustration to their name ; and now he was in the hands of a horde of needy adventurers, who were represented as the most unprincipled and cruel of mankind. Oh, how bitterly did the Count and his brother repent having permitted him to enrol himself under Santa Anna's banners ! They had done so, indeed, in the idea that the expedition could not prove difficult, and would be nothing worse than a military *paseo*, from whence the heir of the family would return, adorned with fame and improved in experience, without having incurred any peril. They had, nevertheless, been deceived in their expectations, as well as many others, wiser than they, and now they began to consult upon the means of repairing the sad effects of their condescension. But was there any possibility of effecting it? Would it be practicable to rescue their beloved Ambrosio from captivity? Could they, for this purpose, avail themselves of their influence with men high in office, under the federal government?—Alas, no!—Corro's administration neither held, nor permitted any correspondence with the rebellious colonists, and would not allow even the admission of flags of truce.

In this sad emergency, and well nigh driven to despair, the old Count took a resolution, which, in a man of his age and habits, might seem to border on extravagance. It was to set out, himself, for Matamoros, and, thence, try to get into Texas, by the way of New Orleans, and ransom his grandson with money. "At all events," said he, "the Texians are poor. Their government, if such it can be called, must be in need of resources, and I will offer them such a sum as will purchase his liberty."

His brother, however, would not consent to his departure. "No," said he, "if any one is to go, I will be the man. You are, now, past travelling, dear brother, and quite unable to resist the fatigues of such a journey. Moreover, I have more experience of the world than you, who have always lived in retirement. And if it be necessary to cross the gulf of Mexico—have I not beheld the sea, from the peak of Colima, while I lived in the state of Jalisco?"[4] It was not necessary for the Abbate to insist with much perseverance, in order to persuade the Count to accede to the proposed change, for the good man dreaded travelling beyond expression, and nothing short of the agony of grief he felt at the loss of his grandson, could have prompted him to so strange a resolution.

It was, therefore, settled, that the good ecclesiastic should immediately set out on his journey towards the mouth of the Rio Bravo, a distance of more than twelve hundred miles;

and the servants received orders to make the necessary preparations forthwith.

When it became known in Pascuaro, that Abbate Letinez was going to Matamoros, with the purpose of penetrating into the heart of Texas, every body was in the greatest amazement, and not a few people supposed that the good man, through grief, had lost his wits. The Texians were reported to be monsters in human form—worse, if possible, than cannibals—for whom it would be a special delight to put to death any Catholic clergyman who might fall into their hands. They were reported to have taken Señor Valdez, parish priest of Goliad, to Harrisburg, and there to have burned him alive. Could it be any thing but sheer madness which now prompted the good Abbate to expose his life among such a people ? A number of female devotees, whose father confessor he was, moved heaven and earth, to induce him to alter his mind. They prayed and wept !—They burned blessed candles before every image in the parish church, and caused masses to be said upon every altar, but all in vain. The day of his departure at last arrived, and in spite of all their tears and supplications, he set out.

A new coach had been bought for the occasion, and no less than fourteen servants were engaged to accompany him. Provisions of the best quality, with a large and commodious tent had also been provided ; so that our good clergyman had the chance of enjoying every possible convenience upon the road. But as we have already described the mode of travelling, in the interior of that country, we will abstain from repeating, here, what could not but prove fastidious to our readers.

We have once hinted that the period marked by our hero's father for paying him a visit had elapsed. The great trouble to which the family of Letinez had been a prey, prevented them from resenting this want of punctuality as much as they would otherwise have done ; still they had several times thought of it, particularly, after learning the news of the battle of San Jacinto, for they imagined that, had Mr. Faring been in the country, he might have gone to the rescue of his son, with greater probability of success, than Abbate Letinez could expect.

Our hero's father was, nevertheless, faithful to his promise, and he arrived at Pascuaro, shortly after the departure of his late wife's uncle. He would have got there, sooner, and in time to save the old man his long journey, but he had to remain some time in Vera Cruz, in order to transact business for a commercial house of New York, with which he was connected, and this had been the cause of his delay. His arrival, though late, was hailed with the utmost joy by the old Count : " Welcome," said he, as he embraced him, " a thousand times welcome, my dear Faring.—You will be in time yet to overtake the *padre*, and assist him in rescuing your son.—I hope there is no danger of his life !"

" My son !" exclaimed Mr. Faring, alarmed. " Ambrosio's life is in danger ! Where and how ? Is not the boy here ?"

" Alas, no, my dear friend," resumed the old Count. " When it was ascertained that President Santa Anna was to march, with the flower of the army, against the rebels of Texas, the lad was seized with an irresistible desire of joining our troops. The padre and myself did all in our power to prevent him, but he so teased and besought us, that we gave way. In fact, we did not think the Texians would make any resistance—imagining that the campaign would be nothing but a military *paseo*, and that, as the boy had always lived in seclusion, he wanted some knowledge of the world, and a little *desenvoltura*, which he could not fail to acquire in his intercourse with the superior officers, to most of whom he was especially recommended. But *Valga me la Virgen de los Dolores !* The affair has turned out contrary to our expectations, and he is now a prisoner among the Texians."

" Gracious heavens !" interrupted Mr. Faring, " My son, my poor son ! Perhaps he has perished by this time, in expiation of the Goliad massacre !—But are you certain that he is prisoner, Count ?—Have you any official news ?"

" Alas !—It is but too certain," answered the old man, and, thereupon, he detailed all the information he had derived from his communications with various officers, who, after surviving the campaign, had returned to Matamoros. The unfortunate father, having become possessed of those details, immediately took his resolution, and told the Count that he would set out, on the spot, in order, if possible, to overtake the Abbate.

" Heaven be merciful to us !" returned the old man.

" You cannot be in a greater hurry to depart than I wish, but it is impossible to undertake such a journey, without a coach and servants, or, at least, without a gig. And, wo is me, it will take time to make things ready! The house has been turned topsy turvy with my brother's departure, and I do not know how, or where to find trusty servants."

" Put yourself to no trouble about it," replied his son-in-law. " I will not tarry here, twenty-four hours.—Two servants and a good sumpter mule will be sufficient. I came from the city of Mexico, hither, with no larger retinue, and I need very little baggage on the road.—It is not time to study my own convenience, when my child's life is perhaps in jeopardy."

" Verily, my dear," resumed the Count, " I will not permit you to expose yourself in the way you propose. Madness itself would not undertake so long a journey—and, partly, through desert countries—without provisions and a number of attendants capable of defending you, should you be attacked. Moreover, something is due to the standing of the house of Letinez, to which you are so closely allied!—Consider what would be thought of us, should one belonging to our family travel with no more state than the merest *ranchero*."

"And would you," said Mr. Faring, " postpone, for one single day, the succor I owe to my son, for the sake of so paltry a consideration ?—Oh, Count, Count! is it possible that your mind can be set upon such frivolities, when the only scion of your house—the worldly honor and feudal glory of which you esteem so highly—is in danger of his life, or, at least, straightened with want ?—No, sir, I will set out immediately. You may give orders to your *Mayordomo*, in case you are disposed to speed me on my way. I want fresh horses, for mine are jaded, a strong sumpter mule, and two servants of approved fidelity. Your resources, undoubtedly, can command all this in twelve hours' time. If a proper degree of speed be used, I may yet overtake the padre, and then travel in state and with all the pomp suited to the son-in-law of the Count of Letinez."

It was as a kind of anodyne that Mr. Faring threw in these last words, and in order to bring the old man to accede to his proposal ; for, though he had, as yet, no idea that the weakness of intellect peculiar to old age had begun to creep upon his mind, he knew, of old, his vanity and pride of ancestry, and did not think it beneath him to indulge a little that foible.

The bait took effect accordingly, and the Count gave orders to his *Mayordomo*, to furnish his son-in-law with what he wanted. These commands being promptly executed, Mr. Faring took his departure from Pascuaro, and rode with all possible haste, in order to overtake Abbate Letinez, which he entertained well founded hopes to effect, for he knew the good clergyman would be slow in travelling.

His expectations were not, however, realized as soon as he had imagined, for the old gentleman rode hard and had already reached the frontiers of the state of Cohahuila, before Mr. Faring came up with him. He could not even have overtaken him, had not our clergyman been detained by a singular occurrence, which arrested his further progress and caused him to prolong his stay in the little mining town of Mapimi, from which the extensive desert, mentioned in the beginning of this work, derives its name. There, Mr. Faring found him—and under such circumstances, as excited his astonishment and required all his energy to extricate him.

# CHAPTER XIII.

They see with great exactness, but at no great distance. And to show the sharpness of their sight towards objects that are near, I have been much pleased with observing a cook pulling a lark, which was not so large as a common fly; and a young girl threading an invisible needle with an invisible thread. *Gulliver's Travels.*

THE place where our reverend traveller had stopped, although its population amounts but to five thousand souls, ranks high among the *minerales* (mining districts) of the state of Durango, and supplies a considerable portion of the precious metals which enrich that province. About ten silver mines, in which the abundance of the ore makes up for its poverty, gives occupation to two thousand miners, who spend five days of the week, in the bowels of the earth; descending into the subterranean caverns, on every Tuesday, and returning to the broad daylight, only, on Saturday evening. The silver extracted from these deep recesses is distinguished by what is, in the language of the country, styled "*ley de oro*," that is to say, a portion of gold which cannot be separated from the less precious metal, with which it is combined, save by a long and intricate chemical process, that was, in ancient times, solely practised at the mint,([5]) in the city of Mexico; but which a Frenchman, of the name of Bras de Fer, has lately introduced into the *casa de moneda*, at Durango. By this improvement, the profit of the owners of mines, in the northern provinces, has been much increased; for they were, previously, obliged to sacrifice that portion of gold, for a trifling consideration. These circumstances, how unconnected soever they may appear with our history, had the effect of suspending, for some days, father Letinez's progress eastward.

In order to enable our readers to understand the connection of events, which seemingly bear no manner of relation to each other, it is proper to premise here, that, in conse-

10*

quence of such a state of things, and for the purpose of levying an indirect tax, by means of the *seignorage*, in coining the precious metals, the Mexican government has strictly prohibited the egress of bullion. This nation is still far from appreciating the economical theories of Smith and Say, and they think that the greater the quantity of silver and gold they keep stagnating at home, the richer the country is likely to prove. For this purpose, they have, also, established very high duties on the exportation of specie. But not satisfied with this, and, as if it were not sufficient to cramp trade and industry ; they have continued a transit duty, which, under the Moorish name of " *Alcavala*," existed in Spanish times, and prevented the circulation of bullion and coin, from one province to another—unless with a permit from the officers of government—under pain of confiscation. It is not only the precious metals which are subject to this enactment, but every kind of merchandize ; even goods manufactured in the country being placed under the same restriction, and debarred from passing freely from parish to parish.—It would be difficult to imagine any thing more opposed to the development of industry and the progress of commerce, than the present Mexican plan of finances. The ideas by which the leading statesmen of this nation seem to be governed are absolutely those of the eleventh century—when cramping and restriction were the only policy known, and the limits of a parish were accounted sufficiently extensive for all the purposes of internal trade.

It was the law we have been inveighing against, which, now, caused our reverend traveller's embarrassment ; for, as the reader may remember, the Abbate had taken with him a large sum of money, and by a singular oversight, had neglected to get a pass from the *Alcavalero*, id est, the custom-house officer charged with the collection of the duties. Nay, he had, contrary to law, taken some bars of silver, and ingots of gold ; and the purpose of his journey being divulged by his servants, the collector of the revenue, in Mapimi, became aware that our good ecclesiastic was carrying specie and bullion out of the country without permit. His office gave him the right of searching the stranger's baggage, and, in case of discovery, awarded him a large share of the confiscated property.

As the traveller was a priest, the revenue officer felt some repugnance to interfere ; but the prospect of a valuable windfall easily overcame those scruples.  He would not, however, proceed to the intended search, while Padre Letinez was in town, for fear of giving scandal ; as well as out of respect for the curate of the place, at whose house the stranger was lodged.  He said nothing, then, of the resolution he had taken ; but, having secretly summoned six guards, over whom he had authority, he lay in wait for Señor de Letinez, at the little village of Vinagrillos, three leagues distant from Mapimi ; and when the latter's caravan came on, in the morning, his servants, as well as himself, were disagreeably surprised, at seeing their further progress impeded by the *Alcavalero*, who presented his begrimed face at the door of the carriage, and with a profusion of bows and congees, called upon the padre for permission to search his baggage.

The servants, indignant that a man of their master's quality should be treated in such a fashion, were ready to resist the unpleasant request ; but the Abbate would not permit them to make use of their arms.  He relied upon the respect inspired by his cloth, and supposed that the examination would be only for form's sake ; or, even, he thought, that, at the last extremity, he could bully the collector into terms, and make him consent to accept a gratification.  He was, however, mistaken in his expectations, and the Alcavalero insisted upon the rigorous discharge of his duty.  " I hope your paternity will forgive me," said he ; " but the laws of the republic prohibit the exportation of silver in bars, and it is my duty to see that none be carried eastward : therefore, I humbly beg you to rise from your seat, in order that I may examine this carriage."

" How, now ?" interrupted Señor de Letinez, " is it thus the officers of a Christian government treat a Catholic clergyman ?—Do you think we have overthrown the impious faction of the Yorkinos, to be now dealt with in this manner ? How dare you stop a priest of the Lord, on his journey ? Do we live in a Christian country, or amongst Moors ?"

" Really, sir," replied the officer, " notwithstanding the reverence we are bound to pay to men of your order, and which we render most willingly, I feel myself under a conscientious obligation to follow the dictates of the law, in every thing which concerns temporal matters. I pray you, therefore, do not think hard of me, if I again request you to rise from your seat, and allow me to do my duty."

"Well, be it so," replied Abbate Letinez; "since you are so rude. Only, I hope you will permit me to take out my travelling chalice and other sacred vessels—these being utensils which you cannot even touch without sacrilege, as you are a mere layman."

"Santo cielo!" exclaimed the revenue officer, "the most important portion of what I am in search of will escape me, after all. But I must be plain with you, sir, I see. If I cannot touch your chalice, I may, at least, look at it. You must, therefore, uncover it for my inspection, and it will be safe from my unhallowed grasp, as well as the *cruets*, if you have brought any with you!"

"Hear! now, how the creature is scoffing at religion," resumed Abbate Letinez.—"O seculum nequam!—That a Catholic clergyman should be stopped on his way, by Catholic Christians, under pretence of obeying revenue laws, and have his baggage searched, like a common smuggler!—O shame! O abomination!—Gracious heavens, in what times do we live!"

"It is too bad,—it is too bad, indeed," exclaimed the servants, "and we cannot permit the brother of Count Letinez to be treated so unworthily. The Alcavalero shall not prevail. Shall we smite him, padre?"

"For God's sake, commit no violence, my children," replied the pacific clergyman. "Better for me to submit, than to see blood spilt in a quarrel like this.—I command you to make no resistance. I am going to alight. But, Juan Fades, open this box, and let me take out my chalice and breviary, together with the diurnal—and the box of holy oils—and my ritual, also,—and my portative altar stone. The unhappy man shall not dare to put forth his sacrilegious hand to touch these consecrated objects! If he should, I will resist unto the death—even as the high priest resisted unto the impious monarch of Israel, when he put forth his hand to seize on the censer."

So saying, he helped his servant to select the articles he had mentioned—which, being wrapped in many folds of paper and linen cloth, defied scrutiny. To tell the truth, while he fumbled about, in haste, and, with well feigned confusion, threw every thing topsy turvy ; he contrived to conceal several ingots of gold, in the folds of the paper which served to wrap up the chalice, ritual, breviary and diurnal ; and Juan Fades, catching inspiration from his master's alertness, secreted two *silver bars*, under pretence that it was the altar stone—only the altar stone, wrapped up in consecrated linen !

But the Alcavalero was resolved not to be balked, and insisted upon looking at that pretended altar stone, as well as on examining the smaller bundles, which they had snatched away with so much precipitation ; and, as they dared not offer him positive resistance, he had the satisfaction of seizing upon more ingots of gold, than it had fallen to his lot to clutch, at any time before. A few silver bars became also his prey, and the milled dollars, which the Abbate was carrying away, fared no better, because he had no permit from the custom-house officer at Pascuaro.

By the zeal of the minister of the law, our good clergyman was left nearly destitute, and, in the utter impossibility of prosecuting his expedition, saw himself obliged to retrace his steps, and throw himself again upon the hospitality of the parish priest of Mapimi.

There he was, now, without funds—equally unable to advance, or to recede—and with too numerous a retinue to render it tolerable for the *cura* to keep in his house any length of time. The only resource left him was to write to his brother, and send some of his men in order to get wherewith to continue his journey ; but the shame of having been the dupe of his overweening confidence rendered this application for money highly repugnant to his feelings. Moreover, the Count might find himself staightened to comply with his wishes, for it was not without difficulty the *talegos* with which the Abbate had set out had been made up. The loss of so considerable a sum as that which the Alcavalero had seized upon was, also, no trifling cause of grief to our traveller, for the amount was too large, to be overlooked by any one in his senses.

All these reflections were bitter and galling, but regret could bring no remedy ; and he, at last, saw himself forced to write to his brother a statement of the case, and despatch four of his most trustworthy servants, to convey to him this sad piece of intelligence, and ask for more funds.

The servants had just reached the frontiers of the state of Zacatecas, when they were met by Mr. Faring. The latter would have passed them unknowingly, but his *peones* recognized those of father Letinez, and both parties having come to a stand, an explanation ensued. Our Marylander was a man of resolution, and after a few minutes' reflection took his determination. He directed the Abbate's messengers to retrace their steps, and return to Mapimi, promising that he would settle the difficulty, and there would be no need to trouble the Count with so disagreeable a piece of news as the confiscation of the money and bullion. The servants were at a loss to imagine by what means he would recover what was in the Alcavalero's power, but they obeyed, and all pursued their march to rejoin the Abbate.

Señor de Letinez's joy at the sight of our American was not a little damped by a sense of the embarrassed situation into which his neglect had thrown him ; but when the latter proposed the scheme he had framed for the recovery of what had been confiscated, he became alarmed, and, for a long time, refused to give his assent. The plan, really, was exceedingly rash, and, in any other country but Mexico, would have exposed the perpetrator to severe penalties ; but as *Anahuac* is a republic where any illegal act, not amounting to an enormity, can be executed with little or no danger from the courts of law, Mr. Faring knew he did not venture much, and insisted upon the old clergyman giving his consent.

He intended entering the Alcavalero's house, with his men fully armed, and retaking possession of the bullion and money.—Should the scheme fail, he thought he could laugh it off as a joke ! but he had very little doubt of its success, for revenue officers are generally detested, and there was no probability of any of the neighbors coming to the help of the man upon whom he intended to make an inroad.

How strange soever the assertion may appear to the inhabitants of more civilized countries, the plan succeeded. Thus, about ten thousand dollars, confiscated according to law, were, in the face of a town of five thousand souls, and in broad daylight, abstracted from the house of the officer who had them in custody, without any resistance being offered—the neighbours only laughing at the adventure,

and applauding the dexterity with which it was executed.

Mr. Faring, well knowing that it would be no part of discretion to prolong his stay after such a feat, had been careful to have every thing in readiness, before repairing to the
Alcavalero's. The sumpter mules were all loaded, and
waiting a little way out of town—the horses were harnessed
to the coach—the good Abbate snugly seated inside, reciting
his breviary, and all prepared to set off, at a moment's
warning ; when our gallant merchant, at the head of a posse
of his servants, well armed and guided by Juan Fades, of
whom we have already made honorable mention, went to in-
vest the dwelling of the revenue officer. Leaving a guard
of four men at the door, he, with the remainder, proceeded to
search the interior of the house, and had no need of long
perquisitions, for the Alcavalero, frightened by the invaders'
first threats, immediately returned the confiscated property.
Mr. Faring, not content with recovering it, and in order to
prevent a recurrence of the same accident, forced the officer
to give him a *guia*, or permit, in the most ample form. This
exploit happily achieved, our American marched off in triumph to the place where the old ecclesiastic was waiting.
His men mounted their mules, the coach-driver gave the signal of departure, and all trotted off in great glee.

Soon after they had left Mapimi, however, the Alcavalero,
having no longer an immediate danger before his eyes,
picked up courage ; and, enraged at the taunts and jests
which his neighbors were showering upon him, made a formal petition to the Alcalde of the town for a party of the
civic guard, in order to go to the rescue of the money and
bullion. Such a request the Alcalde could not refuse. In
consequence he summoned thirty of the citizens, commanded
them to get horses and arms, and when they were fully
equipped, put them under the orders of the revenue officer.

The parish priest, however, having got wind of it, despatched a swift messenger, who overtook father Letinez, and
gave him information of the impending danger, advising him,
at the same time, of a cluster of mines, situated at about two
leagues from his road, in a very precipitous *cañada*, or glen,
and the *sobresaliente* of which,* being a particular friend of

* The sobresaliente is a kind of police office, stationed at the mines,
to watch over the miners' conduct.

the cura, would afford him a place of concealment for his
effects and money.

It may be easily imagined that this advice was received
with gratitude, and the means thus offered to escape the ra-
pacity of the revenue officer, joyfully embraced. Leaving,
therefore, the high road, they turned into the glen, and began
to ascend the rocky acclivity, by which they were to penetrate into one of the most remarkable mining districts of the
State of Durango.

The group of mountains where those mines are situated
is called "la Buffa de Mapimi,"—by which generic term
Mexicans designate any insulated cluster of small extension,
rising abruptly in the middle of a plain, without connection
with any of the longer and more important chains, to which
they apply the name of *Sierra*. The Buffa of which we are
now speaking,—about ten leagues in length, and five in
breadth—is, on all sides, surrounded by an extensive plain
and rises abruptly, on the left side of the Rio Nasas, which
meandering round, and washing its base, environs two thirds
of its circumference. It may be considered as an immense
block of secondary lime stone, cut by various deep ravines,
and intersected to its inmost recesses, by fissures, or caverns
in which nature has lodged an inexhaustible quantity of ores
of various metals.* Few spots offer such an amazing variety
to the geologist. Copper, in the state of green oxide ; lead,
in immense quantities ; silver and gold, gypsum, alabaster
and sulphur are among the products of these mountains, towards the internal fastnesses of which, our travellers were
now hastening.

* The Bolson of Mapimi has not yet been investigated by any scientific geologist, but the author of this work can, out of what he has collected, from very intelligent rancheros, assure his readers, that it abounds
in mines. It is not as destitute of water, neither, as had been generally
supposed ; since, in these latter times, large bodies of Comanches are
known to have crossed it, from north-east to south-west. The waters
of the lakes of Parras and Mapimi sink into the earth at their northern
extremities, and re-appear, as is generally supposed, at the *Agua verde*,
forming the laguna and river of that name, which empties itself into the
Bravo, under the twenty ninth degree of north latitude. It is highly
probable that these waters do not flow that prodigious distance, altogether underground, but re-appear on the surface, in several places, as is
almost always the case with subterranean streams !

## CHAPTER XIV.

In those deep caverns Nature works unseen,
But not less wondrous—in her mineral realm,
Than on the surface of the earth.
            *Delisle. Les trois regnes.*

It was impossible for them to drive their coach to the appointed place of refuge. They were, therefore, obliged to leave it in a thick *palmar*,* situated in a nook, at the entrance of the glen, where the winter torrents had accumulated a little vegetative earth. There they concealed also the bulkiest portion of their baggage, leaving the whole under the care of three of their most courageous servants, with strict orders to keep themselves and their charge out of the officers' way. In the meantime, our travellers, with the remainder of their retinue, proceeded up the glen, on mules, a kind of conveyance exceedingly painful to the Abbate, and rendered more so, in this instance, by the precipitous nature of the road. It mostly lay in the narrow bed of a torrent, now dried up, but full of large fragments of rock that had fallen from the neighboring eminences, and over which the mules had to scramble, with a pace so irregular—now, sliding—now, jolting their riders—that our travellers had hardly proceeded half a league, when the padre declared all his bones were unhinged ! "I cannot stand it, my child," said he to Mr. Faring, for it was by this endearing title he used to address him, "I cannot stand it any longer.' I will even alight and take it on foot. Oh, blessed St. Peter of Alcantara, what a road !—Oh, holy fathers, wo is me !—I shall never get over this !—It once fell to my lot, while I was teaching metaphysics, in the University of Guadalaxara, to go to exhort

* The plant very improperly called *palma*, in Mexico, is the Yucca gloriosa, which, in many places, forms large forests and attains the height of sixty, or seventy feet.—Its blossom, properly prepared, makes a fine salad.

a poor French Huguenot, who had been thrice put on the
rack, in the dungeons of the inquisition, and the sight of the
miserable patient struck me with such horror, as actually
made me shed tears—yes, I wept over him—though he was
a Frenchman, and it was at the time of Bonaparte's war in
Spain—but what he had suffered was nothing to *this*. And,
methinks, if the inquisition had been informed of the existence of this glen. they might have saved themselves the expense of the rack and other engines of torture, and sent all
the Protestants they apprehended, to pace up and down this
*cañada*.   Three turns upon it would have brough them to their
recantation, I trow !—I bet it would have crushed the obstinacy of old Calvin himself, and made him as pliant as the silk
of my *solideo*."*

With this, the good padre alighted and began to walk, but
soon gave out ; so that the servants were obliged to carry
him, on a kind of hand-barrow, which they made, on the
spur of the occasion, out of a strong piece of linen, and two
stiff batons.   Sometimes, their path rose on the crest of lofty
eminences—when it was bordered, on either hand, with deep
precipices.   Sometimes, it descended into the deepest gullies,
when towering cliffs nearly concealed the light of day,—but
which way soever they rode, they frequently crossed veins
of precious ore, marked out, on the superficies of the ground,
by a red oxide of silver, as bright as a trail of cinabar, which
streaked the clefts of the rocks.

This spectacle was highly entertaining to father Letinez,
who piqued himself upon being something of a naturalist, and
who, much relieved, by his new way of travelling, found, as
he went along, leisure to indulge in scientific disquisitions.
Their guide, who had received from the parish priest of Mapimi strict injunctions to give them all the assistance in his
power, was ready enough to amuse the padre, by communicating all the information he possessed, in relation to the
mines the mouth of which they saw, at a distance, on the
sides of the acclivities.   " That opening, which your paternity beholds, yonder," said he, " near the top of that perpendicular cliff, shining with hues as bright as if it had been
painted with vermillion, is called *el Gato*, (the cat) because

---

* A skullcap of black silk, used by the Mexican clergy, to cover their
tonsure, when they travel.

it was originally supposed that no other animal could ever reach it. A gachupin, however, discovered the means to get at it. He caused himself to be let down, by means of strong ropes, from the top of the cliff, and having, as he thought, found the ore rich enough to justify the expense, he cut a road, in the form of a cornice, through the live rock ; but, after all that cost, he found the mine very poor, in the interior of the cave. The best specimens of metal were at the mouth, and it turned out a perfect *chasco*, (disappointment.) The man, having lost all he had, became, out of despair, a lay brother in the convent of the barefooted Carmelites !— That other gaping cavern, which you perceive, a little above *el Gato*, is, from its great height, called " *la Luz*," (the light.) Nature had provided a scrambling path to reach it, but it ruined its first owner, for all that. The way was so narrow and steep, that a goat would have hardly been able to tread it, and he, without thinking, drove a large *atajo* of mules, up to the mouth of the mine, to load them with ore ; but the poor animals never came down again, by the way they went up. A large fragment of rock fell across their path—the beasts got scared—they could not turn round, and most of them tumbled down the steep and perished."

" Friend," interrupted the Abbate, " it is but a poor account you have to give, I see, of the mines of this celebrated Buffa."

" Oh ! but wait a little, Señor," resumed the guide, " and we will presently come to something better.—Here, now, you see this deep pit, yawning at your feet.—It is the mine of San Juan. It has, in its time, proved a little Potosi ! It belonged to a certain padre Don Roque Arce, who was the most determined miner, in these parts. For seven weary years, he sweated and toiled—running up and down the whole country—climbing up rocks and hills, like a she-goat that has lost her kids, and squeazing himself into every hole, like an armadillo, in search of food—reducing to cinders every loose stone which bore any indication of metal—and saying masses at half a dollar a piece, to support himself—until, at last, he lighted upon this *creston*. Nay, I am wrong in saying that he lighted upon it, for it was a goat-herd, whom he assisted for death, who told him of it—and by the same token that he buried the boy gratis, and made his

mother a present of a gold doubloon and a green plush petti-
coat, which she still wears on grand festivals—she had it
on, last Easter—and may I never see St. James of Compos-
tella's face, if it did not look as good as new! But it is
neither here, nor there. Padre Don Roque had a lucky hit
of it. He had hardly dug sixty varas, when he reached a
criadero, that is, a large insulated chamber, in the rock,
which was partly filled with *polvillos*,* the most precious kind
of ore we have in these parts. The padre realized ninety
thousand dollars in seven months, besides what was stolen by
his workmen, for he was a careless man."

"And what became of this padre Don Roque?" interrupted Señor de Letinez. "I have not seen him among the clergy of Mapimi."

"And good reason there is why you should not," replied
the guide. "The man became mad, sir. His good fortune
turned his brain. He ran into every kind of excess and rioting—gave balls—followed cockfighting and horse-racing—
gambling and drinking—until, at last, in one of his mad
frolics, he undertook to say mass with *pulque whiskey;*
whereupon the Illustrissimo Señor Castañiza, Bishop of Durango, caused him to be shut up in the prison of the officialty.
Some folks thought that he should be burned alive, in punishment of so dreadful a profanation; but the chapter of the
cathedral being consulted, all the prebendaries were of opinion that it would be an unsightly thing to behold a priest tied
to the stake, now, that faith had grown so cold and the inquisition was gone. They thought, therefore, it would be more
advantageous to religion, to treat the padre as a crazy man,
whereupon they sent him to the mad-house of San Hyppolito,
in Mexico."

"Upon my word, the owners of mines, in these parts, seem
to be unlucky!" observed the Abbate. "I wonder any
one dares to undertake a new work."

"Oh, Señor Padre," replied the guide, "you have not seen
the lucky ones, yet; but presently we will come to them.
They are situated in a cluster, at the upper part of that sharp
crest, you see, yonder; and are probably only ramifications
of one and the same vein, the main trunk of which has not

* Ore in dust.

yet been reached by the miners. Each mine occupies from one hundred and fifty, to two hundred men, and produces four or five *tejos** of silver, a week. There is, besides, the profit on the lead, which is immense, and the *ley de oro*, which is no trifle."

" But do not the poor miners lead a miserable life, in those dark and pestilential caverns ?" inquired father Letinez.

" No, indeed !" replied the guide. " They are, on the contrary, happy and well paid.—You will presently see what buzz—what life and what gaiety ! The bottom of the Caña-da is the abode of perpetual joy, sir ; the Indians laugh, crack their jokes and dance !—Why, the life of a miner is one of the merriest upon earth. He is under no compulsion, he may labor as little, or as much as he pleases. He is paid in proportion to the quantity of ore he brings up."

With these and several other discourses of the same kind did the guide beguile time and amuse the padre, until they reached the mouth of the Ojuela, where they intended to conceal their effects and money. The director of the mining operations and the sobresaliente, being informed, in a whisper, by the guide, of the quality of the new visiters, and the protection which the parish priest of Mapimi extended to them, did the honors of their subterranean domains with a courtesy which one would not have expected in such a place. They sent their men to help the new comers to unload their mules, and put their effects under shelter, and prepared every thing for their accommodation.

The entrance into the mine of the Ojuela is by an horizontal gallery, of three hundred yards in length, till one reaches the first perpendicular shaft. That adyt is wide enough for several persons to walk abreast—having originally been a cleft in the rock, which nature had filled with precious ore, but that has, long since, been cleansed out. As all the mines, thereabouts, are perfectly dry, the owners have saved themselves the expenses of a *tiro general*, by which, in *wet* works, they draw out the water, that would otherwise, inundate them. The miners of Mapimi are content to go on, according to the

* *Tejo de plata*, designates the cake of refined silver, after the second smelting. In this state it is sent to the mint, where it is cast into *bars* and returned to the miner, unless he choose to exchange it for hard dollars.

old imperfect method, introduced immediately after the conquest, and the ore is brought, on men's shoulders, up steep
ladders, which reach from the mouth, to the bottom of every
shaft. Each of these is generally sixty or seventy feet in
depth, and they recede from each other, in the fashion of
steps ; so as to afford room for fixing and securing the tim-
bers. By the term *ladder* our reader is not to understand
any accommodation similar to what bears this name elsewhere ; but, merely, an uncouth piece of wood, with notches,
cut into it, sufficient to support the foot. Up such ladders,
planted nearly perpendicularly, the poor miner is obliged to
climb, with a heavy load on his back—when his support
creaks, shakes and bends under his weight, at every step he
takes upwards. It is, particularly, when the ladders are
overloaded, if a large number of miners happen to be ascending at the same time, that the danger becomes more imminent ; and one single accident, such as a sudden swoon, or
the missing of one's footing, might be sufficient to cause the
death of as many as three or four scores of men.

On the other hand, the spectacle is interesting, and a sense
of awfulness raises it to sublimity. Shaft succeeding shaft,
disposed so as to permit the lights which shine along the de-
scent to be perceived to an immense depth, and a string of
miners ascending those ladders, each with a candle fixed in
a kind of helmet which he wears on his head, afford a most
curious subject of contemplation. Thank heaven, too, a
sense of religion is not unknown in those places. In the
midst of the dangers which accompany their every step, the
poor miners are mindful of their Creator. " Out of the
depths" they call unto him ; and do call in a manner worthy
of him—in a sublime manner ! Every now and then, all
join in singing the following simple, but noble rhymes.

> " Santo Dios, santo fuerte, santo imortal
> Libra nos, Señor, de todo mal."

It is the " Ἅγιος ὁ Θεὸς, ἅγιος ἰσχιρὸς," &c. of the Greek church.
Nothing more than these few words !—No monkish little-
ness—no superstitious conceit !—When those sounds proceed from one of those rocky caverns, being echoed by the
surrounding hills, they are responded to by the inmates of

the neighboring mines, and the barren mountains become vocal with praise.—The wilderness seems to rejoice, and "the solitary place exults in gladness !"

It was with a singular emotion the padre witnessed this spectacle, and he was melted while every *tenatero,* after unloading the cargo he had brought up,* came to him with a cheerful smile, to bid him welcome to the ojuela, and kiss his hand. The priest's visit was accounted an important event in the annals of the mining establishment, and one which could not fail to bring down great blessings.

To derive from it all possible advantage, the miners were anxious to carry him down into the interior of the mine, in order to make him bless a new gallery that they had opened, a few months previous, and which promised immense profits. This was what Mexicans term a *bonanza,* but as these bonanzas are frequently of short duration, and commonly end by disappointment, our miners wished to render this favor of fortune permanent, and they supposed that the blessing of such a man as father Letinez, would produce that effect. It was not, however, easy to convey him to the spot. As soon as the proposal was humbly made to him, he shuddered with horror at the idea of venturing down those ladders, which we have already described, and declared that nothing upon earth would induce him to do it.—No,—not even if he were sure to get the Popedom !—But he knew not what a bait his presence held out to the miners, nor what an immense value his reputation for sanctity gave to his blessing. The sobre saliente, head miners and others, had set their mind upon it, and were not to be frustrated. The occasion was too precious to let it slip through their fingers. The padre was a man of great fame and character—a holy man—a professor of metaphysics, *emeritus !*— A similar chance would never probably occur again. They teazed the priest, therefore, till he was, through sheer vexation, nearly out of his wits, yet their supplications proved ineffectual, till they bethought themselves of constructing a

* The tenateros are carriers who bring up the ore from the lower works, in a leather hod, as already noticed. The ore is weighed at the mouth of the mine, and each tenatero, immediately credited with the worth of his labor, in a book kept for that purpose. This is termed *Rayar.*

kind of arm-chair, which, by means of pullies and ropes, could be let down from shaft to shaft, both with convenience and safety. In this rolling throne, father Letinez was snugly seated—well propped with cushions, pillows and bolsters—and made his descent, rather more quickly than he wished, to the new gallery. There, he was, nevertheless, well re-paid for his trouble, by the magnificent spectacle which of-fered itself to his view, and he confessed that nothing he had ever beheld, or imagined, could compare with it.

A gallery adorned with the richest stalactites gave admit-tance into a hall of large dimensions, where nature seemed to have displayed all the magnificence with which she can deck inorganic matter. The roof was lined with concre-tions of the brightest hues. Fluoride of calcium assumed, there, all the variegated tints of which it is susceptible. In some places, it glittered with diamond lustre, and almost transparent purity, forming splendid crystals, of octohedral shape, regularly grouped *en mamelons*, which bore the ap-pearance of fretted work. In others, the spars were color-ed with violet tints, in perfect imitation of the amethyst.—Here, the color was dashed with various lighter shades :—It was waved—curled—veined and diversified in every pos-sible manner!—There, the fluor was of the most uniform golden yellow, and mocked the topaz ! But divers other minerals, besides these magnificent spars, concurred to give to this grotto an air of enchantment. One recess was in-crusted with malachite, which, when the light of the many torches by which the grotto was illuminated fell upon it, might have been mistaken by a vulgar eye, for an incrusta-tion of emeralds. The pavement of the grotto itself offer-ed, in several places, specimens of chloruret of silver of the most gorgeous appearance ; and when all the miners had as-sembled, and all the alcoves and recesses were lighted up, the blaze of effulgence was such as nearly overpowered Ab-bate Letinez.

The survey of this splendid *sala*, was terminated by the religious ceremony which had been the occasion of this de-scent. They brought him a crucifix that he placed in a su-perb niche, after which he pronounced a solemn blessing on the miners' new works and hastened to return to the light of day.

Our worthy ecclesiastic was hauled up safe and sound to the mouth of the mine, and there feasted in a splendid manner. He did not, however, stay above two days ; for, having received information that the Alvacalero, with his armed force, had returned to Mapimi, he resumed his march and soon crossed the river Nasas.

As our travellers were entering a little town called " El Alamo de Parras," they witnessed a curious scene between the tithe proctor and the inhabitants. While the *Yorkinos* wielded the political power of the Mexican republic, they abolished the *civil* obligation of paying tithes, and suppressed the temporal jurisdiction of the chapters of cathedral churches, but still left the *moral*, or conscientious duty, existing ; so that any of the faithful who had a regard for his soul was yet bound to pay over the tenth part of the produce of his land to the Bishop and chapter. But, as the latter had no longer any earthly tribunal to recur to, in order to see themselves righted, the *moral* obligation, which had been left untouched, was but little regarded; and the poor canons were nearly in a state of starvation. Their fat livings, of ten and twelve thousand dollars, a year, had been reduced to as many hundreds ; and the incumbents, driven to desperation, had had recourse to excommunications and anathemas. The refusal to pay had been denounced as a heresy, condemned by the ecumenical council of Constance, and a kind of crusade actually preached against the wicked opinions of Wikliff, John Huss, and Jerome of Prague ; heresiarchs, who had, in their time, endeavored to despoil the church of her wealth.

Strengthened, as he thought, by all the spiritual terrors that had gone forth, the proctor called upon the villagers of the Alamo and insisted upon their discharging, not only what was due for that year, but even all the arrears, they had neglected to pay. Nevertheless, the people, in general, proved refractory ; and, in the end, the nonconformists raised a mob, in consequence of the proctor's extravagant demand upon an old woman, who had already paid the tithe of her fowls and garden *stuff*. The collector of the holy revenue required her to pay the tenth of her *melon* and *pumpkin seed*, which is, in Mexico, an object of some importance, it being used in the preparation of a delicious beverage called orchata.

" How, now, *picaro !*" exclaimed the old woman, when she heard the exorbitant request ; " I have already paid the tithe of the melons, themselves, and must I still pay the tenth of the seed of those I have eaten ?—who has taught you such a way of reckoning ?"

" The chapter, good woman—The chapter !" replied the proctor. " The canons of the Holy Cathedral church of Durango have prescribed it, and you shall pay, or be a here- tic.—A Jewess—you understand !—And your portion will be with Wikliff, John Huss and Hyeronimo de Praga, three Turks, from England, who were burned alive, at the coun- cil of Constance, by order of the Holy Inquisition, and of the old king of Spain—as his m&st illustrious Lordship says."

" I, a heretic !—I, a Jewess !—And all for three or four handsful of pumpkin seed !" exclaimed the old woman, great- ly incensed. " *Vaya !*—If it is so, I will, at least, retake my own." So saying, she threw herself upon the chickens, which the proctor still held in his hand and a scuffle ensued, during which the fowls escaped his grasp, and flew off as fast as their wings could carry them. The old woman and the proctor ran after them, through the public square of the vil- lage, each loudly calling for help and showering vituperative epithets upon his antagonist, so that a large crowd was soon gathered round them, and, as was natural, sided with their townswoman.

The proctor had the indiscretion of facing the populace He invoked the canons and fathers of the council of Constance, and waved, before the mob, a pastoral letter of the Bishop of Durango, as if to shake some excommunication out of it, against the insurgents, but all in vain. They began pelting him with stones, and he ran an imminent danger ; when fa- ther Letinez's coach drove into the square. This attracted the people's attention and suspended the fray, and the good padre, being informed of the cause of the uproar, harangued the multitude and succeeded in pacifying them. He, how- ever, seriously advised the tithe proctor to desist, and leave the place, which the latter did, but not without giving the padre to understand that he suspected him to be a favorer of the pestilent heresy of John Huss and Hyeronimo de Praga.

We have related these petty incidents which befell our

travellers, thinking that they might prove of some interest, as having a tendency to illustrate the manners and customs of the country ; but, for fear of rendering our narrative tedious, we will pass the remainder of their itinerary over in silence, and return to Matamoros, where we left our hero anxiously waiting for letters from his family.

## CHAPTER XV.

We have an interpreter with us, my lord ;—a fellow who has got the gift of tongues !

*The self sent Embassador.*

Captain Letinez would have spent his time pleasantly enough in Matamoros, had he been allowed to give himself up to the cares of love ; but the wretched condition and precarious situation of Urrea's troops, who, nevertheless, continued to be styled the *army of operation against Texas*, kept the general in a continual state of perplexity and embarrassment. From that disagreeable position, he sought to extricate himself, by endeavoring to open a correspondence with, and excite movements among various tribes of Indians, in the west of the United States ; and he employed our hero in carrying on these diplomatic communications, or methodizing the various schemes which he was daily hatching to that effect.

By a strange coincidence, there was, at that time, a general discontent prevalent among the aborigines, on the western frontiers of the Union ; and, from Canada to Texas, they were preparing an insurrection, which would certainly have taken place, had the Florida Indians been able to make a decided impression on the blacks of the neighboring states, and given, thereby, more importance to their contest with the whites. The rapidity with which Santa Anna had, in the beginning of the campaign, chased the Texians from the southern parts of the country had served to buoy up the hopes of the Indians. They expected a powerful diversion in their favor, as soon as he should reach the frontiers of Louisiana, and in that expectation, several of their tribes sent him ambassadors, who did not, however, arrive at the Mexican head quarters, till the retreat of Filisola had blasted the hopes they might, otherwise, have conceived, from that quarter. Yet the Indians, who are not endowed with much shrewdness to distinguish the " nick of time ;" did, after their arrival, propose to enter into arrangements with Urrea, as readily, as if he had been scouring the plains of Texas, in triumph.

There were three Cherokee chiefs that treated publicly, and who, in order, as they conceived, to render their treaty more binding on the Mexicans, caused themselves to be solemnly baptized.

Besides these Cherokees, there were other emissaries sent by some of the northern tribes, who remained in Matamoros *incognito;* but held frequent communications with Urrea, during which our hero acted as interpreter. All diplomatic intercourse, between the high contracting parties, being carried on in such French and English as it had pleased God to endue the Indians with, it formed a jargon so difficult to understand, that Captain Letinez was frequently at a loss to take their meaning. This was the source of several mistakes, that fretted the general in chief; to obviate which, it was resolved to call in the aid of one of the chaplains of the army, a clergyman who had occupied eminent posts in the United States, and possessed considerable literary knowledge.

This worthy was an ex-Jesuit, bred in one of the establishments the society possesses in Maryland, but from which he had been dismissed, on acconnt of an unconquerable propensity for certain alcoholic liquids, whereby he had frequently derogated from the upright standing of a child of St. Ignatius. Save this little misfortune, the chaplain was an exemplary clergyman, with so ardent a zeal for the faith, that it had prompted him to come all the way from Louisiana, to offer his services to the Mexican army, at the time Santa Anna was sweeping every thing before him in Texas. Unfortunately he had reached the theatre of war too late, and, at his arrival at St. Patricio, the news of the defeat of San Jacinto came to dissipate certain splendid visions of schools, colleges, Catholic settlements, and fine sugar and cotton plantations, all intended " ad majorem Dei gloriam."

He undertook, nevertheless, to serve the army in its retreat, inasmuch as the soldiers were nearly destitute of spiritual succor, for Santa Anna's chaplain had been taken prisoner, at San Jacinto, and the Texians had detained him, in order to administer spiritual consolation to their captive.

Whatever assistance our worthy priest could give to Captain Letinez, in translating and explaining the extravagant proposals of the Indian emissaries, was freely bestowed, and he was in so far successful that he made the Mexican chief understand the purport of some singular documents, with which these deputies had been intrusted by certain eminent divines, residing in the United States, but accustomed to fish in troubled waters, and to mix politics with theology.

The first paper was presented by a warrior belonging to a tribe of Indians, living in the west of the union, and was in the Latin language. It consisted of a certificate of Christianity, in favor of the bearer, and, as our readers may chance to be curious to know how those things are done, we will transcribe it, here, literally.

"Nos Fredericus Von Rusé Epps. &c. &c.

Cunctis hasce nostras litteras inspecturis, fidem facimus latorem hujus, Romualdum, vulgo dictum *l'oiseau blanc*, ex Indica gente *des Otowas* oriundum, et a nobis baptizatum, esse pium sincerum que Christianum, et auctoritatem foederis faciendi, cum quibuslibet quorum interesse potest, a sua gente accepisse, necnon fidem ei, ab omnibus Christi fidelibus, adhiberi posse.

Datum apud Petit Gouffre, in fœderatis Americæ septentrionalis provinciis, pridie Idus martii. Anno Domini MDCCCXXXVI.

+ *Fredericus Von Rusé Epp.*

De mandato suæ Illustritatis,
        *Vicentius Brigandeau, Secretarius.*"

Now this paper appeared to Urrea an unintelligible riddle. "It seems to have been given by some ecclesiastical person," said he. "There is an authoritative form, and it is in good Latin. But what are these words in italics, "*l'oiseau blanc*," and "*des Otowas?*"—It is not Latin. I remember enough of my Lebrija, to be convinced that it must belong to some modern lingo.—Do you conjecture what it can mean?"

"I take it to be some nickname, by which this fellow, (this commissioner, or emissary, I mean,) is distinguished, in his own country," said Captain Letinez.

"Well, that may be," replied Urrea—"but what does

it mean ?—and this *Petit Gouffre!*—what is the purport of it ?''

" Why, Excellentissimo Señor, exclaimed the priest, " it is French.—*l'Oiseau blanc*, means the white bird !—It is the man's name, according to the fashion of the northern Indians, who, generally, select some animal, to be their spiritual patron, as we do the saints, that are in heaven ; and in consequence of such a connection, adopt their names. The Otowas are a powerful tribe of Indians, who anciently lived in Canada, and *Petit Gouffre* is probably the name of some town, where the document was signed and sealed. It is a quaint name ! but they are reduced to great stress, in the United States, to find names for the prodigious number of towns which every day brings forth, and they make any singular term answer the purpose.—They have exhausted all the proper names of antiquity, sacred and profane !''

" The *Otowas !* exclaimed Urrea,"—I never heard of such a nation !—The *White Bird !*—*Petit Gouffre !*—Upon my word, it looks, or rather, sounds worse than quaint. This fellow is quizzing us—as I take it. But wo to him, if it is the case. I will send him to a *presidio*, yet we must investigate this somewhat more deeply. Can you guess who has signed this paper ?''

The priest, thus appealed to, answered : " May it please your excellency, in order to make matters plain and intelligible, I must enter into some details, seemingly bearing no manner of connection with the subject now in hand.—I fear it will be with me, as Horace says, ' Trojanum bellum gemino orditur ab ovo,'—But I will abbreviate, and give you no reason to be tired with my prolixity—taking care, nevertheless, to inform you of all the facts necessary for a clear understanding of the purport of this paper,—as well as any other which might be presented by the same individual, or other Catholic Indians, from the United States. Otherwise I might fall into the opposite extreme, no less to be dreaded than prolixity,—according to what the same Horace says : ' Brevis esse laboro, obscurus fio,' and futher———''

" Padre," interrupted Urrea, out of patience, " if you go on at this rate, you are not likely to get through, before the end of the week.—Let Horace alone, man, and speak to the purpose.''

"Well, General, I come to the point," resumed the ex-Jesuit.—"You must know that when Pius VI., of blessed memory——"

"O Lord!" exclaimed Urrea, "he carries us back to the eighteenth century.—It is intolerable!—I wish thou wert not a priest, I would teach thee to condense thy ideas!—I would teach the ' brevis esse,' I assure thee."

"Well, then, at once and in four words," returned the chaplain, "since your Excellency is so fond of a precise style, all I have to say, is, that this certificate bears the signature of a German Baron, who left bright prospects in the world, to enter the church, for at the time of his conversion, he was a corporal in the Duke of Brunswick's *Schwartz yagers.*"

"A corporal!" interrupted Urrea, with a broad peal of laughter, "and you represent him as a man of consequence! —Sir, your cloth gives you privileges, by securing impunity!—We will not, however, suffer ourselves to be trifled with.—Your jesting in this manner is in bad taste.—By my santiguada, if you were not a priest, you would pay dearly for this!—Ha, ha, is it come to this, that a simple chaplain dares to trifle with Don José Urrea, general in chief of the Mexican army?"

"I am not trifling with you, general," replied the ex-Jesuit. "Your excellency is certainly the last person at whose expense a prudent man would venture to jest.—Had you given me time to proceed, you would have seen that the very circumstance which shocks you as improbable is perfectly credible. The Duke of Brunswick's celebrated legion of *Black Chasseurs* was exclusively composed of noblemen of most ancient pedigree, and the least soldier in it was, at least, a belted knight. Now, to have been a corporal in such a regiment might be accounted an honor any where.—But, to resume, sir; this Von Rusé found military glory unable to satisfy the aspirations of his heart: he found that the world and its vanities are nothing but an empty sound—*œs sonans vel cymbalum tinniens !*—He found the truth of what the blessed St. Austin says, in the book of his confessions, ' irrequietum est cor nostrum donec'—"

"And I find," interrupted again Urrea, quite enraged and stamping with his foot, "that you are enough to drive a man out of his wits.—Come to the pith and marrow of the thing, at once, without dragging us through Germany and Flanders, at this rate.—What have we to do with the Duke of Brunswick and his legion ?—Tell us what degree of influence this Von Rusé enjoys.—With whom does he correspond, in Europe.—Is he, really, a man of consequence ?"

" You may judge, yourself," replied the chaplain, somewhat terrified by the general's violence ; " how high in dignity he must have been, when I tell you, that he had, several times, the honor of officiating as train bearer to our holy father, the Pope."

" Oh, oh !" exclaimed Urrea, in surprise ; " *Caudatario del Papa !*—That is a dignity, indeed !"

" He probably wishes to open a correspondence with the Mexican government, for he is somewhat addicted to political intriguing," resumed the chaplain.

" Well, then," returned Urrea, " we must not overlook so fine an opportunity.—Who knows what may turn up in our favor, in those parts ?"

" I hardly think," said the captain, " that it would be prudent to treat with him, without knowing something more, in relation to his respectability ; particularly when the medium of communication is an unknown Indian, who can hardly be supposed to have an adequate idea of the importance of his mission. But let us hear the father chaplain further. Perhaps he may throw some more light on the subject."

" Why, gentlemen, certainly I can," resumed the priest. " This Von Rusé is supported by the Austrian government, in order to act in their behalf ; but while he appears to husband their money according to their intentions, he is really carrying on a nice underscheme of his own, with which his European constituents have nothing to do. He is filling an eligible territory, in the back parts of the United States, with settlers entirely devoted to him, whom he trains up in a spirit of nationality distinct from that of the Americans. I do not know whether the little *yager* will succeed, but you may be sure the United States will have their Texas, too. I do not think they can escape it.—And there are those who will plant a thorn in their side, just as the Texians have done with you."

" Well, well, we must treat with this Indian," said Urrea.

" This is a good windfall !—By my santiguada, it is not to
be neglected. But look at this other paper which he has
put in my hands.—See, it is full of hieroglyphics !—Representations of various animals, I declare !—There is an
eagle,—here is a turtle,—and there is an armadillo, I
believe."

" An armadillo !" exclaimed the priest ; " it cannot be, for
there are none in the United States. I suppose it was intended for an alligator, which they knew only by hearsay !—
These are the signatures of the various chiefs of his nation,
who have given him power to treat. It is customary for them
to delineate, on their public instruments, representations of
the animals the names of which they bear, and it is this
which imparts to those papers their authenticity, just as signing and sealing do among civilized nations. Now, this is
written in French, but the orthography is so bad, that it is not
easy to unravel its meaning. It must have been composed
by some ignorant *coureur de bois*. From it, however, I can
make out, that *Loiseau blanc* is empowered to treat with the
Mexican President, or any of the generals, and the Indian
chiefs beg arms and ammunition."

" Oh, as for this," said Urrea, " it is impossible. Our
stores are too low. I cannot, without orders from the supreme government, encroach upon what remains."

" If such is your determination," said the priest, " you
need not think any longer about a permanent treaty with
them. I am acquainted with their ways and habits. You
cannot put any reliance in whatever arrangements they may
enter into, unless they be bound on their memory, by presents
proportioned to the importance of their nation. The English
and Americans have accustomed them to it, and the highest
bidder is sure to have them for allies."

" If such be the case," replied Urrea, " they may
return home, and God speed them. We are not able to
buy their alliance. It is a pity, nevertheless, for a diversion on that side would have proved advantageous to our
cause."

" But the Cherokees who are here ?" said Captain Letinez.
" They ask no presents, I believe. They only want lands
in Texas. It is not very costly to grant them what they desire, and they may annoy the Texians until we be able to re-

new the campaign. It is, however, uncertain whether they can bring a respectable force into the field."*

"The Cherokees," interrupted the clergyman, "form a powerful nation, now half civilized. They have already acquired the use of letters and of the principal mechanical arts, and, should you succeed in getting them over to your side, they might relieve you of the present war against Texas, but would, in future, prove no less dangerous neighbors. Moreover, the land on which they live, at this time, is surrounded by establishments of white people, and they cannot emigrate to Texas, without the consent of the United States."

"Well, then, let us drop all thoughts of alliances and treaties with them," said Urrea. "They may go their way. I wash my hands of them.—Our country does not buy allies with gold, but conquers her enemies with iron."

* There are many Cherokees among the Comanches, at this time, and it is thought the latter have derived from them the idea of several improvements.

## CHAPTER XVI.

Who chooseth me must give and hazard all he hath,
Must give—for what ? for lead ? hazard for lead ?
      *Shakespeare.  Merchant of  Venice.*

URREA who had been anxious to make treaties and enter
into alliances with the Indians, no sooner saw that presents
were expected, than he dismissed the subject, with the levity
and carelessness which the reader has seen in the preceding
chapter.  Thus, plans that had cost weeks of labor and consultation were in an instant laid aside, and our hero found
himself freed from the irksome occupation which had nearly
engrossed his time.

Now, he could attend on Miss Quinton with  more  regular-
ity, and pay his devoirs with all the punctuality worthy a
gallant and chivalrous officer.  The young lady, however,
naturally fond of a retired life, was not always inclined to
accept his invitations to balls and other assemblies.  One
night, when there was to be a grand party, given by the superior officers of the army, to which she and her father had
received notes of invitation, and where it was anticipated that
she would play on the piano ; she felt strongly inclined to remain at home, but her lover and her father having earnestly
besought her not to disappoint her acquaintances, she was,
at last, prevailed upon to accompany them.

As she entered the ball-room, her unrivalled beauty attracted the general admiration and she was so often requested to
dance, that, at last, she saw herself, through weariness, obliged to refuse one of the principal officers.  The latter felt
*piqued*, but, conquering his chagrin, with perfect good breeding, he requested Miss Quinton to pass into the music room
and indulge the company with some music, since it was out
of her power to delight them by the gracefulness of her steps.
With this invitation she readily complied, and while she

moved from the ball-room, she was followed by so great a number of gentlemen, eager to hear her, that dancing was suspended.

In the next apartment, the piano was placed between two windows, whence there was a view into the interior *patio*, (court-yard,) and through the grating of these windows, a considerable number of eager faces were looking into the music room. Presently Miss Quinton began to play a splendid sonata which charmed the whole company. Her lover was on one side, bending, in a kind of rapture, over her shoulder, and turning, with the greatest readiness, the leaves of the music book, while her father enjoyed the delightful spectacle with an air of recollection.

All at once, in the middle of a passage of superior power, there protruded a face, from among those which were looking into the room, whose eyes were intensely fixed upon Miss Quinton, and bore a peculiar sinister expression. The young lady, happening to look upon the intruder, recognised him, uttered a piercing shriek, rose from her chair with precipitation, and, with an air of the greatest dismay, threw herself in her father's arms.

It is not necessary to describe the disorder that ensued thereupon. None but Captain Letinez guessed at the cause of the young lady's extraordinary conduct. While her father soothed her and inquired the cause of her fright, an old matron, who had brought to the ball two daughters whose beauty was eclipsed by Miss Quinton's, shrewdly remarked, in a whisper, to three or four old crones, who attended upon her, that those American women were singular, with their *nervous attacks*, and that, for her part, were she a man, she could never admire such babylike things, who would scream, and throw a whole company into disorder for nothing in the world, but to draw the whole attention upon themselves. Father Pafarro, the vicar of the parish, observed that this came from admitting heretics to a *Christian ball*, and that Mexicans could expect nothing but the corruption of their morals and the downfall of their faith, by their criminal condescension to strangers. But the principal officers, unmoved by the insinuations of the priest, or the jealousy of the old woman, thronged around Miss Quinton, and eagerly offered their services, against any one who might have offended her.

In the meantime, the individual whose unexpected appearance had given rise to this commotion had vanished, and when Miss Quinton recovered from her alarm, she was no longer exposed to encounter his odious gaze. However, she no sooner felt her emotion subside, than she desired to be conducted home, and left the party to their surmises, in relation to what they termed "*el accidente de la señorita;*" in which they exercised the acuteness of their wit, with no more uncharitableness than is customary in the fashionable world. As soon as Miss Quinton, accompanied by her father and the captain, had reached home, the latter said to her, "I need not inquire whether you have seen this man, before now. I have no doubt my suspicions are well founded, and he is the villain who made the infamous attempt at Lepantitlan."

"He is, indeed," answered the young lady; "but I beseech you, captain,—nay, I lay my strict injunctions upon you,— to do nothing rashly. As you value my happiness, abstain from any attempt at avenging what is past. I am now, here, out of all danger, and absolutely forbid that *it* should be made a subject of quarrel."

"Leave that to me, my dear Miss Quinton," replied our hero. "We, men, understand these matters better than your sex.—I could not, without disgrace, continue to aspire to the honor of your hand, were I to omit calling him to account. Only I am afraid he will refuse to give me satisfaction."

The young lady begged and threatened by turns, but could never shake the resolution of her lover, who, taking leave of the family, withdrew, in order to make his disposition for the meditated encounter. He thought proper to consult the officer at whose house he lodged, and begged him to act as his second; but this one, also, endeavored to dissuade him.

"You know," said he, "how unusual duels are among us. Not a single one has taken place during the whole campaign; and, in fact, I never heard of one being fought in our army. Take my word for it, it will look excessively odious, —ten times more so, than if you were to pistol your man, in the street. A murder would be less prejudicial to your reputation. In a duel, if one of the combatants dies on the spot, he is deprived of Christian burial; and this, as you are aware, is a circumstance which affects the imagination of our people, more than any thing else. Should you prove victorious, you gather upon your own head the execration of the family of the deceased and the odium of the public. Should you die, you are deprived of the suffrages of the church, and your body is buried, like that of an unbaptized Jew, in unconsecrated ground;—whereby your family is for ever disgraced. Therefore, my dear friend, take my advice, and give up your notion. There are many ways of disposing of your enemy, besides this. I do not advise you basely to assassinate him, but can you not, as we have heard that the northern people sometimes do, in their country, cowhide the man in the street? He that wished to dishonor your bride shall, then, be himself dishonored."

"Come, come," replied Captain Letinez, "all this is childish! The fellow would assassinate me, in return, and be justified in the public opinion. It behooves me to do every thing like a gentleman. I must punish the wretch, but it must be in a manner worthy of Miss Quinton and myself. —Say, at once, whether you are willing to be my second, or not?

"Your second!" exclaimed the other, "God forgive me, I will.—There is an excommuncation against seconds, as well as principals; but *Vaya!*—I never feared man, in your quarrel, I will not fear the devil, this bout.—So much for friendship!"

"Well, then, the affair is settled," said our gallant hero: "I am going to write the challenge, and as soon as it is day, you will carry it to the gentleman."

"I, carry it!" replied Captain Letinez's friend; "cannot a servant do the job?"

"My dear fellow," replied our hero, "such things, among gentlemen, are always done by seconds.—This is the way, in civilized nations.—We cannot depart from the code of civility, you know! To send a servant would be ridiculous and would cover me with shame, because it would prove that I am not acquainted with the code of honor."

"Well, captain," returned the other, "we are not so well informed of the rules of duelling, in this country, that you should fear any improper criticism shall be passed upon your conduct, should you fail in some trifling item of etiquette."

" Still I must and will insist upon every thing being done according to strict form," replied Señor de Letinez.

" Very well," answered the other ; " every thing shall be done in conformity to your wishes. I will start no more objections, but will be as submissive as a child. And, now, don't you think it is time to go to bed ? What, with the ball, the champaign we have drunk, or the idea of the duel, which is to take place to-morrow, I am nearly bewildered, and my head is dizzy."

" Oh ! stop !" resumed our hero ; " We have yet a great deal to do this night. I may be killed, and I must make my will.—We must get witnesses, and send for an *Escrivano*, (notary public.)

" Good Lord !" exclaimed the other, " that will keep us up till day, and I am nearly dead for want of sleep. Where are we to get witnesses, at this time of night ?—Why, you must have five men, besides the Escrivano. Do you think people will get up from their beds for such an uninteresting purpose ?"

" Surely, we do not want so many persons. Two witnesses with the notary public, will suffice," observed Captain Letinez.

" No, indeed," resumed his friend ; " you must have *five*, *with* the Escrivano; and *seven*, *without* him ! So you see it is sheer extravagance to pretend to collect so many persons at this time of night.—Wait till to-morrow.—You cannot help yourself, now."

" If such be the case, indeed, I must wait," replied the captain.

" To-morrow, then," returned the other, and they retired to rest.

# CHAPTER XVII.

There are very few pains, however exquisite, which are not preferred
to death..—*Burke on the Sublime.*

THE next morning, our hero had no sooner risen, than,
according to the preceding night's resolution, he immediately
set about making his will. Thanks to the many and cumbrous formalities prescribed by the Spanish law, it could not
be done without some degree of publicity, and he was aware
that the good health he enjoyed was a circumstance that
would give rise to various surmises, and, perhaps, excite suspicion in relation to his further intentions.

In this, however, he was mistaken ; for, as duels were
nearly without example in the republic, it did not enter the
head of any one to suspect him of such a design. The escrivano and witnesses having been sent for, the instrument
was drawn, signed and sealed, and, though, in less than one
hour's time, it was reported all over the town, that Captain
Letinez, being as yet in good health, had just made his will,
no one guessed at the motive. Some thought he was going
to undertake a journey, and had taken this precaution, in
case of accident in the way ; others pretended that, as he
was on the point of being married to an outlandish woman,
he had made his will beforehand, from fear of some *evil influence* on her part, and some attributed it to caprice ; but
none divined the true reason.

In the meantime, our hero had sent his challenge to the
officer who had so infamously offended Miss Quinton. The
latter was yet in bed, when Captain Letinez's friend was introduced into his apartment, and, upon his perusing the note,
manifested a great surprise. He understood not its meaning, and inquired from the bearer what it might be. " Captain Letinez complains of me, as I understand from this here
paper," said he, " for some wrongs which he pretends I
have done to the young American lady upon whom he was

waiting, last night. To be sure, I found her very handsome, but did not know, till lately, that she belonged to a family of distinction—though, by the bye, her father is nothing but a rebel. Yet whatever may have taken place in St. Patricio, I do not see what right Captain Letinez has to interfere.— She is neither his sister, nor relation.—And what does he mean by demanding satisfaction ?—Is it money for the young lady he asks, in order to make up for the Lepantitlan business ?—By St. Corolampio, I am sorry for *that*. I did not think, at the time, she was more than a common *ranchera*. But, *vaya !* If she want money, money she shall have, though it is but little I have to spare."

" Major Firaña," interrupted our hero's friend, " I am sorry that you do not seize the meaning of Don Ambrosio's note. The young lady is his promised bride, and he considers any insult offered to her, as if offered to himself. In St. Patricio, she was under his protection, and you must have known it. Were he informed of the offer of money, which you make, it would incense him still more, I assure you."

" The devil, it would !" replied the other. " What is it, then, he requires ?—What other satisfaction can I give ? He does not intend to make me do penance, in a white sheet, at the door of the church, I suppose !"

" Why, sir," resumed the other, " if I must be explicit with you, such offences, among men of honor, are atoned for only by a duel.—Do you understand me, now ?"

" A duel !" echoed Major Firaña, in surprise. " Does the fellow mean to introduce that foolish thing amongst us ? It did well enough in the times of Don Quixote ; but, now, it is passed away !—It is worn out, and become ridiculous !—It smells too much of feudal times to be acceptable to modern Mexicans."

" You will find," resumed the other, " that the suspicion of cowardice is still apt to attach to the character of those who prove recreant, and that such a suspicion, in a military man, is equivalent to complete disgrace."

" But what would you have me to do, my friend ?" resumed Firaña. " Duelling is not customary among us. I do not even know how it is to be gone about. What arms are we to use ?—When, and where are we to fight ?—Must I not have a second—a *padrino*, as it is called, and he, another ?"

"Certainly," replied Señor de Letinez's messenger. "You must appoint one of you friends to act as padrino for you. Captain Letinez has appointed me on his side, and when you have named your man, he and I will regulate every thing, so that you shall have no trouble, except that of fighting."

"We will be much obliged to our seconds for their courtesy," replied Firaña, with a sardonic grin, "in taking so much trouble off our hands, and leaving us but the trifling matter of handling our arms, and cutting each other's throat. But I must have some time to get a padrino : it is not a thing to be done in the twinkling of an eye. It will, at least, take two days to make my dispositions. So, tell your friend to wait patiently. As soon as I am ready, he will hear of me."

"And what arms will you select ? As you are the challenged party, it is your privilege to take your choice, you know," said Captain Letinez's friend, "will you prefer the sword ?"

"We will see as to that.—I must reflect," replied Firaña. "But, for God's sake, be not in such a hurry, and give me time to breathe ! Sure, the meeting is not so attractive, that I should jump out of my bed, and run to it, without having taken my chocolate."

With this verbal answer, our hero's friend returned to his principal, and faithfully related the conversation which had taken place between Firaña and himself. Captain Letinez was not a little disappointed at the result, and began to suspect that the Major sought to shuffle off. Nevertheless, he kept some hopes till night, supposing that a sense of military honor would prompt his antagonist to accept ; but, towards sundown, he received a summons from the general-in-chief, to repair to his house, and found there a council of officers, assembled to deliberate upon the challenge he had sent to Major Firaña.

At his entrance into the apartment, the paper signed with his own hand was put under his eyes, and he was asked by Urrea whether he owned it ; being, at the same time, reminded that the ancient ordinances of the kings of Spain, which were still, in those matters, the supreme law of the land, prohibited, under severe penalties, the fighting of duels and sending of challenges, and that this frightful evil, having, as yet, gained no footing in the country, it became the duty of the chiefs to see that the first attempts to introduce it should be carefully suppressed.

Though this explanation was added with a view to warn him not to commit himself by owning the challenge, and the captain perceived Urrea's design, yet he had too much honor to deny the truth. He, therefore, boldly admitted that the note had been sent by him, and added, by way of comment, the history of Major Firaña's attempt on Miss Quinton, concluding by proclaiming him as cowardly as beastly, since, after so shocking an offence against a defenceless female, he had not the heart to face her protector, but must take shelter under the ægis of the law.

Thus confessing, without any palliation, what the code of the country considered as criminal, and against which it awarded a severe punishment, our hero brought himself into danger. The officers who were present, acting as a court of inquest, saw themselves obliged to send him to prison, and though every one admired his spirit and approved his gallantry, still a legal process was commenced against him, for a breach of discipline, which threatened a very disagreeable delay to his marriage, if not some danger to his person.

Upon learning what had befallen the captain, Miss Quinton was thrown into the utmost grief, accusing herself with being the cause of it. She bitterly regretted the imprudent manifestation of her alarm at the ball. Had she had presence of mind to suppress it, when she unexpectedly beheld Major Firaña, her lover would have preserved his liberty. But, now, entangled in a criminal accusation, to which no speedy termination was likely to be put, how much he would have to suffer, and all for her sake!—was there any thing she could do, in his behalf?—She would go, accompanied by her father, and throw herself at the feet of the general-in-chief.—She would present her supplications to the superior officers, who were to compose the court-martial, in whose hands her lover's fate was placed.—But was this compatible with female modesty ?—Was it even practicable with such men as these officers were supposed to be ?—Would not such a step be considered as a degradation of her maidenly character, of which she was still more jealous than of her life, because she felt that it was dearer to her lover ?—Alas, was there nothing she could do ?—Her father, at least, could, without impropriety, interfere and solicit in behalf of the captain. But who would pay attention to the prayers of a mere prisoner of war, without friends or influence in the country ?—While her mind was agitated by these cruel reflections, and her tears evinced the bitterness of her grief, she received some consolation from a letter which our hero sent her from his prison. The tone of cheerful playfulness with which it was fraught, gave her some hopes that there was not as much danger as she had, at first, anticipated. It was worded as follows.

Dear Miss Quinton,

" As I hope you have too much sense to be seriously alarmed at what has happened, I will not exhaust my rhetorical powers in pouring forth the balm of consolation. What was begun in the real tragic vein has dwindled down into sheer comedy. The hero of Lepantitlan has acted in perfect keeping with his former conduct, which I might have foreseen. I am, however, better avenged than if I had lodged a bullet in his brain, for he has covered himself with ridicule, and though duels are not much in use amongst *us*, sarcasms and epigrams are by no means strangers to our country, and I am told they fall so thick upon the poor Major, that he cannot possibly stand ' the pitiless storm.' He has brass enough, but yet the shafts directed against him must penetrate to the quick. I give him but three days to stay in town, and in three days more, I will be at your feet."

Yours, &c. &c.

It was exactly as the prisoner had foretold. Major Firaña became the subject of so many pasquinadoes, that he was forced to leave Matamoros, and went to visit his family, on a furlough, which Urrea gave him to understand he was welcome to render perpetual.

After the Major's departure from the city, Captain Letinez did not remain long in prison, for all the army took a lively interest in his fate, and looked upon the treatment he had received as an indignity ; but while there, he made a little acquisition, which, at the time, appeared unimportant, but

13*

had, nevertheless, some unpleasant consequences upon his peace of mind. It consisted in a little miniature portrait, set in gold, which he bought of a soldier that had been in the campaign. It attracted his attention, on account of the similitude of the features to some one with whom he was conscious to have been acquainted, but without exactly recollecting who it was.

The portrait was bought at a low price, and our hero's interest being awakened, he examined it for a long time, endeavoring, by the closest reflection, to clear up his remembrance, in order to find out when and where he had seen the face which the portrait represented. It was the effigy of a middle aged man, of handsome features and prepossessing aspect, but our hero taxed his memory in vain; it furnished him with no clue to unravel his confused ideas, and, though fully convinced that he had been familiar with the original, yet he remained uncertain whether it was in Texas, or Mechoacan.

## CHAPTER XVIII.

——What damned minutes tells he over
Who dotes, yet doubts, suspects, yet strongly loves !
*Shakespeare. Othello.*

Our hero felt a pettish disappointment, and impatiently turned the portrait round and round, till, at last, the thought occurred to him that it was rather massy, and must contain another portrait, inside, or some token from the original owner, whereby he might be led to a discovery. He was not mistaken: upon a closer scrutiny, he discovered a small spring, ingeniously contrived in the rim, on the pressing of which, the portrait flew back, like the lid of a snuff-box, and showed, within, an elegant cipher, embroidered with human hair, upon a piece of white silk, set in a frame of fillagree work, which, he had no doubt, was a token from the person by whom the minature had been presented.

On further examination, he perceived some words written in diminutive characters, beneath the design, and judge of his surprise, when he read the following, ' *To Sophia Quinton.*' —" Is it possible," exclaimed he, " that this portrait belongs to her!—But there can be no doubt: here is her own name. —This was got among the Texas plunder.—Whose picture can it be ?—I am acquainted with these features—nay, they seem those of a person with whom I have been familiar, and yet my treacherous memory cannot clear up the uncertainty ! —Is it some relation of Miss Quinton ?—Is it not, rather, some lover, whose memory she still fondly cherishes ?—Oh ! If she have loved any one before me, her heart can never be wholly mine ; and yet, how perfectly new did love appear to her !—How modest and unobtrusive has she always shown herself, even when I had the conviction that her heart was won and pleading in my favor !—But what, if I had mistaken gratitude for love ?—Would real love be compatible with so much coolness and self-possession, as she always manifested ?

Did she not dread my presence, even at the time she owed me the greatest obligations ?—Did she not always endeavor to render our interviews as short as possible, and seek for pretences to prevent me from declaring my sentiments ?—Yes, I see how it is.—Her heart belongs to another, and it is merely through necessity she consents to wed me. It is out of regard for her father, and in order to insure *his* welfare, that she agrees to become my wife.—But I will not press myself upon her. I will not build my hopes of conjugal felicity on the inspirations of mere gratitude. I will tell her that I leave her at liberty, and her more favored lover may claim the accomplishment of the pledges, which, in more happy times, have passed between them.—And yet, can I part from Sophia Quinton ? Is there another woman in the world like her ? No. There is none. None at least for me. My felicity is intimately connected with the hope of obtaining her. My soul is identified with hers ; and life, without Sophia Quinton, were but a burthen."

Thus was our hero plunged into all the torments of jealousy, and without knowing who his fancied rival might be,—though he was conscious of having seen him somewhere. In vain he inquired from the soldier who had sold him the miniature, how he had come by it ; he received no information capable of clearing up his doubts. It had been found in a house abandoned by its owner, not far from Gonzales, at the approach of Santa Anna's army, and was secreted with several valuable jewels, in a piece of furniture, which, from the description the soldier gave of it, Captain Letinez concluded must have been a writing-desk. This meagre account left him in the same perplexity and ignorance. He resolved, therefore, to come to an explanation with Miss Quinton, for the trouble of his mind had become so excruciating as to be intolerable.

As soon as he was liberated from confinement, his first visit, as our readers may guess, was paid to the Texian major, who received him with the greatest joy and testified the deep concern he had felt, when informed of the danger our hero had incurred, in order to avenge his daughter. " But I was glad when I learnt that you were in prison, my dear friend," said the good old man, " for, there, I knew your life would be safe. In spite of Firaña's villany, I owe him some thanks for his prudent conduct. Confess that you were too warm, and that such a scoundrel was beneath your notice."

To these felicitations and parental expressions of regard the captain answered in a confused manner. His brow was overcast, and a heavy anxiety sat upon his mind. His conversation with Miss Quinton was unmeaning, and his serious demeanor and cold address, appeared unaccountable, and almost offensive. He had come with the intention of presenting the miniature to the young lady and asking an explanation ; but, *now*, when in her presence, he could not screw up his courage to the proper point.

The embarrassment of his manner was visible, and surprised no less than displeased Miss Quinton and her father. The latter, however, attributed it to the mortification, the captain's military pride must have suffered in his imprisonment, and proceeded to administer well meant consolations, in the jocose strain peculiar to him,—but which sounded, in the captain's ears, like so many bitter taunts.

" Come, come, cheer up," said the Major. " Be not cast down for such a trifle—what are a few days' imprisonment ?—All in the way of your profession, man—And it was for an honorable cause. Although I scolded, yet it rejoiced my old blood to see you acting so manly a part, and so ready to avenge my daughter. A woman knows better the worth of a man, when she sees him thus willing to shed his blood in her quarrel."

But, notwithstanding all the Major could say, and he said much to enliven the conversation and put the captain in spirits ; he could not succeed in dispelling the cloud of deep anxiety that overhung his brow, and the interview ended in the same cold and embarrassed manner it had begun.

Our hero returned to his lodgings, angry against himself for his want of resolution, and, in order to remedy it, made up his mind to send the miniature with a letter, but he found it nearly as difficult to indite an epistle appropriate to the circumstance, as he had found it to make the verbal communication. He wrote several letters, and, unable to please himself, tore them up, one after another. Sometimes, he found the style too vehement, and sometimes it was too humble, and did not sufficiently express the feelings of an offended lover. Then, again, the thought would recur to his mind, that the picture was, perhaps, the portrait of some relation, and had been received as a token of family affection, in which case, his peremptory demand of an explanation would prove the most awkward thing in the world. But further reflections showed this supposition was improbable, for he had never been acquainted with any of Miss Quinton's relations except her father, and he was firm in the persuasion that he had seen the original of the portrait; though he could remember neither when, nor where. After long debates with himself and scribbling over and tearing to pieces, nearly a quire of paper, he was unable to take a final resolution, and went to bed, despairing to come to a conclusion.

But we must not omit informing our reader of the conversation which, after the captain had withdrawn, passed between the Major and his daughter. The old man started the subject, by observing that he could never have supposed a few days' imprisonment could have such an effect upon a lad of spirit, like the captain. "One would think," did he observe, "that he is bewildered, and has become stupid.— How absent minded was he not, and what foolish answers did he not give to some queries you addressed him. Sophia, my dear, did you ever before remark that he was subject to such *tantrums ?* And yet, he kept his eyes constantly fixed on you ! He seemed to be grieved in mind, and one would have thought that you were the cause of it. Have you done any thing to wound his feelings ?"

" No, indeed, father," replied Miss Quinton, " and I am still more surprised than you, at his strange behaviour ; the more so, as I cannot imagine his imprisonment has soured him to such a degree. His manner amounted to positive rudeness !—There must be some other reason besides what you suspect. But I will know from him. I will put him in the way of making an apology ; and should he not tender it of his own accord, I will not be in a hurry to give him further encouragement.—The Lord preserve me from caprice and sourness of disposition in the person to whom I am to be united !"

" This is well said, my daughter, and is a magnanimous disposition of mind," resumed her father, playfully, "adhere to it. Be not too rash, however, and do not take offence at trifles. You are young and lack experience. Think that such a conquest is not to be effected, every day. I speak not of his wealth, nor of his rank; for, were he the poorest of mankind he would still be the son of my choice.—Believe me, child, a pure virgin heart, in a man of his years and profession, is a treasure which will never wear out,—if once put in the keeping of a woman of feeling and intelligence. Be not rash, therefore, and though I am of opinion that you should maintain your maidenly dignity and pride of worth, with proper spirit, still do it with discretion, and beware of going too far."

" Father," replied the young lady, " I am astonished to hear you speak in such a manner. Would you advise me, in order to secure an advantageous match, to put up with a treatment which I conceive to be unworthy of me? I am aware of the captain's good qualities; but he must respect as well as love me, if he wishes to secure my regard. Whatever you may say, I will expect an apology from him, and if he is not able to appreciate *me*, it will be an easier task for me to console myself for the loss of him."

In such a disposition of mind Miss Quinton retired to rest, so that the captain and herself might be considered as in a state of mutual coolness and suspicion.—It was too painful to last long, and the captain being, as he thought, the offended party, and the one whose anxiety of mind was greatest, was the first to break the ice.

After spending a sleepless night, he, next morning, took heart of grace, and paid Miss Quinton a second visit. He found her alone, and the first greetings being over, he took the miniature out of his pocket, and with a peculiar solemnity of manner presented it to her, saying, " Here is something that belongs to you, madam, as I conjecture, from your name being written under this design."

At the sight of the portrait, Miss Quinton manifested the most lively joy and exclaimed; " My uncle's miniature!— How did you come by it, captain?"

Now, the great mystery was cleared up!—Our hero's countenance lost the dignity of offended worth, to exchange it for an air of awkwardness, bordering on the comical. He felt how strange his conduct, on the preceding visit, must have appeared to Miss Quinton, and began to stammer forth an apology. The good natured girl did not give him the trouble of going through it, but, interrupting him, with a smile, said, "now, you need not enter into an explanation.—I see how it is.—You were jealous! It will do well enough, for once, and I am disposed to overlook it; but, from henceforth, beware!—You must put an implicit confidence in me, or we cannot promise ourselves any happiness. Enough of this, however: tell me, now, how you came by the picture?"

Thereupon the captain recounted in what manner he had bought it, and what he had learned from the seller, touching the house where it had been found; ingenuously confessing, that his suspicions sprung from the consciousness of having seen, somewhere, the person whom the miniature represented.

Miss Quinton was not a little surprised at the assertion. "Are you sure," said she, "that you are not mistaken? some similarity of features may deceive you, considering, chiefly, that you do not recollect the individual to whom you allude. My uncle has never been in Texas, neither have I myself seen him, since my infancy, for shortly after my mother's death, my father removed from Maryland to Alabama; and though we have, of late, kept up an amicable correspondence with her family, we have never visited. It is true, my uncle has travelled much, both through Europe and America; but you can hardly have seen him in Mexico, for I have understood it was in his youth he visited this country, and you must have been too young yourself to become acquainted with him."

"Well," interrupted the captain, "if he has travelled through this country, it makes good my surmises, and shows that I was not mistaken. But pray, my dear Miss Quinton, do you know what parts of Mexico your uncle visited, and at what particular time?"

"Indeed, I do not," replied she; "I have already told you all that I remember about him. He was my mother's youngest brother, and there had been some estrangement between him and the rest of the family, on account of his grandmother's entire fortune having been settled upon him. It is only of late years, that the difference between him and my father has been made up, and in consequence of that reconciliation he sent me his portrait."

"May I inquire what was your mother's maiden name?" said Captain Letinez.

"Claughton," answered Miss Quinton. "My uncle, however, took his grandmother's name, in consequence of her whole estate being made over to him. But if you are anxious to know further particulars, you must consult my father, for, I confess, my information is neither exact, nor extensive on the subject."

The old Major not having yet returned, all further eclaircissement was postponed.

# CHAPTER XIX.

Speed the match! Speed the match!
*Marriage in a hurry.*

MISS Quinton did not fail to communicate to her father what had passed between herself and the captain, and he was as much astonished as she had been, upon hearing that the latter had a notion of having been personally acquainted with her uncle, though unable to remember when or where. The thing seemed too romantic, and he would have pronounced it absolutely incredible, had not the captain possessed all his confidence. He, therefore, impatiently awaited a second visit, in hopes that, by imparting to him what he knew of his brother-in-law's history and peregrinations, he might so far refresh his memory, as to enable him to recollect whether his surmises were founded, or not. Major Quinton's knowledge of the particulars which the present moment exhibited as possessing a capital interest, was not, however, so extensive as to induce him to believe that he could throw much light on any peculiar circumstance which might have made an indelible impression upon our hero's mind during his infancy ; for he supposed if he had seen his brother-in-law at all, it must have been in a very juvenile age.

The captain, no less desirous than the major to clear up his doubts, and tormented, besides, by an indescribable anxiety of mind, the cause of which appeared unfathomable, and seemed to portend some strange discovery, did not fail to return to Major Quinton's, as soon as he judged it likely he should find him at home, and obtained from him the following account of the Claughton family, from which the major's wife was sprung.

They were the descendants of one of the original settlers of Maryland, under Lord Baltimore, and made a considerable figure in that province until the revolutionary war, when they began insensibly to dwindle away. They had remain-

ed zealous Roman Catholics, until the major's wife's mother married into the family, who, being no less zealous a Protestant, instilled her religion into the mind of her daughters
and youngest son. This bred continual quarrels between
her and her husband, and, at length, she died broken-heart-
ed : yet those among her children who had imbibed her religion, could never be prevailed upon to abandon their faith,
in order to win their father's favor, but rather looked upon
him with some rancor for the treatment he had caused their
mother to undergo. " In that state of things," continued the
Major, " James, the youngest son, left the paternal house,
and turned his attention to commerce, while, about the same
time, I married one of the daughters, of whom I have been
deprived by death these nine years. My brother-in-law
having publicly conformed to the Church of England, it so
much exasperated his father, that he declared he would entirely cut him off from his inheritance, and this very circumstance was the cause of his fortune ; for, his grandmother,
who was as zealous a Protestant as himself, settled upon him
all her estate, as an indemnity for what he had lost. His
sisters and elder brother, saw this with a jealous eye, and he
was so much vexed by their ill-will, that he resolved to absent himself for a time, and obtained from the commercial
house he served, permission to visit Mexico, where he managed the interests of the firm with great success. He may,
then, have travelled through this country ; but it is nineteen
or twenty years ago, and you cannot have been acquainted
with him at that period."

" Has he never, since, visited the Mexican republic ?" interrupted the captain.

" I am not able to say," resumed the Major, " because
since that epoch, a great coolness existed between us, and I
was not informed of his movements ; though it is not impossible, for he has been a great traveller, partly for commercial purposes, and partly for the sake of collecting information. We are on good terms, now, the more so, that he
was the first to seek a reconciliation, though, perhaps, the
greatest share of blame was on my side."

This short account gave Captain Letinez no clue whereby
his doubts might be cleared up. He took the miniature into
his hands, viewed it again and again, muttering to himself,

" Claughton ! — Claughton ! — Have I ever heard this name ?"

But, suddenly an idea seemed to flash across his mind, and he asked Major Quinton, " Did you not tell me that your brother-in-law changed his name, in order to receive his grandmother's bequest ?"

" Certainly," replied the Major, " it was one of the old lady's special conditions, for she was proud of her family name ; and an act of the legislature of Maryland was obtained to that effect."

" And what was the old lady's family name ?" eagerly interrupted the captain.

" Faring," answered the major.

" Faring !" exclaimed the young man, in the greatest amazement ; " is it possible ?—Great God of Heaven, it is my own father !—Yes, these are his features !" and eagerly kissing the picture, he gave way to a flood of tears.

The major and his daughter kept a profound silence, exchanging, however, significant glances, as if they could have read each other's thoughts. Being unacquainted with the captain's history, the discovery he had just made appeared to them the most improbable thing in the world, and they feared lest he should be under some strange hallucination of mind.

The first burst of passion being over, our hero perceived their astonishment, and became aware that his emotion must have appeared unaccountable. He hastened, therefore, to lay before them a brief history of his mother's marriage, and the manner in which *he* had been brought up by his grandfather, the Count of Letinez. He had, hitherto, postponed giving them an account of his birth, because, expecting papers and legal vouchers from Mechoacan, he thought the communications which courtesy required of him, would be best accompanied by the written documents ; but now, when a proper occasion offered to give the information, he did so with modesty, when speaking of the wealth and rank of the house of Letinez, and with such a tone of tenderness and filial affection, when alluding to his father, that the old Major was melted. The latter had, nevertheless, a difficulty on his mind, of which he asked the solution with great frankness. It was about the captain's name. " Be not offended with me," said he, " if I make so free ; but whence comes it that you do not bear your father's name ?"

" It is usual, in this country, as well as in Spain," replied the captain, " for children of families of distinction to bear the mother's, as well as the father's name ; but the old Count would never hear of any other preceding his own. He had retained many prejudices of the ancient times, and consider- ed it as a species of degradation for the name of Letinez to be linked with a plebeian appellative, and, as it were, drag- ged in tow by it. There might also have been some illiber- ality on the score of religion. My father being a Protestant, his name was, I believe, considered heretical, and would have been thought inauspicious for me ! But the arrangement was made with his consent, and he has never shown himself dis- satisfied with it."

" Has your father frequently visited you, in Mechoacan ?" inquired the Major.

" I remember having seen him thrice, since my childhood," replied the captain. " He was with us, four years ago. I was then entering in my fifteeenth year, and he promised to return to take me to travel, much about this time ; but I doubt whether the old Count and my grand uncle would have consented to it. It was only by protracted importunities that I extorted their consent to go to Texas,—and yet they thought the campaign would only prove a military paseo and a kind of recreation !—Travelling abroad would appear to them fraught with much more danger. However, I have no doubt, my father will keep his word, and he either is *now*, or will *soon* be in Mechoacan."

" Well, captain," resumed the Major, " it is you who im part to us your own history, and therefore we believe it ; but were it any body else, it would strike us as a disjointed ro- mance. Egad ! I will have many a jest at your expense, for having had your father's picture in your hands, and been un- able to make out who it was, till prompted to the name."

" Certainly, it looks very odd," exclaimed the captain, laughing ; " but yet there have been thousand similar in- stances, when an idea deeply engraved in the heart, and with a perfect hold on the powers of memory, cannot be fully de- veloped, for want of some leading circumstance which has escaped remembrance, and is, like a match, absolutely indis-

14*

pensable for setting the train of gunpowder on fire. Though the miniature is not well executed," added he, looking at it, " yet the features present the general expression of my father's countenance, and I felt that I had been familiar with the original ; but there was a vagueness in the impression, which did not vanish, till you uttered his name.—It was like a mist, suddenly rolled away ! Now, the whole appears so clear and plain, that I am astonished at myself for my want of penetration."

" It is then certain," said the Major, " that you and Sophia are cousins.—I give you both joy of it."

" And I think, my *prima* should do the same," interrupted the captain, stealing a kiss, " and from this moment give me leave to call her *coz*, and call me *Ambrosio*."

" Though we be cousins," replied Miss Quinton, playfully, and disengaging herself, " it is no reason that you should grow saucy and familiar, *Señor Capitan*.—I must make you keep your distance and teach you discipline."

" Will you, indeed ?" replied our hero, who was now in a fine flow of spirits, and in a witty vein. " But what do you say about going to a ball this evening, at Madame Larronie—the French lady's house ?—It will evaporate all the remainder of ill humor against me, for my foolish conduct of yesterday."

Miss Quinton's father urging her to accept the captain's invitation, she consented, and the latter took his leave.

As soon as he got to his friend's, this one perceived by his radiant countenance, and the peculiar buoyancy of his manner, that some happy circumstance must have turned up, but the captain did not wait till he should inquire the cause of his joy. He broke forth in a tone of exultation : " Give me your felicitations, Troles,—we have made an interesting discovery.—Miss Quinton is my cousin !—Her mother was my father's sister." And, thereupon, he repeated the account which the Major had given him of the Claughton family, and showed in what way his own father had come to change his family name ; manifesting, at the same time, that the idea of such a connection rendered Miss Quinton still dearer to him.

" His friend was, nevertheless, far from congratulating him upon such a discovery.—On the contrary, he told him it was rather unlucky for him, and that he would find it a serious obstacle to his marriage.

" An obstacle to my marriage !" exclaimed the captain— " What do you mean, my dear Troles ?"

" Why," answered the latter, " are you not aware this is an impediment which renders your marriage null and void, unless it be released by a previous dispensation from the Holy See, and that such a grant is not to be obtained without a large sum of money ?—I wonder that a man of your standing should have so imperfect a knowledge of the canon law !—By the virgin of Guadelupe, you should be sent back to school.—There will be a postponement of your marriage, now. It will take one year, at least, to send to Rome and get an answer."

" Is it even so ?" exclaimed Captain Letinez, " then, confound the canon law."

" Hush, hush :—for God's sake, my dear friend, do not blaspheme," cried Troles. " The canon law is a part and parcel of the law of this country, and besides, it is a holy thing, the prop of the church."

" But what are we to do ?" asked the captain.

" Why," resumed his friend, " I would advise you to visit Padre Rapiñez, the great canonist of this place, who will inform you of the measures necessary for procuring a dispensation. He is a venal soul, and has the greatest reverence for wealth. You may be sure he will smooth the matter for you, as much as possible. There are no canons capable to withstand sixty five thousand dollars income."

" Well, then, I will go and see this father Rapiñez," said the captain ; " and if money be all that is wanting, he may have cause to call this marriage one of the best wind-falls he was ever blessed with." And, as there was yet a long time before the hour when he was to accompany Miss Quinton to the ball ; away he went, to consult the above mentioned clergyman, who was considered quite an oracle, in matters of canon law, and was, moreover, ecclesiastical judge and rector of a parish more extensive than any diocese in Europe.

# CHAPTER XX.

Laws are like cobwebs, which detain small flies, but the big ones break through them.

*Anacharsis, the Scythian.*

PADRE Rapiñez, of Matamoros, with an ecclesiastical income of about eight thousand dollars per annum, was, in all things, the reverse of the good clergyman whom we have depicted in the beginning of this work ; yet he possessed that fawning address, which too many among the Mexican gentry mistake for politeness. An affectation of humility, which amounted to baseness, and a hypocrisy of benevolence that made him press his favors upon such as needed them not,— accompanied by perpetual smiles and mellifluous words— covered a heart as hollow, and a temper as wrathful as it is possible to find. This worthy was a great respecter of the rich, for it was his principal aim to keep up his popularity with the upper classes. Of course, he received our hero with the utmost civility, and had no sooner been informed of his business, than he hastened to relieve him from his anxious forebodings. "It is true," said he, "that the dispensation which you need for your marriage, being for the second degree of consanguinity, is, by the canons, reserved to the Pope ; but his Holiness, considering the unsettled state of the Republic, has, in his fatherly mercy, sent an *indultum* to our Bishops, whereby they are enabled to grant these dispensations to the diocesans. Now, there is no doubt but a gentleman of your house has a peculiar right to the favors of the church, and his most illustrious Lordship, our Bishop, will delight in having it in his power to oblige you. I must, however, forewarn you that there will be a trifle to pay,—not as a price for the dispensation,—you understand,—but as a *multa*, (fine,) for the violation of the laws of the church— which is employed in pious works."

"Well," interrupted the captain, "this will be no difficulty with me.—Unless the amount should prove enormous."

"Enormous!" replied the padre. "No. The Mexican Church is too tender a mother. It will, on the contrary, be very light. I dare say, not above a thousand dollars."

"A thousand dollars!" exclaimed the captain, in amazement. "And do you call *that* a trifling sum?"

"Why!" said the priest, "for such a man as you, it is certainly insignificant. Consider, Señor, that our most illustrious Lord, the Bishop of Monterey, was a poor friar, without a cent in his pocket, and that, upon being raised to the mitre, he had to go in debt to the amount of forty thousand dollars, to procure the episcopal insignia, and after taking possession of his See, he found his income could not even defray the expenses of his household; much less enable him to pay his debts. Now, he is reduced to live in the convent of San Francisco, in Mexico, for the sake of economy, and to apply the proceeds of those *multas* to satisfy his creditors. So, it will not be too much for you, to contribute to this good work. But take notice that I do not include in this sum, the various fees of office,—church rates,—*paraguantes* to the sacristan and choristers,—beadle and bell-ringer,—notorial fees, and my own charges for brokerage—without mentioning the singing boys, who are left to your generosity."

"Brokerage!" echoed the captain, with a smile which was any thing but flattering for the *Señor Cura*.

"Ay, brokerage!" resumed the priest, a little confused. "The word was, perhaps, ill chosen; but I meant the proper fees for my trouble and intervention in the matter. You are aware, no doubt, that the drawing of the petition to his Lordship must be in Latin, and that it requires no little skill and some labor to compose it, and detail the canonical reasons, which alone can prompt the church to grant the favor sued for. You do not expect these things shall be done out of mere charity, as for a beggar, (*de limosna*.)

"I expect and desire nothing to be done for me through mere charity," replied the captain, with haughtiness, (for, the idea of obtaining the rites of the church gratis, or de limosna, as the Mexican clergy express it, in order to stimulate the pride of their parishioners, is one of the greatest humiliations the latter can possibly undergo.) I confess, however, I was not prepared for the manner in which these things are carried on. I did not expect to see an explicit contract entered into, as for the acquisition of a piece of property. I had supposed it was left to the generosity of a gentleman. But, since every thing is done above board, and in a merchant-like manner, I will draw up the petition myself."

The priest, who saw that he was going to lose this rich windfall, wanted to repair the effect of his indiscretion. He apologized, and said the sum would not, probably, amount to a thousand dollars—that it was the maximum, and that he could obtain the dispensation for eight, nay, perhaps, for seven hundred :—all would not do. The captain was inexorable, and taking leave of him, returned home, where, by recalling to his remembrance various scraps of Latin, he had learned in his youth and with the help of his friend, he succeeded in composing an elegant petition to the Bishop of Monterey, and despatched it, that same evening, with a strong letter of recommendation from the general to back it.

This business being over, his mind felt at rest, for he doubted not, but, he would receive a favorable answer from Mexico, in less than a fortnight. He, therefore, thought of nothing but paying his court with assiduity to his fair cousin ; and for that purpose, was very importunate to take her to balls and assemblies, which the people of fashion frequently gave to the superior officers of the army.

It happened that five days after Madame Larronie's party, Don Gregorio, Francisco de Paula, José, Maria de Castro, with his spouse, Doña Catalina, Teresa de Jesus de Meragua, (I like to give both names at full length, because, in Mexico, a wife preserves her own, distinct from that of her husband), gave a splendid assembly ; which, it was intended, should surpass any thing ever seen in Matamoros. Madame Larronie, they confessed, had stolen a march upon them, in causing her *gran sala* to be floored with fine wrought plank, imported from New Orleans, for that express occasion. This was an unheard of piece of luxury and had been extolled beyond measure, on account of the wonderful ease and grace it imparted to the movements of the dancers.

Don Gregorio and his wife could not offer the same convenience to their party, but still they were anxious to out-do Madame Larronie ; for they held it a kind of stigma upon the Mexican character, that a foreign lady should know better than they, how to order these things. To carry, therefore, their scheme into effect, they borrowed all the fine furniture they could cram into their hall. Four mahogany sideboards, placed at equal distance, two on each side, displayed an immense quantity of china, lent by an importing merchant. Four large looking glasses, all borrowed, decorated the walls and afforded to the beauties of the place peculiar facilities for contemplating their charms. Sofas of the latest fashion filled up the empty spaces, between the side-boards, and afforded superior convenience for lolling with grace and elegance. But what capped the climax and commanded the general admiration was a cut glass chandelier, suspended from the ceiling ! Such a piece of furniture had never been seen in Matamoros and was accounted the *ne plus ultra* of magnificence ; so that Madame Larronie was, by the unanimous voice of the company, declared absolutely out done.

All the principal officers of the army and not a few of the inferior ones were present, and participated in the festivities of the night ; appearing in a variety of costumes, which, without being elegant or picturesque, were sufficiently varied for the purposes of singularity. A colonel presented himself in the summer *negligé* of the country,—white vest—trowsers and roundabout of the same, with an enormous silk sash, of some brilliant color, round his breast—the only insignia of his military rank being two small embroidered strips on his shoulders, in lieu of epaulets. A captain danced in his cumbrous regimentals, loaded with more gold than is, in Europe, lavished upon a general : the seams of his pantaloons covered with broad gold lace—the collar, cuffs and skirts of his coat, richly embroidered with the same, and two epaulets, nearly as large as frying-pans, spreading their fringe down to his elbows. Close to him a lieutenant appeared in a citizen's dress, without the least mark of his profession. There was, however, a point in which, notwithstanding their variety of costume, they all agreed—it was the wearing of glazed hats of prodigious thickness—an absurd fashion, in a country where it seldom rains, and of which it is not easy to discover the motive.

The ladies were no less fanciful in their habiliments than the gentlemen. The elegant *gala* dress of the Spanish fe-

males, consisting of a white tunic and mantilla, trimmed
with the richest Flanders' lace—at once the most modest
and coquetish of female costumes—did not, however, make
its appearance.    It seems that Mexican women are in-
sensible to its charms.    In ordinary circumstances, they use
their pitiful *rebozos*, to cover their head and part of their
face ; but, in their balls, they appear bare-headed, while their
gowns are generally more gaudy than tasteful, being furbe-
lowed all over with gauze and ribons, and not unfrequently,
bedizened with spangles, like a doll's frock.    Their necks,
hands and ears are loaded with jewels, without taste, chiefly
set with pearls ; and when they move in the mazy dance, with
all those meretricious ornaments dangling about them, and the
noisy castanets in their hands, they look rather like Indian *Bay-
aderes*, than Christian females indulging in decent recreation.

It was in this style they were dancing at Don Gregorio,
José, Maria de Castro's, and Sophia Quinton, though she assisted at the ball with a certain degree of repugnance, commanded, nevertheless, the admiration of all the men by her
superior beauty ; while the women did not fail to criticise the
simplicity of her costume, with all the bitterness of envy.
She had been just led down, for a *volero*, by Colonel Passa-
monte, next to Captain Letinez, the finest looking man in the
army, and all eyes were fixed upon them, the young lady's
lover enjoying with a kind of rapture the elegance of her
movements, and listening with a secret pride, to the praises
which he heard on all sides lavished upon her, when two
strangers entered the ball-room.

They created no sensation, for there was, at first sight, nothing remarkable in their appearance.    Both wore soiled
clothes—as if just arrived from a long journey.    One was a
reverend looking old man, with a mild countenance, and sil-
very hair ; but so feeble, that he needed his companion's arm
to support his tottering steps.  The second was much younger,
and of Herculean frame.  His complexion indicated the most
vigorous health, and the shrewd expression of his handsome
features, marked him out as a man of superior intelligence.
Both of these new comers stood for a while, gazing at the
assembly, and successively fixing a scrutinizing glance at
the various groups that filled the hall ; when, at last, the elder one suddenly sprung forward towards Captain Letinez,

who, having recognized him, met him half-way, and received him in his arms.

It was his grand-uncle, from Mechoacan, who had just arrived at Matamoros, and having learned that he was at liberty, had not even given himself time to change his clothes, before embracing him. Now, he pressed on his bosom the child of his promise—the only hope of his family—the dear pupil, whom, from the first dawn of reason, he had carried through the various stages of instruction, and fashioned according to the wishes of his heart—another himself, as he thought, and as dear as if he had been his own son.—Now, he held him in his embrace, and there was no danger of their ever being separated again!—The young man's arms were cast around him, to support his weak frame, while the venerable old man literally lifted up his voice and wept! "Oh! Ambrosio," said he, as soon as his emotion, a little subsided, allowed him to give utterance to his feelings, "I find thee safe at last.—Heaven be praised for all his mercies, but mostly for this last one.—Ah! child of my heart! Little thou knowest the mortal anguish to which I have been a prey; yet this one embrace repays me for all!"

The good clergyman's companion, who was, in fact, no other than our hero's father, was more successful than the good Abbate in mastering his emotion, for he was descended from a more phlegmatic race, yet a *tremor* of pleasure shook his frame, as he took his son's hand into his, and his voice faltered, when he articulated a father's blessing on his head. The tall, beautiful form before him, that shone with all the grace of youthful manliness, was his child!—O joy!—Oh! had only his long lost Maria been alive now, to share with him the pleasure of contemplating the son of their love!—But though alone, what did he not feel, when the young man pressed him to his bosom? The whole father yearned within him, and he felt it as one of those few moments of rapture, when the human soul seems on the point of being overpowered by a trance of bliss, and a spasm of mental pleasure well nigh reduces her to the brink of annihilation. Some few such moments are interspersed through life—being, perhaps, a glimpse of that immortal bliss, for which mankind were ordained,—but to no one are they vouchsafed as frequently as to a parent.

O God of nature, condemn those who have refused to
know thee to bodily enjoyments, and, to avenge thyself,
plunge them into the degradation of bestial sensuality ; but
grant me the pleasures of the soul—grant me the delights of
paternal love, which never cloy the inward taste.—When
thou hadst created man, thou didst rejoice at thy own work,
and when he stood before thee, in the beauty of manhood,
" thou crownedst him with honor and glory ;" but of all the
privileges thou grantedst him, none was like this, save that
of knowing thee !—Oh, let such be mine !—That I may, one
day, behold the son of my bosom, standing before me, in
the full bloom of youth, and smiling on me, with gratitude
and filial love !—Then I will be content to lay my head in
the cold lap of the grave, for I shall have enjoyed the greatest of human pleasures,—the one that comes nearest to thy
own unspeakable joys !

Such thoughts as these had frequently crossed Mr. Faring's mind, especially at the sight of parents fondling on
their children—when he was reminded of his own dear boy,
far away—but *now* he saw his utmost wishes realized.   His
affection for his son was probably greater than it would have
been, had the latter been brought up under his immediate
inspection ; for he possessed one of those ardent and imagi-
native souls for whom the remoteness of objects lends them
higher charms, and the rarity of the enjoyment enhances
its worth.

The scene which the meeting of our friends exhibited
suspended the amusements of the company, who were now
gazing at them, with the most lively interest ; till the old
clergyman, his first transports being over, reminded Mr.
Faring of the strange figure they made, in the middle of the
dancing apartment, and manifested a desire to withdraw.
But our hero stopped them, telling his father that he had
another relation at the ball, besides himself ; and immediately presented Miss Quinton and the old Major to the new
comers.

The Texian could hardly believe his eyes.—The scene
of recognition between the two brothers-in-law was not so
pathetic as the one which had preceded it, for they had been
once at variance : it was, nevertheless, sufficiently cordial,
and, after apologising to the master of the house and the as-

sembly; they left the ball, and hastened to Major Quinton's house.

As they went along they formed a joyous band,—Miss Quinton between her father and her lover, and the old Abbate, between the latter and Mr. Faring." It was such a confusion of queries and answers! "But you are a bold and brisk traveller, Faring," said the Major, "You, *Tranche-montagne*, as your grandmother used to call you!—To pay us so unexpected a visit and in such a spot!—After having not seen us for fourteen years!—Ay, it does my old heart good, however, to have, before death, sealed our reconciliation by a hearty embrace."

"I was preparing to pay you a visit, in Alabama," replied Mr. Faring; "when I heard of your removal to Texas. I knew that my niece had grown up into a fine woman, and I had to make an interest in her heart for some one."

"Ah, you old fox!" interrupted the Major. "There, also, you have been more lucky than wise, and *we* have done the work in your absence.—My daughter is all but married to your Ambrosio.—You may, however, thank Texas, and the Comanches, and a thousand strange circumstances which have concurred in bringing it about, for, without it, you might as soon have hoped to pluck the *Sierra Madre* from its foundation, as to get your son out of the old Count's clutches, to make him take an airing through the world.— But I have not yet asked you when did you land, nor by what vessel you came."

"Oh," replied Mr. Faring, "I have not landed at this port. I come from the interior. It is now more than two months since I landed at Vera Cruz, and after visiting the old Count, from whom I learned what had befallen Ambrosio, I made haste to overtake the Abbate; which I was happy enough to effect, at the time he stood most in need of my assistance."

"Well, I admire the rapidity of your movements," resumed the Major, adding in jest, "only I fear you will not find the world large enough for your perambulations, and, that, like Alexander, you will be reduced to shed tears, that there is no other which you can overrun."

"Never fear, brother," answered Mr. Faring, "my peregrinations are now at an end. This marriage will oblige me to settle down."

While the two Marylanders were thus conversing together, the captain was communicating to the Abbate a brief account of his adventures, and had not yet finished the recital, when they arrived at Major Quinton's house.

" The travellers' mules and equipage had been left in the *plazuela de los arrievos*, under the care of trusty servants, and it being now too late to look for a house, it was settled that the old clergymen should take possession of his nephew's apartment, in Sonora-street, while Mr. Faring would return to the *plazuela*, where his servants had been ordered to erect his travelling tent. Our hero, therefore, after taking leave of the Quinton family, and seeing his good uncle snugly bestowed in his bed, and in a fair way of enjoying a comfortable night's rest, accompanied his father to his tent and spent the night with him.

They were no sooner alone, than Mr. Faring opened a confidential conversation with the young man. " Well, my dear Ambrosio," said he, " in my absence, I find you have been making up a match for yourself. Though Sophia is all I could wish, and the very person upon whom I had cast my eyes—and though this singular coincidence appears an interposition of Providence ; yet, was it dutiful, on your part, to take so important a step, without my counsel and permission ? Youth is heedless, blindly impelled by passion, and needs the experience of age. Now, suppose you had made a choice which I had reason to blame, and to which it were my duty to refuse my consent, what an estrangement would it not produce between us ?"

" Father, father, blame me not," answered the young man ; " it was not passion I followed, but judgment. My love for Sophia, grew in proportion with my esteem and admiration for her virtues. I was perfectly convinced you could not but approve of such a choice. She will prove equal to what you have so often told me my mother was, and I hope, God will grant us a greater share of happiness than fell to your lot. But, after all, can you complain ? Had you acted yourself according to the rule you wish I had followed, should *I* be here now ?"

" Come, come," interrupted his father; " you grow naughty. But let *that* rest, and let us speak of our ulterior projects. I do not wish to deprive the old Count and the good Abbate, of your company. With them you must remain as long as they live ; yet, in the course of nature, they cannot last long, and my earnest wish has been, that, when the ties which connect you with this country are broken, you should settle with me in Texas. The marriage you are going to contract will greatly facilitate the execution of such a plan ; for you do not imagine that Sophia would part from her father, or that the latter would consent to spend the remainder of his life in Mechoacan. The Mexican republic will now become a prey to anarchy and be divided into several states. Confusion and misery await the inhabitants, and it will be the part of prudence to leave the country."

" I confess, sir," replied the young man, " that, ten months ago, I would have felt great difficulty in conforming to your wishes ; but, during my captivity, I have had more lights on the advanced state of civilization in the north, and it will cost me very little to give you my promise. I am persuaded, like you, that the fate of Mexico is sealed. I have not the least doubt, that, although arising from such a small beginning, Texas will ultimately sweep *westward*, even to the shores of the Pacific and become a considerable nation ; neither do I consider it as a misfortune for the inhabitants of our northern provinces. It will certainly improve their civil existence and enhance their happiness. By removing to Texas, we will only anticipate by a few years the fate which is sure to overtake us ; for, Texians we must become, whether we will, or not. I make no objection, then, to your plan. But we must keep it carefully concealed from the Abbate, as well as from the old Count : it would give them incredible pain, particularly to the latter."

" Well, thank you, my child," said Mr. Faring, affectionately. " Now, indeed, I hope my old age will be spent in peace and happiness. For your sake and the remembrance of your dear mother, I have abstained from a second marriage. You are my only child, and with you I was determined to end my days, at whatever sacrifice, but it would have been gall and wormwood to me, to live and die in this country. My fortune is considerable, nearly about half as much as what you are to inherit from your grandfather, and it is my wish that we should form but one family—the Major, yourself and wife, and myself, together with a sister I have in Maryland, whose husband has left her in poverty."

"Your desires, sir," replied the son, "shall be my law, and all those who are dear to you shall be dear to me."

In those fine sentiments of mutual love and reciprocal condescension for each other's wishes, father and son fell asleep, and when they awoke, the next morning, the most urgent thing they had to do was to look for a house, to lodge in, during their stay in Matamoros.

As they were leaving their tent, the captain happened to cast his eyes upon some *arrieros*, who had spent the night in the square, along with his father's men, and was not a little surprised to perceive Flambeau among them. He approached him and kindly addressed him, in French, saying; "*Eh bien, mon ami*, do you still bear rancor?—Had you not better return to me?—Harkee, my fate is now determined. Almost all my family have, by an unexpected concurrence of circumstances, met in this place, and in a few days, my union with Miss Quinton will be consummated, when we will set out for Mechoacan.—Had you not better be one of the party? I have an old uncle, among the rest, who is a priest, and a man of science and literary taste. I will place you with him, rather as a companion, than as a servant.—The old gentleman will be delighted to have a *scholar*, to serve his mass, every morning, and to take care of his library, and he will never find fault with you, provided you listen with patience to his metaphysical disquisitions when he is in a chatty humor. You, that, once, so much envied the librarian of Scratchnoodle college, and thought him the happiest man in the world, have it now in your power to secure the same bliss for yourself." Flambeau had already repented having left the captain; he relented, therefore—suffered himself to be coaxed into the family—and having briefly wound up his *commercial* affairs, was, the next day, introduced to Abbate Letinez, who, upon a further acquaintance, was delighted with him, and treated him with the utmost condescension.

We will not enter into the detail of all the trouble our travellers had to undergo, in order to procure a house suited to their purpose. The best part of the day was spent in inquiries, and it was only just before twilight, that their equipage and servants were enabled to leave the square, which, in Matamoros, serves destitute travellers, as a caravanserai, to go and take possession of their new lodgings. We will suppose them already installed in them, their apartments set in order, their kitchen in operation, each of their servants punctually discharging his alloted task, and the whole family in the full tide of house-keeping; for, though they intended to stay only one month in Matamoros, to such a strait were they reduced, through the want of houses of entertainment in that city, which is the second sea-port town of a republic boasting nine millions of inhabitants!

## CHAPTER XXI.

Here come the lovers, full of joy and mirth—
Joy, gentle friends!   Joy and fresh days of love
Accompany your hearts.

*Shakespeare.*

ONCE settled in their new habitation, our friends had very little else to do, than to wait for the arrival of the papers from Mechoacan, and the dispensation from the Bishop of Monterey, necessary for the marriage of our hero ; who, either on account of the qualities of his mind, personal beauty, or the circumstance of his being the only scion of a wealthy and noble house, was a perfect idol in the family.   Old Abbate Letinez, who, as we have already observed, was a man of learning, much addicted to thinking and very shrewd in his observations, found an agreeable employment in examining the curiosities of the seaboard, which he had never visited before.   He was delighted with the splendid shells found on that part of the coast, and collected several precious plants, entirely unknown on the table land of the interior, besides attending to various other objects of natural history.

Without having ever travelled out of his country, he was well acquainted with geography, and pronounced the locality at the mouth of the Rio Bravo, the most important for commerce, on the gulf of Mexico, next to that of New Orleans.([6]) But at the same time he thought that, if Texas could secure her independence, these natural advantages would be rendered useless by the superior facilities which the immense extent of frontier between that country and Mexico, would give for the smuggling trade.   He wondered much to see nothing was exported except coarse wool, raw hides and silver ; when that *port alone* might furnish immense quantities of copper, when lead, sulphur, cochineal, vegetable gums, for manufacturing purposes, wine and other articles might form considerable items.   But his wonder ceased, upon being informed that there was a general conspiracy between the government and the inhabitants to prevent the navigation of the river, (though they seemed to be anxious for it) and that, by the multiplication of formalities, so many obstacles were thrown in the way of exportations, that it was a much more difficult operation to ship off a dozen hides, than to introduce a whole cargo of foreign goods. "Now you would hardly believe it, *Mon reverend*," said to him a French merchant, who acted as his cicerone, in his rambles ; "but we have never, got here, a pint of wine from Passo del Norte, although the poor vintners, there, find hardly any sale for it, and it might be brought down by water. My neighbor, on the other side of the street, brought, last year, from the interior, a quantity of copper, to ship it to the United States ; but he was prevented from embarking it, under pretence that there is a law forbidding the exportation of the precious metals in bullion, and that this copper contains, perhaps, some gold.—Not only your people oppose the exporting of many commodities, produced here in abundance, and precious abroad ; but even they absolutely refuse to believe in the existence of those which were not pointed out and recognized by the Spanish government, in times previous to your revolution. You will tell me, this is too absurd to be believed ; but you may try an experiment, if you choose. Essay to make your Mexicans *believe in the coal mines* found some hundred miles up this river ! They will laugh in your face !—This is an article I quote, among twenty."

"Is it so, indeed ?" said the Abbate. "My dear countrymen run the risk of becoming the poorest and most miserable nation upon earth. They should change their maxims of political economy."

"Yes," interrupted the Frenchman ; "for, those they follow, *now*, seem to have been borrowed from Morocco."

This conversation suggested to the keen sighted Abbate many reflections and remarks, which it might be accounted pedantic to relate in this place. We will, of course, pass over a period of about five weeks, and hasten to the happy marriage of our hero—which forms the *denouement* of our story.

Mr. Faring, who was careful to visit the post-office every time the post arrived from the west, was so happy at last, as to receive two huge packets at the same time. With these he hastily returned home, his face radiant with joy, and the sanhedrim of the whole family being immediately convened, they began to examine whether any thing was wanting which might retard the nuptials so ardently desired.

They met with no disappointment.—All the papers were in order, and not the least formality prescribed by the canon law, or the ordinances of the kings of Spain had been neglected. There came, first, the certificate of baptism of our hero, extracted from the registers of the parish church of Phelipa,—duly authenticated by the ecclesiastical notary of the place, and afterwards endorsed, signed, sealed and legalized by the Bishop of Durango.—Fees, forty-six dollars!—There came, in the second place, an attestation in due form from the parish priest of Pascuaro, diocese of Mechoacan, by which it was made known to all men, that Ambrosio de Letinez, captain of cavalry in the Mexican service, was a *single* man, and at full liberty to contract marriage, no other impediment intervening, &c. &c. This instrument of writing was also endorsed by the Bishop of Mechoacan, and charged only twenty-two dollars. The third piece was a dispensation from the last prelate, whereby our hero, being his diocesan, and under his jurisdiction, was permitted to contract marriage, *in facie Ecclesiæ*, with Sophia Quinton, without any publication of bans, the above said bishop being moved to grant that favor, by good and canonical reasons; and, on the back, this pious condescension was rated at two hundred and sixty dollars,—as a *multa*, (fine) to be spent in pious works, by the bishop aforesaid. This, with a paternal letter from the old Count, and a notarial act, by which he gave his consent for the captain's marriage, did well enough for Mechoacan.

Now came the other packet. It was from the Bishop of Monterey, who mercifully dispensed our hero from the publication of bans, likewise, seeing that the marriage was to be solemnized in his diocese, and exacted, for this act of kindness, the light sum of seventy dollars. A second paper contained the dispensation of what is technically called *disparitas cultus*, that is to say, the religion of the bride. But, as this was a matter of great consequence, and a bad precedent for the diocesans of his most illustrious Lordship, the grantee was ordered to pay six hundred dollars, and, moreover, to fast, and recite the seven penitential psalms, on the first Friday in every month.

With these papers in his possession, our hero was not more than half way through his difficulties, for the same formalities, should, in rigor, have been required of the bride. But how could she prove that she was *not* a married woman ?—She was a stranger in the country, and before she could get an authentic certificate of *solteria*, (singleness) as the Spanish law terms it, the marriage would be delayed at least, six months ! In this emergency, our hero remembered what his friend had told him of the pliability of principle of father Rapiñez, and caused him to be spoken to by his uncle and his father. The curate was easily prevailed upon to receive Mr. Faring's declaration, as a complete proof of the young lady's being at liberty to contract marriage, whereupon the old Abbate, who attributed it to his eloquence and insinuating powers of persuasion, was not a little elated ; but he did not know that a secret douceur to a certain Doña Olympia, who passed for the curate's cousin, three times removed, had preceded their visit to the padre.

The difficulty being thus smoothed over, the day for the ceremony was appointed, and, on the happy morn, the *cortege* proceeded from the house of the bride to the parish church, where father Rapiñez awaited them, in his most splendid vestments. A number of officers waited upon the bridegroom, in order to do him honor, and during the marriage mass, a fine band of music played national airs.

The priest being expeditious, the ceremony was soon over, and our hero led his bride in triumph to his own house, whither Major Quinton also immediately removed. At night, there was a superb ball, which, according to an ancient promise, was opened by Captain Alvarez dancing a *volero* with the bride. To him, besides, were paid the principal honors of the *soirée*, the family thinking that they could never do enough, to manifest their gratitude towards the noble hearted man, who had saved Major Quinton's life, with so much danger to himself.—And we wish we had the power of a Homer to immortalize his name, as well as that of his wife, for they are not fictitious personages, and well deserve to be honored for their humane heroism.

Our task is now drawing to a close. A few days after the marriage, the whole family left Matamoros for Mechoacan ; the captain, his wife and Major Quinton riding in one coach ; and Mr. Faring, Abbate Letinez and Flambeau, in another. They met with no accident on their journey, unless we should call by that name the fright of the bride and her father, at a place called *los Coyotes*, where they encamped, the first night after leaving Matamoros. Some prairie wolves, which prowled round their tents, made so dreadful a noise by their cries, as alarmed them seriously. Unaccustomed as they were to these visits, they supposed themselves surrounded by several scores of ferocious animals, and their surprise was great upon being assured that there were not probably more than three or four creatures of the fox species, dangerous only to lambs and poultry.

They could not pass within reach of Phelipa, without paying a visit to the excellent Don Fernando de Larribal. Ever since he had become acquainted with father Letinez, in the manner related in the beginning of this work, he had kept up a friendly correspondence with him, and continued to take a lively interest in Mr. Faring's son. His delight was inexpressible in seeing, now, in full and blooming manhood, the being he had parted from, with so much grief, when only an infant. As he embraced him, he could not help calling him *hijito*, and when this *babe*, of five feet eleven inches high, presented to him his bride, he kissed her, also, for the sake of his child, (en favor del muchacho.)—Of the old inmates of the house, none remained alive, but the old Ama de llaves, who manifested nearly as much joy as her master, at the sight of father Letinez whom she recognised immediately, and could not refrain from tears, when told the captain was the babe she had nursed nineteen years before.

Our travellers' joy was damped by a mournful ceremony. Mr. Faring, of course, wished to visit his wife's grave and his son was no less anxious than he, to kneel on the sacred spot. But tearing themselves, at last, from the mournful recollection, they resumed their journey and arrived at Pascuaro in eighteen days after leaving Phelipa. When the old Count saw his brother and grandson, he was so overjoyed as entirely to lose his gravity.—He rubbed his hands together,—skipped about like a child—actually gave two kisses to his grandson's bride, and began to talk about a *great grandson*, as if he expected one on the very day of her arrival.

Mrs. Letinez, or the young Countess, as she is called by some of the people, thereabouts, is becoming accustomed to the town, and greatly admires the scenery of the surrounding country, which she finds superior to any thing she ever saw before.

The old Abbate is delighted with Flambeau, who has now learned Spanish enough, to discuss with him questions of metaphysics, which furnish both with subjects for interminable conferences. He has, moreover, availed himself of the knowledge he acquired, while a servant in Scratchnoodle College, to construct for the old man several philosophical instruments that have enabled him to perform certain experiments he had never seen before. A galvanic battery, in particular, has thrown the good gentleman into raptures, and a rotary magnet he has set up in his library has caused a great run of the gentry, from a considerable distance.

Mr. Faring, curbing his erratic disposition, has promised to stay in Pascuaro, until he sees the birth of a grandchild; but still, by means of a correspondent, in New Orleans, he is making preparations in a snug corner of Texas, where he intends to establish himself definitively. He has even ventured to drop some hints of his design to the Abbate, and imagines that, were the old Count once removed, his brother might be prevailed upon to settle in the territory of the new republic, with the rest of the family.

# NOTES TO VOLUME II.

Note 1, *page* 11.—Account of the affair of San Jacinto, as given by Santa Anna, in his official communication to the Mexican government.

" Early on the 19th of April, I sent Captain Marcos Barragan, with some dragoons, to a point on the Lynchburgh road, three leagues distant from New Washington, in order that he should watch and communicate to me, as speedily as possible, the arrival of General Houston ; and on the 20th at eight o'clock in the morning, he informed me that Houston had just got to Lynchburgh. It was with the greatest joy that all the individuals belonging to the corps then under my immediate orders heard these news, and they continued the march already begun in the best spirits.

" At my arrival, Houston was in possession of a wood, on the margin of Bayon Buffalo, which, at that point, empties itself into the San Jacinto creek. His situation rendered it indispensable for him to fight, and my troops manifested so much enthusiasm that I immediately began the battle. Houston answered our fire, but refused to come out of the cover of the woods. I wished to draw him into a field of battle suited to my purpose, and, in consequence, withdrew about a thousand yards distance, to an eminence affording a favorable situation, with abundance of water on my rear, a thick wood on my right, and a large plain on my left. Upon my executing this movement, the enemy's fire increased, particularly that of his artillery, by which Captain Fernando Urriza was wounded. About one hundred cavalry sallied out of the woods and boldly attacked my escort, which was posted on the left, causing it to fall back, for a few moments, and wounding a dragoon. I commanded two companies of cazadores to attack them, and they succeeded in repelling them into the woods. Some infantry had also sallied out, but seeing their cavalry in full retreat, they withdrew. It was five o'clock in the evening, and our troops wanted refreshment and rest, which I permitted them to take. Thus was the rest of the day spent. We lay on our arms all night, during which I was busy in posting my forces to the best advantage, and procuring the construction of a parapet, to cover the position of our cannon. I had posted three companies in the wood, on our right ;—the permanent batallion of Matamoros formed our body of battle, in the centre—and, on our left, was placed the cannon, protected by the cavalry, and a column of select companies, (de preferencia,) under the orders of Lieutenant Colonel Santiago Luelmo, which composed our reserve. On the 21st, at nine o'clock, in the morning, General Cos arrived with four hundred men, belonging to the batallions of Aldama, Guerrero, Toluca and Guadalaxara, having left one hundred, under the orders of Colonel Mariano Garcia, with their loads, in a swampy place, near Harrisburgh, and these never joined me.

"I then saw that my orders had been contravened, for I had asked five hundred select infantry, and they sent me raw recruits, who had joined the army at San Louis Patosi and Saltillo. I was highly displeased with this act of disobedience, and considered the new reinforcement as trifling, whereas, before its arrival, I entertained well founded hopes of gaining some decisive advantage with the new succour, which was to give me the superiority in point of numbers.

"I disposed myself, however, to take advantage of the favorable spirit which I perceived in our soldiers, on the arrival of General Cos. But the latter represented to me that, having made a forced march, in order to reach my camp early, his troops had neither eaten nor slept during twenty-four hours, and, that, while the loads were on the road, it was indispensable to grant some time for refreshment to the soldiers. I consented to it, but, in order to keep a watch over the enemy, and protect the loads which were coming on, I posted my escort in a favorable place, reinforcing it with thirty-two infantry, mounted on officers' horses. Hardly one hour had elapsed when General Cos begged me, in behalf of Don Miguel de Aguirre, the commander of the escort, to permit his soldiers to water their horses, which had not drunk for twenty-four hours, and let the men take some refreshment. Being moved by the *pitiable tone*, in which this request was made, I consented ; commanding, at the same time, that Aguirre and his men should return to occupy their position, as soon as they should have satisfied their necessities, and his disobedience to this order concurred to favor the surprise which the enemy effected.

" Feeling myself exceedingly fatigued from having spent the whole morning on horseback, and the preceding night without sleep ; I lay down under the shade of some trees, while the soldiers were prepaing their meal. Calling General Castrillon, who acted as major-general, I recommended to him to be watchful, and to give me notice of the least movement of the enemy; and also to inform me when the meal of the soldiers would be over, because it was urgent to act in a decisive manner.

" I was in a deep sleep, when I was awaken by the firing and noise. I immediately perceived that we were attacked, and had fallen into a frightful disorder.—The enemy had surprised our advanced posts. One of their wings had driven away the three select companies, posted in the woods, on our right ; and from among the trees, were now doing much execution with their rifles. The rest of the enemy's infantry attacked us in front, with two pieces of cannon, and the cavalry did the same on our left.

" Although the mischief was already done, I thought I could repair it ; and with that view, sent the batallion of Aldama, to reinforce the line of battle, formed by that of Matamoros, and organised a column of attack under the orders of Don Manuel Cespedes, composed of the permanent batallion of Guerrero, and the pickets of Toluca and Guadalaxara, which moved to the front, with the company of Lieutenant Colonel Luelmo, in order to check the advance of the enemy ; but my efforts were vain. The line was abandoned by the two batallions that covered it ; and notwithstanding the fire of our cannon, the two columns were thrown into disorder ; Colonel Cespedes being wounded, and Captain Luelmo, killed. General Castrillon, who ran to and fro, to re-establish order in our ranks, fell, mortally wounded, and the new recruits threw every thing into confusion ; breaking their ranks, and preventing the veterans from making use of their arms ; while the enemies were rapidly advancing, with loud hurrahs, and in a few minutes, obtained a victory which they could not, some hours before, have even dreamed of.

All hopes being now lost, and every one flying as fast as he could, I found myself in the greatest danger, when a servant of my aid-de-camp, Colonel Don Juan Bringas, offered me his master's horse, and with the most urgent and tender expressions, insisted upon my riding off the field. I looked about for my escort, and two dragoons who were hurriedly saddling their horses, told me their officers and fellow-soldiers had *made their escape.* I remembered that General Filisola was only seventeen leagues distant, and I took my direction towards his camp. I darted through the enemies, but they pursued me, and after a ride of one league and a half, nearly overtook me, on the banks of a large creek, the bridge over which had been burned. I alighted from my horse and with much difficulty succeeded in concealing myself in a thicket of dwarf pines. Night coming on, I escaped my pursuers, and the hope of reaching the army gave me new strength. I crossed the creek, with the water up to my breast, and continuing my route on foot, I found in a house that had been abandoned, some articles of clothing, which enabled me to change my apparel. At eleven o'clock, A. M., while I was crossing a large plain, my pursuers came up with me again and seized on my person. Such is the history of my capture. On account of my change of apparel they did not recognize me, and inquired whether I had seen Santa Anna? To this I answered that he had made his escape; and this answer saved me from instant death, as I have, since, been given to understand.

NOTE 2, *page* 70.—The lime-stone ponds, in the mountains of Texas, as well as the lagoons, on the coast, abound in fish and water-fowls, and offer almost every variety found in North America. Among the best kinds of the former are the perch, trout, pike, carp, chub, pout and buffalo. In the bays and inlets of the sea are found the cat-fish, sturgeon, mullet, sheepshead and the red-fish, which is particularly abundant in Galveston bay. Many of these attain a large size. In addition, there are crabs, shrimps, soft and hard shell turtles and oysters of excellent flavor. The latter, in particular, are in beds that seem inexhaustible, in some places, the continuous banks extending thirty miles in length, by one or two in breadth.

Of wild fowls which make the water their haunt, there are immense flocks, chiefly in the winter, more particularly around Galveston bay, and their eggs are found in great quantities upon the shores of the islands, and harbors. The principal kinds are the pelican, crane, goose, brandt, duck, curlew, swan, loon, teal, stork, snipe, water-hen and fish-hawk. As many of the prairies are intersected by considerable lakes, even at a distance from the sea-coast, these water fowls are also found in the interior, between the Trinidad and the Brazos. Cane lake, in the midst of a prairie, with an expanse of water, about ten miles long, and from one to three wide, is one of their favorite places of resort.

NOTE 3, *page* 79.—The *Rio de Santiago* crosses the state of Jalisco, from east to west. It is a considerable stream which communicates with the lake of *Chapala*, and can be navigated from Salamanca, to the port of San Blas, meandering through a country of unsurpassed fertility. The *Mescala* is further south and can be of little service for navigation, unless by the help of locks. The *Panuco*, which falls into the sea at Tampico, can be navigated by steamboats, one hundred miles. The waters of the Valley of Mexico and the river *Guautitlan* disembogue into the Panuco, by the tunnel of Huehuetoca, one of the most stupendous works ever executed by the genius of man, and by which the city of Mexico has been, in great measure, secured against the recurrence of the inundations which, before, used to deluge it, along with a great part of the valley. As the lake of Tezcuco is the lowest, it receives the waters of that of Chalco, from the

16*

south and those of San Cristoval from the north, which latter was anciently the recipient of the Rio Guautitlan and several lagoons that extend from its northern extremity, nearly to the foot of the hill of Sincoque. The communication between the above mentioned river, and those lakes is now regulated by locks, and no more water is suffered to flow towards the south, than is necessary to keep the lake of Tezcuco up to a certain level.

NOTE 4, *page* 108.—Jalisco is, in point of population and wealth, the second state (now, department) of the Mexican Republic. Its capital, Guadalaxara, boasts a population of eighty or ninety thousand souls. It is built on the left bank of the river Santiago, is the seat of an university, and the residence of a bishop. The climate is delightful, though warm, and provisions are exceedingly cheap.—The peak of colima is the most occidental volcano of all those of Mexico, which are placed nearly on a line, running north and south. It frequently emits prodigious quantities of cinders, and the smoke can be seen at a vast distance, at sea. Its elevation above the Pacific ocean is estimated at six thousand feet, by father Abad y Queipo.

NOTE 5, *page* 113.—The mint, in Mexico. This establishment has, at all times, commanded the attention of foreigners, and been celebrated throughout the world, on account of the prodigious quantity of precious metals which have been coined in it. Till fourteen years after the conquest, that is to say, till 1535, no other money was current in Mexico than what was struck in Spain; but as this was not sufficient for the necessities of the country, the inhabitants made use of pieces of silver of a fixed weight, and hence the introduction of the word *peso*, to designate a dollar. This, giving birth to many frauds, a royal decree was issued, on the 11th of May, 1535, for the establishment of three mints, in America, one in the city of Potosi, one at Santa Fe, in New Grenada, and the other in Mexico. The last named building cost $1,004,493. Its principal front faces the north, and is one hundred and twenty *varas* in length, and that which faces the east is one hundred and seventy. It is solidly constructed and in good style. All the principal officers lodge in it, and the apartments of the superintendent are sufficiently sumptuous for a prince. There are more than three hundred men employed in it, and anciently many of the offices were sold by government and passed from father to son. As high as $60,000 were, at times, paid for the office of treasurer. Some of the most lucrative posts, about the mint, were in possession of religious communities—as, for example, the office of first smelter and assayer, which belonged to the convent of carmelite friars!

Now this establishment presents but a faint image of what it has been. The stream of precious metals which, once, made it so noted, has been nearly exhausted, and it has, of late years, served for little else than to coin copper. There are now other mints in the country, such as at Zacatecas, Durango, &c. &c.

NOTE 6, *page* 176.—Geographical sketch of the lower parts of the valley of the Rio Bravo, with a description of the principal towns on its banks.

These settlements, some of which were begun as far back as eighty or ninety years ago, received the refuse of the Mexican population, and this district of country thus became the *Botany Bay* of Mexico. The convicts whom the vice regal government of the capital sent by thousands, to people those desert regions, were settled in large villages, termed *presidios*, (forts) from the circumstance of their being protected, or, rather, kept in awe, by small bodies of soldiers, generally residing in some adjoining stone inclosure, which the grandiloquence of the Spaniards dignified with the title of fortress. Several of those presidios have, in process of time, grown into considerable places, and the immorality of the original settlers has been somewhat modified, by the accession of more honest persons; yet the population of those districts is, at this day, much more vicious, than that of any other portion of the Mexican Republic.

The largest of these places is the city of Matamoros, situated on the right bank of the Rio Bravo, about sixty miles above its mouth. Originally called El Refugio, it continued an inconsiderable village, till it was made a port of entry; from which time, its growth was so rapid, that its population lately amounted to sixteen thousand souls. The present war against Texas has greatly checked its progress, still it must, ultimately, become a place of great importance, as it is at the mouth of the largest river, next to the Mississippi, of all those which empty themselves into the gulf of Mexico. Even, at this day, the commerce of Matamoros is considerable; coming next to that of Tampico and Vera Cruz. It will certainly, before long, surpass that of either of those two cities, and as soon as steamboats can ply in safety on the Rio Bravo, the trade of four or five large states must centre in this place. Chihuahua can send its precious metals and copper to the banks of this river, by the way of the *travesia;* Passo del Norte can send its wine, Taos can float down its timber and New Leon produces sugar in abundance; while cotton can grow every where, along the margin of the stream.

Between Matamoros and the mouth of the river, the country is thinly interspersed with small villages and solitary farm-houses, and the sugar-cane is already in successful cultivation; though not to any considerable extent. The few settlers who inhabit the Texian side are yet almost exclusively Mexicans, and limit their attention to grazing. Even this kind of industry has been much checked by the incursions of the Lipan Indians, and the robberies of the Mexican soldiery.

Matamoros, being a new city, is regularly laid off; with broad streets, cutting each other at right angles, and adorned with several handsome squares. It possesses some fine private houses, built in the American style, several stories in height, with elegant balconies; but most of the buildings are in the Mexican fashion, only one story, with flat roofs—and the dwellings of the lowest class are little better than wretched cabins, of unburnt bricks, covered with thatch. The scite of the city, being perfectly level, is subject to be overflowed by the Rio Bravo; the waters of which, at the season of its periodical inundations, cover the prairies to a vast extent; but, in spite of the yearly recurrence of these floods, the country is perfectly healthy. Never has any epidemic, save the last general cholera, visited these parts of the Mexican Republic, neither has the yellow fever shown itself. Chronic diseases themselves seem to be milder and rarer than in the healthiest parts of the United States.

Sixty miles above Matamoros, on the same side of the river, is found the town of Reynosa, a place of three thousand inhabitants, and the seat of a parish which extends twenty-five leagues on both sides of the Rio Bravo, and boasts a population of six or seven thousand inhabitants. Here, the first high lands are met, in ascending the stream; and the town itself is built on a rocky ridge, the base of which is washed by the Bravo. The people of this parish attend chiefly to raising cattle, or burning lime. The farms are extensive, stocked with immense flocks of goats and sheep, or herds of horned cattle. Few of the farmers attempt to raise corn; the land is, nevertheless, of amazing fertility, and the river offers great facilities for irrigation, but the people are not acquainted with any kind of machinery to raise the water.

Sixty miles above Reynosa, we find the town of Camargo, the population of which amounts to six thousand inhabitants. It is situated on the same side of the Rio Bravo, at the place where the river San Juan empties itself into it. This is one of the most important tributaries of the Bravo, draining an immense extent of country—to wit, the best part of Tamaulipas, all Nuevo Leon and the southern half of Cohahuila. It heads in the lofty range of the *Sierra Madre*, twenty-five leagues west of Monte Morelos; and, forty miles above its mouth, it receives the river of Saltillo. It is subject to high freshets, particularly at the time of the equinoxes, when it rises so considerably as to become boatable; and did the inhabitants but know how to avail themselves of this facility, the trade of those states might be greatly enhanced. Part of the lands, at the foot of the mountains, is extremely fertile, extensively cultivated, and produces immense quantities of corn and sugar, as well as many of the fruits peculiar to tropical climates. The course of this river may be estimated at five hundred miles. The two largest towns in the regions which it drains are Monterey, the capital of the state, or department of Nuevo Leon, and Saltillo, the metropolis of Cohahuila ; which has about twenty-five thousand inhabitants and is the seat of a considerable commerce and some rude attempts at the manufacture of woolens. *El Pueblo,* a large village, close to that city, consists of descendants of a colony of old Tlascalans, who have preserved the language of the ancient Mexicans and make use of it among themselves.

Fifty miles above Camargo, we find the town of Mier, on the right bank of the Bravo, the population of which amounts to four or five thousand inhabitants. The parish is extensive, and the land, occupied mostly by graziers.

A place which, in process of time, must attain more importance, is Revilla—fifty miles up the river. A little west of this town, on the river Salado, are found mines of stone coal, which will, at no distant period, prove of immense advantage for the navigation of the Rio del Norte by steam. These mines are a continuation of a large coal-field which crosses Texas from east to west. It has not been yet employed to any useful purpose by the inhabitants of Mexico, though some American blacksmiths, in Matamoros, are acquainted with its existence.

Laredo, another town of some importance, above Revilla, is situated on the left bank of the Bravo, and, of course, belongs to Texas ; although its inhabitants have not yet recognized her jurisdiction. Steamboats have ascended the river as high as this point; but it is navigable much farther up by boats of a light draught of water. It will even, probably, be found practicable for small steamers, during high freshets, to penetrate into the state of Chihuahua, by the Rio Conchos.

From Laredo, there is not any town of importance in the immediate vicinity of the river, till we come to *Presidio del Rio Grande.* At this place, the high road from Saltillo, to San Antonio de Bexar, crosses the Rio Bravo ; and in case of an invasion of Texas by the Mexicans, this will be the first point aimed at, chiefly on account of the great fertility of the San Antonio valley, which offers greater resources for the subsistence of an army, than any other district of western Texas.

Between the 29th and 30th degrees of north latitude we find the mouth of the river Agua Verde, which proceeds from two lakes situated on the edge of the Bolson of Mapimi, from whence it is inferred that there must be some subterranean stream in that vast desert, the discovery of which would be followed by prodigious results; as the *Bolson* is full of mines, which nothing but the want of water has prevented being wrought. Above Agua Verde, the river makes a great bend to the south, and the country, on the right side, has a number of villages, such as St. Vincent, St. Charles, Chiricote, Presidio de la Consolation and Alamo.

The Rio Conchos, which pervades a great part of the state of Chihuahua, and flows from south to north, empties itself into the Bravo in 30 deg. 21 min. north latitude. Fifty miles above it, north of *las Yuntas*, at some distance from the Rio Bravo, is a remarkable warm spring, the volume of water of which is sufficient to turn a mill.

The last place we will notice, on this river, is Paso del Norte in 30 deg. 37 min. north latitude. The town is considerable and surrounded by a populous, well cultivated district, famous for the wines it produces. They are reckoned superior to any other in Mexico, yet such is the supineness of the people, that not a drop of it has ever reached Matamoros.

At a distance west of the Bravo, is the little town of Santa Rosa, in the vicinity of which are found silver mines, whence large quantities of bullion are daily smuggled into Texas. These mines are important and though hitherto worked neither methodically, nor on a large scale, much precious metal has been extracted from them. Besides what has been exported through Texas, a considerable amount has passed through Matamoros; though, of course, unknown to government.

The description of the country bordering on the left bank of the river will be more brief. The Rio Puerco, the largest tributary of the Bravo, heads in 35 deg. north latitude, not far from the town of Sibileta, and empties itself into the Bravo, south of the thirtieth degree. Its course is nearly parallel with that of the preceding river, at the average distance of one hundred and fifty miles; but between the two, intervenes a high chain of mountains, known under the name of Sierra de Chamate, del Diablo; and, higher up, towards the north, under that of Organos,—from the immense quantity of *cacti cylindrici* which grow in its glens. A higher chain separates the valley of the Puerco, from the head waters of the Colorado of Texas, and the Brazos. Below Paso del Norte, it is called the Guadelupe ridge, and north of that town, it bears the name of Sierra del Sacramento, some of whose peaks attain a prodigious height. All those mountains are metalliferous and must, in process of time, become the seat of a dense population, the valley of the Puerco being well adapted to agriculture and consisting chiefly of a rich loam. The upper parts of New Mexico are already well settled, and numerous villages are found on the Rio Bravo, both above and below San-ta Fe.

The river Nueces, which derives its name from the immense quantity of peccon-trees growing on its banks, has an estuary parallel to that of the Bravo. The intervening district abounds in prickly pear and fine grass, but is scantily watered. Several settlements had nevertheless been made, chiefly on the road from Matamoros to San Patricio ; but, in consequence of the war, the settlers have withdrawn to Mexico.

St. Patrick, on the left bank of the river Nueces, was, at the time of Santa Anna's invasion, a thriving village, almost exclu-sively consisting of Irish people. These colonists were divided in politics ; some sided with the Mexicans, and these, at the time of Filisola's retreat, followed his army to Matamoros. The oth-ers, who embraced the party of the Texians, have returned, and their village bids fair to become a flourishing place. Being situ-ated only thirty miles up the river, in a healthy and fertile coun-try, its future prosperity seems to rest upon a solid basis.

East of the Nueces, the country improves, being better water-ed, and at this particular period, towns are springing up about the sea-shore, as if by enchantment, between Matagorda bay and Aransazu. This latter part of the country is, nevertheless, un-healthy and the plague of the musquitoes is worse than in Lou-isiana.

San Antonio de Bexar, one hundred and forty miles from the sea and two hundred from the Rio Bravo, had been selected as the future metropolis of Texas, by the government of Charles IV., king of Spain. It it very well built, has, till now, been the most important town in Texas ; and must, from the peculiar felicity of its location, ever continue so. It is situated at the head of the river San Anton, a stream formed by the confluence of some large springs which issue from the ground four miles above the city. This stream would be navigable, were it not for the rapid decliv-ity of its bed, chiefly after it has received the Medina, which comes from the northwest ; yet the rapidity of its course multi-plies facilities for farming, since, in consequence of it, its waters can be conducted by canals to almost any part of the valley.

The land in this neighborhood, and, indeed, as far east as Gouzales, is the richest it is possible to imagine, well adapted to the production of cotton and sugar, no less than to the cultiva-tion of the grape vine and tobacco, for which a very advanta-geous market is found on the Mexican frontier. Somewhat to the north of Bexar wheat succeeds well, while flax grows any where. To these advantages may be added the salubrity of the climate—no epidemic, save the last general cholera, having ever visited the country, though it has been settled by white people

more than eighty years. Winters are hardly felt, ice being seldom seen. The air is extremely pure and transparent and
minute objects can be discerned at such distances as would appear incredible to any one who has not visited the country.

The parallel of latitude in which this district is situated and
the direction of the mountains of St. Sabas, which defend it from
the northern blast, concur to make it the favorite spot where
tropical productions meet those of northern climes and blend with
them "in gay confusion" for the benefit of man.

In the fields, maize indigo, rice, the sweet patatoe, beans and
divers kinds of capsicum, an infinite variety of melons and sweet
squashes, with many other useful plants, which it were endless
to enumerate, solicit the attention of the husbandman. In the
orchards, the orange and shaddock, the peach and apricock, the
pomegranate, the avigate, or alligator pear, the peccon and several kinds of Indian figs, along with many of the northern
fruits, succeed to perfection, while several others, such as the al-
mond and the olive, might be introduced. In the gardens, every
kind of useful plant and poth-herb known in Louisiana will grow,
and others, known but by name in the United States, will thrive
with luxuriance. Lastly, the whole world cannot afford a better
country for the grazier, stock being raised without any trouble on
the part of the owner and the wild grass being of the best quality.

The town of Bexar, in consequence of the war and the incursions of the Indians, has lost a part of its population, but it
boasts yet about three thousand souls. It possesses water-power
sufficient for a large number of factories, and its locality must
render it, one day, the emporium of two important mining districts, for all the mineral wealth of the sierra of St. Sabas and
Santa Rosa must altimately centre here.

Though the mouth of the Rio Bravo affords but an indifferent
port, on account of the bar at the entrance, the Brazo of Santiago,
about ten or twelve miles west of it, offers a fine harbor, accessible to vessels drawing nine or ten feet water. It is, in consequence, the place of resort for most foreign merchantmen trading to this part of Mexico. The Brazo de Santiago is within the
limits of Texas and as soon as the latter will enforce her jurisdiction over this spot, it is highly probable a town of importance
will grow here. For the present, there is, at that place, as well
as at the mouth of the river, nothing but a wretched village, but
the land in the vicinity is fertile. South of the mouth of the Rio
Bravo, are seen high downs, of white sand, beyond which rich
prairies stretch to a vast distance, sometimes intersected by
bayons, or lagoons. Between Boca del Rio and Matamoros, the
land lies pretty high, is beautiful and not destitute of wood ; it is
one of the most desirable spots on the face of the earth, yet in a
manner, untenanted.